The novel that goes back to Nina Reilly's
first legal case. . . .

A paralegal by day and law student at night, Nina
has her hands full fighting for custody of her young
son and overseeing her mother's medical malpractice
suit. Then a woman takes a fatal plunge near Big
Sur—and Nina, with the help of homicide cop Paul
von Wagoner, sets out to prove her death was no
accident. . . .

SHOW NO FEAR

"O'Shaughnessy knows how to spin a diverting tale."
—*The San Diego Union-Tribune*

"Nina's balancing act and independent streak
make her an admirable heroine in a solidly plotted
book. . . . A good starting point for those new to the
series."

—*Library Journal*

"Engaging characters, intriguing plot."
—*Booklist*

"O'Shaughnessy is in fine form."
—*Lansing State Journal*

"Fascinating. . . . Nina Reilly fans will enjoy meeting
her younger self."

—*Freshfiction.com*

"Intriguing. . . . Surprising twists."
—*Publishers Weekly*

ALSO BY PERRI O'SHAUGHNESSY

PERRI O'SHAUGHNESSY

A NINA REILLY NOVEL

DREAMS OF THE DEAD

POCKET BOOKS

New York London Toronto Sydney New Delhi

Pocket Books
A Division of Simon & Schuster, Inc.
1230 Avenue of the Americas
New York, NY 10020

This book is a work of fiction. Names, characters, places, and incidents either are products of the author's imagination or are used fictitiously. Any resemblance to actual events or locales or persons, living or dead, is entirely coincidental.

First Pocket Books paperback edition May 2012

POCKET and colophon are registered trademarks of Simon & Schuster, Inc.

For information about special discounts for bulk purchases, please contact Simon & Schuster Special Sales at 1-866-506-1949 or business@simonandschuster.com.

The Simon & Schuster Speakers Bureau can bring authors to your live event. For more information or to book an event contact the Simon & Schuster Speakers Bureau at 1-866-248-3049 or visit our website at www.simonspeakers.com.

Manufactured in the United States of America

10 9 8 7 6 5 4 3 2 1

ISBN 978-1-4165-4974-1
ISBN 978-1-4391-6064-0 (ebook)

Dedicated to Nancy Elizabeth Mason, M.D.
For bringing three precious lives into our lives, and
for thirty years of friendship and caring.
And, as always, Brad.

—M

To Harry Berger, Jr., an inspiration to many, and
good friend.

—P

PROLOGUE

The dreams of the dead are unimportant to the living. Once they were told to loved ones, turned into reality, and whispered in prayer, but now they were locked away. Silent and unreachable, such dreams are.

Lake Tahoe lay passive under the long rays of the April afternoon, a repository of more than water. I tacked in an easterly breeze toward Meeks Bay with its still-snowy promontory. All around the lake the white Sierra peaks were the only witnesses to the small sailboat.

Maybe the dead dreamed even more vividly now, with activated souls. That they no longer moved meant nothing.

Why do modern people ignore these extended sunsets of their ancestors? I know the dead exist for a long time after death, as long as the disintegrating flesh and bone.

Safe from possible pursuers and witnesses now, under control again, I screwed the lid off a second bottle of beer and drank some, guiding the tiller, the boat moving smoothly out to the spot I had chosen on his map. Some sages said the dead spent their time redreaming the time when they were alive. They wouldn't know they were dreaming. They would fly, love, win the one they wanted in life. They would lose their teeth, not be able to find their lockers, be pursued by stupid trolls, think they were talking to the dead and living, fall harmlessly off cliffs.

Maybe they relived death. I hoped Jim would. And I hoped this time he would feel the deaths of the people he had killed. Yes, why not? Dreams contain strong emotions. Jim would live the killings over and over and maybe even feel something unusual happening now— bewilderment, and distaste at being disturbed, removed from this frigid mountain bed.

A scientist once said that after cremation much of the body is lost, not released to the air or anywhere. Where did it go? Cremation, then, would unnaturally and instantly kill the dreaming soul. Burial was the proper way to treat the dead, or plucking by vultures, or insufficient burning as at the Varanasi ghats, so the dead could have their centuries to dream as they returned particle by particle to the soil.

I tied off the tiller, loosened the sails, and rattled the blue tarp as, grunting a little, I pulled and pushed the body up from the hold. The tarp was filthy but I felt little repulsion as I laid it onto the low, long seat, hard on my knees, my arms around it as if to embrace it and show it the glorious scene in which we were performing our parts in this drama. I felt I could almost hear him talking to me, whispering, moaning, trumpeting in a low register like an elephant, but it was only the flap of sails, the wind against the sides.

This final burial would be worse than cremation, in its way. Maybe he knew he was going to lie on the frigid bottom forever, never decomposing, forever retaining a faint shadowy connection to one end of the spectrum of life. His dreaming flesh would be preserved indefinitely in the lake's almost-freezing deep temperatures. There would be no release.

And if dreaming meant reexperiencing the events of life, he would not wish to dream forever.

The tarp unwrapped slightly at the top and I saw a clump of familiar brown hair. I propped myself against the open hatch to the tiny cabin and put out a gloved finger, touching the hair lightly. Something stirred within me even as I shuddered.

Then I hardened my stomach muscles, crouched, picked it up tarp and all, and tipped the reeking thing into the lake. The boat was at the deepest fractured depth of the lake, about sixteen hundred feet, the second-deepest lake depth in the United States.

Down there it would be utterly lightless.

As it sank, last blue on blue, I took out a small, soft, flattened leatherbound book from my pocket and read an old poem I had chosen for this occasion:

> we are white floating
> in an unknown firmament
> our faces loom from the black
> then recede as impassive

as winter branches
our lips fall into disarray
we stare harmlessly
wide-eyed we dream—

I didn't feel like finishing. When I closed the book, I could no longer see anything over the side. I threw the book into the water, removed my gloves, leaned out over the lake, and washed my hands and face. The water cooled me.

Then I reset the sails, freed the tiller, and headed back toward the Tahoe Keys Marina.

Let the dead dream. Let the living act.

PART
ONE

CHAPTER 1

Sandy Whitefeather walked into the inner office, closed the door, and sat down in one of the orange client chairs, wearing her usual expression of firm dignity. On the phone with a probation officer who was preparing a sentencing report for one of her criminal defense clients, Nina raised her eyebrows, but Sandy's expression did not alter.

The secretary and lone staffer in the Law Offices of Nina Reilly, Sandy ordinarily stood at Nina's desk, so either she was tired or some cataclysm was afoot. Since at 8:00 a.m. Sandy usually was well into her fourth cup of coffee, she probably wasn't tired. She had been hard at work when Nina arrived, and Nina had meant to ask her what was bringing her into the office so early these days, and why she would close out the file on her computer whenever Nina came near.

Outside, the weather had turned cloudy, the thick white clouds that meant they would have snow. This was the tumultuous season, as the mountains left winter and moved into spring.

"Sorry, gotta go. Call you back later," Nina told the officer, and hung up. "So?"

"Scumbags have been sitting in these chairs for four years now," Sandy observed. She wore a belt with small silver conchas and tan leather cowboy boots under a long skirt. A member of the Washoe tribe, Sandy had lately gone country-western in her dress, and the appearance of a snorting stallion in the parking lot one night would not surprise Nina.

"They do the job." Nina got up, spun one, and tried not to notice the ugly brown stain not exactly adorning its back. When had that got there?

"We need new chairs. Comfortable. Leather so they clean easier."

"That's low on the list." Nina indicated the stack of files and phone messages stacked neatly on her desk. "Today, we work on generating cash, not spending it. As I recall, you told me Friday that we are low on the accounts receivable front, no surprise, considering that nobody in town has a dime to litigate these days."

"Fine, if you like cooties."

"So hire a steam cleaner. Do we need to have this conversation right now? Is that why you came in? I'm working."

"I saw brown leather chairs at Jay's Furniture over in Reno this weekend. Four hundred apiece, but your clients can rest their heads and they won't have to put their arms on this cold chrome."

"No money for extras now."

"How about if you could make five thousand bucks in ten minutes?"

Nina waited, but Sandy sat, arms crossed. Unable to stand it any longer, Nina asked, "New client?"

"Someone we know awaits outside."

"Who?"

"Philip Strong."

"Strong?" Nina felt a nasty stirring in her gut. For two years, she had tried to put that name out of her mind.

"Jim Strong's father."

"No."

"Yes."

"That's over."

"You'd think."

"What did Philip say?"

"He'll pay a big retainer for a problem he has."

Nina covered her eyes with her hand.

"You look peaked. Maybe you ought to see a healer. I know one up at Woodfords everyone says—"

"Philip Strong's waiting in our outer office?"

"Marched right in five minutes ago. I was busy writing something important, but he didn't mind interrupting. Says it's urgent."

Nina heard herself, voice higher-pitched than usual. "I don't want to."

"You may not want to, but you oughta. Listen. You have an appointment with Burglar Boy in twenty minutes. Just hear Philip out and I'll scoot him away when you're done."

"Send him upstairs to John Dominguez."

Sandy shook her head. "Claims he needs to consult with you. Only you."

"Why is he here?"

"No details, but I'm thinking it's about his ski resort."

Paradise Ski Resort. Nina pictured the lodge up the mountain behind town, the enormous stone fireplace, handsome people pulling off their rigid boots, downing hot toddies, beers, and champagne, singing loudly, throwing arms around each other before eventually venturing out into the night, heading for their rented condos or a long night of gambling. Straddling the border between Nevada and California, a neighbor to Heavenly Ski Resort, Paradise was a hidden gem. The lifts cost less, the lodge had delicious food, and the runs rivaled world-class Heavenly in their variety.

Those really in the know, though, remembered that two years earlier the resort had seen a serious family tragedy, one Nina didn't care to remember.

"I don't know why, but the phrase *deep pockets* popped up in my mind the minute I saw him," Sandy continued. "You should fit him in."

Nina leaned back in her chair. The sharp sunlight of Lake Tahoe in March lanced through the window. Only a few miles to the east in Nevada, across the Sierra massif, in the high desert, the sun reigned most of the year. Outside in the well-plowed street of the mountain town, old Hummers and other full-size trucks and SUVs tankered by as though the price of gas had never been close to five bucks a gallon, the vehicles spattered brown with slush.

Nina made her palm into a stop sign. "I never want to hear Jim Strong's name again."

Sandy nodded. "Neither does Philip, I'm thinking. Look, he's one of the few people left in this town with money." Sandy scratched at the metal arms of the chair, then leaned forward to see the result of her handiwork. "But what strikes me is that you need to know what's going on here even if we don't accept him as a client."

"Why?"

"'Cuz if it's about his son, it affects you. You'll get lassoed into his stuff sideways if you're not careful. At least find out why he came." Sandy had the strongest fingernails of any human on the planet, it appeared. They continued scratching on the chair arm in one tiny place. The chrome began to disappear as though she were using a tiny Brillo pad.

"Direct him upstairs."

At the door, Sandy turned once more to Nina, her eyebrow cocked into a final question mark.

"Tell him I'm sorry," Nina said. The door closed, and Nina went to the tiny mirror by the door, examining the blowy hair, the darkness under the eyes, the brown eyes that now appeared almost amber, translucent in the reflection from the light behind her.

No one had ever hated her, hurt her, or scared her as Philip Strong's son had. Nina would never recover from the blows, never. Knowing Jim would never come back helped her to sleep at night. She walked a few more steps to the corner of the big window, where she liked to look out over her personal shimmering sliver of Lake Tahoe.

In the outer office, voices competed for airspace, Sandy's mostly prevailing. Nina recalled Philip Strong as a quiet man, and Sandy seldom raised her voice, so why all the shouting? A crash made her rush to open her office door and take a look.

Sandy, feet stuck to the floor, sturdy as a tripod, gripped the back of Strong's parka like a bouncer. Sure of her hold, she shoved him implacably toward the door. Strong grabbed the jambs, preventing her from propelling him out, yelling, "I need to see her!"

"Sandy?"

Sandy paused and looked back at Nina, eyes her usual cold coal black. "Told him you had other plans for him. Upstairs."

"I'm not leaving!" Philip cried. "This is important, damn it!"

Sandy's grip tightened. Nina, recalling some old business between Philip and Sandy's mother, something vague, something that probably made Sandy nuts, said, "It's okay, Sandy."

Sandy held tight. Was that a hank of hair stretching between the fingers of her left hand? Philip yelped again. "Really?" Sandy asked after a few moments of Philip's twisting left and right, bubbling with anger but unable to free himself from her hold.

"Yes," Nina said.

Sandy let go.

Philip, caught off guard, nearly fell to the floor, tried to regain his balance, and set a hard hand against the wall to steady himself. He pulled a hand through his thinning hair as if to recapture his lost dignity.

Sandy adjusted her belt and brushed off her skirt.

Then they both looked at Nina. "I found a minute," she said.

"Thank you." Strong righted himself and said, "Sorry, Sandy."

"Hnf." Sandy went to her desk and plopped down to a ringing phone. While she answered it and Philip Strong tucked his shirt back into his pants, Nina took a good look at him.

He had aged. Thick, dark hair that once curled around the bottom half of his skull had diminished to wispy white strands since she last saw him. He had lost weight in two years. He must be in his sixties by now. Even so, he maintained an attitude of physical health, wearing a red parka and jeans that accentuated stringy, once athletic legs. He stared back at her as if he'd forgotten what she looked like. He looks haunted, she thought.

"Come in," she said, holding the door.

Almost as the door clicked shut, he was saying, "I have news, Nina. It's killing my family. It might kill you, too. But you need to know."

She tensed. A threat, not even two minutes into the conversation. She had been right to want him upstairs, not here, in her face, frightening her.

"Jim's alive. My son's alive."

CHAPTER 2

Nina felt her insides turn out. Her heart slapped against her chest. She knew Jim was dead. What his father said, what he believed, couldn't be true. She shook her head, smiled slightly, resumed breathing, and waved for Philip Strong to sit down.

He swiped a sleeve across his sweating forehead. The office, kept at a stable sixty-six degrees by Sandy, the energy czar, was not warm.

"Why do you think that? Jim's been gone for years. It makes no sense. None," she said, going around to her chair.

"I know he hurt you and your family. I imagine how hard this must be for you to hear."

"He's in contact?" No way was this possible.

"He's out of the country, but, yes, he's in contact."

"Where?" Pulling out her yellow pad, she wrote down the date, March 27, the time, 8:25 a.m., and that she was having a conference with Philip Strong, taking notes, a nice, normal, routine thing.

"I can guess your immediate reaction. Nothing will bring your husband back. You don't want to get involved with my family again. You'd prefer never to see me again."

She compressed her lips into an impersonal and unemotional line. "What's going on, Mr. Strong?"

"Philip, please. We've been through enough together, haven't we?"

"Philip."

"I have to lead up to this. It's been upsetting, these past couple of years. Jim caused such turmoil for my family and yours."

"We've moved on. We don't think about him."

Strong nodded, although his expression said, Yeah, right. "Kelly—obviously, you know my daughter. She's working for your brother these days, right?"

"He says she's capable, reliable, all kinds of good things."

"She's very good at anything she tries. You know she was first in her law school class?" Strong's hands kneaded each other. "I thought she'd make a great lawyer."

To make up for her wayward brother, Jim? Nina wondered. A rap on the door interrupted. "What?"

Sandy stood back to reveal Kelly Strong.

Kelly stepped into the room. "Been a while," she said, holding her hand out to shake Nina's.

"Your ears were burning," her father said.

Nina liked Kelly. Not long after her brother's disappearance, she had suffered some sort of breakdown and dropped out of law school. She came to

Nina one day and asked if she might have some legal research for her to do. Nina had nothing, but it was winter, and Nina's brother, Matt, was looking for people to drive tow trucks and snowplows. Kelly signed on, finished the specialized training in style, and turned out to have had the fingers and brain of an auto mechanic all along. She'd been working for Matt for over a year now.

"Good to see you again." Nina didn't like Kelly's expression at the moment, but she looked physically healthy, at least. She was taller than Nina remembered, or maybe it was the work boots. She wore jeans and a tow-service jacket, a baseball cap hiding her newly short hair. Her cheeks were reddened from the outdoor work.

"I'm sure Dad appreciates you seeing us without an appointment. And of course"—Kelly looked her in the eye—"you're totally pissed about seeing us at all."

"What are you doing here?" Her father didn't reach for his daughter.

"It's my company, too. Marianne called me. She said you decided to drag Nina into this."

"Why not?" Philip said. "Who else could help us—"

"I'm not saying it's a bad idea, if she's willing."

Nina interrupted. "Your father was about to tell me why he thinks your brother Jim is alive."

"Then I got here in the nick."

"Kelly—"

"Press on, Dad. As long as you're here, fill her in." Kelly pulled over a second client chair, put her elbow on Nina's desk, and took up a listening position.

"No one's seen Jim for the past couple of years," Philip started, then stopped.

Nina took a pull from her water bottle. Her guts snaked around in her abdomen. Why did the man have to drag this out? Jim Strong was dead.

Philip had propped his elbows on the other side of her desk and buried his head in his hands.

Kelly watched him and said nothing. She was only in her twenties, but events had focused the face that had once been pudgy and soft. There was black under her fingernails, oil maybe. She had probably come straight from a tow job.

"Philip. My time and my patience are limited," Nina said as gently as she could. "You've got fifteen minutes to organize yourself and tell me exactly why you barged into my office." She got up and went into the outer office. Sandy clicked away intensely on some document, unusual for her, not listening at the door.

"Sandy, can you please call my next client?"

"Burglar Boy."

"I know you don't approve of him."

"I approve of his rich mama."

"Maybe you can catch him. Reschedule him for four p.m."

"Already did."

Returning to her office, Nina settled herself behind

her desk and looked again at the pair sitting across from her. They didn't seem to have exchanged a word. Kelly looked at her father with an expression Nina would have to describe as conflicted. Philip raised his head. He looked furious rather than tearful.

"Where do I start? Jim's come back to ruin my—Kelly and my—and Marianne's life again. You remember my son Alex—I guess you didn't meet him before his death—"

"No."

"His widow, Marianne, is still working at Paradise. Remember her?"

"Of course." Marianne, the dark French girl who had never seemed quite authentic to Nina.

"Jim was the middle child. And Kelly's youngest here. Who was halfway through law school."

"Fat lot of good that did me," Kelly said.

"You'll go back to school."

"I'm proud I can pay my rent." Kelly looked at Nina. "And even that's thanks to Nina's brother. Law school's a thing of the past. Besides, there's nothing like working hard for a living to teach you what crap life can bring your way, as you always said."

Philip's angular face reddened. "Driving a tow truck? Cleaning snow off the streets in winter? What kind of a life is that for a woman? It's too hard for you, honey. You won't last."

He looked at Nina and said, "Not that I'm not thankful your family pitched in when she needed help. But it's been a while—I expected—" Kelly's jaw had jutted out, and Nina thought, Why is he riding her? She's got a job in a bad economy, what's the problem?

Still, his obvious disappointment had made Kelly turn to face him directly. "Guess what? My job makes me happy. I come home at night knowing I helped people out."

"But you won't let me help you."

"How?" Kelly turned to face her father. "You owe everybody. You were wealthy for so long you don't know how to live without money. Well, I do. I'm young. I can work. Now I pay my own way. That's the way it should be."

"I know everyone in this town. I could help you get a better job. Why won't you let me?"

Kelly's face had turned sullen. She patted her jacket pocket for cigarettes, probably. Or Mace, or a gun; nothing from this family would surprise Nina.

"Please," Nina said, "can we stay on track here? Let's focus on Jim."

Frowning, Philip shifted in his seat. "I'm trying. All right. To unload some more really unpleasant family history which I have never told you about, I found out a few days after Jim disappeared that in addition to everything else he had been embezzling from Paradise for several months. He managed the Lodge and the ticketing gates. He was skimming off cash. He had taken about fifty thousand dollars from raw receipts. He hated me, Nina. He didn't give a damn about our family. I suppose his real crimes started with the skimming. I think in those last days he was breaking down. There was that, and—"

Philip didn't go on, but Nina knew what he couldn't stand to say. Philip had had an affair with his daughter-in-law, Jim's wife, Heidi. Jim had killed her in a jealous rage.

"How long did he steal from you?" Nina asked.

"Maybe two months?"

"You didn't report it?" She reflected that it wasn't a huge amount of money and under the circumstances hardly an awesome scandal.

"I knew it had to be someone in the family or on the staff. Because I couldn't bring myself to call the police, I hired a local investigator named Eric Brinkman. He talked to people and examined our records, told me he couldn't pin it on Jim, although he strongly suspected him. Jim made a very talented criminal in some ways. Personable. Good at lying and covering up."

"You're convinced Jim took the money?"

"I am. I had changed all the passwords, but then something much more damaging happened. Before he disappeared, Jim somehow got into our capital account. We had taken out a large loan to finance an expansion of the Lodge. He had all the numbers, knew what to do. He managed to get the money wired to an account he had opened with Charles Schwab in Sacramento, then had that wired to a casino account in Reno, then went gambling and somehow got the rest of the money converted to cash."

"How much money, Philip?" Nina asked.

"Almost a million dollars. We had to pay out another million to cover it."

"A million," Kelly repeated, then fell silent. "You didn't tell me."

"You weren't even speaking to me. You didn't want to have anything to do with the business at that time. I had to decide whether to call in the police. I didn't, because it would be the end of the business. Turned out to be the end anyway."

So in the end Jim had found another way to screw his family. Philip had to have foreseen some of this. Jim had shown signs of his predilections from his teen years.

"Bottom line, he did destroy the resort. Receipts at Paradise started to slide as the country went into recession, and some of our other loans started becoming pressing problems. We didn't have the capital to make some safety improvements to the quad lifts and almost got shut down. The money Jim stole might have got us through, but—the point of all this, Nina, is, I have to sell Paradise. It's been on the market for several months."

"*We* have to sell," Kelly corrected. "You, me, and Marianne."

"I can't tell you how humiliated and sorry I am to lose the place I've loved and fought for my whole life." Philip turned back to Nina. "Paradise has been in our family for over a hundred years. I put it on the market in January in a very quiet way."

"And here we are," Kelly said.

"The broker mostly looked internationally. It took him about three months to find us some buyers in Seoul, Korea, and they want to close the deal quickly."

"How did you determine the price?" Nina asked.

"Heavenly sold for roughly a hundred million seven or eight years ago. But real estate everywhere is down severely right now. Paradise has about fifteen hundred skiable acres as opposed to Heavenly's forty-eight hundred. Paradise is not as luxuriously developed as Heavenly, but it offers tax advantages, being partly on the Nevada side of the mountain and incorporated there. I figured we could sell it for about twenty million, and that would pay off our debts and leave us a little, and that was the best we could hope for. That was the offer, twenty million dollars.

"We have to sell, but the accountants have told us that the resort is completely overwhelmed with debt. We owe about seventeen and a half million dollars including the costs of sale, and we couldn't get an agreement from the buyers without a condition that all the debts will be paid before the company receives any of the purchase price."

"That's standard," Nina said, "to pay the debts prior to sale, but what an enormous debt load you're talking about. Technically, you're not bankrupt, but I don't see how you could continue doing business with the credit needed for the ongoing operations."

"Precisely," Philip said.

"Is Paradise still privately held?"

"Incorporated in Nevada, yes. A Subchapter S corporation, kept within the family, no public stock. Paradise is now owned by four people, Nina. My wife and I owned the resort, and when she passed away years ago, she left her share to our children, share and share alike. So I hold fifty percent, Marianne holds one-sixth as my son Alex's widow, Kelly owns one-sixth, and Jim theoretically owns one-sixth. Lynda Eckhardt—she's handling the purchase and sale agreement—thought we might be able to get court approval on the sale even though we can't get Jim's signature on the deal." Strong's speech tumbled out as he leaned forward again and laid his palms on the desktop.

"Kelly, didn't you sell your share to Marianne two years ago?" Nina said.

"Oh, I tried," Kelly said.

"I had that agreement annulled," Philip said, "for Kelly's protection. She wasn't able to make financial decisions at that time. Marianne gave up and we didn't have to slug it out in court. Of course, in hindsight, Kelly would have done very well two years ago, and now—well, anyway, it seems I made another mistake. Kelly's still angry about it." He didn't look at his daughter.

"It sounds like you both have had a very difficult time with the fallout."

Philip hung his head. His face screwed up as if he

were going to weep, but he didn't. He said quietly, "You have no idea."

"Oh, she knows all right," Kelly said.

Nina had been working out the figures on her calculator. "So that means you would net two and a half million dollars from the sale after the debts are paid. One and a quarter million for your half-ownership, and Kelly, Marianne, and—and, well, Jim's heirs would each receive about, let's see, four hundred seventeen thousand dollars. Am I close?"

"Yes, in a simple world. If only it were so simple."

Kelly's pager made a sound, and she gave the display a quick look. She stood up. "I have to get back to work. Been out since six thirty this morning. Nina, the point is that the sale is a legal mess right now, and Dad is right about one thing, that you may be the only person who can step in and help us. If I were you, I wouldn't take the job, though. You might run into Jim, ha-ha, the homicidal maniac who won't go away. Well, somebody's got to make an honest living around here." Kelly shook Nina's hand again and left the office.

"She's gotten bitter," Philip said, watching her go. "Won't take anything from me, you know. Lives on that job your brother gave her and on disability."

"She gets state money?"

"After all this stuff with Jim, she's never been the same. Emotional problems."

"I'm sorry."

"Listen, hey, don't forget, I'm responsible for triggering a whole lot of this. I had a relationship with Jim's wife. I regret that every single day. If I hadn't, maybe none of it would have happened. Kelly would be a lawyer by now. Alex would be alive. Your husband would be coming home for dinner every night. I've paid for my trespasses, but other people—Alex, Heidi, Kelly, you—paid much more."

Nina swallowed.

Philip leaned forward. "The buyers have given us thirty days to close escrow."

"That's monstrously tight for a business."

"They have complicated financing that involves several banks, and they can't hold the deal together any longer than that. I have to say, given the current economic climate, I'm afraid if we miss the deadline, our buyers may not be back. We may go bankrupt. We have another court hearing coming up in a few days, and our attorney doesn't know what to do."

Nina held her fingers to her lips. "Judge Flaherty?"

"Yeah. He's presiding over the hearing coming up."

"And Lynda Eckhardt is your attorney?"

"Right. But you know, she doesn't do court work. She was only handling the purchase and sale of the business. She recommended you, but she knew the history, and frankly, I doubt she thought you'd take over."

"That's the background then. Tell me now. What's your evidence that Jim's alive?"

Philip reached inside his fleecy vest and pulled out a heavy legal file. He handed it gingerly to Nina. "Okay, here's what happened yesterday, Nina. I went over to Lynda's office. She had been served with these papers. Here, take a look. Lynda made up the file for you."

Nina pulled out the sheaf of pleadings and skimmed them as he talked. They were perfectly organized. They were so sensationally organized that Nina wondered, not for the first time, if Lynda might suffer from a mild obsessive-compulsive disorder. Anyway, she wasn't resilient enough for court work and had the sense to know it.

"Basically, and you know I'm not a lawyer, there was an objection from a local law firm to the sale. Another outstanding firm in town, Caplan, Stamp, and Powell. Michael Stamp is the lawyer from the firm."

Nina couldn't help feeling pleased at being compared to that firm, with their mahogany wainscoting, Ivy League partners, and longtime universal respect from the community.

"They say they represent Jim, that he has retained them using a lawyer in Brazil as a go-between. He's supposed to be in Brazil, Nina!"

"No," Nina said, shaking her head, because it was impossible.

"He had all that money he stole from the resort to get away. Look, there's an affidavit attached here that's in his handwriting. Look."

The papers in front of her felt heavy as she picked

them up. A petition had been filed by Lynda to approve the resort sale, which was set for a hearing, with a consolidated petition to have Jim Strong, a missing person, declared dead, to be heard on the same date, two days away.

But a new, third matter consisted of a complaint in intervention and motion to have a conservator appointed for Jim Strong under the California Probate Code, along with supporting papers, all prepared by Michael Stamp's office. Nina went straight to the notarized affidavit, the last document appended before the proposed orders:

I, James Philip Strong, declare:

1. *I am over the age of twenty-one and a resident of the City of Porto Alegre, State of Rio Grande do Sul, Country of Brasil.*

2. *I own 16.667% (one-sixth) of the shares in Paradise Ski Resort, a private corporation licensed to operate in the States of California and Nevada. A copy of the duly-probated will of Yolande Strong, my mother, is attached hereto and incorporated herein by this reference, and is the source of my ownership interest.*

3. *On or about February twenty-eight and for two weeks thereafter, a Notice of Proposed Sale appeared in the* Tahoe Mirror *newspaper regarding the sale of all assets, stock and goodwill in the above-named corporation.*

4. *My consent as a minority shareholder has not*

been obtained, and therefore the sale is not approved by all owners of more than 5% of the stock as required by the Bylaws of Paradise Resort, Inc., attached hereto as Exhibit "B and incorporated herein."

5. *I am informed and advised and thereon aver that the reason my consent has not been obtained is that the majority stockholder, Philip C. Strong, my father, plans to deprive me of all proceeds due and owing as a result of my ownership interest, due to personal animosity and without any legal reason.*

6. *As a resident of a foreign country I am requesting permission to make a Special Appearance in this action* in absentia, *represented by my counsel, Michael Stamp of the law firm of Caplan, Stamp, and Powell. I am unable to travel to the United States at this time due to pending Warrants of Arrest in the States of California and Nevada which I intend to contest in due course.*

For all the above reasons, I request that this Honorable Court deny the motion of Petitioners to approve the sale of the said company unless and until I have been contacted through my attorneys and my consent or declination of the transaction has been obtained.

In the alternative, if the Court for other reasons decides to approve the sale, I request that my entire share of the gross proceeds be placed in

*an interest-bearing trust account pending a final
determination of my claim to the proceeds and
my obligations as to resort debts and sales costs.*

*This Declaration is made under penalty of
perjury pursuant to the laws of the State of California on or about the 15th day of March, at the
City of Porto Alegre, State of Rio Grande do Sul,
República Federativa do Brasil.*

The document was signed, dated, witnessed, and
notarized. Nina stared at the signature. She remembered Jim Strong's writing, the aggressive hook of
the *g*, the pressing-down, the size of his writing.
She was interested in graphology and remembered
signatures.

It looked like the real thing. She said, "Do you
know if the requirements for notarizing documents
in Brazil are as careful as they are here?"

"No idea. I've never been to Brazil."

"The signature looks like Jim's to you?"

"Looks exactly like his. I can't tell you the impact
it had on me, when I first saw this."

"Brazil," Nina said. "Why?"

"Don't know. He's far away, at least, and it doesn't
seem he has any plans to show up in town, but I
wanted to tell you myself, he still seems to be walking this planet. And look here." Philip reached into
his briefcase and unearthed a letter from Michael
Stamp dated March 24th. "It's a demand letter for a
complete accounting of the anticipated sale proceeds

and for twelve and a half percent of the gross sale, not even the net, to be placed in escrow. That would tie up everything, Nina—the entire two and a half million!"

"It stinks," Nina said. "It's a dual attack. The strategy seems to be this: to demand that Jim's share of something over four hundred thousand net be paid to Jim in Brazil, or in the alternative Mike Stamp will try to tie up the entire net proceeds in an escrow account, which may well sit for years. The object is to put pressure on the rest of you to accept the affidavit as valid and sufficient proof that Jim is alive and get the four hundred thousand freed up quickly. It's nasty, but very effective. Very smart." Stamp was a chess player. Nina played chess, too, and was familiar with a forking maneuver when she saw one.

"Lynda's unwilling to try to deal with it. Of course I'm not going to send the money to Brazil. Kelly has been in therapy—I went into a depression myself and had a minor heart attack because of him—look what he did to— I am not going to do anything to benefit Jim except help him surrender. If he's alive, he can come up here and ask for his share in person."

Nina nodded and reached for the bottle of Pepto-Bismol in the bottom drawer and poured herself a slug.

"Bellyache?" he asked.

"You got that right."

Philip smiled sadly. "He always was."

"This signature appears to be authentic." She

couldn't understand how she could be holding a signed document from a man she firmly believed to be dead. "Of course, we would have it checked."

"And after everything, he is my son. I loved him, once. It's all beyond me. I've been torn apart so many times I—"

"Do you know of any connection he had to Brazil?" Nina thumbed again through the legal pleadings. A *pro forma* proceeding had exploded into real litigation.

"Marianne's mother lives in Brazil," Philip said, "but she says they aren't in contact. That's about all I know about Brazil. Samba. Ipanema. The Amazon."

"The other side of the world. Philip, is there any evidence Jim is alive other than this affidavit? Is this it?"

"Yes. According to his lawyer in Brazil, he doesn't want to contact us as family anymore. He only wants money. You know, he told Kelly once, he took his anger out on other people by taking away what they loved most. I guess he thinks I'm all about the money. It's true, it was my hope to use the money to start a new life. This is my punishment. Endless punishment. It's eerie. The strength of his jealousy and vindictiveness—maybe he is alive."

They were both silent for a moment. Nina patted Philip Strong's gnarly, cold hand.

He said, "Lynda suggested I try to get you involved. Did she call you?"

"Not yet. I appreciate you coming here, Philip,

but I can't help you. As you know, I have a close personal stake in this. Your son was my client." The unspoken flowed between them. Not only had Jim Strong been her client. He had killed her husband.

"That's why you should be involved, if you can stand it. You withdrew from handling his defense. There's no legal conflict. And if Jim is alive, you can find out where he's living, what he's up to, what he's planning. You can track him. Maybe you can get an address or something from his lawyers. Extradite him. Get him tried. Find a silver lining. I don't know."

"Philip?"

"Yes?"

"He's dead. This is a fraud."

"So help me prove it. You're familiar with us, familiar with him, and you are a good lawyer. Hardly a week goes by without news about some case you won."

"It's a small town, once you deduct the tourists. Not so much to write about."

"We need you, Nina. I'm sorry, but we do. You know the criminal case against Jim and you practice civil law. Kelly wants you to come on board, too. She told me she'd prefer that any money we need to spend on this case goes to you."

"I'm grateful for your faith in me. But—"

"And Marianne would like it, too."

This, Nina did not believe. Philip's daughter-in-law had always troubled her.

Philip continued, "I know this might take some

time. I'll give you a generous retainer and front all the expenses." This all came out in one breath, a plea.

Nina's intercom line rang. That would be Sandy. "Excuse me," she said to Strong, and glanced toward the doorway that led from the outer office, and which sure enough was cracked for Sandy to now catch the gist.

"Ask for ten," Sandy said in her ear. "And they pay you to watch over a guy you should watch over."

"I'll get back to you on that." Nina heard her friend Paul's voice in her mind. *A screw loose*, he would say about Jim, as if that explained everything about a boy with the empathy of a slug who grew into a man who killed other people.

She turned back to Philip. "What exactly do you want me to do?"

"Talk to Lynda about taking over the sale."

"When?"

Philip said, "Well, right away. The hearing is coming up pretty fast."

"I see that. Wednesday at three." Two days away. For the millionth time, Nina wondered why every single damn legal problem had to be complicated by some sort of insane deadline.

"Lynda doesn't know what to do. She realizes she's out of her depth. We seem to be in a dangerous and chaotic and urgent situation, Nina."

"What about the buyers for your resort? Any chance you could convince them to be a little more patient?"

"It's not up to them. They have bank deadlines."

"So a continuance might be fatal to the sale?"

Philip spread his hands. "Please. I know it would be smarter for you to not get involved. I know we have no right to ask. But—I don't know, at least help us complete the sale and prevent the money from going to Jim in Brazil."

"He's dead, Philip. I truly believe that. I would take that position rather strongly, and that would mean that you would take the position that this is some sort of con."

"Take whatever position you think is right."

She could imagine nothing more satisfying than a final resolution, Jim declared dead, all of them able to move on without his ghost coming around to haunt them. She was excited, infuriated; the signature on the foreign affidavit she was fingering was like the return of a ghost she had to do battle with, had to fully defeat this time.

She opened her appointment book and studied it. Philip waited. She could hear him breathing.

"All right, Philip, I'll represent you. I can put aside some commitments to get to this right away. I'll check with the Ethics Committee of the state bar first to make sure there isn't a legal conflict, but if I get an okay, I'll do my best to complete the sale."

"And you'll deal with Jim?"

"And deal with whatever."

"Thank you so very much." Strong reached again into his briefcase and said, "A starter." He handed her a corporate check made out to Law Offices of Nina Reilly.

Twenty thousand dollars. A sign that this wouldn't be easy.

She stood up, and that urged Strong to get up. His back seemed to hurt him as he did so, and he gave the orange chair a dubious look and arched his body carefully.

Great.

"I've already hired the same private detective who investigated Jim's embezzling. Eric Brinkman. Do you know him?"

"I know of him. I usually use an investigator from out of town."

"Eric speaks Portuguese—he's American, though. He's willing to go to Brazil. I'll call him and tell him to make an appointment to see you right away."

At the door to the hallway, Philip leaned in close and whispered, "I hate him. My own son."

"I can relate. He hurt me, Philip."

"He's a pain. A bad one."

She allowed herself to let out a dry chuckle. "He always was."

CHAPTER 3

As soon as she saw Philip Strong out, Nina made a quick call, then stuck her head out her office door and said to Sandy, "Can you get hold of Paul?"

The left side of Sandy's lips turned up slightly.

The *Mona Lisa* half smile: Sandy ecstatic, Nina thought.

"About time you talked to him."

"I don't have much choice. He's involved." Nobody had a more intimate relationship with the Strong family than Paul, however much he might wish to forget it.

"I already put in a call to Carmel."

Sheer gall or mind reading, Nina could never decide about Sandy. "That was jumping the gun. But okay, thanks."

"I knew you needed him. Meanwhile, you have a meeting later with Burglar Boy. I'll lock up the silver and the files good before he shows."

"Fine. I can't put that off. I'm going to read these

papers from Philip Strong and talk to Paul. I've got some things to think about."

Sandy pulled at her lower lip. "Jim Strong's in Brazil?"

"So his father believes."

"I can hardly stand to say his name."

"Me neither."

"Bob told me he was dead."

Bob was Nina's fifteen-year-old son. He, too, had been terrorized by Jim Strong. Paul had talked to him and somehow allayed his fears. With lies?

"Bob doesn't know anything."

"He said Paul said."

Nina felt a cold finger scratching her spine and shook a little to knock it off. "I heard what Paul told him, Sandy. He was reassuring a scared kid."

"Don't worry, I didn't even tell Joseph. I didn't even tell God about it in my prayers. But now I gotta say something. Paul told Bob he took care of Jim. He shouldn't have done that to make Bob feel better."

"Maybe Paul needed to make us feel safer."

"Maybe Paul knew what he was talking about."

Nina didn't know what to say to that.

"In spite of what Paul said, if Jim Strong's in Brazil, can he be extradited?" Sandy asked.

"I just found out from Sergeant Cheney that the authorities down there have been informed about the contact. I get the feeling that law enforcement is going to let the Strong family do the legwork of confirming it or proving it's wrong before they try to start any kind of extradition proceeding, Sandy. It's true, though, if Jim's alive, the sale of the resort is flushing him out. He has to come forward or forfeit a fortune. There's so much money involved." About all Fred Cheney had been able to tell Nina was that murder warrants were still out on Jim Strong.

Sandy rubbed her nose with a finger. "If he's alive, we'll have to kill him."

"An affidavit does not a live man make." Nina went back to her desk and looked at the file pile. Her concentration was blown, but she was used to forcing herself to work in whatever mood she was in. She opened a file and got efficient and busy and let Jim Strong ride a high current in her mind, float there not doing much, waiting. She could hear Sandy in the outer office, clacking on her keys, and the sound was comforting. Sandy sure was working hard these days.

At noon Nina and Sandy put on their coats and drove through the slush to the new Chinese restaurant near the Y. Nina ordered wine and Sandy's eye went to the glass. Sandy did not drink, drug, smoke, or tolerate fools.

"My choice was this or Jack Daniel's straight," Nina said. "It's wine, Sandy, not whiskey. I'm not falling-down drunk in an alley, happy but semiconscious. I'm upset."

"Me, too, which is why I'm keeping my wits about me." Sandy had ordered a plate piled high with cashew chicken over rice, with a side dish of broccoli. She ate, studying Nina.

Nina sipped her wine slowly, knowing she could not order another without inviting an intervention. Two glasses of wine at lunch was the beginning of the end for a lawyer. The food didn't attract Nina at all, which on its own was highly unusual.

"Lynda Eckhardt called." Sandy delicately sipped her iced Darjeeling. "She'll cooperate all she can, but you need to decide pronto."

"I've told Strong I'm in, but I wish I could have talked to Paul first."

Sandy speared a piece of broccoli and ate it, mouth closed, chewing methodically. "I like Paul."

"Don't we all."

"But he'd lie if he thought he had a reason to."

"Yes."

A couple of grains of rice remained on Sandy's plate. She picked up her chopsticks and hunted them down. "Paul hasn't been up here in the mountains in ages."

"His choice."

"Not exactly. Yours. Yours and Kurt's."

"No. Paul's problem."

"Still."

"Still what?"

"Still got a thing for you."

"Oh, for Pete's sake." Nina sucked down what was left in her wineglass, gulped some water, and took a bite of her egg roll. "I'm trying to make it work with Kurt right now. Paul understands that."

"But," Sandy said, then sucked down the rest of her tea, "no contact for months."

"I don't know why guys get that way, Sandy. It's never made any sense to me how they cut you off when things change. They seem to need to go cold and quiet. I'd love to see him."

"Really."

"Of course."

"Why not stay in contact?"

"I've been busy."

"And there's Kurt to think about."

Nina looked out the window at the happy people moseying along the sidewalk. "You're right. Paul understands. He stays away because that's appropriate. I'm with Kurt. I guess I actually don't like it when people do that, stay in touch with old lovers, like, if things don't work out, they've got an alternative lined up."

"Well, you picked Kurt over Paul."

"I did."

"Kurt's your son's father, I get that," Sandy said. "Aside from that, I wish I knew why you stick it out."

The doors to the restaurant opened, letting in a frigid blast of air, but the doors shut and nobody came inside. Nina shivered. "I only want to do my job, make some money, raise my son, and find someone to love. Why's that so hard?"

"Yeah, why is it?" Sandy said, her standard impassivity restored. "I think you should get a horse."

"What?"

"Get outside. Do some riding. Do something normal on the weekend besides working."

Nina left some money on the table and pushed her chair back.

"Nix on the horse," she said.

"You go ahead." Sandy scraped up the last of her chicken, steady and deliberate as always. "Don't worry. I'll get the receipt."

That afternoon in Nina's office, the young burglar took the news that his case was going to be reduced to a misdemeanor with aplomb. "Time served?" he said.

"That'll be the recommendation, along with three years of probation. But, Josh, listen, okay? You need to pay attention."

He raised his eyebrows as if attending, but his eyes were glued to his smartphone.

"You'll go to prison if you do it again."

"You mean, if I'm caught." He was nineteen, with a shaven head and blue tattoos covering his left arm. His lost eyes, when they finally looked up, bothered Nina. His crying mother had paid his legal fee. Like many young petty criminals, he thought he'd just had a spell of bad luck, when what he had had was a foreshadowing.

Nina handed him an appointment card. "Nine a.m., tomorrow. Be there. Do not under any circumstances get in any trouble before then."

He grinned at her, stroking ornately carved facial hair, then got up and said with a formality that astonished her, "May I ask you a personal question?"

"What?"

"How old are you?"

"Thirty-eight."

Her youthful burglar looked her in the eye and said, "I hope when I'm that age, my wife looks just like you."

Half her age, he almost had her fluffing her hair. "See you tomorrow."

Before leaving for the day, Nina read the paperwork on the Paradise Ski Resort sale again. She called Lynda Eckhardt. She called the state bar ethics hotline to see if she'd have some sort of conflict of interest, considering that two years before Jim Strong had been her client. The answer was no. This was an entirely different legal matter.

She called the South Lake Tahoe police station and talked again to her buddy Sergeant Fred Cheney, then had Sandy make copies of all the legal paperwork and deliver it to him.

She called Michael Stamp's office to say that she would be stepping in.

Nina did some online research. In the library, which with its long table doubled as her conference room, she looked up the law on special appearances, in which a party in a lawsuit either didn't appear personally at all or appeared only for a limited purpose.

The law was vague on the question of whether Strong could carry on his litigation from Brazil. Other legal issues stemmed from Jim's status as a missing person and from how to handle his share of the sales proceeds. Was there a chance she could convince Judge Flaherty that Jim was dead? Probably not, not until they had dealt with the bombshell affidavit.

Jim couldn't be alive. She had it on good authority that he was not.

Before she left for home, Paul van Wagoner called her back. "Remember me?"

"Who's calling, please?"

"Why, you naughty, naughty girl."

"Paul, I'm so happy to hear your voice." Nina felt an automatic lift just talking with him again. He knew her better than anyone else and forgave her for what he knew.

"Got your message, sweet cheeks."

"What have you been up to?"

"Played hooky today and went for a hike at Big Sur."

"With Susan?"

"Susan?" He said it as if he needed to think in

order to remember the name, although Nina knew better. He had known her for years. According to gossip, Susan wanted marriage and had agitated hard. Nina felt uneasy about how relieved she had been when she heard through the Monterey grape-vine that Paul didn't jump at the chance.

"I went alone," he said finally. "We're over."

"Sorry to hear it," Nina lied. She had no rights over him. Still, Paul swam into sharper focus with this pronouncement.

"She moved to San Francisco. That's a long way."

Nina herself was over 250 miles from Carmel, and yet they had managed, at one time. In spite of months of silence, they always picked up in a happy place, when they picked up.

"Somewhere along the line we stopped caring a whole lot."

"No need to offer details."

"Ah, but if I don't, you don't have to give me details about you and Kurt."

"Paul, I didn't call about—"

"Please don't say you're getting married again and I'm not invited."

"Philip Strong came to my office. He believes Jim Strong is alive." She listened to Paul's breath catch over the line and remembered how it smelled like cloves sometimes, or peppermint.

"Now, why would he believe that?"

She explained about the affidavit.

"From Brazil? It's a con."

She imagined Paul in his office, feet up on the polished desk, looking out the window at the attractive patrons below. Paul had a prosperous practice as a private investigator in Carmel, California, where he had found an office in a building that overlooked Clint Eastwood's old restaurant and bar, the Hog's Breath Inn.

"I won't discuss Jim Strong with you. You know that."

"I have been over this in my mind, Paul, and I've developed this awful suspicion that Jim's alive. Maybe you lied. You let me think he was dead."

He didn't say anything.

"I have a right to know the truth. I thought I did for these past few years and now I need reassurance."

"I never lied to you, Nina."

She heard heat in his voice, but was it the heat of truth or the heat of deception? "You have to know how this affects me and Bob."

"Look. I'll come up to Tahoe tonight. Stay at Harrah's. See you in the morning. Been meaning to do some gambling anyway. My jar's full of quarters and my fingers ache for cards."

"Why not tell me now?"

"All in good time."

"What about your work?"

"Just finished a big job. Wish is hanging things out and I can leave for a day or two. Hire me. What do you say? We'll deal with this, get it over with, hit the beach, and let the sun work its magic."

"Philip already has a PI," Nina told him. "I told him I'd take the case, Paul, but I may not be able to bring you in."

"Take it. Let's see what's up."

They had been lovers and they had been friends, and they had done things together that gave her night frights. "Probably it wasn't a good idea."

"Philip's PI won't be as good as I am."

"Not up to me."

"I don't know what's going on yet, but we'll find out. There's money in the pot somebody wants, and it ain't Jimmy. Listen. I'll be by in the morning. You got court?"

"Short stuff."

"Good."

The intercom buzzed. "Sandy wants me," Nina said.

"Well, then, hustle. Never ignore the boss. See you tomorrow. Can't wait. There's ass waiting to be kicked up there."

CHAPTER 4

Nina drove home with much on her mind. With law, a great deal of thinking went on between three and five in the morning, and Jim Strong had instantly become both a personal and professional awakener. Sometimes jogging a few blocks around the neighborhood with her dog, Hitchcock, helped her sleep better, but the slushy spring roads lately had made that risky.

Oh, hell, she wasn't going to sleep much no matter what.

News nattered on the radio and she listened to the local report: snow showers tonight, a high of fifty, clear weather tomorrow. Tahoe's dry climate had plenty of sunny early-spring days. If only Jim Strong hadn't bobbed up like a jack-in-the-box, she might be thinking about the weekend and her new skis.

At least Paul was coming. Maybe he would take over and figure it all out. How to feel about Paul? She plonked him on a dusty mental shelf with all her other past indiscretions, knowing he would instantly jump off. He had a way of crawling into her heart whether she invited him or not.

She turned onto Jicarilla off Pioneer Trail and, after a few more twists in the forested streets full of cabins, went down Kulow Street and turned into the slick downhill driveway.

These days she drove a sensible RAV4, a compact SUV that never broke down and had enough cargo space for trips to the lumberyard and the dump.

Bob and Hitchcock must be out for a walk, though it was already dark. The cabin emitted a warm, damp smell. Bob had turned on the lights in the big room and even tossed a Duraflame log into the orange Swedish fire stove. She sat down on the couch to pull her leather boots off, then went to the kitchen to check her messages and pour her nightly glass of Clos du Bois.

Blinking.

"Hi," Kurt's voice said. "Can I come over tonight? We need to talk." The world is a cliché, Nina thought, as she refreshed her glass.

After a long sip, she called back and got Kurt's message phone. "How about eight? But I have to get to bed early."

She had noticed that when Kurt's latest temporary job had dried up, he began staying up late and got up later. This disrupted their relationship, since she began to yawn by 9:00 p.m. most nights.

In her small, cozy kitchen she boiled water for

spaghetti, clicking on the television news, watching with one eye on it, one on the food. A bear had been sighted wandering down Golden Bear Street. Made sense in an ursine way. She felt a small pang of worry about Bob and Hitchcock. She would have to equip Bob with pepper spray and teach him how to use it; he took the dog onto all kinds of trails, and the bears had lately come to view South Lake Tahoe as their neighborhood Safeway. The big animals were supposed to be hibernating but with food available year-round, their ancient habits had shifted. They broke windows and garage doors and came into people's houses, ransacking fridges and pantries and scaring everyone.

She dumped tomato sauce into her potion of ground beef, onions, garlic, and peppers, turned the heat down, and stretched out on the couch for a moment of peace.

The front door flew open. Bob said, "Mom?"

"Shoes off!" she called. "Wipe Hitch's feet!" Too late—the big, mostly black malamute bounded to her and propped both his muddy, wet paws onto her leg. She gave up, petted his coarse fur, chatted with Bob for a minute, then went back to her kitchen duties while Bob changed the station to a show about affluent kids who lived in a Neverland where snow never fell and teens never got acne.

At dinner Bob, age fifteen and on the edge of some sort of revolution, said, "I have a test in Spanish class tomorrow. I'm going to blow it."

"Why? You have tonight to study."

"It's too hard."

"You've talked to your teacher?"

"He despises me. He plots my death."

"Bob, have you been acting up in class?" Bob seemed to develop a new annoying mannerism every day, from foot-tapping to humming to restless shifting around that Nina only had to look at at mealtimes, but the teacher had to watch day after day for an hour straight.

Bob got up. "How come you always blame me? I'm trying to get through without dying of boredom. Mr. Acevedo doesn't like me and I don't like Spanish." Bob pulled out his cell, read it, and began texting. "It's Kurt. He says he's coming over."

Bob hadn't met Kurt until he was twelve years old, and it had seemed too late to all of them for Kurt to be called Dad. Bob and Kurt had taken to each other like puzzle pieces finally slotted together correctly. Nina found some aspects of their reunion almost uncanny, as if Bob had been somewhat of a mystery that suddenly resolved. Their coloring, their volatility, their musical talent; they were very alike.

They loved each other now, that was the main thing. "You have to study, so say hi and disappear upstairs while we visit."

"Don Quixote de la buncha crap," Bob said. "Got it."

"Go to work, now, kiddo."

He whined and complained for another minute.

"Fine, your choice. No B average, no piano until

you bring your grade up." Bob loved playing his old stand-up piano so much that Nina occasionally used deprivation of piano time as a punishment. As a result, Bob considered the piano a luxury and pleasure. She drained pasta into a bowl and added the sauce, hoping it would pick up heat from the noodles.

Bob's future swam into view: a musical career of some sort. He often played late into the night after Nina went to her room. Looking at his lips, set in a teenage snarl, she allowed herself to hope he could make a living from music because a college degree would never hang on this boy's wall.

"How the hell would you know if I have a B average right this minute or not?"

"Don't swear, Bob. Do you?"

He looked exactly as he had as a four-year-old, as he considered lying. Unlike when he was four, he realized he'd get caught. "No."

"Think of Spanish like you think of music. Listen to it. It can be beautiful, too."

He snorted and started to leave.

"Um, but you know, clean off the table first."

He cleaned the table and even rinsed the dishes, although the whole time he sang loudly, songs he knew offended her. Then he went upstairs, and Nina didn't have the energy to check whether he was playing video games or studying. She cleaned up the rest of the kitchen, threw a load of laundry in the washer, watered the houseplants, petted and fed the dog, fluffed her long brown hair, and changed out of her work clothes into a pair of fresh jeans, finishing as the doorbell rang.

Kurt Scott wore his usual denim and fleece jacket and suede work boots. He carried a six-pack of Coors, which he set on the floor while he gave her a hug and stripped off the winter outerwear, hanging the coat in the small closet in the foyer, and stacking his boots over the layer of melting boots that already lined it. "Almost had an accident on the way in," he said. "Slid out a little on Pioneer, and sure enough a Chevy Suburban was piling by in the opposite direction at that moment. Missed it by an inch. You could hear his horn all the way to Reno. I hate the melting spring slush that comes with a warm spell almost as much as I despise the apocalyptic winters here."

"Cheerful as always, eh, Kurt?"

He laughed.

"Sit." She brought him a pint glass for his Coors and sat down with him in front of the fire. Kurt actually did look weary and glum. He had Bob's black hair and blue eyes, an elegant man with a long face and narrow chin who always looked a little out of place in the mountain-man clothes he wore. Of his two dissimilar careers, concert pianist definitely fit him better than forest ranger. His hands were long and smooth. He had recently lost weight, and his face seemed thin and drawn.

The move from Europe to Tahoe hadn't worked out well. Kurt barely made his rent from his savings and the unemployment checks for his last layoff, and the next stop would be operating a ski lift at minimum wage. She moved closer and put her arm around him, angling up for a kiss. A butterfly flew by her lips.

Nothing had been right for some time. "Rough day?" she asked.

"Usual day. You?"

"Yeah." Nina told him about Philip Strong wanting to track down his son, and how Paul was coming up, and what he had said.

Kurt frowned, listening without comment, then said, "Somebody's full of shit."

"You mean Philip? Or Jim Strong? Or Paul?"

"Let's not get into that. I don't care about Paul. Truth is, I don't care about your case at the moment. What matters is that you care more about your job than me."

Nina studied the way the logs burned, listening to their crackle. Kurt hurt her so often lately. Was this what it was like when sweet turned to sour? Every tap felt like a blow.

"*Care*," she said. "That seems to be the operative word."

Kurt set down his beer. "Let's talk. I came back three months ago hopeful for our relationship, wanting to mend everything. I wanted us to be a family. And it was a beautiful vision, one you bought into, too."

Past tense.

"Instead I'm broke and this—unity I hoped for didn't happen."

"Three months isn't long," Nina said.

His brow creased. "Listen, Nina. I won't go to work as a cashier at a casino or sell lift tickets. I'm too damn old to go back to tromping around for the Forest Service, making trails and scaring off poachers. I'm a concert pianist. Not playing for people is killing me."

"But since you had physical therapy, you've been able to play in the community orchestra. I thought you loved that."

"I do, but it's not enough. I built a reputation for fifteen years in Europe. I have six CDs. I have a following. There's nothing to challenge me here professionally."

He sounded confrontational. Nina felt herself heating up.

"I got this today." He pulled out a letter and handed it to her.

She looked at it. "Swedish. What's it say?"

"I'm invited to tour Scandinavia and Russia for four months with the Royal Swedish Philharmonic. Short notice, but they want me to sub for Bengt Forsberg. He broke his leg. The Bach pieces I already know."

Memories of the two of them, young, swept through her mind. She remembered them kissing on a rotting porch at Fallen Leaf Lake and how much she had loved him, trusted him. She had felt abandoned and lost without him, a young, pregnant, unmarried woman.

We can do without you if we have to, she decided.

"Roughly one hundred twenty days. A summer apart. We'll be okay."

"This offer could work into a full-time gig."

"Wait a minute." She paused to think about what to say. "You came here tonight to give up on our family? You'd do that?"

Kurt stood, got close to her, then put his hand on hers, a gesture so familiar it hurt. "You chose me for the wrong reasons. To be a father to Bob. To avoid other hard truths. Maybe you thought I'd fill in the part of parent you don't do because you work so much."

"Someone has to make a living. Someone has to support us!"

"That's right, and you love it. I'm not criticizing. I love that about you, too. But see, you don't love the same thing about me, that I also love my work and won't give it up."

"You won't stay here and I won't follow you. That's the grand idea?"

"No." He shook his head. "The insight here is that I don't think you love me."

Nina tried to say she loved him unconditionally and madly. Her mouth opened. She cleared her throat. Nothing came out.

He watched her try, waiting patiently as she struggled. "Bob will be fine. He knows how much we both love him. He'll adapt. Tell him I'll call tomorrow." Kurt turned her so that he was facing her, then he kissed her on the forehead. "Think about what I've said. Let's talk again soon."

The sound of his old pickup made her run to the window and look out. Orion shone down like a brilliant number seven playing card on this moonless night, on snow piled roundly all across the yard. She drew the curtains, locked up, turned off the lights, and went upstairs. Peeking into Bob's room, she said, "Kurt had to go. He'll call you. How's the Spanish?"

"*Muy malo*," Bob said, looking up from the Facebook wall he was writing on.

"Good night, Bob."

"Did you fight?"

"We talked about how we both love you, and 'that's about the size, where you put your eyes.'" She sang a favorite childhood song of his. Then she couldn't resist a compulsion to kiss him on the cheek. He used to smell of talc and baby oil, now he smelled of boy.

"Urk."

"Sleep well. Love you."

"Love you, too." His reply, automatic though it might be, warmed her.

The evening called for a long shower, then a nightcap. Passing through her room en route to the bathroom, she looked at the case file on her bed, taken home to ready her for tomorrow's work. Stripping off her clothes, throwing them on the floor, she changed course. Quick shower and then a pot of tea instead.

Kicking her shoes toward the closet, she thought about the young boy Sandy had dubbed Burglar Boy. He lived as she had in her youth, without consciousness, hurtling forward, too busy snatching at opportunities to give a thought or a damn about consequences. Hence Bob, the precious outcome of the most important mistake she had ever made, falling for Kurt that summer so long ago.

After her shower, she turned on her night-light and studied Burglar Boy's paperwork. Yeah. The probation office was recommending time served. The judge wouldn't go against that. The sentencing hearing would go smoothly. She plotted out her moves to get the kid off, hoping he would do good, not bad, in the future. That was out of her hands, however. Her job had been to earn him a second chance to be the innocent they all wanted him to be.

Eyes drooping, she ticked off her blessings.

Bob. Brother, Matt. His wife, Andrea. Their kids, Troy and Brianna.

Sandy and her family.

Her job. Her good health.

She pictured Kurt. Where did he fit in?

Angel or demon? Or both?

Paul? Same questions.

Nina clicked off the light and closed her eyes. Imprinted on the inside of her eyelids was an image: Jim Strong, murderer. He had killed her husband and come after her and Bob. Some nights you never forget. The image of a handsome, empty, resurrected face disturbed her dreams.

He was dead. He had to be.

CHAPTER 5

She called at ten on Tuesday morning while I was at work. "How about a quickie?"

Crude but effective; she was gorgeous. I was in love, and her roughness excited me. I laughed. "When?"

"Noon. Room 102. Ground floor of the new building. You can park practically at the door from the back parking lot."

"You have until one?"

"I'll make it feel like longer. Can you get away?"

"Yeah."

"Yeah, you're coming?"

"Yeah."

As I drove into the half-full parking lot, I noticed only a couple of tour buses—there used to be a hundred. In April, when the skiing gets messy and a few boats are starting to come out on the lake, the doldrums come and the tourists do stay away, but this had been a remarkably poor season. The mountains behind me looked pristine from far away, but a closer look would show the runs had gone to slush. Dark clouds bellied in from Nevada, a hopeful sign. We could use one more blizzard before the skis schussed off for good.

I felt vulnerable, which was unusual for me. With ten minutes to wait, I didn't want to stand at the door of the room and have people who might know me see me. I'm not great with words, so as I locked up and leaned against the truck and pulled my baseball cap down low against the bite of the wind, I did some rehearsing.

I'd had shit for a life and a ton of disappointment. Now I needed to talk to her again about my plans. I was pretty sure this time she'd go along with everything, but then again, it's hard to tell with women like her, who haven't had it easy either, who don't always live by the rules of the straight world.

Cyndi, I said to her in my mind, in my fucked-up life, nobody else has come close; that's the truth. I love you. I want to give you the life you deserve. You didn't understand last time when I tried to explain, but today you'll change your mind.

Saying these things to myself, I felt touched enough to wipe my eyes. I could hardly believe I had it in me to fall this hard for anyone. I've never been in love before, though I've had plenty of women. It took a lifetime to learn that there's a chasm between loving someone and being in love. Being in love is an uncanny thing.

I watched her walk from the main hotel in tall leather boots, all streaming hair and blowing coat. She saw me. We met at the door. I didn't say anything or touch her while she inserted the card into the lock and swung the door open, because anybody in the lot could see us. We both took a long look in.

Everything as it should be: bed unmade, bottle stuck in the wastebasket with the cardboard remains of last night's Thai takeout, lamp and heat left blowing energy. On the little table next to the window, a $20 bill for Housekeeping awaited plucking.

We rushed in together, shoulder to shoulder, and I kicked the door shut. Cyndi smiled, her mouth mischievous. She held up a finger. One hour until she had to be back at her job at the desk. One clear hour before the maid would come to clean the room. Cyndi would know that. Meantime, for this short space of time, the room was a free zone.

Cyndi threw off her coat, stuck out her tongue at me, ran into the bathroom, and slammed the door. I stripped, laying my clothes on the chair, then pulled up the cover and stretched out right on top. I put my hands behind my head and thought about her, and, man, I started heating up. She came out wearing a blue bra and black tights, swinging and grinning. "What a beauty!" she said, looking at me, before she jumped on and straddled me. And we went at it.

Limber as a gymnast, she was light and sweet to taste and it went on and on, all kinds of moves. Not shy, Cyndi was an expert; she had danced with a lot of poles in her career. She liked a lot of energy from her partner and I gave it to her.

I gave it to her good.

A couple of my women I had loved with that respectful, law-abiding love that meant you couldn't totally forget yourself in bed. Most I had slept with without feeling any connection. You have to keep a guard up; you have to calculate things, make sure she has equal time, fake things, lie. During my year with Cyndi, though, I had given her complete power over me and my lonely heart. She could make me cry. We didn't ever have quickies. That was just her little joke.

She was the one.

Finished, we lay on our sides, me pressing against her back. I ran my hands up and down her, slow and calm, enjoying that dancer body, the curvy stomach of a woman who'd had kids.

"I could use a drink," she murmured in a sleepy voice.

I handed her the half-pint of Martell cognac I had brought. She downed a good slug and handed it back. I powered down the rest.

She turned to face me, stroking fingers on my chest. "You are mine."

"I am."

She took another long minute or two to kiss me again. Then she breathed, "I'm sorry. I better—" She began to get up.

"Wait a minute." I held on to her. "We need to talk."

"Better spit it out then, sweet one." She put a bare leg over me and got into a position where she could see the clock radio on the bedstand. "I have to go."

"Do you love me, Cyndi?" That broke an unwritten rule because we only said that when we were right in the middle of it. "I need to know you do."

"Ah, c'mon. You're my sweetie, bad boy. Let's not get technical," she teased.

"I can show you how much I love you if you let me, but I need to know first. What are you willing to do to be with me?"

After a long silence, she sat on the side of the bed, hair hanging over her eyes so I couldn't see them. "We had this discussion. You promised me you wouldn't bring it up again."

"Yes, but I don't think you thought it through. We could live together in a beautiful, warm country in a beach house with a pool, a staff, a view of the world, a soft bed, privacy at last."

"I told you, no."

I came up behind her, pressed against her back, wound my legs around her body. "Listen one more time." I held her close and told her about it again, laid it out a different way, sure I could convince her this was the only way, and it was the right way.

When I finished, she turned sideways, her body against me, almost melting in the heat between us. "Forget it. I won't commit a crime. I won't go to prison. You should never have told me any of this."

"There's no risk."

"Right. Sure." Her body tensed. "My friend who went to the Nevada State Penitentiary for selling drugs? He died there."

I suppose my nerves and the time pressure got the better of me. "We'll be rich and free. We can live our lives like we deserve to, not in a hellhole limbo like this. I need more time to explain all this, that damn second hand moving around is all you see—"

"Because I have to go!" Cyndi struggled to stand up and leave.

I tightened my hold.

"Let me go. It's twelve forty-five, and the maid could come in anytime after one. I have another life and it's time to get back to it."

"Fuck your other life! You love me, I love you, I'm trying to talk about our future together and you're—"

"Let me go!"

I felt my heart beat against her back. I felt her sweat on me, smelled perfume mixed with her body.

After another minute, she quit fighting me. She turned her head away and closed her eyes, speaking so softly I had to work to hear her.

"Should have known. Get close to somebody. Fall in love. It's never enough. I should know by now, crazy shit every time." Her eyes opened and she stared at me coldly. Her voice rose but held steady. "You need to let me get up now and put on my clothes. Then I'll go back to work and you forget about me. We're done. I mean that. Okay? I won't tell anyone about your plans. I won't do anything to stop you. But leave me out of it."

She meant it. I could hear it. She had detached

herself right then with no return possible. I knew because I'd done it myself. She might as well have taken an ax and chopped right through my brain. I felt pops, storms. All thinking ceased. Memories attacked. I thought of the day I met her. I thought about how I have failed so many people and how life has failed me.

"I told you from the start," Cyndi said, shaking, pushing. "I won't leave my kids. I won't run with you. I won't go to prison because you've got another set of cheap dreams. Fucking fool. Jesus." She managed to pull away from me, but I jumped up and pushed her back down against the bed. I could see her sneaking furtive looks at the clock, the clock that read five minutes to one.

"You're gonna listen, and you're gonna say yes."

"You're hurting me, asshole!"

She's small but strong. She made a fist and right-hooked me in the side of the jaw. The pain made me lose it for a second. I hit her with the palm of my hand hard on the side of the head—a reflex, that's all it was—and she went limp for a second, so I laid her on her back on the bed. Her mouth opened and kept getting wider and wider and she took in a breath as she got herself ready to let out a shriek that was going to bring witnesses and ruin. Her face went red, snotty, and nasty, transforming her into a new person who didn't love me after all, who'd played me for gifts and thrills.

I put my left hand over her mouth and held her

down with my other hand, trying to keep her quiet, saying, "Cyndi, Cyndi," in a soft chant, but she squirmed like a python, a big snake who had turned against me forever, vicious and out of control. Some small part of my rational mind arrowed its way through the chaos of my emotions to one clear thought: She would tell. If I let her go, she would call the police about my plans.

As if reading my thoughts, she bit me suddenly on the arm, a deep bite, as if she were trying to eat me. The clock, the one she had watched so avidly, flashed one o'clock.

This time reflex played no part. I hauled off and hit her hard again, connecting with her chin, knocking her head back to the pillow. She didn't move. I rubbed my forearm, groaning. White teeth marks, no blood yet, purpling under the skin. I looked at her. Silence, for now.

In emergencies I go cold. Time slows down. In the middle of one now, hardly any blood around, I noted that I hadn't even sat in a chair. Other people slept here every night. The room was full of prints. I had touched almost nothing. Cyndi had even handled the key.

She stirred.

Her black nylons lay on the rug beside the bed in easy reach. I picked them up and wrapped them around her neck. I don't believe at that moment I really meant to kill her, but when she started fighting me, everything snapped into place. The thought had entered my brain, the possibility. I fought back. I held my position even though she struggled through every dying second.

Finally, she stopped. I held tight long enough to look at her pretty hair, her body, anywhere but her face. I wrapped and stretched the black material tighter, muscles straining, encountering no more resistance.

The clock's second hand moved. Round and around it ticked forward as I waited, holding the cloth against her neck. Three times around. Three minutes of hell past one. I had to be sure.

I let go.

Eyes open, she looked dreamily at the ceiling as if she had spotted something interesting there, face now a mottled, swollen gray, fog-colored. I felt a mental storm coming on, not a storm of rage and self-preservation this time, but a storm that would soon lead to decompensation.

I had never killed anyone before. She had forced the situation, put me in serious danger.

I checked the room, ears wide-open for the clank of a cart. I dressed quickly, looking around for signs of my presence. Ten past one. I maneuvered her into bra and panties, unwound the black material from around her throat, and settled her on the bed, wondering at the changes. She looked removed. Distant. Spent. This was the sum total of her life, one stupid mistake.

I had no time, but still I arranged her tangled hair.

Did she think of her children and her husband, in those last moments, when she gasped and I became a maniac?

Her hair felt silky, alive, twisting between my fingers.

Was she sorry? Had there still been a chance?

Her mouth dropped open. I closed it. It dropped open again. I closed her eyes. They opened. She was still fighting me. Her skin moved between life and death in front of me, changing from an interim dusky color to something like salt, inert.

Time to go.

I had the door open and was ready to leave when I realized I didn't have my wallet.

Leaving the door ajar, I crept back inside to look for it. I was so screwed up from the liquor and pain and the rest of it that my eyes couldn't focus anymore. Nothing on the rug, nothing on the bedside table. Seventeen past one in the afternoon. Brilliant sunshine. Fucking Tahoe clarity.

I found my wallet under the bed nestling near a used condom, not mine. I grabbed it, stuffed it into my pocket, and left, pulling my cap down low. I hit my hand on a cart full of towels on the way out. No blood, just another scream in my head. What I had done to Cyndi barreled around my mind like a bad dream. I felt like someone slugged by a piece of king-hell bad luck.

As I hustled out, a maid leaned against the building. She looked my way from about a hundred feet, long-haired, gray-rooted, a good ol' girl. I ran out to the lot; at least the car keys had stayed in my pocket as they should. I took off, but I wasn't relieved to turn onto the highway. My skin had gone cold and my hands on the wheel shook.

What had the maid seen?

See you shortly, honey, I thought, and strength came back, resolve came back, fury came back. Women trying to ruin my life, what I had left of it, trying to destroy the one chance I had left. I wouldn't allow that.

CHAPTER 6

Brenda Bee had been yawning all day because her new husband, Ronnie, husband number three, took Cialis and wouldn't give her any peace all night. She was fifty-five and sex was pleasurable, but have a heart, baby. Don't make it so hard to sit down the next day.

Right now, she was eating lunch at the restaurant on the gaming floor. Employees of Prize's got food at a discount, and since casino buffets cost practically nothing, she could have loaded up on starch, beef, and rich desserts, but she chose wisely, going for lettuce, soggy fruit, and two cups of hot black coffee. At her age, you had to make a choice, sex or food, and she chose sex.

She watched the gamblers' numbing routine. Not long ago you put in quarters and pulled a lever, watched the rows roll for a while, watched them clack clack clack one by one. These days, you inserted a money card and punched a button. The machine gave a digital approximation of sevens rolling along for about two seconds, then lights insisted on another punch, preferably of three quarters, not one. Bells used to blare when even a small pot hit. These days the casinos played it cool and quiet.

Of course, back then you could hardly see the machines for the ciggie smoke, and nowadays the gaming floors were well ventilated. Win some, lose some.

She watched a girl with bleached-blond hair almost faint as three sevens lined up on her machine. A newbie, now hooked on winning, destined to lose her fun money, and it wouldn't take long. Three sevens weren't worth what they had once been. Inflation had hit the world of slot machines in this way, too. Good. More money for Prize's, and that meant better job security for her. How much had the girl won? She couldn't see the jackpot amount on the machine, though it was only a few feet away. The girl wasn't squealing anymore, so it wasn't worth getting up.

Ronnie had been nagging her for ages to get glasses. She couldn't imagine wearing them, the weight on her nose, the ugliness. He said, "Brenda, are you saying female pride won't let you get glasses, even though you're blind without them?"

Pride? No. This was a survival technique, the way she saw it. As soon as she could, she would get LASIK surgery. She hated being nearsighted, had spent her whole life fighting it. If only she had the money. Of course, then she wouldn't be able to see as well up close, but that would be fine, she would welcome drugstore magnifiers for reading. They cost like what, ten bucks? Plus, she didn't read all that much, and Ronnie could read her the menus.

Up here in the mountains, working at a place where showgirls reigned, a girl needed to look her best. That required intervention and vigilance. She had beauty tricks Ronnie would never know about. She had recently had her lips permanently tattooed with color. Lips got pale in middle age. She remembered how perplexed Ronnie had been when she wouldn't let him kiss her for a week after because her lips, swollen and a little crusty, hurt so much. Then, her breasts had shrunk when she lost weight. They hung like her grandma's until she got the lift and implants. She made him wait again until everything healed and she could appreciate his appreciation.

Then came her hair extensions. Yes, hard to believe how cute they made her feel. She had never expected to watch her hair thin, but that it had done. One morning, she had followed her brow to her hairline and discovered—a bald spot! Up the street, right off Highway 50, was a hair/nails place where a Vietnamese lady, singing to herself in her own language the whole time, carefully wove strands of someone else's lovely thick hair into Brenda's own, until you couldn't see where the other person's hair ended and hers began.

Worth every penny, especially the previous week when Ronnie took her out to Harrah's to a live show, and she curled her new hair and looked fantastic and sexy.

How else could a girl compete in this culture of ski bunnies and entertainers who looked twenty when they were thirty, and twenty when they were forty, the dyed-blond boob-babies?

Wiping the dressing from her lips, she rose, then climbed downstairs and down a long hallway, where she picked up her cleaning cart. An extension of Prize's Casino-Hotel, the two-story motel part of the complex had some cheap rooms that opened directly on the parking lot.

Pushing the loaded cart seemed hard today, even though a thin springtime sun warmed her. Her partner, Rosalinda, was home sick, so, doing double duty, she was running late. A few of the rooms she should have finished in the morning she hadn't yet done. Oh, well. She'd skimp on the bathrooms. You could run a dry cloth quickly over water drips and toothpaste blow, fold down the ends of the toilet paper rolls, and keep the customers happy.

She rolled up to Room 102, where the guests had checked out according to her schedule, and saw that the door was ajar. A DO NOT DISTURB sign dangled from the knob.

Ah, jeez, they hadn't left yet after all.

Once, a bad thing had happened—she had busted in on a couple making love on the bed. Brenda had backed out again, and nobody had ever said anything about it to her.

She put her hand on the door, ready to give a swift knock and push it open.

Then hesitated. Something was making her nervous. It was—boy, was she ridiculous—it was as if she could feel that someone was in there, and listening for her. She looked down. Someone had blocked the door with a pillow. Odd, a pillow of all things. It would be hard to step over that with a suitcase.

Not a sound within. It looked dark in there, though it might only have been the sunlight she stood in, contrasting with the interior light.

Fucking Tahoe. All this beauty, but you couldn't ever forget the Donner Party, the starvation, the cannibalism—fucking place, mysterious always.

One thing she believed: when you felt something wrong, something was wrong. How many movies had she seen where the heroine walked right into a situation, a dark alley, toward a couple of lurkers with hoods, when any sane person would turn right around and head for the lighted, busy street? Also, Rosalinda was an astrologist and had been talking about Saturn being ascendant, which meant strange things, occult things, afoot.

She slid back into the hall, skittered under an outside staircase at the end of the block of rooms, and waited.

And waited.

The door opened all the way and she caught a glimpse of someone stepping over the pillow and coming out. A man's leg, that was all. But then the leg was pulled back in and the door softly shut.

Huh? The whole thing was giving her prickles. How could a hotel ground-floor corridor feel so spooky and lonely? Where was everybody?

What was wrong with people? You're in a hotel. Every day, someone comes to clean the room. Where's the surprise in that? Unless you're up to something. Another time she had found a little baggie of white powder on the sink. She and Ronnie had been dating at the time, and she had given it to him. He never mentioned what he did with it, but he took her to a nice place in Carson City the next night.

Now the door opened again. A figure stepped outside the room, peering up and down the shade of the hallway as if looking for her. She shrank back, though she was a long way away.

He seemed to look right at her, but that was impossible. She could barely see him. Although Brenda squinted, she couldn't make out features, except for his build—tall. She stepped back behind the building.

Now she watched passively, hidden, as the man slipped out of Room 102 into the parking lot and disappeared behind a line of hulking SUVs. He wasn't carrying anything.

Okay. Fine. She had let her imagination go wild.

Brenda dragged the Dyson vacuum cleaner, purple and red, something new and expensive the hotel liked because the cleaners were bagless and cheaper in the long run, from under the stairway, edging toward the door. She frowned. He had left the pillow blocking it.

She got closer to the door and could peek inside a little. Heavy drapes held tight, closed against the daylight. The furniture all appeared gray and gloomy. Brenda listened.

To nothing.

A slight breeze rustled the curtains.

"Housekeeping!"

Nobody came. No sound came out of the room. She turned the knob to push the door open wider.

Curious and bolder now, she stepped inside. For a few moments, her eyes needed to adjust. The furniture turned itself from shadows into innocuous things, the usual TV, desk, chair.

She flicked the light switch.

On the bed the body of a woman lay, arranged with her hands folded on her stomach. She wore a blue bra. Brenda came close, breathing fast, and looked into open eyes, a slack mouth. She grabbed the woman's hand. It felt too cool but not cold.

Brenda knew her. "Cyndi! Cyndi, wake up!" It was one of the receptionists for Prize's, Cyndi Backus.

Cyndi didn't move. Something had fled from her. A chill swept over Brenda.

Brenda had seen Cyndi the day before, such a pretty girl with a husband and babies and—

Brenda stood there, overwhelmed for a second. More clothes lay on the floor . . .

He might come back!

She ran screaming out the door.

Nearby guests came out of their rooms blinking, tucking in shirts, pushing back scraggly hair, and made a bunch of cell phone calls. To her surprise, her boss's wife, Michelle Rossmoor, appeared out of nowhere, put her arm around Brenda, and tried to settle her down. Pretty fast, three guys from Security cordoned off the room.

The El Dorado County Sheriffs arrived within five minutes. Brenda sat on a chair in the hallway with a bottle of water, sick in her gut, Michelle by her side murmuring quietly. They closed down the whole hallway and made Brenda stay and Michelle go. She got hungry, but knew she couldn't eat. There were sirens and detectives arrived, then technicians, a woman doctor she had never before seen, and finally a couple of men who looked like lawyers. No one talked to her. Inside that room, she heard them scurrying around, important, taking calls, making them, coughing, speaking, moving furniture.

Her boss, Stephen Rossmoor, arrived to talk to her and the police. He had a long face above the sport coat he always wore when she saw him.

"The police need to talk with you, but then you need to take the rest of today off," he advised her, looking at her badge. "You recognized her, Brenda?"

Brenda nodded. "Cyndi Backus. I saw her yesterday!"

He looked down and shook his head. "She's worked here for what, five years? Who did this, Brenda?"

"How should I know! I only found her! I saw the man, but I didn't recognize him, nothing like that. Why kill her?"

"You saw him? Have you told the police?"

"I will, but it won't do much good. Do you think other employees are in danger, Steve?"

Rossmoor bit his lip. "I don't know anything yet. Take some time off, Brenda, as much time as you need, okay?" He and Michelle had two young children to worry about and a big business to run. They always looked so happy together, so solid, but right now, he looked as shell-shocked as Brenda felt.

"Can I borrow your cell phone?" Brenda said. "I want to call my husband."

After about forty-five minutes, they put her into a police car and took her to the police department building in Al Tahoe to be interviewed and make a statement. At least ten law enforcement people were swarming about the motel room when she left, like on a TV show. Raised not to trust cops, Brenda kept a little secret as she told her story into the tape recorder in a room where a female officer sat with her at the conference table and questioned her.

The secret was that she had seen the Housekeeping tip lying on the table in the room and put it into her pocket before she ran out of the room. Twenty dollars wasn't much for what she had gone through. She really needed the money after Christmas and deserved it. She knew she'd keep it.

Brenda arrived at her home, the knotty-pine cabin, in the winter dusk. Walking up to the cabin, she noted that the kitchen window had a steady bulb burning, the one above the sink. She could almost smell the gray woodsmoke the fire was shooting out the chimney that rose above the living room, where orange light flicked against the window like fireflies trying to get out.

She came in through the side door, throwing all her stuff on the bench beside it. Ronnie, making a pizza without salt, his latest food fad, saw her and came toward her, saying, "Aw, poor baby, what a mess, are you okay?" He took her into his arms and they both sighed and relaxed. Feeling his heart beat next to hers, she felt able to let go and cry a little.

"Why didn't you let me come get you?"

"I didn't know when they'd finish with me."

"I woulda waited."

"It was awful," she sobbed. "I never saw a dead body before." Outside, snow drifted into the window mullions. His hand roamed to her breast. She liked him comforting her like this. She turned a little so her mouth could meet his. "I should have let you pick me up."

"You should have."

"I feel like shit."

"Let's have a drink."

"I told you not to take that job," Ronnie said later, after they'd wolfed down the pizza and drunk a bottle of red wine, his favorite, a sweet one, disgusting, gave her headaches, but she never said no to wine.

They went straight to bed after that, and Ronnie

got up on his elbow and started asking her questions. "Those big Tahoe hotels—anybody can rent a room. People go to casino-hotels to get wasted and do stuff they wouldn't dare do at home. Crime, drugs, prostitution—"

"We need the money." Lying in the warm bed next to her husband, Brenda felt guilty about keeping the latest windfall from him. Twenty dollars sat in an envelope in her purse, and she had already decided to give it to her ex for Isaiah, for school supplies.

"You're not going back there."

"We need that job." Brenda shivered, pulling the red plaid flannel comforter up over the sheet to cover her shoulders. "We need the income, and we need the health benefits. Honey, we've discussed this before."

"What'd the big man say?"

"You mean Steve? Mr. Rossmoor?"

"Yeah, him, the owner. What did he say? Come back tomorrow, work your ass off like you saw nothing, heard nothing, and didn't get totally unhinged by finding your friend murdered on a bed?"

"Correction. I hardly knew her. And why the attitude about Steve? He's good to us. Good benefits. Supports the union. Mostly. He told me to take as much paid time as I needed to recover from the shock."

"Huh."

"If I didn't know you know you're my handsome

lover, the only man I adore"—she gave his goatee a gentle pull—"I might just imagine you were jealous."

"He's rich. And young. He's got you all day. I'd rather you stayed home."

"Yeah, but you're bigger. And don't ask me how I know that, okay?" She punched him on the arm.

He ran his hand along her hip. "You say that to all your guys."

She laughed. "As if you leave me energy for anybody but you."

Ronnie kissed her for a long time, but to her surprise and disappointment pulled away before the part where she went nuts, moaned, and forgot about everything except for where he was touching her, and how awesome it felt.

"Really, now. What did Rossmoor say?"

"He said for me to take my time."

"Easy for him."

"He told me he would pay me lost wages."

"Dude! Now's the time for that vacation in Rio, expenses paid, courtesy of a freak who killed his girlfriend."

"As if we'd take advantage of him like that."

"You think he cares about you?"

"I do. He cares about his employees."

"I'm the one that cares about you." In a swift change of mood, now that he'd cooled her down, he got hotter. "Put your hand on me, babe. Come on."

"We're talking!"

"That's why I said use your hand. Do you think it's a sex crime? Any signs of—violation?"

"No!"

"No?" His fingers, usually so welcome, suddenly felt like bugs crawling along her thigh.

She batted him away. "Shut up, pervert."

"Tell me what you saw one more time." When she said nothing, he said, "Brenny, I want to understand."

"Fair enough." She sighed. "I was cleaning per usual, but this one room, well, I got a bad feeling."

"I don't get the whole psychic thing. So many shows about it now. Never met one I could trust."

She nodded and shrugged her shoulders. "I can't explain it. I just felt nervous. The door was open a little—but I couldn't go inside. So I went around the corner of the walkway—you remember how the walkway's kind of L-shaped?"

He nodded. "And then?"

"And then—I hid under the stairs."

"What?"

"That's right. Ducked away like a kid scared of a bad dad."

"Jesus, Brenda. Sometimes I don't get you. Your father was the nicest guy—"

"I'd say maybe five minutes passed. Then—a man came out."

"What man? Someone you know? What did he look like?"

"I was hiding, not looking. But I did not, repeat

not, know this guy. What I saw was standard Tahoe, a man in a parka, jeans, and a baseball cap like every other guy up here. He seemed tall. Athletic."

"He could have come after you." Ronnie looked distressed, and Brenda loved that. She let herself melt a little more into his body.

"I was really scared he'd spot me, but I think he didn't because he moved at a regular pace, never paused. But for sure he didn't want nobody to see him, okay?"

"Okay."

"So I wait until I'm sure he's gone. And then, I go inside the room. I mean, it's my job. I can't exactly say, 'I did floors one, two, and three, except for Room 102,' can I?"

"Someone else would show up in the morning and make you look bad."

"Right," Brenda said. "So I went inside. One side of the bed had been turned down. On the other side was this woman. There was no blood, but she was dead. I realized right away it was Cyndi Backus. Our chief receptionist. She looked awful."

"Wow. Was she nude?"

"There you go again! I don't want to think about it! No, she was not nude! She was wearing her underwear."

Ronnie nibbled her neck. "You're disgusting," she said, but not so he'd really think she meant it.

God, men, smells, sex, incorrigibility. She sat up so that he had to stop what he was doing and she could think. "Honey, the body lay there like someone paid attention to how it looked. I think he must have been sorry for what he did. He had folded her hands and made her look peaceful."

Turning the edge of his hand absentmindedly along the curves of her body, Ronnie said nothing.

"Here's a weird thought. What if he had got rid of it and I hadn't known and I went in to change the sheets and just thought they were extra dirty or something—where Cyndi was killed?" Brenda thought back over all the iffy towels on the floors of all the bathrooms, wishing she had worn gloves the whole time. Ronnie was right. She should get a less nasty job.

"If you saw him again, would you know him?"

"No, like I told the cops."

"You didn't say that to protect yourself? Not that I would blame you a bit. Hell, if he saw you——"

"I guess there's that chance. I'm blanking him out, okay? I don't want to see his face. If I ever did."

"You're shaking. You're fine, babe. You're with me."

"I'm cold." She snuggled closer. It was midnight, but she was too messed up to sleep yet.

"Do you believe he saw you? Do you?"

"I don't know."

He pushed his body so that every inch could match up to hers. "I'll keep you warm. You've got Ronnie watching out now. I know you're upset, but don't worry. We're in this together forever."

Oh, she had waited her entire life for Ronnie!

When she considered all the losers and abusers, well, she was glad she had made it this far, to a man who appreciated her as much as she appreciated him. She smelled him, the mix of sweat, wine, and cologne, and tried to fit her curves to his hard edges.

Squeezing in close, he pressed against her, this time not to fit, but to intrude. Brenda realized they were going to have sex again if the hints from his body told her anything, and she felt happy about it.

"Say it. 'Ronnie, you're the best,'" Ronnie demanded, pushing from the rear, harder, and she knew what would happen next, knew it with a mix of shame, terror, and desire.

"You're the best!"

"Damn straight! Is this okay?"

"Yes! No! Stop that! I have to tell you something!"

"Sure, babe, tell, can't wait to hear, c'mon—"

"He left money!"

"Huh? Who!"

"Him! On the bureau. Twenty dollars! In the tip envelope!"

"Hallelujah!" Ronnie said, not a bit put off.

"I didn't tell you—I want to—ouch!—give it to Isaiah!"

"DNA," Ronnie said. "The envelope. Prints. The money."

"No! I want the money!"

"Honey. Ahh. God, that feels good." Long pause. "Look. He killed a girl."

"This is no time to be discussing— Ooh! Ooh!"

Brenda tried to wriggle away but Ronnie had her where he wanted her. He pinned her down, saying, "I'm not letting you out of my sight. You gonna tell the cops or do I?"

"Don't you dare."

"I'm gonna."

Brenda moaned. Ronnie always said her moans sounded like a spring wind in Kentucky caverns, loud and batty.

"I'm gonna, I'm gonna."

"You're the one I'm in danger from! Ah! Ah! Ah!"

"That's right. Don't forget how good this feels. And this. Do you like this?"

"No, no, no."

"Ooh, I love it when you moan."

"Ronnie, oh!"

"We'll give it a couple days, but we have to give it to the cops. I insist." Flipping her onto her back, he loomed above her in the dim light. For the next few minutes, she welcomed his lust; she welcomed the enveloping arms of oblivion, forgetting all about the sad body she had seen and smelled in the hotel bed.

She moaned again, louder. He better not ask any more questions. He could read it in the mornin' paper. He could hear it on the radio.

CHAPTER 7

I consulted my watch. The luminous dial told me it was 6:30 a.m., dark, temperature twenty-three degrees, clear and icy on the street where I waited near the Minden bus stop.

Here Brenda Bee usually caught the bus up the mountain to her cleaning job five days a week. Although I'll never know exactly what she saw at Prize's, I recall her eyes flickering at the sight of me. That scared me. I slept little, after that, reliving the whole mess and the fact that there was a witness.

I waited by the side of the road. Today the crowd arrived and left but she was a no-show so far. I thought, Brenda's running late. She'll be here any minute. I had done my homework: her shift started at eight in the morning. Her commute up to the mountains took a long time. She seldom missed a day. She needed the money.

I had already consumed two hot coffees and an almond-covered sweet roll along with several exhilarating pills courtesy of a corrupt Reno doctor. Now I had a third cup in the holder beside the driver's seat. I drink too much coffee but the alternative is to succumb to alcohol, other addictive drugs, or Jesus. Thank God scientists always try to help us think better, and thank God for all the enhancements people in bug-eyed glasses have invented that involve nuanced alterations of the human body on a subatomic level that make you feel so good when you're so bad.

I felt good anticipating the bad, loaded up.

A time comes when you're committed. You've done so much, betrayed family, lied, stolen.

Brenda Bee was the last boulder in my way, and she needed removing. Death for me would be a relief. I never thought of it as the end of consciousness. I thought of it as a leap into somewhere new.

I wanted this over. I wanted money. I wanted freedom. I needed not to be caught. I needed her dead.

I sat upright in the driver's seat, feeling my eyeballs jump around in my head, hepped up. I checked for the knife, accidentally jabbing myself. I examined my finger. No blood. No DNA. Good.

When the old pickup pulled up in front and the good-looking, middle-aged woman got out, kissing her hubby good-bye lovingly, lugging a backpack with a Prize's logo, I recognized her. She, Brenda Bee, took care of the floor where Cyndi died. She vacuumed, dusted, wiped surfaces. She cleaned that room. Seeing her get out and smooth her hair, blowing a kiss to the man in the car, I felt for both of them, for a moment anyway.

Giving her a fond wave, he drove off. She plunked her

backpack down and sat on the bench inside the covered kiosk bedecked with graffiti.

I looked up and down the street. Not a soul drifted in this light fog, but something could come soon, such as the next bus, due in five minutes. Conditions were not ideal, but I was fast and strong. I felt sure I could handle whatever needed handling. Her time had come, in a way, nothing to do with me. We all die.

She hadn't said much about what she saw that day—I knew this from an associate at the South Lake Tahoe Police Department. She had taken a look at me though, and at some point she would connect me with that moment, Cyndi's death moment.

That husband of hers had been with her every second since.

Until now.

Time to take her out, decision made.

I breathed in and out. You must stay tuned with your body. When you ski down a hill, when you drive fast, when you take physical risks, you must be vital. I took the time to analyze how I felt at that moment because that had helped me all the way through my life. I closed my eye for one moment to calculate and decide I was rip-cord hard in body, mind, and spirit.

Brenda slouched on the bench, headphones in her ears, parka wrapped tightly around her. The sky lay cold across the mountains.

I took one more long look down the street. I jumped out of my car, knife in hand, and ran at her as if she were a deer to be hunted down and killed in a forest.

Somehow able to ignore the music blaring in her ears, she saw me and recognized danger hurtling toward her as forceful as a train. She ran. I ran faster. I caught up a hundred feet beyond the kiosk. I seized her hair and forced her head back. My sharp knife slid across her throat. She accepted the assault without making a sound.

A gout of blood gushed out onto her parka. She fell limp.

I pushed her forward. Her head knocked against the curb. Blood dribbled out of her like a mountain stream.

Red.

I couldn't take my eyes away. Her own opened briefly, but she looked at the tall pine along the road, not at me.

Then, a sound.

I looked up.

From far down the cold and empty street a bus rolled toward us.

I ran to my car, set the knife on the newspaper-covered floor on the passenger side, and drove off in the opposite direction. I couldn't help speeding a little, but at this hour and in this weather the cops must also be drinking coffee somewhere, since traffic kept up with me as we all made our escapes.

In five minutes I had joined the commuter dance, light traffic heading toward Carson City. The sun lit the dry, black desert mountains on my right a cheerful peach. Flipping on the police scanner, I made myself move to the right lane and stay there. I put in Etta James and let her sing "Got My Mojo Working."

I looked into the mirror, thinking about the husband waving good-bye. I imagined his pain for no more than a moment, then set it aside. I will not go to prison. I will not be executed. I deserve to live. I deserve to live well.

When I could do so without violating any traffic laws, I pulled over and gave myself a reward popper for doing what had to be done.

This time had been much easier.

CHAPTER 8

In the parking lot of the Starlake Building, Nina stepped out of the car and into six inches of spring slush. Though she hopped nimbly to the curb, her open-toed shoes let her feet get soaked.

On the carpet in the hallway she took off the shoes and carried them into the office, wondering if a fresh pot of java awaited her in the conference room, or even an old pot.

She had spent an hour at Burglar Boy's sentencing hearing. When the moment had come, her client had read a contrite statement; then several of the homeowners he had victimized read statements. They finished before the midmorning break. The judge subjected Burglar Boy to a harsh lecture followed by a lenient sentencing recommendation, a coup for the defendant and his counsel, Nina Reilly, proud graduate of the Monterey College of Law, defender of the innocent—or losers who deserved a little due process.

Removing her coat, Nina glimpsed Sandy through the half-open inner door talking to someone. "We have a pretty good mix of clients right now, the respectable ones and the bozos. I found gum under the seat last week. That's what I get for looking where I shouldn't."

Nina stopped in the doorway.

"Hello, beautiful." Paul van Wagoner stood and wrapped her into a hug. She got up on her toes, but he had ten inches on her with her heels off, and for a moment she thought he'd get carried away and lift her. He bent down nicely, though. His blond hair had grown over his ears. Her fingers ran through it.

Holding on, examining his face, she said, "You hardly resemble a cop these days."

"Because I haven't been a cop for a long time now." He allowed her to move slightly away from him but kept her close, like family, or a dancing partner, or someone in bed, trying to touch as much of her body as he could. "Then again, you never looked like a lawyer."

She pulled back, releasing his arms, freeing herself from the touch that sometimes felt a little too much like a burning brand. "Is that so? Well, how do you think a lawyer looks?"

"Controlled. Not like you, with that shiny, brown hair like a halo fighting its way out of Hades."

"Well, now." Nina regarded Paul. He kept his tall frame muscular these days. He had given up tennis after a knee injury and taken up free weights, which had broadened his shoulders even more and shortened his belt. He looked trim and tan and happy.

Nina made a silent vow to go to yoga twice a week from now on.

Sandy said, "He won two hundred bucks on the Wheel of Fortune slots at Crystal Bay last night, so he's feeling pretty good."

"A bad moment," Paul said, smiling. "I won enough so I had to quit. If you lose slowly, you can play all night. Nobody wants to win early. Then you have a moral obligation to try to hang on to it."

"I wouldn't mind that problem," Sandy said. "But Gamblers Anonymous is the biggest social club in this town, and not one I want to join."

Nina picked up the towel they kept by the door for Hitchcock's occasional visits and dried her cold toes. "I should have worn my boots." She told them about her court appearance and suggested lunch.

It felt like every other visit Paul had made to Tahoe, but this time another urgency was between them that she felt in that first touch, a recognition that important matters would have to be dealt with soon.

After some vigorous back-and-forth and reminders of dietary preferences, they all decided on the Driftwood Café past Ski Run Boulevard, past the ski shops and law offices, Paul driving. The remaining snow on the freshly plowed streets had melted under a parade of white-encrusted vehicles and now looked like an oil slick.

A new building complex, keeping the château motif going, sat at the foot of Heavenly Mountain beside the entrance to the Marriott. A lift nearby carried visitors to the lodge at the eight-thousand-foot elevation, for snacks and the view from the broad deck of skiers flying down. The gondola was climbing the mountain just as they drove by on the highway and appeared to have plenty of passengers.

Not long before, South Lake Tahoe had also opened a grand skating rink, a big attraction. But the biggest industry around here after skiing remained gambling, and Nina kept hearing from her clients who dealt cards at the casinos that gamblers were gambling bigger than ever, losing more, and seeking solace in the free booze passed out to good customers. Gambling was like law; there were profits to be made in both happy and unhappy times.

While Paul looked for parking, Nina watched the buildings whirl by in the town she had come to love, enjoying what was new along with the old places, small inns and restaurants that hung in there.

Beyond all the buildings and green trees, the lake lay under the clouds, so much bigger than their cares.

Sandy, in her suede jacket, ten-gallon hat set neatly on her black braid, advised Nina what to order for her, then stopped to chat with a threesome of ladies leaving the café as they walked in. Paul and Nina found a table in back. As always, Paul insisted on sitting with his back to the wall with a clear view of the front door and, when questioned about it, would only refer cryptically to Wild Bill Hickok's brutal ending. "It's been a long time," Paul said.

The waiter came, and they ordered, starting off with shrimp.

"How've you been?" Nina asked.

"Consolidating. Pretty good client base right now. Carmel's hoppin'."

"That's not what I meant. Personally."

"Personally? I've been working out a lot, running on the beach, that kind of thing. Recovering from yet another failed relationship."

Nina was silent. She wanted to know who had replaced Susan but didn't have the guts to ask outright.

"Give it to me quick now," Paul said playfully, "anything you don't want Sandy to note for her novel, before she gets back."

"What novel?"

"You know. All about a small-town law office?"

The waiter brought their order. Nina speared a shrimp, dunked it in cocktail sauce, ate it, and said, "So that's what she's been coming in early to work on. She said she had a project."

"She has a project all right. She's gonna pull a Proust on you."

Across the restaurant, Nina could just make out Sandy's cowboy hat. "But—she never wrote any fiction before, as far as I know."

"Even Hemingway had to start someplace."

Nina put this latest strangeness aside as a puzzle to be dealt with later. "Until Sandy gets back, let's talk about why you're here."

"Fill me in."

"I've told you most of what I know. I'm sorry I didn't call you before I told Philip Strong I'd take his case. He had a hearing coming up fast and he needed help. The sale is in trouble because of this Brazilian thing, and—"

"You have a conflict of interest, don't you? Maybe not a legal one, but there's definite conflict between my interests, our interests you might even say, and the resort." Paul gave her a knitted-eyebrow look that she couldn't interpret, then went back to nibbling shrimp.

"If he's alive, Jim's actively engaged in ruining his family. If he's dead, he's causing harm, too. But here's the problem. He can't be alive, can he, Paul? Because you told me he would never threaten us again, and you told Bob you took out the garbage. Bob told Sandy."

They both searched out Sandy's cowboy hat with their eyes this time. She was listening to the earnest speech of another woman. She noticed them looking across the crowd and gave a nod. Nina noticed what a handsome nose she had. Some noses can handle cowboy hats; Nina's nose couldn't.

"So I indulged in poetic license, honey," Paul said. "The bit about the garbage pieces. Bob needed reassuring. Tell me it's okay to stretch the truth with a kid who's having nightmares."

She nodded.

"As for Sandy? She can handle the truth. Jim

Strong was garbage, garbage who killed a man you loved and went looking to kill you—that's the truth."

Nina sipped her ice water, admiring his chin, his clear hazel eyes, his square shoulders. "Where is this garbage, Paul?"

He put his fork down.

"I need to know now."

"Puts me in a hard place. I wish the evil had been interred with his bones," Paul said. "Who imagined Jim would turn up again, a vengeful ghost?"

"I wouldn't demand to know something unless it was necessary."

Paul watched a couple, smiling, toast each other with red wine at a table near the door. "I can see our future, and it's not so pretty." Paul had small laugh lines around his mouth and eyes that at the moment looked more like deep, dark pits. "San Quentin has no indoor pool, I hear, no gym, and a bunch of fellows I'd rather not know better." He fell silent, then said, "I'd do it again. I fought to save your lives, damn it!"

"My life and Bob's." She waited but he didn't respond. "Now tell me what happened that night."

Paul gave himself enough time to imagine himself in prison. He had visited San Quentin, seen the Northern California oaks and eucalyptus trees leading the way, deceptively alluring, sweet-smelling. Then you got to the prison, and the protocol leading up to a simple visit—well, it stopped just short of an anal search. He shifted uncomfortably in his seat.

He had also visited Alcatraz when he was a kid growing up in the city. He recalled the clank of the cells when the doors shut, and although nobody lived there anymore, he had no trouble imagining the misery and noise of its inmates, the smells, the hopelessness.

In prison, he would hate his fellow criminals and they would hate him more. His life, with the charms of jogging on the beach, loving a woman in the mountains, feeling the sun, thrilling with the power of his car's engine—all that would end in such ugliness.

All this because he had killed a man who needed to die. Relying on the law in this case was not an option. The man would have lived on, evading the law as he had always done, protected by an enabling family, a lifelong threat to Nina and Bob.

So here in Paul's heart, Jim Strong remained alive even in death, a ghost, haunting. He wanted to unburden himself, confess, but he found it hard to trust his instincts in this case. What was right? Killing Jim? Burying him? Confessing? Going to prison for killing a malignant killer?

Paul did not often think of himself in moral terms, but right now, he saw no other option but truth, whatever the cost.

"I hope you know what you're doing, Nina. Taking on knowledge like this is a burden. I'm afraid it may hurt you."

"I've accepted that."

"Do you consider this information protected by the attorney-client privilege?"

She hesitated.

"I told you there was a conflict. You may need or want to pass this on to Philip Strong sometime. But I want to retain control over the information."

"I—"

"So right now I'm going to tell you a story I heard about a guy who took out a murderer who tried to kill his own lawyer.

"This guy followed the murderer to your, I mean *her*, house. He watched the murderer break the lock on her door. She was inside asleep. The men struggled. The murderer had a knife, a long, deadly bowie knife. He had killed her husband and his own wife. He was almost in."

Nina looked down, recalling the snowy night. Bob had not been home. She, alone, had felt afraid but brushed off her fear. Foolish. Outside, a killer crept. If it hadn't been for Paul—

"This guy jumped the murderer and there was a hell of a struggle. One of the strangest fights ever. They were both quiet to keep you out of it. He was quiet so that he wouldn't alert you. He was in good shape, Nina, younger than the guy and tough. The guy didn't murder him. The murderer was trying very earnestly to kill the guy. They fought a fair fight and the good guy won. The guy put him down. He took the body of the murderer away and buried it in the mountains."

Paul finished without emotion. He rubbed his palms together. "He never meant to kill, but he'd never allow someone to hurt you, Nina."

"And he didn't." She put her hand on his arm. "I'm right here, right now, thanks to you."

"But now I have to ask you for something. Can you help the Strong family, what's left of it, by proving Jim's dead without involving either of us? Without getting me put away for the rest of my natural born days?"

"I wish I could promise. I'm not sure."

The waiter returned. Paul asked for a pint of Hefeweizen.

"As a minimum," Nina said, "we have this obligation: we have to make it possible to push the Paradise sale through. That should be the goal. At least that way the family is not ruined and publicly disgraced. They won't go bankrupt."

"It would be nice to find the money Jim stole from the resort."

"It's gone by now. Spent. It has been a couple of years. Life's expensive. No. Wait. He's dead. I'm confused, Paul."

"How much money do you think Jim stole?"

"Over a million dollars, including smaller thefts over a period of time, and the big theft right before he—"

"A lot, then." Paul leaned back, drank some beer.

"The embezzlement started a cascade of financial problems that leads straight to this sale."

"I get it. I do. I wouldn't necessarily be feeling all that helpful," Paul said, "but I'm reeling from reading this affidavit. Someone has big ideas. They want some of the sale proceeds. But how could anybody lay hands on Jim Strong's share?"

"I don't know. The situation is starting to shape itself. There are several different moves ahead, but I just set up the ongoing game on the board and haven't got a real picture as to where the pieces go yet."

"I need to spend some time up here. Such a quaint little mountain town it is, too."

"About that night, Paul."

"That dark, bloody night."

"I took photos of the scratches on my doorknob a few days afterward. I wish you'd pounded on the door and come in and called the police."

"I never wanted to involve you." He spoke hoarsely, head down. He meant this.

Nina put her forehead to Paul's and said softly, "He's dead? You're positive?"

"Positive." Paul watched as Sandy's ample denim-clad hips swayed their way. "Cue our conscience."

"Did I pretend to be having fun elsewhere for long enough?" Sandy asked. "Figured you had catching up to do." She sat down next to Paul. She liked him and sometimes showed it by suddenly slapping him on the back or chucking him on the chin. The ice had melted in her iced tea. They had polished off the shrimp.

"*Salud*," Nina said, tapping Paul's beer and Sandy's tea with her water glass. Glug glug.

"Is Wish doing his job down there in ol' Carmel?" Sandy asked.

"He's fine. I think he has a girlfriend," Paul said. "He answers his phone, turns red, goes into the store-room, and shuts the door. Then I hear the whispers."

"Glory be," Sandy said. "I hope she can cook. I'll call him tonight." Wish hadn't lived at home for several years, but Sandy still concerned herself actively with her son's love life. "So are you gonna get involved with this new case?"

"Have to," Paul said.

"True," Sandy said. "No choice there."

Paul looked at her. Sandy squeezed lemon into her tea as if nothing mattered but the lemon, the tea, as if the world moved in stately sequence and untoward emotions never occurred.

Paul looked at Nina. She gave a slight nod.

"Sandy?" he said. "I apologize. I've made some missteps that hurt Nina and you."

"I'm well aware," Sandy said.

Their lunch arrived.

"I screwed up," Paul said. "I should have knocked on Nina's door that night and gotten you and the police involved."

"True," Sandy said. "Who'd you think you were? This is America."

Paul cleared his throat. "Sorry."

"Apology accepted," Sandy said.

They talked about Paul's kayak trip, where he had almost been overturned by dolphins gamboling all along the Pacific shores that year. The dolphins came at Christmas. Nina thought it amazing that dolphins took a regular route down to Mexico for Christmas, not a whole lot different from seniors taking their winter vacations. "You grew up on the Monterey Peninsula," Paul said to Nina. "Don't you miss the ocean?"

"I used to think I wouldn't be able to stand it, but it turned out for me that Lake Tahoe had the same effect, you know? It's a huge body of water, alive like the ocean."

"So you don't miss Pacific Grove?"

"I sure don't miss the fog."

"Well, Pacific Grove misses you, honey," Paul said, and both Nina and Sandy laughed.

After coffee, Nina got back to the case.

"There's a hearing tomorrow regarding the sale of Paradise Ski Resort, and the lawyer who has been handling all of it, Lynda Eckhardt, needs me there. It's possible Judge Flaherty will insist on proof of Jim Strong's death or signed permission before he allows the sale at all. That's the worst possible result, and I can't believe he'd do that, even with this new claim that he's alive."

"Can't he be presumed dead? It's been two years," Paul said.

"Probate Code section 12401 says the person has to have been missing for five years in almost all cases," Nina said.

"Wow, long time for the family to wait for their money."

"That's right. And even worse . . ." Nina explained that the judge was likely to put the full $2.5 million net after the sale into escrow, not charging Jim's gross share with a proportionate share of the debts, since Jim had not consented to having that share taken out.

"What does that mean in terms of what the family gets right now, then? If that amount goes into escrow?"

"They get zilch. All the other money will go toward the debts, and these net proceeds will all be tied up in an escrow for the indefinite future."

"Especially since Jim'll never show up to take possession of it and work out a settlement with his family. Any idea who might be involved in this affidavit?" Paul asked. "It's a forgery, and according to you, a credible one."

"I have thought about it." And so she had, with Jim's face glaring at her from underneath her eyelids at three in the morning. "Michael Stamp and his firm are representing Jim Strong. They've been retained through the Brazilian attorney. Mike is smart and articulate. He's got plenty of international business. He might have a deal going with a Brazilian lawyer. Maybe he's got a brother down there desperate for money? Maybe he's run into problems with his stocks being worth nothing, and he's close to retirement age? Maybe he promised his wife five carats for her fortieth?"

"I like the greedy-trophy-wife angle. Always

blame her if you can. Yeah, sure, maybe it is Stamp. That's a good first guess, anyway."

Nina smiled at him, knowing he was working hard to be his usual carefree self, when he appeared far from it. "Hard to know what will push someone over the edge. You might spend your whole life honorable, and then blow it all because you didn't get what you thought you deserved in the end, and you see all of your hard work turning into nothing."

"We have a forged affidavit and a possibly compromised attorney so far. Got anything else?"

"Philip's daughter-in-law, Marianne, has some sort of connection with Brazil. She always said she wanted to run the resort, along with her half brother, Gene. Maybe this is a twisted way of taking control of it."

"How do you mean?"

Nina shook her head. "I'm not sure. But they don't get along, any of them. Then there's Kelly, his daughter. Remember her?"

"The law student, right?"

"She has changed so much, Paul, you wouldn't recognize her. I don't know. Something off there. She's hiding something. Maybe she's hiding a lot of things."

"I bet the scammers figured they had a crack at getting the money sent down to Brazil, getting hold of it down there. Lynda Eckhardt—she wasn't exactly putting up a fight, right?"

"It's risky, Paul. How could they know Jim

wouldn't hear about it on Twitter or something and make another claim himself? They don't know for sure he's dead."

"Good question." Paul shook his head. "But I do know he's dead, so Brazil is a scam. I'll go down there."

"No. Philip's investigator's going. Eric Brinkman. He speaks Portuguese. We'll get this figured out."

"I don't know this guy, Eric Brinkman."

"He'll be at the office at four," Sandy told Paul.

"And I'm not invited?" Paul said.

Nina said, "I just heard about this myself. Can you come?"

"I wouldn't want to impose."

"Ho, ho." Sandy slapped a hand on the table. "You know you want to be there."

"Okay. I'll be there. So how's the novel going, Sandy? Nina's dying to hear more."

Sandy discovered something interesting on her plate.

The waiter stopped by. Nina refilled her black coffee but felt too full to finish it.

"Wimp," Paul said, finishing his second mug. "Sandy, you coddle her. It's a good thing I'm here."

CHAPTER 9

Confession of Guilt
a novel
by Sandra Whitefeather

*P*roud descendant of a master basket maker of the Washoe tribe, Sondra Dat So La Lee Filoplume woke up early that morning, almost as if her dreaming self realized the day would be tough. She put on her clothes carefully, choosing a tight skirt that best showed off her fine-looking legs, kissed her current boyfriend good-bye, and climbed into her new Lexus, a gift from her employer for last year's job well done.

Sam, a tall, rangy Washoe cowboy from down Minden way, stood on the porch waving her off, his hooded eyes tired-looking after last night's exercise.

It being March and a dry, sunny day, Sondra drove the road from Gardnerville up to Lake Tahoe in record time, admiring the small signs of spring that brought out early birds along with pesky bicyclers that made negotiating the mountain road a little annoying.

Brushing off her mood, which had most to do with

Sam's telling her last night how he wanted to marry her—why did they always want to complicate a good thing?—she decided she would leave work a little early this evening. She and Sam would take the horses out for a sunset ride, and she would set him straight.

She arrived at the foot of Ski Run Boulevard at South Lake Tahoe, where the ten-story high-rise held the offices of Fox, Wagoner, and Josephson, and pulled into the brand-new underground garage after nodding to the guy in the booth, who had been pestering her for months for a date.

In the elevator to the penthouse suite, she rode up with Barry Manilow. He stared at her beauty through bloodshot eyes.

"Beautiful day," Sondra commented.

"It's daytime? Shit," said Barry Manilow.

By the time the elevator reached the tenth floor, Sondra was alone, with enough time to adjust her coral-colored lipstick in its mirrored surface.

War paint, she chuckled to herself, clicking the lid shut and popping it into a dedicated pocket of her new designer bag. She needed lots of it these days. Her boss hadn't been herself since her husband had died tragically, smothered by snow, killed by a madman. Sondra had had to pick up the slack in all departments, including creating a cheerful, professional mood every single day.

The doors parted to reveal one of the slickest offices in South Lake Tahoe, the envy of all the other lawyers in town.

[Insert action. Sondra does something—saves Riley. Runaway horse? Then: kick from Sondra that makes

Riley Fox get skeptical, like she should be. Then back to the real story of a deceptive client.]

Sondra's door flew open. Her boss stood outside, wet with snow, the outfit that appeared so immaculate that morning now bedraggled and muddy around the cuffs.

"You okay?" Sondra asked.

Her boss sighed and pushed wet hair off her forehead. "Dandy."

"You know what you have to do now, don't you?"

"Sure wish I did."

"Sit." Sondra directed Riley Fox to one of the plush waiting-room chairs. "Listen. I can help with this. I've studied the paperwork and news reports. A good thing is, you trust people. You defend people who look guilty to everyone else. But this is different. This is your life on the line. Now you should examine that instinct to trust, okay? Time to look on the dark side. He's bad, Ms. Fox. You need to take him out."

Her boss tossed her a rare smile. "I'm so lucky to have you on my side," she said, leaning forward to listen.

[Add that her boss has a hot love life and has to decide between two very different men. Sondra nudges her the right way.]

Sondra had totally accidentally overheard a few strained conversations taking place in Ms. Fox's office. "Busy day ahead," she said, keeping the mood light but professional.

Riley slipped gracefully out of her light jacket and

hung it in a spacious double closet flanking the entry-way. She stood for a little longer than usual, looking unusually troubled. "I need time this afternoon. An hour."

Sondra reviewed all the appointments she had booked and how hard she had worked, organizing them, and nodded. "I'll take care of it. Take an hour and a half, two o'clock on."

Her boss's eyelids looked huge as they drooped over unhappy eyes. "Thanks."

Sondra watched the door close on her office. She would cancel urgent cases, but that's what she did, watched her boss's back.

Another relationship bites the dust, she thought. She flipped through the contacts list on her computer, writing down the relevant three, picking up the phone, thinking about what she needed to say to cancel 'em and leave 'em happy regardless.

Another hour and a half wasn't going to solve their problems, she thought, punching in the first number, but Sondra had never mistaken this guy for the right guy anyway. Her boss would get over it and figure out what was what eventually.

"Hello," she said into the phone. She explained about the double-booking of clients, all her fault, such busy times, her boss so hugely successful and all. While the client squawked and she took it, she straightened files on her desk and pondered the future. Things in the present appeared so blighted.

Five minutes later, after being subjected to some pain-

fully accurate verbal abuse, she could finally hang up the phone and allow herself a silent parting thought:

Things would end happily.

Somehow.

An hour after lunch, Sandy glided into Nina's office. "Mr. Brinkman is here." She often gave non-verbal cues about new people coming through the door. This time she betrayed nothing, not even the cock of an eyebrow.

Perplexed, Nina came around her desk and went into the front office.

The man standing there turned around. She had to keep herself from staggering back. He seemed to fill the small office. Well over six feet tall, he had broad shoulders and brought a scent of leather and the outdoors. She reacted to that, partially. She registered a few details: Prada sunglasses, rugged cheeks, creases in his cheeks even though he must be in his midthirties. The smile—whoa! Shiny, happy, expensive dentistry. Harley jacket and jeans, right for the weather. He looked like an advertisement for an outdoorsman. A slender outdoorsman. An elegant man dressed as an outdoorsman?

"Hello, Mr. Brinkman."

He took off the sunglasses and parked them negligently on his head. "Eric, please." His eyes were blue, the eyebrows darker than his hair, which was cropped short. He gave her a polite smile.

Sandy, at her computer, watched sidelong while

her fingers moved at a hundred words per minute, no doubt on her novel, since Nina hadn't given her any work this afternoon and the files were in excellent condition.

Nina held out her hand, also smiling, in her usual greeting to professional strangers. Brinkman looked at her hand, took it, turned it over, and bowed and touched his lips to the palm. He had long, white fingers and a thick gold ring with an onyx stone on the index finger.

Resisting the urge to pull back her hand, she wished that she had applied some wonderful-smelling hand lotion.

He returned her hand. "Thanks for seeing me. Phil Strong suggested I stop in."

"R-right. Sure. Come in."

He followed her into her office.

"A colleague of mine might join us." She watched him take in the sliver of lake view, the decor, such as it was, and the banged-up desk.

"Fine." He sat down and crossed an ankle over his knee. "My card." He handed it across the desk to her. The embossed card said only BRINKMAN INVESTIGATIONS with an e-mail address and website. "I've seen you in court. You have a way with a cross-exam."

Rubbing the card between her fingers, she said, "I'm glad you came. Where's your office, Mr. Brinkman?"

"Eric, please. I mostly work the Nevada side. Like

to play golf, so I set myself down close to Edgewood Tahoe. I share an office with someone you might know—Ed Quinn?"

She had heard of Quinn, a security specialist. She nodded. Brinkman went on, "Actually I work mostly out of my home office, or on my boat."

"You're a sailor?"

"I am. Do you like to sail, Nina? May I—"

"Sure, Nina's fine. I don't get to sail that often. The demands of my practice, you know. Have you been working at Tahoe long?"

"Just a couple of years. I'm originally from Germany. I was working out of Vancouver before I came here."

He continued smiling. His confidence was overwhelming as he looked around her office, studying her certificate from the Monterey College of Law, her admissions to various California state and appellate courts, and the Washoe prints Sandy had hung around the office, but he seemed relaxed and reasonable. Nina wrote him up in her mind as a European with a supplemental income who had visited and fallen in love with Tahoe. There were plenty around, especially among the skiers.

She had barely sat down when he started talking again. "How is this going to work, Nina? I've been working with Lynda Eckhardt, and before her involvement, you know already, I was looking for Jim Strong in connection with an embezzlement. The hearing on the Paradise sale is tomorrow. You're stepping in very, very late. Will that be a problem for you?"

"I've been in close touch with Lynda. I'm up to speed."

"You know that Philip needs me to get to Brazil and get some information? It seems we may be out of time."

"No. We'll get the time for you to go. I'll get you the time."

"Great! Great! I'm glad you're with us."

"Between you and me, Eric, I think you need to assume this is a fraudulent scheme and bring us the details."

"Really? You think there's no way Strong is alive?"

"I don't think so."

"Why?" Brinkman said. "What about the affidavit?"

Nina got a funny feeling. "Are you recording?"

"Are you?"

"No. We're on the same side. Besides, this conversation is privileged as attorney work product."

"I'm not recording." Brinkman folded his hands in his lap as if waiting for her to spill some beans, as though he already knew what had happened to Jim Strong.

She told herself, watch out, he's an investigator. "I'm a lawyer. Paranoia is unavoidable."

"I'm glad Philip retained you. I remember you from the events around the time of his son's disappearance. You were in the avalanche he caused, I read about that. And your husband. That was terrible. I'm very sorry."

"Thank you. So you were investigating the embezzlement at Paradise?"

"That's right."

"I'm curious. Did you advise Philip to go to the police regarding the theft from the capital account, when he asked you to handle it privately?" Nina said.

"Of course. He said it would ruin his business, and I had to keep it quiet. And as we both know, Jim Strong disappeared off the face of the earth over two years ago. I looked for him then, all over the world. I was stunned to see this affidavit. Like you, right?"

Nina nodded.

"Stunned. I hadn't caught up with him, and now he was coming out of the woodwork in Porto Alegre of all places, in the southern part of Brazil, not too far from Argentina. I know that city. He picked a sensible place to disappear. The local government will turn a blind eye to a well-behaved foreigner with a little money."

"I believe you won't find him there."

"You sound so sure." He was studying her harder than she was studying him and not bothering to hide it.

She shrugged. "Did you obtain proof he was embezzling from the resort?"

"There were accounting discrepancies, and soon

afterward, one day the whole capital account was emptied. That same day, Jim Strong seems to have left the area. That's pretty good circumstantial evidence he was involved. But, and this has continued to bother me, I couldn't find his mark anywhere. Couldn't find the money trail. It's one of my few failures, actually, which is why I'm gung ho about having the chance to follow up now."

"But you're convinced he had that money when he disappeared, aren't you?"

To Nina's surprise, Brinkman answered, "I'm not positive. I don't know if he had a well-thought-out plan. He was in a highly emotional state, decompensating you might say, during the days before his disappearance. I'm not at all sure he was even sane. I think if he committed the thefts, that it was an opportunistic crime." Brinkman got up and stood by the door, where Sandy would be getting her earful. "This will surprise you, but I was zeroing in on someone else for the embezzlements. I thought it possible that someone else knew Jim Strong was gone and proceeded to take advantage of the chaos. It was an online theft, you know, a matter of passwords."

"But who on earth are you talking about?" Nina asked. "I thought—Philip said—"

"Oh, he's sure it was Jim. He also seems sure Jim is alive. But I think—can you keep a secret?"

"My job in one word."

"And how about you?" Eric said, getting up and throwing open the cracked door to reveal Sandy.

"Come on in and join us, Sandy." Nina couldn't help but crack a smile. Sandy came in and sat down.

Eric smiled at her, too. "To continue, then, I was working on the theory that Marianne Strong, Philip's daughter-in-law, and her half brother, Gene, stole the money."

"Was there evidence of that?"

"Opportunity, primarily. Motive. Knowledge. But, no, I never managed to make the linkage. I'm not sure of that now. It would have been easy for anyone with the password to do it. And Philip was bad with passwords. He had written it in his address book, which he left on his kitchen table most of the time. Anyone in the family could have taken note of it. Though I will say if Marianne stole it, she hasn't deposited the money into any known bank account, and we haven't caught her spending any of it over the past two years."

"There was no dispositive evidence as to who did it?" Nina asked. "I find that hard to believe."

"Believe," Brinkman said. "So you think this affidavit is bogus." He was still standing by the door. Nina let herself waste a moment enjoying his posture, the belt, the chest —that rare event, a man with a sense of fashion.

She had almost missed the change of subject. "Yes. Bogus."

"You think he's dead."

Nina said firmly, "I think it's fraud, Eric. I want

you to know my opinion because I don't want you to waste a lot of time."

"I appreciate that." Brinkman looked away. "He killed your husband. I can only imagine."

"So you're going down there?"

Eric half smiled. "As soon as you get me the okay. I'll enjoy it even though it's a job assignment. I know Porto Alegre. The inland mountains contain some of the last Atlantic jungle habitat on earth. A lot of Germans immigrated to the area over the past hundred and fifty years. I'll fit in well. I'll see what I can come up with."

The door opened suddenly, and Brinkman stepped back. "Oh, hi, Paul," Nina said. "Come in. This is Eric Brinkman."

Paul had to look up at him as they shook hands. Powerful masculine chemistries clashed as the two big men looked around the small office, each angling for the best spot. There were only the two empty paltry-looking orange client chairs. They pulled out the dueling chairs and sat opposite each other, Nina presiding.

Sandy had gone to the door. "There's the phone. It's been fun," she said, and moved without haste into the outer office again.

"Don't shut it all the way," Eric said. "Wouldn't want you to miss anything." But it sounded witty, not mean.

Nina felt a bristling thing happening in the air. Eric and Paul had glanced at each other's eyes long enough to decide not to befriend each other. Nina brushed the moment aside as irrelevant. She wasn't interested in their testosterone issues, and she was sure they could set them aside to do the work. They were professionals on the same side and they would all get along.

"Heard of you," Brinkman said to Paul. "Ex-homicide detective in the Bay Area, right? Currently working out of Carmel?"

"That's right. I'm surprised I hadn't heard of you," Paul said, "considering you're local."

"Most of my work is in San Francisco and Silicon Valley. My clients like a low profile. I like a low profile. It's a relief to meet someone with a lot of local knowledge. Hope you'll allow me to pick your brain."

"Yeah. Okay," Paul said. "Maybe it'll be the other way around. You've been on this a lot longer than I have."

Eric said to Nina, "Is Paul on this case?"

"If Nina's involved, I'm involved," Paul said.

"Paul isn't formally part of the case but he's my associate," Nina said.

"Did you know Jim Strong?" Eric asked Paul.

"I knew him," Paul said. "I'd recognize him if I ever saw him. Thing is, I find that prospect unlikely."

"Why, Paul?" Brinkman said. "What do you know we don't know?"

"Jim Strong's not the type to sit quietly in some remote corner of the world for years, murder warrant or no." Paul said this calmly and carefully, and

Nina felt the tight grip on her heart loosen. He had it under control.

"You sound so sure," Brinkman said.

"I know human nature."

"He's a fugitive from justice. Seems like he'd have to hide somewhere far away, where he might feel safe. Why not Majorca? Why not Brazil? Is that really so far-fetched?" Brinkman asked.

"If he ran, he could be anywhere, I'll grant you that. But if he ran south, you'd hear some news out of Brazil that would not be pleasant. He's a killer. He would never stop killing."

Brinkman nodded.

"I've done a lot of reading on the subject," Paul continued. "People don't jump up and kill several other people, unless we're talking about domestic murder-suicides, which are an entirely different realm. No, men like Jim develop. They start off cruel when they are young, bullying, hurting animals, that kind of thing. It's easy enough to hide, so they do. Their families might know nothing. Of course, his mother has been dead a long time."

Nina said, "His father and siblings saw signs of how troubled he was, but they were in denial about what it all meant. Who would imagine your son might kill his wife, his brother, and—" She stopped.

Both men looked at her with sympathy.

"Yes, what parent can stand to think their precious little boy is a monster?" Brinkman asked.

"Exactly." Paul nodded. "And a monster might disappear for a while, but he would come back to do the things he's compelled to do. There's been no sign of him here in South Lake Tahoe in years. In my opinion, what you're going to end up doing is finding out who is trying to defraud the Strong family of millions of dollars. It's too bad you have to go all the way to Brazil to do that."

"Well, you and Nina seem of like mind about that," Brinkman said, looking back and forth at them. "Old friends get like that."

Paul shrugged it off. "I am wondering, though. What's your strategy, once you get down there?"

"Well, I'll see the lawyer and the notary who executed the papers. I've already called the Brazilian lawyer. Her name is Gisele Kraft. She claims a man who looks like the photos I sent down did come to her to get the affidavit prepared and showed her an American driver's license and a passport."

"Since it isn't Strong," Paul said, "I'd look into Gene Malavoy's travel arrangements—he's the half brother of Marianne Strong and he works at Paradise, too."

"I know Gene. I'm way ahead of you on that."

"Nina's also looking at Michael Stamp, the lawyer who threw this phony paperwork at the court."

"Yeah? Yeah, I see your thinking, Nina, very good. A crooked lawyer, routes the whole thing through his office, gets the money sent to another crooked lawyer."

"If Gisele turns out to be young and gorgeous, I'll buy that," Paul said.

"Stamp is married," Nina said. "Happily, I think. I think he's got the skill and nerve to try to carry off something like this. The problem is, he has a very good reputation. He should be checked out anyway."

"I'll bring a photo of him," Brinkman said. His expensive boot moved close to Paul's retro Hush Puppies. The tension in the air increased infinitesimally. Nina found herself staring helplessly at the boot, hoping it would not accidentally on purpose kick Paul's shoe.

An angel passed over, apparently, because the room went silent. Nina was facing two good-looking men, and it felt good at least to receive the vibes coming her way. It had been a while. Eric seemed to be playing up to her. She found herself looking down, blushing a little at the intensity of his stare.

"Nina? I'm confused. Has Paul been hired independently of my company to work on this case?" Eric said again. They had taken a long detour on that question.

"Not at this time," Nina said.

Eric got up and opened the door. "I'll be on my way, then. Nice to meet you, Paul, see you around. Nina, I am glad we'll be seeing a lot of each other."

Then Eric was gone. Paul said to Nina, "Is that true? You can't get me the gig? He's got it?"

"Philip can't afford both of you, and Lynda, and

me, too, Paul. Brinkman seems to be doing a good job."

"He's too smart for his Rolex. He's going to divine all this fast, Nina. He's going to catch the con and he's going to catch me. It's not good that I can't work for Strong, too."

"I'll talk to Philip again."

"Let's get a drink."

"Sorry, I have to get home," Nina said.

"What? But we haven't caught up yet."

"That may be, but I have supper to make and homework to enforce and other clients whose files I have to work on tonight."

Paul said to Sandy, who had come in again, "She won't have a drink with me, can you believe this? A stand-up old friend like me, drives all this way, and she won't have a drink. And I know you're with Joseph, Sandy, so I can't keep you out at a bar."

"Joe wants to show you his new circular-saw projects. Says he's fixing you dinner."

Paul said, "Sounds great. I might jump in the hot springs while I'm out near Markleeville."

"Come on out to the house at six," Sandy said. "Bring a bottle of beer."

Nina said, "See you tomorrow morning, Paul."

The outer door closed on Paul. Sandy and Nina turned to look at each other.

A lengthy silence led into the exhalatory sound of a long day finally over with.

Sandy broke it. "Now that was fun. In my single

days I would have locked the door so neither of them could get away and pulled out a picnic basket and a bottle of gin."

Nina said, "Why, Sandy. Are you commenting on the, er, looks of the gentlemen we have been meeting with today?"

"Ya think? Smokin'!"

CHAPTER 10

Jim Strong's face, progressively less human and uglier, showed up again on the inside of Nina's eyelids when she tried to sleep that night. He smiled at her with those big white teeth of his, a smile that devolved into a leer when she looked hard.

She went down to the kitchen and poured herself a tot of whiskey, usually enough to conk her out for the night. An hour later, she changed the sheets on her bed and stuck an air filter machine in her room to make white noise. She closed her eyes and concentrated on a glowing white dot in the middle of her forehead and blanked out her mind. She tried counting backward from one hundred.

Jim kept staring, baleful on the inside of her eyelids. She lost count around eighty-eight.

Her eyes felt dry with all the staring and staring back.

About two, she made herself hot chocolate in the dark, cold kitchen, sniffing at the greasy pans Bob had left to soak in the sink. Back in bed, she drank the chocolate, fluffed up her pillows, closed her eyes, and watched Jim, no longer smiling, now actively malevolent.

When she failed again to obliterate his face, she turned on the radio, the dullest station she could find, waiting to be soothed by murmuring voices perseverating about war, capitalism, consumerism.

She went into the bathroom and opened the junk drawer. A minute's rummaging brought forth her treasure, an allergy pill. She swallowed it and backed it up with an entire glass of water. Then she made sure for the twelfth time that the alarm was set, paced until she felt too tired to walk anymore, and once again lay down on her comfortless bed. At last, sometime around four in the morning, she sank into a nightmare she lived through to the end.

They turned around and headed as swiftly as they could back the way they had come, clumsy on the snowshoes, deep in powder, scared.

The snowmobile took off, straight up the mountain. It peaked almost two hundred feet directly above them and roared down the other side into the trees they headed toward.

Suddenly Nina felt tired, her feet as heavy and awkward as bowling balls. She remembered how mountain climbers at high altitudes take eight breaths after every step. She didn't want to go toward that revving motor in the trees, but Strong was much faster and could cut them off easily no matter which way they went. She took sharp, shallow breaths and tried to prepare herself as they trudged forward.

Jim Strong gunned the snowmobile and roared away from them, up the mountain, higher than she would have thought possible. About two hundred feet above them now, he sat on the snowmobile, silent.

Cold crept into the gaps between her gloves and her hands and up the legs of her pants. She felt her nose harden and hurt with it. Panting with exertion, barely balanced on her snowshoes, she turned once more to look up.

With a mighty roar, Jim's machine lurched to life. It cut back and forth above them as they turned, struggling down the mountain as fast as they could. They realized what he was doing now. All that snow, the tons and tons that had dropped from the sky—

The mountain came alive.

They moved even though they stood immobile, Nina's hand at her throat, her husband's hand reaching toward her, moving downhill faster and faster as the huge slab of snow they were standing on slid down the mountain toward the valley below. For a second that lasted forever, they watched the snow above them break into massive, bricklike slabs accelerating at different speeds down the mountain. Right in the middle of the face, traveling down with it, they had no escape. Nina saw Jim Strong, a tiny figure in the blinding sun up above, racing for the side.

Changing direction, desperate, they traversed franti-

cally, trying to sidestep the onslaught of snow, of fate, of death somehow.

The air around Nina darkened with snow crystals. Her hair whipped around her face. Something hit her in the back. They were moving faster! She threw herself at her husband, held him in a fierce embrace, bracing herself.

No sound. No air. Knocked forward by a wall of snow, she somersaulted down the mountain, wiped out in a tidal wave.

She slammed into something, a rock or a tree, and a mountain slid past. She continued free-falling, out of control, struck over and over by rocks, conscious in spite of the awful pain. As if struggling in the ocean, she tried to swim up, get her head up so she could breathe—but the snow was so deep, and she was drowning . . .

"**M**om! Mom!" Bob shook her awake.

She clutched a pillow tightly to her chest, unable to control her sobs.

"It's okay, it's all right, you're okay, Mom. You had a nightmare. I'm here to tell you it's over, and look, here's Hitchie." The dog had jumped up beside them and begun to lick her arm. "See, Mom? Good old Hitchie. Big old slobbering Hitchie."

She tried to get a grip and found herself safe in her bedroom. The LED display on her clock read 5:20 a.m.

"Look out the window, Mom. See?"

She blinked and looked.

"Late snow. Maybe I can snowboard a couple more times before they close the lifts for the season."

The black window shifted like a screen saver, marshmallows drifting softly down over a changing landscape.

"Are you crying?"

She wiped her eyes on the pillowcase.

"I'll be right back."

While Bob ran down to the kitchen, Nina turned on the bedside light and pulled on her kimono. She sank down under the covers to stop the shaking. A wonder I never dreamed about his death before, she thought.

Bob came back, holding a glass. She took a big gulp and choked, holding the glass up to the lamp. "I thought it was water."

"I figured wine might work better."

The impact was already fading fast. "Sorry to wake you, honey. I had a nightmare." She thought of the great painting by that very name, which she had seen at an exhibit at San Francisco's Legion of Honor Museum, by the symbolist precursor Henri Fuseli. In that painting was a ghost horse with white eyes. A maiden, disheveled. Something awful was about to happen.

"No shit. I heard you through Opeth and two doors."

She put the wine down and found her bedside water glass.

"Was it a bad one?" he asked. "Was it about Collier? The avalanche?"

"Yes."

"Don't tell me details and give me a nightmare, too."

"Okay. I'll only tell you the good part: there was no ghost horse in it."

"Are you sure you're okay?"

"Thanks for the—drink. Who's Opeth?"

"A Swedish metal band."

"You were listening to music at this hour?"

Bob smiled. He seemed to have a shadow on his cheeks.

Nina reached out a hand and felt the beginnings of a beard. "We need to get you a razor."

"We need to get you to sleep."

"You know why I'm awake. Now I want to know why you were awake."

He sighed. "It's a twenty-four-hour clock these days, Mom. People in Sweden are ahead by nine hours. It's afternoon there. Everybody's up."

She shook her head, feeling thick. "And?"

"And we can communicate in real time." As always when they discussed such things, he seemed to chafe at her ignorance.

"You're on the computer? Listening to music? Writing to people in the middle of the night? Writing to Nikki?"

"Yep."

Nikki was a few years older than Bob, a Tahoe

native and accomplished musician he had met, who now lived in Sweden. "No wonder you're grumpy in the morning." She felt too tired to come up with a lecture.

"I'm okay in school, not using drugs. Quit worrying."

"Ha. That will never happen."

Bob petted Hitchcock while Nina pushed up pillows behind her and sat up higher in bed.

"What's Paul doing up here?" Bob asked.

"How did you know?"

"What's the difference? The point is, why is he here?"

"Humor me. How'd you know?"

"Wish has a blog. He said Paul was going out of town. I guessed he came up here."

Well, Bob had known Sandy's son, Wish Whitefeather, for years. No doubt they tracked each other in the ways that younger people did.

She had plucked out three gray hairs that morning. She had wondered before if people her age, midthirties, okay, late thirties, could get gray hair. Now she had proof positive they did.

"Mom, how come Kurt didn't come over tonight? We were going to watch *Sherlock Holmes* at nine."

She felt her lack of sleep as irritating as bugs on her skin. Now she wanted nothing more than to put her head down and conk out. But she said briefly, "Some problems have come up."

"What kind of problems?"

"He has professional options he's considering. Work."

"Aha! In Europe, huh? Not here."

"Right. A tour."

"Well. I guess you don't like that."

"Do you think he'll go?"

Bob shrugged. "I don't know. It makes sense."

Was that what it meant to be male? Men looked at options in list form. They weighed them, assigned points perhaps, and made their decisions according to a logic any woman would find troubling and inadequate.

Bob lay on the thin rug beside her bed, petting the dog. Hitchcock lay sprawled beside him, his damp black fur exuding smells best left undescribed.

"If he goes to Europe, I want to go."

"Not if I have anything to say about it."

"I know you get lonely without me. But you need to think about me and not you for a change." Bob got up. "Yo, I have to get back online."

She punched her pillow as the door closed. Bah, she thought. I have lived for you, punk.

Her mind went back to the dream; she couldn't stop it. She remembered her first meeting with Jim Strong, so fit and healthy in his red, white, and black ski jacket. She wondered, as she often did in her criminal defense work, how it was that people with such severe psychosocial impairments made it to adulthood without intervention.

This night was turning into some kind of

summing-up that had been building for a long time. Her mind wandered to Eric Brinkman with his cool eyes and his macho posturing, then on to Paul.

Paul had proposed to her a few years before. She ground her teeth at the memory of her reaction, not that there's a graceful way to turn a man down when he's taken a big risk, laid out his heart before you. All you can do is cut, and she knew her refusal had cut deep. Upset, angry, he avoided her for a while, but now, here, she sensed nothing from him but the usual deep affection and friendship. She felt the same exasperated, playful love for him she had always felt, and worry for him, and—the same complexities.

And Kurt? Aside from his being Bob's father, how did she really feel about him? Where did love come in? Did it? Shouldn't she be devastated about their latest conversation? She searched the crannies and found—

Found she was up for good, ruminating as if she had any kind of control over any of it, or as if there were a solution, a nice clear solution that would work for everybody. Rationality, though, is a veneer. We are not in control of our thoughts.

She got the dog up, bundled in her warmest coat, and took a walk at dawn, wary of bears, watching the sun come up and the snow diamonds melting.

CHAPTER 11

Lynda Eckhardt called Nina at the ripe old hour of 6:00 a.m. Stars shone through the big window that looked into the backyard, and all the lights in the cabin were on as Nina and Bob prepared for their day. The outside thermometer read twenty-eight degrees. The nightmare and lack of sleep had left Nina feeling fragile, but she intended to ignore that.

"I know I said I'd be there this morning to introduce you and so on, but I'm calling to ask if you'll take over completely," Lynda told her. "I have stage fright. My IQ drops by half in a courtroom. I freak out. Can't do it. I didn't sleep last night. I'm getting out of law if I can't find a way to keep my deals from turning into litigation. Is there any chance you would, Nina? I'm really sorry about the notice."

"Sure, no problem." Nina wondered which of them, Lynda or herself, had gotten the least sleep the night before. Nina dabbed on concealer to hide the circles under the eyes squinting at her in the bathroom mirror.

"You have to get Eric some time for his trip."

"I know."

"I don't like this escrow notion. I don't like any of it. The sale has to go through."

Nina tweezed a man-hair that was stalking the soft little female hairs of her brow. She picked up a light brown pencil and began outlining her lips. "I'll take care of it, Lynda. Drop off the Association of Attorneys at the clerk's office on the second floor by eight and leave me a couple of copies to pick up and give to Michael Stamp. And don't worry. Nothing big will happen today."

"You need time. This is turning into an international matter. The notice period wasn't long enough to talk to everybody, make a decision, find the investigator, file responsive papers, get him down to Brazil—"

"Not to worry." Nina hung up and reconsidered her face. One should not wear dark eyeliner to court, especially at an early-morning court appearance, especially using the kind of eyeliner that starts at the tear ducts and traverses the entire pink interior lining of the eyes and remakes them to look like the eyes of Lady Gaga. Not to mention pale pink lipstick.

Although Paul would be there. And Eric Brinkman. That called for a certain ladylike sultriness. Not that she was looking for anything, she just wanted to keep up her end.

Nowadays, a lot of women skipped the eyeliner in

favor of false eyelashes so realistic men never knew, so feminine and glamorous, but too many had fallen in this very bathroom and wedged forever in cracks in the floor. She didn't have the time or fine-motor skills.

Conflict, conflict, always this conflict for a woman lawyer. Nina wiped off some of the eye makeup and observed the more serious-looking result. Her lips she recolored with a deep pink. Her hair she left to hang, as it would anyway. At the last moment, she rubbed a little pink lipstick onto her cheekbones.

It was getting late.

She dressed in a red push-up bra, bikini panties, black slacks, turtleneck sweater, and the usual tidy blazer, all over sheer black tights.

At least one person would register that she was sexy. Kurt might not notice it anymore, the judge might not give a damn, and opposing counsel had other things to worry about. Eric and Paul would see only her lawyerly jacket and slacks. No, she might not demonstrate it to anyone else, but by golly when she was arguing this matter today, she herself would know she was hot. One does what one needs to do for confidence when one is a female entering the judicial bastion. Her attitude would be better and impact the proceedings favorably for her client.

Now—the Louboutins? She could bring them in a bag and put them on at the top of the stairs to the second floor—there was much to be said for triviities of this sort. They distracted one from the real pressure of the hearing. And other, more personal things that weighed upon the mind. If she started thinking about all that now, she'd get so upset she wouldn't be able to—

One more look in the mirror. Spiffy, if sleep-deprived. She zipped downstairs to make scrambled eggs for Bob, whose bus left at seven twenty.

"I don't see how you can sell the business with a new claim like this pending," Judge Flaherty said. "On the other hand, an affidavit from a foreign juris-diction signed by a fugitive from justice who isn't willing to risk extradition by appearing today might not be enough to settle the claim. Seems we have a conundrum, gentlemen. And lady," he added, nod-ding at Nina.

The courthouse was almost deserted this morn-ing. More snow had fallen in the night, and Nina had followed a snowplow along Pioneer Trail, arriv-ing, even so, fifteen minutes late. With supernatural luck, all the other participants—Philip Strong, Paul, Eric Brinkman, the lawyer who was representing Jim Strong, Michael Stamp, and Judge Flaherty and his clerk—had apparently made it right on time. The prospective buyers had sent a representative, a young Asian man in a blue suit who was sitting in front of an older African-American man who appeared to be texting, something the court frowned on but found it difficult to control.

Kelly Strong, freckled and scowling, a real contrast to everyone else in her family, wore a battered brown leather jacket. She sat a row behind Philip and, other than for a perfunctory greeting to him, sat alone and said nothing. She nodded to Nina when she saw her, then turned back to look at the empty court beyond.

Kelly's sister-in-law Marianne Strong, and Marianne's half brother, Gene Malavoy, sat across the aisle near the prospective buyers' rep. They had been pushing for the sale of the resort ever since Jim's brother, Alex, died and Marianne inherited his one-sixth of the resort. How close were Marianne and Gene to the potential buyers? Close enough to converse familiarly, Nina noted, observing smiles, nods, and bows with the man from Korea. Look into that later, she told herself.

Petite Marianne looked the same as she had the first time Nina had seen her: all black clothing, styled to show off her sublime athletic body. Her dark hair was cut short and shiny. Gene, the younger of the pair, had a boyish, long, angular face, his hair shorter these days. His broad shoulders dwarfed Marianne's tight physique. They both looked upset at the turn of events.

Nina dredged up what she could remember about Marianne and Gene. Their father was a ski instructor in France, in Chamonix? Yes. Marianne had told Nina her mother left her when she was six.

But—as Nina sat down at the counsel table and quickly unpacked her laptop and files—she recalled that Marianne had also told Nina her mother was born in Florianópolis, Brazil. Now, wasn't that something to ponder? Her half brother, Gene, shifting in his seat, obviously as uncomfortable as his sister to be stuck here instead of flying down slopes or doing something physical, anything at all, shared the same French father.

Gene wanted to own a resort of his own someday. He had told many, many people that. Right now he ran only the dining room at Paradise.

Judge Flaherty had a certain regard for Nina. Notorious for his apoplectic moods, he had never exploded at her, and he appeared relieved as she explained that she'd associated with Lynda and would be handling the litigation aspects of the sale. He must have known about Lynda's dread of court. He seemed to be in unusually fine spirits, actually, which would have pleased Nina except that some of his geniality appeared to be due to the presence of his sports buddy, attorney Michael Stamp. She suspected Stamp and the judge spent many a lunchtime regaling each other with their skiing exploits at Heavenly. They looked as cozy as a couple of aunts by the time Nina rushed in, the straps on her fab shoes not yet properly fastened.

Stamp had been in practice in South Lake Tahoe for twenty years and had served as a city councilman for twelve of those. He had attended law school at UC Davis, and before that he had been an undergraduate track star at Cal State Hayward. He had a new baby and a lot of business clients who paid their bills. He was on his third wife, and his quest, Nina believed, was to be forever young. She got along with him and had never thought he was dirty, but now he had produced these papers, and that was making her wonder.

Brinkman, Paul, and Philip Strong sat together behind the lawyer's bar, the two PIs flanking Philip like bodyguards. Philip seemed to languish between the younger, bigger men, and Nina wondered if he had some illness he wasn't telling her about. Maybe it was the chronic emotional turmoil his son had put him through. She found it hard to look at him without feeling a pang of empathy.

No testimony would be taken today—the judge would make his decisions based solely on the paperwork filed by Lynda and Michael Stamp, and on legal arguments.

Through the tall windows a few stubborn snowflakes drifted through the firs. The courtroom was drafty and yellow-lit. At eight thirty in the morning, almost all of them had brought in a mug of coffee, including the judge. Nina began scanning Lynda's responsive papers again. They were fine, no technical problems, and Lynda had left Nina plenty of room to wiggle through the legal argument; that was the main thing.

Stamp got up and in conversational tones made his argument. Jim Strong, son of Philip, owned a one-sixth interest in Paradise Ski Resort and had apparently belatedly learned of the plan to sell it. He had gone to a Brazilian lawyer named Kraft, who had advised him that, due to the extradition treaty between Brazil and the United States, he should not provide any information regarding his location and business in Brazil and should submit all paperwork through his counsel. This had been accomplished by associating in the South Lake Tahoe, California, law firm of Caplan, Stamp, and Powell.

"As you can see from our Points and Authorities, Judge, his attorney has opened a bank account for him in Porto Alegre, Brazil, where the sales proceeds can be wired. The corporate papers as well as the copy of the probate-proceeding papers clearly establish his ownership interest—there can be no issue about that.

"Therefore, an order is respectfully requested confirming the ownership share based on the corporate papers submitted previously, and further ordering that the net proceeds be distributed by wire to the bank account as stated."

And, of course, if these orders weren't forthcoming, the abyss would open. Nina watched Philip and Kelly Strong blanch as Mike led up to this point and highlighted it. In the galley behind, Marianne Strong and Gene Malavoy reacted, letting out subdued bleats of unhappiness. A good lawyer makes things sound so simple, so reasonable, as if no other interpretation of reality is possible except the one he's selling on a particular morning halfway between winter and spring in a small mountain town.

Nina's turn. She stood up behind the counsel table. "Let's return to Earth, Your Honor. We are talking about two and a half million dollars, most of which should actually go to the rest of the Strong family and an address in some remote corner of the world where a dangerous fugitive may or may not have found refuge. Let's keep in mind that Jim Strong can't set foot here without being arrested and very likely convicted of multiple murders, and—"

"I need to interrupt here, Judge," Stamp said. "Yes, there are charges against him, but he hasn't been convicted of anything at this point. He has a legal right to make this claim and to receive these proceeds. He may be innocent of the crimes he is charged with. The charges are irrelevant to this proceeding."

Flaherty said, "He's playing a dangerous game here, isn't he, Counsel? Aren't the American authorities interested in extraditing him?"

"It is my understanding that the American authorities don't have any way of extraditing him, even if Brazil allows it, because Mr. Strong's location remains unknown. Brazil is a big country, Your Honor."

"But he's an American citizen. He can't be that hard to track."

Stamp said, "It's possible Mr. Strong is concealing his identity from the authorities in Brazil."

"You can bet he is," Nina interrupted. "Let me go on. Let's talk some more about what Mr. Stamp said. If Jim Strong were alive, he'd obviously be residing illegally in Brazil, probably under an assumed name. Even if he weren't wanted for murder here, common sense has to put us all on our guard. If he's alive in Brazil, he is devious; he's a liar, and he's faked an identity, Your Honor.

"But let me now take this further. What if, as seems possible, someone else has faked his identity? It's not as if this fugitive goes to the same church every Sunday, coaches Little League, says hi to the neighbors. This is a shadowy man on the run. How do we know the signatory on this affidavit is in fact Jim Strong? Did Jim Strong actually execute this affidavit? Or did some third party learn of the proposed sale and his disappearance and try to defraud the Strong family? Enough money is involved that this is an enormous risk. The Strong family cannot permit millions of dollars to be wired to Brazil because somebody down there rigged up an official-looking piece of paper. It's a joke. Plus I've just provided the court and Mr. Stamp with information that Jim Strong may have been stealing from the resort. How is it fair to ask that he receive monies based on the sale, when Paradise Ski Resort is unable at the same time to make counterclaims against Mr. Strong?" She had taken a risk here. Philip had not authorized her to make that allegation in court. She threw a glance at him. He appeared unhappy but not particularly surprised by her release of this information publicly.

"She's ignoring the fact that a duly appointed Brazilian notary examined his identification and determined that it was Jim Strong," Stamp said. "The affidavit is duly witnessed. We have made a *prima facie* showing that he is alive, and there's no countershowing."

"Has Mr. Stamp spoken to his client by phone or used some Internet program such as Skype to permit him to personally interview the signer of this affidavit?" Nina asked, turning and looking directly at Stamp.

His face reddened. "I can't answer that and she knows it. My contacts with my client are—"

"I thought not," Nina said. "Your Honor, the Strong family has retained a private investigator, Mr. Eric Brinkman. He's here in court today—please stand, Mr. Brinkman. He's prepared to go to Brazil, interview the author of this affidavit, and get to the bottom of this. The buyers are willing to allow an additional two weeks for this purpose. Surely this Court will let no stone"—ugh, clichés, so important in this business—"remain unturned." She had carefully chosen the word *author*, too. It reeked of fiction.

"But we have a presumption of regularity and you have made no evidentiary rebuttal, Counsel," Judge Flaherty said. "Why hasn't this trip already been made? It's not enough to opine that the man is dead and that this is a fraud."

"It's not like a trip to L.A., Your Honor," Nina replied. "It takes sixteen hours on a plane, and then a long ride to the coast to an area near the border of Argentina. Mr. Brinkman has a ticket to leave tomorrow. We're not asking for anything unreasonable when we ask for a little more time to investigate this matter, Your Honor. Millions of dollars are—"

"There isn't a shred of hard evidence that this affidavit is faulty in any respect," Stamp said. "Families get greedy. In this case, they don't want any money to go to Mr. Strong because they want to believe the charges. They prefer to believe the hype."

"Hype? This isn't hype. How about arrest warrants? How about—"

Flaherty held up a hand to stop Nina.

"They want Jim Strong dead. He's an inconvenient truth, Judge, and they have written him off. But have they come up with one single piece of evidence that—"

Angry, Nina interrupted again personally and sharply. "Mike, you seem to have forgotten that I was present when Jim Strong started an avalanche that killed my husband." She wouldn't let the lawyer talk bullshit on that point.

Stamp stopped, had the grace to look chagrined. Then, doggedly, he said, "But the fact is, he was never tried on that charge or on any other. He remains innocent in the eyes of the law."

Reason struggled for dominance but failed. "Innocent? He killed his brother, Alex; he killed his wife,

Heidi; he killed my husband, Collier." Some shred of sense made Nina leave out that he had come to her house that night to kill her, too. Paul was shaking his head slightly at her. Calm down, she told herself. It had been more of an emotional risk taking this case than she'd realized.

Stamp turned back to the judge. "There are no convictions. Counsel practices a lot more criminal law than I do, and she knows she shouldn't be making all these prejudicial statements, which I'm sure the Court in its wisdom will disregard. He's innocent until—"

Now Flaherty held up his hand, palm first. "We're talking about a lot of money, Counsel, and a man who has led his family to believe he's dead, a man who may have murdered several people. His character's dubious; I don't think what you offer is enough."

"I agree, Your Honor," Nina said quickly.

"We object to a continuance. We request a ruling today, Judge," Stamp said. "We're entitled to it. We have met the burden of showing he's alive."

"Ms. Reilly?" Flaherty said.

"Give us a week, Your Honor. Jim Strong's a murderer, and as I said, recent revelations have given us reason to believe he was also an embezzler from his family business." Repeating the allegation, she remained unsure about this tactic. She didn't like giving Stamp a heads-up on what she knew, but she didn't know what he knew and what he was prepared to do to win his case, so the previous insomniac night, she had decided to go all out.

She went on, "No one has heard from him for years. If by some wild happenstance he's alive, he has incredible gall trying to take advantage of his family's hard work after gutting the family business, almost destroying his family emotionally, and putting them in this position. Technically he owned a one-sixth share of Paradise. We can't permit him or much more likely some other criminal agency, to cause further harm." Nina said these strong words with absolute conviction. Even Stamp seemed affected. There was no point in being mealymouthed about any of it.

Judge Flaherty said, "So you think it's some con artist from Porto Alegre trying to make big bucks?" He seemed fascinated with the idea.

Nina nodded at the judge. "Exactly. You have your finger right on the problem, Your Honor. As usual."

Stamp saw that it was time to switch tactics. "If the Court is inclined to give the Strong family more leeway here, there's no need for a continuance. Lynda Eckhardt and I have already agreed the sale could go through and the money could be placed with Tahoe Sierra Title Company here in town pending any further investigation of this claim. We would then request that the Court order the money be placed in such an account pending a final deter-mination of this issue. If the two and a half million is safe in a trust account, that serves the interests of the Strong family, in that they can still complete the sale in a timely fashion."

"We object to the placement of that share of the proceeds into trust, Your Honor," Nina said. She explained what it would mean for Philip, Kelly, and Marianne. All debts of the resort would then be paid from their shares, leaving them nothing to start new lives, while the net proceeds might sit in the trust account moldering for a long time. Nina stressed that the buyers were willing to wait until Brinkman could get down to Porto Alegre and investigate the matter, and that the Strong family would pay all expenses.

"Maybe," Flaherty said. "I won't make that order until we find out a little more. Now, then, Mr. Stamp, you have asked that this Court appoint a conservator for Mr. Strong, as he is officially a missing person pursuant to Probate Code section 1845. I have no problem with setting it up as you suggest, with Nelson Hendricks acting as conservator, with the view that if I do order the opening of an escrow, Tahoe Sierra Title, where Mr. Hendricks is an escrow officer, he will also be appointed to handle the escrow account."

"No objection, Your Honor, the family doesn't dispute that Mr. Strong is a missing person and that a conservator should technically be appointed." Nina didn't want any legal mistakes to allow any further complications down the road.

Flaherty made some notes. The courtroom was quiet. The judge pooched his cheeks as he thought.

"Let's give her a week so her investigator can travel," Flaherty told Stamp finally. "Why complicate things further? What's a week for confirmation?"

Stamp took on the rigid-jawed look of a loser. Nina knew it well. There was a stir in the audience.

"Thank you, Your Honor," Nina said. "What's a week? We'll be back in court lickety-split, and Mr. Brinkman will have more information for us. Give us a chance to show this whole thing is a con—"

"I take that personally, as impugning my character and the excellent reputation of my—"

"Oh, can it, Mike," Flaherty said. "One week. What date is that, Madam Clerk?"

Outside in the courtyard, Philip Strong shook hands all around. He looked ghastly, and Nina had a feeling he wouldn't sleep until Eric Brinkman came back from Brazil.

"Who is that, Philip?" Nina nodded toward the man who had been texting in court. He walked with urgent speed toward the parking lot, now muttering into his phone.

"Nelson Hendricks. He's the escrow officer at the title company." They both watched as Hendricks, distracted by his conversation, slipped on an icy patch of concrete and barely recovered himself. "Poor guy," Philip added as they watched him climb into an old

BMW. "I see him at Chamber of Commerce meetings. His wife was recently diagnosed with MS. He almost cried when he told me, and he isn't the type to be crying in the office." Kelly caught up to Philip, thanked Nina, then walked near her father toward the parking lot, not with him, Nina noticed, but a few steps behind, as if she was watching him. The rift between them was wide.

Far from the building, Marianne Strong and Gene Malavoy smoked brown Sherman cigarettes, stamping their feet in the cold, exhaling smoke with cold bursts of angry French chatter. Neither nodded or acknowledged Nina, Paul, or Philip for that matter.

Eric Brinkman and Paul stood right outside the courthouse doors with Nina, a couple of rock-star apostles. Eric was well turned out in his tan sports jacket. Paul wore a tweed jacket that made his shoulders look wider than usual. One of the court clerks, a buddy of Nina's, walked by, glanced at them, caught Nina's eye, and gave her a discreet thumbs-up.

"Okay, we've got the time," Nina said.

Eric looked at his watch, gold and heavy, a Rolex Datejust, Nina noticed.

"I'm ready. Gotta go," he said.

"When's the flight?" Nina asked.

"Two p.m. United Airlines out of San Francisco to São Paulo," Eric said. "Then on to Porto Alegre. I'll go straight to the lawyer's address. We have been in e-mail contact and she's cooperating." He pulled on Prada sunglasses, which made his cheekbones stand out like hard knobs. "The lawyer says she'll give me whatever other authenticating evidence she can. Obviously we won't get Strong to sit down for a filmed deposition. I'll spend as much time as I've got trying to track him through the law office. He's going to be living near there somewhere. Porto Alegre is a very long way from São Paulo or Rio."

Nina nodded. "Okay. I see that you're handling a complicated situation as efficiently as possible. But please remember what I said. This is a con."

"A fiasco," Paul said suddenly.

Eric turned to him. "So you say. So you keep telling Nina here. That's why you think he's dead, am I right, Nina?"

Nina said nothing.

"You drove up to Tahoe right after Nina lost her husband, after Jim Strong became a fugitive, didn't you, Paul? To help out your friend here?" Eric indicated Nina.

"That's right."

"Did you see Strong at any time? Get a line on him? Or obtain some sort of information that he was dead? Because if you know anything factual, Paul, you could save me a trip and save Philip Strong a considerable sum of money."

"Yeah," Nina interjected. "Tell us where he's buried and we can all go home and relax." Her light tone disguised the fright she felt hearing Eric coming after Paul like that.

Paul stared at her, then at Eric. "Hey, man, you talked yourself into the job, even though you don't seem to have been very effective when the murders were going down. Now run with it."

"No need to get offended. I'm asking a legitimate question. Maybe you're hiding something, or you might open yourself up to the possibility that maybe whatever you think you know could be wrong." Eric pulled out a pair of soft leather gloves, slipping them onto his narrow fingers.

"How do you come to speak Portuguese, Eric?" Nina asked, trying to deflect the energy she saw fulminating in Paul's fists. She needed information, not male strutting.

"An old girlfriend from Brazil. I lived with her there for a year."

"Best way to learn a language," Paul said. It came out nasty instead of funny. He seemed to want to say more but controlled himself. Nina had the uncomfortable realization that the two men might not be able to work together, even if both were needed.

"Marianne Strong's mother came from Brazil," Nina said. "Let's keep that in mind."

"Intriguing, isn't it?" Eric said.

"I interviewed Marianne in the course of my investigations for Philip when I was attempting to track down the missing money from the resort," Eric continued. "Well, I've already told you I have suspicions about Marianne and Gene. I have their photos, too, to show around down there."

Nina couldn't see his eyes now, but she had seen him look into hers too deeply on their first meeting. He was very intelligent, very—sensitive somehow. Sexually conscious. He was watching her now, reading her thoughts, as if he knew all about the red bra— Oh, dear, she was straying from the point at hand.

She couldn't read him well enough. What he cared about, who he really was—she couldn't tell that yet.

"I'll call you from Brazil the minute I have something. Let's meet when I get back. We'll discuss everything then. By the way, it's a pleasure to see a woman wearing a nice pair of heels."

Paul stepped between them, scowling. Several people in the courtyard observed from a distance, pretending to notice nothing.

"No, Paul," Nina said.

"No, what?" Paul said.

"No, uh, telling what Eric might stumble into, right? If there's a con, it's a lot of money. People will do a lot for a few hundred thou."

"People will do a lot for a crappy television," Paul said, still scowling.

"I suppose you would know more about that than I," Eric said.

"What do you mean by that?" Now the two men were staring each other down.

"As a former detective, I'm sure you saw plenty of random violence. Why did you leave police work?"

"And not so random," Paul said, ignoring that last question.

Nina had a sudden flashback to being fourteen at school in Monterey, the one year a couple of boys liked her at the same time. She liked the feeling then, how they jockeyed for her attention. Now she was old enough to understand that she had merely served as a handy justification for two hormone-ridden boys to punch each other.

"Please remember, your safety is the most important thing," she said.

Eric smiled at her again. In contrast to his reaction to Paul, he seemed to like everything about her, including her motherly prudence. "I promise to be careful. I look forward to giving you a full report. Let's hope this trip takes care of all the issues. Strong's alive or he's dead. We find out. We solve Philip's problems, and we clink glasses."

Eric didn't kiss her hand this time, a good thing. He shook it professionally, the entire time moving his gaze between her eyes and Paul's.

Nina watched him walk over to the parking lot, beeping the door of the eggplant-colored Porsche Cayenne he drove.

Paul took her elbow. "Coffee?"

"I have a bunch of appointments this morning. Got to get back to the office."

"Okay. I'll call you tomorrow. I have a couple of errands here in town this morning, then back to Carmel. Got to keep the real business rolling, however Sisyphean the task, under the circumstances."

"Don't say that. We'll come out of this. We will," Nina said.

"Don't worry, I'll be back. I'll call tomorrow." He walked her to her little truck, chatting about Wish and his misadventures, showing not a hint of trouble or pain. Nina did the same.

At the truck, he leaned over and kissed her lightly. "Sorry," he said. "Forgot to ask. But you needed one." He strode off.

"Grr," she said, throwing the RAV into reverse.

CHAPTER 12

"The sliced tri-tip with garlic mushrooms and a bottle of cabernet sauvignon." Kurt handed the waiter his menu and said to Nina, "A bottle okay?"

"Why not? I'll go with grilled blackened salmon with a coconut-almond crust, and molten lava cake for dessert." Nina ordered her favorites, hungry but understanding she would probably not finish all that food. The waiter shot away before they could change their minds.

Kurt and Nina sat together at one of her favorite Tahoe hangouts, Passaretti's. Candlelight, white tablecloths. The wine came first, then food arrived, presented on patterned plates.

Kurt looked relaxed in a black turtleneck, his turquoise bracelet, and jeans. Nina wore a blue angora sweater that showed exactly what she wanted to show, a short skirt, and her Jimmy Choos. She was overdressed; some of the other women eating there wore jeans. However, she was on a mission. She forced herself to feel optimistic and ignore the niggling reality that he wanted to move back to Europe.

Her reggae ringtone. She ignored it.

The music again.

"Oh, go on," Kurt said. "Get it over with." He sipped his wine.

"I'll just step outside for a minute, okay?"

Bob needed some help. She told him where to find some things, then returned to the table to find Kurt tossing back a second glass too quickly. Any spell that might have been in the weaving had broken.

When the dinner plates had been cleared and they sat in their tiny island of silence among the other diners, Kurt said, "Being close to you and Bob over the past few months has been great."

"Nice to hear." She tasted the cake she had so anticipated, but couldn't eat it.

He took her hand. His felt cool. "Remember what I said the other day?"

"You mean, when you said I didn't love you?" Nina thought of her mother, dead for years, and mused about her mixed-up relationship with Nina's father. She thought of Andrea who knew Nina's brother, Matt, so well, with all his failings, and loved him to death nevertheless. Memories of Nina's own past loves filled her, Kurt among them. "You can't believe that. You're my first. You're Bob's father. I'll never stop loving you."

"But there are varying degrees, aren't there? You can love but not be in love. You aren't in love with me, not anymore. It's my observation that since I came back from Europe, we've become friendly. Not like lovers."

"Does that mean you aren't in love with me either?"

"Possibly." That hurt. "I do know I'm very fond of you."

"But we committed to each other—"

"To get to know each other. To try."

Nina's coffee came. She stared at the fumes billowing off it. "I'll loan you money to tide you over. Aren't Bob and I worth changing careers over? You thought you were finished as a professional musician when you came here, and I thought you had adjusted to that."

Kurt looked at his hands, beautiful hands, the nails perfectly square, the skin smooth and white, the fingers curved as if ready to go wrestle down a grand piano. "When I couldn't play, I saw the end of my career. Now I'm better. It's a different game. Don't you see, Nina? It's like a miracle. I'm a classical musician. It's what I was born to do. Without that, I'm just an unemployed man with no special skills and no future."

"Let me think." Nina was hearing her whole life deconstruct, her cabin in the woods, their son, Hitchcock hopping like a rabbit through snow down the steep driveway. She thought of Sandy in the office, the smell of freshly ground coffee in the morning, the pleasure of its heat in winter. She tried to smile and took his hand. "If you really want it, if it's what has to happen, we could think about moving. How's that sound? Starting over together."

He didn't answer right away. Then he asked, "How would Bob react?"

"As long as we're a family, he'll be fine. I could sell my practice." The thought choked her. She could barely speak, but forged onward. "We could pack up, compromise, go to San Francisco. Get a place in Noe Valley or someplace." She was flailing. She had a failed marriage in Bernal Heights and had already rejected working downtown in a high-rise legal firm. "You'll find work teaching piano. There's the big symphony orchestra there, and—"

"Aw, hell, Nina." He stroked her hand. "You don't want to be in the city. You fit right in here."

"I'm willing."

He looked away. "I've looked at San Francisco. There aren't any symphony jobs waiting in the Bay Area for me. The symphonies are in serious financial trouble."

"Kurt, I-I can't move to Europe. I couldn't practice law there."

"I know."

"And Bob's life is here."

Kurt didn't respond to that.

"I feel stupid, dressing up like this. I suppose I expected to seduce you. It's been a month since you spent the night with me."

He avoided her eyes. "I don't think we should do that."

She pushed her already mangled cake around with her fork. "Last resort. Will you see a counselor with me? I can't give up, not so easily."

"Sure, if you think it will help you get through this transition."

"No final decisions tonight?"

"No final decisions." He smiled at her and paid for dinner with his almost-maxed-out credit card.

They went home separately, to their separate, empty beds.

Late Wednesday night, after braving a brief blizzard over the pass at Echo Summit, Paul arrived back at his condo on the hill above the Barnyard Shopping Center on Carmel Valley Road. It was already full spring back here at sea level, genista lining the gulch just past the parking lot. Finding his driveway blocked, he found a spot on the street, unloaded his suitcase, and went inside the cold apartment.

Even with all the lights on, the place didn't have its usual welcoming feel. He looked in the fridge and scored a Sam Adams ale, but most of the food looked old and sad, so he gave up on the idea of eating, stripped down, turned off the lights again, and crawled between sheets that needed washing. He did not sleep much. When he did, he dreamed he was lying on a hard bunk wide-awake, watching spiders crawl across the floor, waiting for his cellmate to attack him.

Early Thursday morning he went for a morning run on Carmel River Beach in the fog. He ran as far as he could, up and back along the shore, passing a couple in a double sleeping bag who had no business doing what they were doing on a family beach. He ran like a guy who might not smell this ocean air or watch the powerful splashing waves again anytime soon.

Back at his condo, he cleaned up, then spent the morning dealing with personal issues—bills, rent, plumbing, a visit to the neighbor who routinely blocked his parking spot.

At noon he sat on his deck, surrounded by Monterey cypresses and curling wisps of fog, and remembered offering Nina a ring sometime past on this very deck. She had turned him down. That memory made him get up to pour himself a Bushmills in honor of one of the worst moments of his life. So far.

Starving, he ate at the pub at the Barnyard, then drove the short distance to his office in Carmel. At the stoplight on Ocean Avenue, lost in thought, he pictured Brinkman in Brazil sitting across from a shady lawyer in some exotic office with ferns everywhere. Who had dreamed up this scam?

He was anxious to get back up to Tahoe, but he didn't have an official reason to be there. He was damn anxious, in fact, but it would be much better to have a cover while he was watching events up there.

A horn tapped in the polite California way behind

him. Dude, the light has totally changed, it informed him. Please stop texting, speaking on the phone, figuring out where a good restaurant is, receiving your blow job, fighting with your spouse, or trying to calm your cranky infant. Have a good day, but get moving.

How the hell had it come to this? He had put Jim Strong into a mental dead file labeled *Handled*. Back he had come, not in the flesh but almost worse now, bigger and more dangerous, more powerful as a ghost.

Maybe everything in his mind now related to Jim Strong, since the ultimate insult, images of himself incarcerated, rushed toward him as implacably as loose rocks at Pinnacles National Monument, his favorite climbing spot. He might never again climb those crumbling rock-towers that scared him in a good way; he would not suck down beers and watch the Oakland A's in his bachelor pad or win at blackjack in a casino; he would not drive his car too fast on Highway 1 along a wild ocean; he would not make sweet love to the love of his life—or anyone else, for that matter. The disappearance of Jim Strong would require answers this time around. Paul might well be found out, especially if he let Brinkman handle things.

All for taking out the trash and deciding not to mention it.

For once he easily found a place on the street near the Hog's Breath Inn and climbed the stairs beyond the restaurant to his office. These days, the dark wood that had seemed so hip when he moved in appeared dated and ever-so-slightly dilapidated. He supposed he should upgrade his digs, but this was Carmel, and the Clint Eastwood connection held, and he wasn't going to move.

Unlocking the door's triple locks, he hoped that maybe Wish Whitefeather, his associate, son of the redoubtable Sandy, might be doing something quietly useful on the computer inside, but no such luck, the office was cold and empty. He worked the thermostat, setting it to warm against the moist ocean air that leaked through every gap: sixty-six degrees these days, no higher. When he had first landed here, the standard was seventy-two. Good old times, he thought, not removing his jacket. He sat down at "his" desk, currently littered with a coffee cup decorated with antlers next to a box of stale pecans. Wish's snacks. He pushed these aside to make room for the monadnock of stacked paperwork he needed to study.

Wish must be off gallivanting around, acting as if Thursday were a day of rest. How late these youngsters learn that business is a full-time affair. He had left files and notes, which Paul pored over. He called Wish, who was actually doing some insurance interviews in Salinas.

For the next several hours Paul caught up on business. He had four appointments set for succeeding days. He sent e-mails postponing them.

Then he tackled the file of outstanding business

bills, approved a bunch, and set them neatly on the table where Wish worked when Paul was there. Like a pet when the master was out of the room, Wish had gravitated to the master's spot, the leather reclining office chair, the better monitor.

After dealing with his business problems, Paul let his mind go back to what lingered under every single thought he had these days: Jim's body. The Strongs needed to know Jim was dead. They needed to know the affidavit was forged, and that someone was making a play for Jim's share of the resort money.

Paul had no contacts in Porto Alegre, Brazil. He had no contacts who knew contacts who had contacts. He suspected that his old buddy Sergeant Fred Cheney, due to budget cuts at the South Lake Tahoe Police Department, also had no pot to piss in, in terms of second-guessing the Brazilian angle.

Nina, he knew, had no ammo without his help. Three more years must pass before Jim could be declared dead by operation of law. He had hoped, hearing about the Steve Fossett case, in which the famous explorer was declared dead only a year and a half after his disappearance, the statute might be waived. But Fossett's circumstances were unusual. A pilot takes off on a routine trip and never returns. Death can be presumed by law from the perilous circumstances. But Jim Strong would have had several good reasons to disappear alive.

Paul stood up, stretched, and started up a pot of

coffee, an exotic blend Wish had found that took up a few minutes of his attention, grinding beans, pouring water, setting a dial.

While the water started to steam and drip, he stared down from the window at the people on the outdoor patio below. The fog had finally broken. Golden late-afternoon sunlight colored the impressionistic scene. Heaters kept the courtyard habitable, and the blurry couples and families smiled, gesticulated, and ate food he could smell up here in his office, some cooked over charcoal. A young couple held hands. An old couple held hands. A plump man blew out a candle on a cupcake, and his whole family clapped.

Turning away, Paul poured himself a cup and sipped it black.

He called Nina at home. "Hey, marmalade girl."

"Hi, Paul."

"My name. It's from the Bible. Did you know that? I personally never liked the guy." He heard sounds.

"Sorry, I just walked in the door, Paul. Let me— Oh, yeah, wood in the fireplace. Hang on."

The phone went down.

"Fire," she said. "It's cold in here."

"Bob and Hitchcock sitting in the cold?"

"They're over at Matt and Andrea's. Home soon."

"Ah." Paul imagined her kicking off her high heels, the small, pink half-moons on her toenails.

He heard her sigh.

"Rough day?"

"I had dinner with Kurt last night. It didn't go well."

He felt bad for her. Then he moved rapidly on to feeling good. Kurt didn't appreciate her. He was a selfish bastard. Paul had intimate knowledge of selfish bastards, having been one more than a few times. "I've been thinking."

"Okay."

"Your coat's off? You're settled on the couch?"

"More bad news?"

"It's nice and warm now?"

"Yes."

"There's something I need us to do. Will you do it?"

"You sound so serious. What is it? You know I'll do anything to fix this situation."

He laughed. "You're too smart to make a promise unless you have all the details in advance."

"I'm a lawyer. The three P's. Paranoid, protective, private. Plus I avoid anything that demands a signature. Anything else, I'll do."

"Okay, well, I can work with that. Here's what I need you to do." He paused, hoping to make her nervous. Her quickened breath on the phone told him he had succeeded.

"Ready?"

"What?!"

"I need you to take off all your clothes. I want to

picture you all warm and stretched out in front of your fire."

An outraged silence, then: "Why you little—! I thought we were having a serious conversation."

"Don't you care about my needs?"

"Your needs? What you need is the old grab and twist, and some screaming on the ground in a fetal position to remind you we're in deep trouble!"

"Ooh. Sexy."

"You're impossible! We need to talk about what is really happening here. You are going down, buddy, unless you've got something better than a thirteen-year-old's fantasies to hold you up."

He laughed and heard her join in.

"I have to admit it feels good, doesn't it? A good laugh, even when you're on the way to hell and can see the flames ahead."

"All right, sorry, I couldn't resist, you're so cute and full of gravitas, I had to tweak you, but here's the thing. I do have a plan, a way to give the Strong family peace."

"But—?"

"They need to know Jim's dead and this fraud about the resort has to be laid to rest. Right?"

"How can that happen without something really bad happening to you?"

"By the way, Brickman's not back for a couple more days, isn't that right?" Paul heard some rustling.

"I'm checking what I wrote in my schedule," Nina said. "I think that's right. Eric left yesterday.

He said four days, and with travel, earliest we'll see him is after the weekend."

"I'm going to get some sort of cover job that will bring me back up there. I'll contact some friends up there. Then we swing into action."

"Doing what?"

"I assume Philip trusts Brinkman."

"He's worked with him for a couple of years."

"But no money was recovered. And they suspect Jim took off with the money. But, honey, you and I know he didn't. We have to look at Brinkman."

"You suspect—Eric? Why?"

"I don't know enough. Not yet."

"But why? He has all the right credentials, from what—"

"So does my uncle. The one the World Court is after."

Paul listened to her pause and tried to imagine her on the couch in front of her fireplace, sipping a glass of wine. Comely girl. Certain physical reactions began to occur. Paul focused on the conversation with difficulty.

"You don't like him, but, Paul?"

"What?"

"Isn't it possible that you're prejudiced? That you view him as some kind of rival?"

A Perry Mason moment. *Isn't it true, Mrs. McGillicuddy, that you hated your husband and poisoned him so that you could run off with—* "Yeah. He terrifies me."

"Stop teasing. I can't stand this! You could end up in prison."

"Okay. I'm coming back up as soon as I can, and the point of all this is that I want to take you for a ride when I do."

"Paul, sorry. I have a call. It's Bob. I have to go."

"Don't polish off the whole bottle alone," Paul said. "See you shortly."

PART
TWO

CHAPTER 13

Meantime, what was really happening was that Sondra's boss was in trouble and only Sondra could save her. She sat down at her desk and didn't even take a minute to savor the comfort of her new surroundings. Instead, she punched buttons on her electronic organizer. She knew that what she was doing was risky and might anger Riley Fox, but she saw no other way. Ms. Fox had gotten herself into a dangerous situation. She could lose her license, her family, and even her freedom. Sondra made a few calls. The last call she made to the one man who could help. It took a lot of persuading, but finally he agreed.

"On condition that you don't say a word to Ms. Fox about me setting this up." She knew her employer disliked meddlers, even when sometimes a firm hand up from a friend was required. No, let everyone think this was all his idea.

She filled him in on the problem. He agreed to come up and help however he could.

She ran her hand along the chilly surface of her new desk, finally able to take a look around, enjoying the

feeling that she had done something urgent today, some-
thing useful. She might not be the one out there fighting
the bad guys with her bare fists, but she was behind this
fine desk doing her own kind of good work.

Paul called Sandy Whitefeather at her ranch outside Markleeville.

"Oh, *ho*," Sandy said. Her voice went up and
down as if she were riding a horse over rocky terri-
tory. "You never call me at home."

"That's right, I'm desperate. Look, Sandy, I want
to come back up to Tahoe tomorrow. Nina needs me."

"'Bout time you noticed."

"On the Strong case."

"Usually, I'm on your side. This time, can't help
you. Philip Strong already hired Brinkman."

"Look, I have a problem."

"Jim's body. Your big problem."

"I'm coming up there if for no other reason than
to give you a spanking."

Sandy withheld her response. She merely said,
"You need to do the right thing. Philip Strong should
know his son is dead. If he is. Which I think he is,
according to what you've implied."

Paul revised his vision of her on one of her
horses, outside. She was in the long wooden house
where she had married Joe, surrounded by Washoe
baskets and arts, a fire burning, pondering the universe, making stew—what the hell did she do at
home?

Basket weaving?

Never. Work on the novel she had mentioned she was writing?

He decided to imagine her filing her nails. He had no doubt she kept them hard and useful, ready when necessary. "I could use a client up there. An official reason to be up there, not to mention I always need the money."

"Going broke in Carmel? If so, please tell Wish so he can come home."

"He's taking care of things." Things had been in good order, and Paul hadn't exactly been keeping track. Good thing Wish had been. "You know everything that's happening up there. Any other case at Tahoe cryin' for a PI? I went on the Net and saw a few possibilities, but it's mostly drug deals gone bad, tourist shakedowns, drunks on rampages, the missing person who skipped town with good reasons, the odd body."

"Hnf. 'The odd body.' Not like you to miss something this big." An infuriating time passed while Paul wondered what he'd missed, then Sandy said, "Joe and I appreciate you hiring Wish. He's a funny kid. Some people say he's not so bright."

"Well, I don't hire losers, Sandy, and Wish is an exceptional person."

Silence.

"He's organized, imaginative, detail-oriented, good at communicating with me and my clients. He's also a person I like working with."

Silence.

"I can't imagine a better assistant."

"Between you and me," Sandy said, "we got a call the other day. Nina hasn't had time to return it. Someone you might want to talk to. I mean, there are so many reasons you might call this person."

"Besides getting tipped off. And who might this someone be?"

"Remember Prize's Casino?"

"Sure." Paul remembered the owner, Steve Rossmoor and his wife, Michelle, Nina's first big client. A babe, reformed. Now a respectable mother and wife of a rich, successful husband. "Oh, yeah," he said, remembering a small article he had skimmed. "Steve Rossmoor must be pissed about having a body found at his hotel."

"Michelle Rossmoor is probably more concerned," Sandy said, obviously having learned the dance of the lawyers: shake it up and admit to nothing.

Misty/Michelle Rossmoor. Prettiest real-life doll you could ever see. Why would she call Nina?

"You remember the details?"

Paul scrolled his browser. "A housekeeper found a body at Prize's. Not much to chew."

"The victim was a receptionist named Cyndi Amore, also known as Cyndi Backus. Like a few of our young ladies here, she moonlighted as an exotic dancer in Reno on weekends."

Of course he liked strippers, but now he understood why he might have overlooked the case. Women in the business of erotica sometimes took unusual risks and sometimes ended up dead. He didn't imagine a mystery there. Someone depended on Cyndi for income, or someone loved and stalked her, and the whole thing had resulted in another disaster that raised a mere blip on the collective psyche. "No suspects?"

"From what I hear, no. There's more, and I bet you haven't heard this. The housekeeper who found the body in the bed at Prize's wound up down the hill with her throat slit at a bus stop in Minden, Nevada, on Tuesday morning. She was on her way to work at Prize's. The Nevada sheriffs haven't arrested anybody, and I heard from my friend who works as a 911 dispatcher in that area that they haven't got any persons of interest either."

"Sounds like she may have seen something. So the two murders are probably connected."

"Exactly. I always said, though others demurred, you had a brain."

"Why did Michelle call Nina, Sandy?"

Silence.

"You can't tell me." Still, worth a try. He flicked through several browsers, trolling for information on the Minden killing.

Sandy was onto him. "You won't find the Minden murder on the Net or in the papers yet. Someone's keeping it quiet."

"The Rossmoors have friends," Paul guessed. "But they won't be able to keep these two stories out of the paper for long, two deaths that hark back to Prize's."

"Steve Rossmoor has a lot of power in this town and a few neighboring ones, too."

Much as Paul despised and envied Steve Rossmoor for his tennis wardrobe, Ivy League background, happy family, and intelligence, he had to respect the man for running a fairly honorable business in a town riddled with its own Western version of the mob. "So Michelle sought legal advice from Nina. Interesting," Paul said. "Going back to the attorney who handled her criminal case way back when. I imagine she and Steve have more than a few other attorneys to consult when they need help. Yet they went to Nina."

"Uh-oh. I hafta go. Joe and I are going to a barbecue in Jackson tonight. It's a long drive."

"Any last helpful tips for your son's employer who respects, supports, and encourages him at every turn?"

Sandy almost never laughed, and she didn't this time either. "The dead housekeeper's name was Brenda Bee, the one who discovered the stripper's body. Lived in Minden. Had a husband named Ronnie. I bet he's in the phone book."

"Got it."

"By the way. Brinkman—he came around with questions. Like, is Paul in love with Nina. Like, is

Paul a Doberman who beats people up. Not in so many words. I told him you're a lamb. He laughed. I didn't see how it was funny."

"He's looking at me?"

"Has a couple canines buried in you. Stay cool, Paulie."

"What did you just call me?"

"Take good care of Wish."

"Or else."

"'Bye, now."

Well, well, Paul thought, making notes. The minute he finished, he called Michelle Rossmoor at Prize's. The switchboard tapped him through to her mobile phone.

"Hey, Paul. It's been a while. You still tall, blond, and handsome?"

"Hey, Michelle, you maintain your babeness after two kids and a demanding husband?"

They both laughed, reminisced for a few minutes, then got to the point.

Paul said, "I heard about the body at your hotel."

"Did Nina tell you I called her?" Michelle asked.

"No." He needed to make that clear. Nina had not violated any client/attorney privileges. "Did you call her? Why?"

Michelle was silent, adding up a couple of twos and making four. "I'm glad you got in touch. What a lucky thing. By the way, how is Sandy?"

Despite her looks, she was a smart woman. "As always," Paul said. "On her horse, riding fast. Now, what's up, Michelle? You can tell good ol' Paul. I'm on your side."

"Steve and I could use your help."

"Let's start from there."

"Hello, Mr. Bee," Paul said into his cell phone. In the grocery store at Carmel Rancho Center, he was stocking up on food that wouldn't rot fast, a tiny bud in his ear connecting him to a man in Nevada. Strangely, nobody stared at him for talking to himself. What a grand new world.

He examined the fresh shrimp. He supposed he could freeze it, but what was the point of seafood if it wasn't fresh from the sea?

"What? Who is this? A reporter?"

"I'm a private investigator representing Prize's resort, looking into your wife's death." Paul put two pints of ice cream into his cart, one chocolate chip, one vanilla. He browsed for fudge sauce. The fridge needed filling.

"My wife's murder, you mean. She never should've taken that job. So you're working for Prize's?"

"Paul van Wagoner is my name. I'm sorry for your loss, Mr. Bee. I know it's terrible to lose someone you love." He did know, and to counteract the mood that thought put him in, he fingered a Spanish vegetable, then sniffed it, taking simple pleasure in the routine.

"I loved the hell out of her; that's the first thing

you should know. My neighbors, the postman—they're looking at me funny, as if I could ever do anything mean to her."

"You deserve to know what happened to her and I can help."

Ronnie Bee burst into noisy tears over the phone. "You think finding her killer's going to help? It won't, you understand? You say Steve Rossmoor hired you?"

"That's right. Why do you think your wife was killed?" Paul loaded two good Chiantis into his cart and began searching for inexpensive-but-good pinot noirs to fill the remaining space in his wine rack.

"Because she saw the killer. She told me. That's what is so awful. She told me she wouldn't be able to identify him or even give any good description! She was nearsighted! He killed her for nothing!" Ronnie Bee lapsed into some creative profanity, which made Paul feel bad again. Still, he had been hoping for that confirmation. There had been the off chance that the housekeeper's murder was a coincidence, had nothing to do with the death of Cyndi Amore, but the husband sounded definite about the connection.

"I'm coming your way. Any chance we can speak in person?" Paul asked.

A slender woman with a phone glued to her ear had passed by while Paul talked on his phone, close enough for him to smell her perfume, but he had only a distracted grin to gift her with. She drifted away.

Paul set up an appointment with Ronnie Bee for Saturday, clicked off his phone, then tossed the last of his purchases onto the conveyor belt. The woman had checked out already and left his life. Five minutes from contact to rejection, and the sad truth was, that was not a record.

The man in front of him finished up his transaction, loading up sacks with chips, beer, nuts, cheese, and crackers.

Party down, brah, Paul thought. No big game to watch, nothing happening except the usual emotional emptiness.

It struck him that he was in danger of joining the fraternity of the taco chips.

Friday, early, Paul combed his hair, put on a fresh white shirt over slacks, and hit the office.

Wish Whitefeather, young and tall, lank black hair longer by the day, tied back right now with a leather string, stood up, almost knocking over Paul's chair. "Whoa. I didn't expect you so early."

"My chair likes staying nice and warm when I'm gone." The antler cup steamed on Paul's desk next to the huge, flat monitor.

Wish picked up his pecans and his cup, blew over the top of his coffee, and moved everything to his own area. Wish's table appeared cozier almost instantly, while now Paul's desk looked rather sterile.

"Hey, no problem that you're here. There's room for both of us. Plus, I forward everything to the laptop," Wish said. "It's good to see you, Paul. I hear things aren't going so good up there at Tahoe."

Wish knew most of Paul's personal business through Sandy. Paul knew most of Wish's personal business through Sandy, too, except for the part about the girlfriend.

While Wish paid bills and invoiced outstanding accounts, Paul met with clients down at the Hog's Breath restaurant, his personal conference area. After he finished with his meetings for the day, he and Wish made lists of things Wish could handle and figured out who on their regular roster they could hire to do some of the routine work. Then Paul headed back to the condo for his bag.

Nina spent the evening with her brother's family.

"Yoo-hoo," she said, slogging up the pathway to their house, Bob following close behind her. Orion lorded it over the semiwinter sky, so clear she could even see the faint patch of nebula in his sword. A sliver of moon helped them up the snowdrifts in front of the house. But the season would change. In a few months, it would be hot. The dead pine needles would let off that dry aroma of theirs, and even the lake would warm enough to let them take dips in it.

Nina's sister-in-law, Andrea, redheaded, small but huge in purpose, met them at the front door with hugs and kisses. "I'm so sorry about the walkway. We haven't had time to shovel it out."

They shook off their coats, and while Andrea

hung them up, she told stories of the old folks trapped behind mounds of snow that blocked entry to their homes, tourists who slipped from side roads into ditches and almost died, bears who bashed in garage doors and bullied through freezer doors, eating everything within reach. Winter at Tahoe was full of such tales, and she seemed to have heard every interesting one of them.

Bob listened politely, accepted a soda, and ran upstairs to visit with his younger cousins, Troy and Brianna.

Games beeped and roared down the stairway.

Nina sighed. "Remember when they used to climb trees and roofs and we were so worried?"

"They're still climbing," Matt said, "in a different way."

"Dangerous in a different way."

"Ha. You're so right."

Matt ran a small fleet of tow trucks in winter, along with a sideline in snowplowing. In summer, he took parasailers out flying on Lake Tahoe. He always seemed busy. Nina remembered his hiring Kelly Strong at a big risk, and how he shrugged off Nina's caveats. "Everyone I hire has issues," he had told her.

Andrea, Nina's emotional bulwark, had contacts with the societally conscious community at Tahoe. She ran a women's shelter and was dug as deep as an archaeologist into the strata of things in town.

"So, how's Kelly doing?"

"Shows up. Does her job. She's good," Matt said.

"I'm not sure I understand her. Can't figure out if she loves her family or hates them."

Nina thought about that. "She seems attached to her father."

"I'd say that relationship is not so healthy."

"Why?"

"Things she says. Her brother was a killer. She loves the resort even though she won't have anything to do with it. Her father offers her financial help she won't accept. Instead, she's plowing and towing for me. I don't know. Nothing jibes. She's from a wealthy family but she lives like a pauper."

"Hmm."

"What brings you here, Nina? What's bothering you?"

"I only come when I'm messed up?"

"Furrowed brow and splotchy flush on your neck, dead giveaways."

"Work. Life. How I wish everyone had a perfect marriage like you guys."

Matt and Andrea looked at each other and burst out laughing.

"Haha! Okay, Andrea, you handle this one." Matt, still laughing, went outside to use a new tripod and photograph the stars.

"I hear you took Philip Strong's case," Andrea said. "I'm surprised. I know I told you once before he's a great supporter of the women's shelter. Every Christmas for at least ten years, he's given us a generous donation. But your history with that family—"

"He has been important to this community. It's so complicated. I know. But Andrea, right now, my problem's Kurt. We're going for counseling."

"Good move. Hard for you, asking for help."

"It's not my style or his. Do you know someone good?"

"It isn't anybody's style." Andrea dug around in her bag. "Here you go. The man's name is Buck Tynan."

"Kurt doesn't like to talk about his feelings."

"And you do?" Andrea snorted. She touched Nina on the shoulder. "He'll get you talking. Buck's a mediator. He knows how to break through to reasonable solutions."

"Can he bring us back together?"

Andrea looked out the window at her husband, puffing through the cold, setting up awkward shots, his breath a fog in front of his face. "If it's meant to be," she said.

CHAPTER 14

Paul hit the road for Tahoe at almost midnight Friday. Another mini-storm near the summit forced him off the road at Pollock Pines to put chains on the Mustang, even though he had a perfectly good set of snow tires. He would have toughed it out, but the California Highway Patrol had a roadblock and motioned him over to the side of the road when they saw the vintage car.

He looked around for someone to hire, but the chain gentlemen were all busy, so he got under the dripping fenders on his back and did the dirty work himself. It felt good and marked the break from the civilized valleys. He accepted it all, the icy mud, the snow falling implacably, the cold.

In the wee hours of Saturday morning he arrived at his new favorite casino hotel, Harrah's, sacked out. After a few hours of alert visiting with his dark soul, he showered, dressed, and went downstairs to the gaming floor, where he rapidly won three hundred bucks playing Texas Hold 'Em. But it was hard work, and his eyes were red-rimmed by the time eight in the morning rolled around and he pushed open the door to Nina's office.

Someone had opened up and must be down the hall. He remembered where Nina kept the espresso machine and went into the library-cum-conference-room. The walls were lined with law books, though they were mostly for effect, since almost everything was online these days, and she had the same old used conference table with the scratches on the surface. After making sure his initials remained etched under one corner of the table, he loaded the espresso machine and started it up. In a moment, hot fumes wafted his way and he gave himself up to the heavenly smell, closed his eyes, and breathed it in.

"Good morning." Nina looked better than ever, dressed in tall black boots and leather. He wrapped her in his arms and she pulled back, smiling broadly, not too quickly.

"Wear jeans and your snow boots tonight."

"You came to tell me that?"

No. He had come because he wanted to see her. "Are you free for a late breakfast of waffles and maple syrup? Or yogurt? Or oatmeal, even?" She looked so winsome and at the same time inaccessible, with her brown eyes and fluffy brown hair and tan leather jacket.

"Sorry, no. I have a school thing with Bob. So you made it."

"Amazing coincidence. New clients. You know,

the Rossmoors." He explained about his double murder case. Nina said with her usual candor, "Did you
take it to keep your eye on the situation at Paradise?"

"Of course not. It just came up."

"Did Sandy have anything to do with it?"

"Sandy is the soul of discretion. You know that."

He made his excuses and headed out.

Entering the South Lake Tahoe Recreation and
Swim Complex, he begged to be admitted as a visitor
to save himself the price of admission and wandered
toward the pool. The air reeked of chlorine, one of
his favorite smells, and he wished he had brought
swim trunks. The long drive the day before had
cricked his back. He couldn't be getting stiff at forty-
two.

A dozen people swam laps, splashes flying. He
calculated four were in perfect shape, and the other
eight more like him, wannabes or former jocks a hair
from making it all work again someday.

In the fourth lane from the left he spotted
Michelle Rossmoor. Her platinum hair fanned out
behind her. She wore a black bikini, an affront to the
ladies beside her in their modest Speedos.

She took a breath every two strokes, not opti-
mum, Paul thought, but fair enough for an amateur.
Watching her chug through the water, he remembered Nina describing her a few years ago as a Barbie
doll, one of the doctor ones maybe, smart and pretty
the way fantasy girls always were.

The next time Michelle's head popped out of the water for a breath, he caught her eye. "Hey, there, Mrs. Rossmoor," he called out.

She crawled to his side of the pool, coughed, and pushed water off her forehead. "You're early, Paul, I have another half mile to go."

"I'll wait."

"Screw my good health." She climbed out of the pool, wiped off her toned body while Paul watched, and encircled it with a towel. Her blue eyes twinkled toward his hazel ones.

"I called your office several times to say I would be early. You have people."

She laughed, picked up a fresh towel near the door, and rubbed her hair. "They help me avoid the likes of you."

"Nah, they make me creative. I'll wait for you in the lounge."

"Meet you in ten minutes. Make that fifteen. Have a protein shake or something."

Paul waited at a table outside the juice bar/coffee shop, sparsely populated at this hour. He sifted through the previous day's *Tahoe Mirror*. Nothing new had turned up about the death of Cyndi Amore, at least nothing the *Mirror* could publish. The police, Sergeant Cheney prominently quoted, had no new information.

That wasn't true. Fred Cheney knew it. Paul knew it. There was a connection with a much loved woman who had died violently thirty miles away and down the mountain, in a small Nevada town.

Brenda Bee, Paul mused. She arrived on time most days, he knew from chatting with the lady on the phone at Prize's reception an hour before. The lady, whose name was Shanti, had known her. She said that, as far as she knew, Brenda had been close to her husband, Ronnie, who often came up the hill from Minden to pick her up. Ronnie was having a hard time getting over the death of his wife, Shanti said, and had visited Prize's to talk to Steve Rossmoor and Brenda's friends on the house-keeping staff. He had wanted to see the Classic Room where Brenda had found the body of Cyndi Amore.

According to Shanti, Brenda had two exes, one deceased and one in Virginia who hadn't spoken to her for years.

Paul had tried to get Shanti to open up regarding any information that might be floating around among the employees about Cyndi Amore, but on that topic, all Shanti would say was that the staff was freaked-out and had asked for extra security in the halls.

How strange, to be taking on a red-hot investigation like this when his real focus was an entirely different and unrelated matter. He had thought of this as a subterfuge really, but was quickly being drawn in.

Several women came in, but not Michelle. It had

been a half hour. Paul's mind drifted. Michelle finally appeared, dressed in gladiator heels and skinny jeans, wet-coiffed and pink-lipped. The last time he had seen her she had been pregnant. She seemed to have grown up with marriage and motherhood. Her expression was serious.

She sat down next to him on a chair at the empty table.

"So, yeah," she said. "Boy, am I glad to see you, Paul. Steve and I have discussed this. We want to hire you to look into this situation at the hotel. We trust you."

"Glad to hear that. I'll do what I can, although it's a police investigation. But first, I'm curious. You and your husband own a casino-hotel, among other properties. Why do you swim here, among the plebs?"

"Oh, no big thing. I do have access to some pools, including one that's just ours at home. But those pools are recreational. I work when I swim. Need the twenty-five meters to stretch out."

Remembering her fast crawl, he nodded.

"How are you, Paul?"

"Same old, same old. You?"

"Completely different." She laughed. "When you last saw me, I was an outlaw girl with issues, not the least of which was a murder charge hanging over me."

"Now you're free to swim and meet up with old cronies. Things appear to have worked out."

She nodded, eyes down, her hair hiding her face,

as if her smile were so powerful she didn't want to blast him with it. "They have."

"Good."

"How's Nina? Apart from the fact that I owe her, I miss her. I guess our lives are so different now—"

"She'd love to hear from you. Invite her for lunch. Ladies love that."

"So you and Nina didn't end up together?"

"No, I've been seeing someone else." He didn't add, *But as usual it didn't work out*.

"Paul, you have to stop falling in love at the drop of a bra."

"Nice talk."

She glanced at the clock on a wall above the bar. "Well, as I'm sure you know, I've got two kids, a challenging husband, and a hell of a work schedule. So let's get to it."

In the background, people had appeared at the café. Some sat expectantly at tables. The newly arrived banged around cups. The smell of coffee wafted through the air.

"Mmm," they both said simultaneously.

"Want something?"

"English breakfast tea," she said.

Paul got up and ordered two cups. He brought back the mugs.

"Are you folks looking for a lawyer, too?"

She shook her head. "Not at the moment. We have our business lawyer, and he's dealing with some staff issues."

"So no Nina?"

"Not right now, anyway. I called her about something else."

He told her his fee.

She handed him a check for five thousand dollars. "Cheers."

Paul tucked it away, got out his recorder, and clicked it on. "You mind?"

"No, I can see why it would be important to record witness statements. I'm witness to more than I told the police."

Paul's eyebrows went up. "You were at the hotel the day Brenda discovered the corpse?"

She nodded. "Yes, we're blessed with lots of help with our kids, so I can help out at the business. I do some of the VIP meeting and greeting and take over quite a bit in Steve's absence. He was at a gaming convention in Vegas when all this happened."

"Who watched the little ones?"

"My parents and I, well, we reunited, I guess you'd say. They retired to Tahoe. They don't push their religion on us, and in return they get to dote on our kids. They're fine grandparents, Paul. My mother comes over all the time to watch them."

"You're lucky."

"I am."

"So you got a phone call?"

"No. I was working in Steve's office when one of the cleaning staff ran in. She said the police were coming, and that one of the staff had found a dead body in one of our Classic Rooms in the Annex, on the first floor. I ran back there with her and found one of the cleaning staff, Brenda, sitting outside the room, the police already there. Brenda looked like she was in shock, like she was about to fall off her chair."

Paul got the room number and a description of the layout. "Stop by the hotel this afternoon and I'll show you the room," Michelle said. "It's been thoroughly cleaned after the police took away the yellow flagging, but we've decided not to put anybody in there for at least six months. You know how it is with gamblers. They're superstitious, and if somebody took a big loss, then found out about the murder, well, who knows what they might do. Anyway, I hugged Brenda and said hang on a sec, then I introduced myself to the El Dorado County homicide detective who seemed to be in charge. They let me in and I saw the body of a woman."

"Describe her for me."

Michelle thrummed manicured fingernails on the table. "It wasn't that she had been maimed or there was a lot of blood around. In fact, she looked—well, you're gonna think this is funny, but she looked stiff and dignified, lying on her back on the bed. It reminded me of *National Geographic* photos of funeral practices in ancient Egypt. She was wearing a blue bra, and she was lying on top of the bed. Her hands were folded—Paul, the killer must have done this—her chest and her legs were staged, pulled together. I suppose you'll get all the police reports and photos?"

"Plan to," Paul said.

"There was something, maybe a stocking, black and bulky and long. It had been loosened by the medics or detectives, I think, removed from her neck. Poor Cyndi. They had already pronounced her dead."

"You knew who it was?"

"I knew her right away. Her name was Cyndi Backus. She was a receptionist at the main hotel desk, a very pretty gal who I know did some, uh, lounge work at a Reno club on the weekends to make a few extra bucks under a stage name. She was on lunch break from desk duty, one hour between twelve and one. That hour, and whatever escapade she was involved in, killed her. She was only twenty-eight."

About Michelle's age. "Any idea who did it?" Paul said.

"None." But her mouth tightened as if she were trying to zip it. Somehow they had entered a sensitive area. Paul's interest quickened, but he didn't let it show.

"Notice anything else about the room that seemed out of place?"

"Her slacks and shirt were on the floor by the bed, and her Prize's jacket was laid across the chair. Nice pair of boots. Her purse was on the floor, too. Not a big mess, no obvious signs of a struggle. The door entry card was on the table. I do know the rooms and I didn't notice anything missing. But the room was in a strange condition. There was an empty half-pint bottle of Martell's, the cognac, you know—"

"I do know."

"Well," Michelle said, "we found that in the sink, rinsed. And in the bathroom the toilet paper was all used up. That told me something. Later, after I went back to the lobby, I checked with Housekeeping and found out that room had been occupied the night before. Reception records showed the guests were a retired couple from Cádiz, Spain, who checked out right before eleven, and Housekeeping said it would be about one p.m. before the cleaners would get to that room normally."

Paul said, "Nice work. Couldn't have done it better myself. Would Cyndi have known about the gap in time with nobody in the room?"

"Housekeeping said she called them at eleven fifteen and asked about the schedule. But—"

"Who in Housekeeping?" Paul noted the name.

Michelle went on, "One of the girls called in sick, Brenda's partner Rosalinda Hernandez, so Brenda was working alone. Behind. Trying to catch up. She was worried she wouldn't finish the rooms, so she was rushing. She actually got ahead of schedule as a result."

Paul said, "The best-laid plans. Cyndi had it all figured out. Made sure she had time for the dude, and—"

"Brenda got there at one fifteen."

"Cyndi was married, right?"

"She was always on her mobile with her husband. I met him once or twice. I thought they seemed very close. I hate to think she was having an affair."

"What else could it be?"

"Hard for me to imagine."

Michelle loved her husband, Paul got that, which meant insight went out the window in this case. "Any signs of a sexual encounter happening or about to happen?" Paul said.

"The underwear was expensive and made to get heavy breathing going."

Paul raised his eyebrows at that. "Good observation," he said. "Anybody you talked to at Reception or Housekeeping have a clue?"

Michelle shook her head. "Everybody's appalled. She would have been fired for using the rooms like that if Steve had found out."

"So you went back out into the hall?"

"Yes, the room was full of people and I was in the way, so I went back to Brenda and put my arm around her. She didn't cry; she had that shell-shocked look in her eyes."

"Tell me about Brenda," Paul said. "How well did you know her?"

"Well, she has—oh, shit, she *had*—an eight-year-old son who didn't live with her, and we'd talk about kids when we met in the hall or the coffee shop. She had a little bit of a Southern accent, I thought. She was a warm person and had a sort of raucous sense of humor. Maybe *raunchy* is a better word. She was in her fifties, but you'd never know it. She had long hair and smiled all the time."

"A fifty-five-year-old woman with a child eight years old?"

"I know," Michelle said. "Brenda told me she started going back to church when she got pregnant. She never dreamed it could happen. But then—she and her husband split up. Not the current husband, Ronnie Bee, the old husband, and he moved back to Virginia where his family was. The little boy went, too, I don't know why. She missed him terribly."

"Hmm."

"The little boy came to her funeral with his dad," Michelle went on. "I couldn't stand to see him cry. I had to leave. Paul, it's not business or Prize's reputation Steve and I feel so bad about. We just hate what happened on our watch, and we want to put it right. We feel hurt by it, you know? The hotel feels, I don't know—"

"Sullied?"

"Good word, yeah." She drank from her cup. "I told Brenda how sorry I was that she had discovered the dead woman in the bed."

There it was again, the quick look away.

"I asked if she needed anything. She said she needed her husband and that she wanted to go home."

"She said something else, though, something that put you on edge."

"No, nothing."

"What happened that you're not telling me, then?"

"Nothing!"

"You can keep saying that," Paul said mildly. "But when you don't tell somebody else, it festers and creeps under your covers at night and bites you. You know all that. About secrets."

Now she was frankly disturbed. She was the metaphorical type, always had been, symbols became symptoms with her. Shame about the lip she was testing with her teeth, though. Paul sat there like a neutral, harmless, receptive lump, a stubborn lump that wouldn't move on without an answer.

Eventually, Michelle covered her mouth with her hand and said through the hand, "Paul—can you help me with something?"

"I'll try."

"Do you think Brenda's murder is connected to the corpse she found on the bed?"

Paul nodded. "Can't prove it yet, though."

"Hell." The hand went down and Michelle licked her fantabulous lips. She was ready to speak.

"You can trust me with it, honey," Paul said.

Her exquisitely sculpted shoulders slumped. "I'm that obvious? Ugh. Brenda's dead and I have two little kids and he may have seen her, but he didn't see me, and I don't want to put them at risk."

"Who didn't see you?"

She looked around. "I went out back to the parking lot to get something from a friend's car. This was right before I went to Steve's office, at about ten past one. I stopped by the ice machine to adjust the package I was carrying and saw Brenda ahead of me at the corner of the building, looking away from me. I'm sure she had no idea I was there. I stepped back into a doorway. I don't know why. I stopped to watch her and see what she was watching."

Paul folded his arms. "At one ten? Well, I'll be. You're a witness."

"Just my luck."

"She didn't see you?"

"She never looked back. She was looking so intently down the walkway. You know, people's body language says things. She was busy watching for something. If I made a noise, even dropped a vase, I don't think she would have noticed. I watched her for a couple of minutes."

"Why would you do that?"

Michelle frowned. "That's a hard question. Hm. I knew right away that something was wrong and that I should stay very quiet. That's all I can tell you. Something was off-key, maybe something management should know about."

"Okay."

"And so I watched."

"What happened next?"

"She stood there on the walkway completely unmoving for what seemed like a long time. The longer she stood, the more concerned I got. Then, when I thought I was going to cough or do something else that would ruin everything, a man came out of the room toward the end of the hallway she was watching—102."

"How did you know it was a man?"

Michelle's clear blue eyes glazed as she thought back to the moment. "I don't know, he moved, he swung his shoulders and moved like a guy, deliberately. He was dressed in black. Black pants even."

"Go on."

"He turned our way for a sec. Bundled up, baseball cap, shades, moving fast."

Paul waited for her to say more.

"I won't make my children targets, Paul."

"Ah. Okay, tell me about it. We'll get back to that in a minute."

She drank a deep breath. "I can't say anything else about him. He was down the hall. He looked our way and saw Brenda, then turned and moved really fast down the hall in the other direction, and then practically ran out into the parking lot."

"Did Brenda tell you that he saw her?"

"She wasn't sure, but I am. She shrugged when I told her to be careful. I suppose that's why she went on with her life, was trying to get her bus to work the next morning."

"When you spoke with her in the hall, did you two talk about this guy?"

"She thought he was trying to cover up. You

couldn't see his hair under the cap. He was in a parka. She told me he was fast on his feet. She shook her head when I asked her other questions. I don't think she got that good a look at him. If she was killed for seeing him, it's a horrible waste of a life."

"He was dressed to avoid being recognized to start with. So you didn't tell Brenda that you were watching her and that you saw the man?"

Michelle looked down. "No. I didn't—I hadn't made up my mind what to do. I was afraid."

"And you haven't talked to the police about what you saw?"

"I haven't even told Steve."

Paul said, "Here's what you need to do, honey. I'm going to take you over to see Sergeant Cheney right now and you're going to give a statement."

"But—"

"Then you're going to pack up and get your kids and take a vacation until this is resolved. Right away."

"B but I'm needed here! It could take months!"

"Steve's gonna say the same thing, once you tell him the whole story. Which you're going to do right now." Paul got out his cell phone.

For a moment Michelle looked at it. Then she took it, said, "Phooey," and called her husband.

Paul moved away to give her some space. He looked out the big plate-glass window and thought about what she had told him. This was supposed to have been a side gig. Tahoe was becoming monstrously complicated.

Like it always does.

Michelle beckoned. "Okay. Let's go see Cheney. Steve's booking the babies and me and my mother on a flight to Honolulu for a week. We leave tonight."

"Wise decision," Paul said.

"I hate leaving Steve in this turmoil."

"Your kids' safety is more important."

"You're right."

She let him take her in the Mustang. She was a king-hell high-school date, and he enjoyed every second of having her sit next to him, sunk into the low seat, her earrings jingling slightly as he bumped over the road. She smelled like soap.

The lake sparkled like a vacationer's dream as Paul drove them back into town. The ski slopes loomed above the town, still with thirty-five-foot base depths. The storm had frittered itself and winter away, and spring brightened the snow with more than a hint of the warmth that made summer here so pleasant, but on a weekday nobody was around because it was only April and people have to earn the money for their vacations sometime.

Not that anybody had much money this year to drop into slot machines or for ski tickets. Several of the small souvenir shops lining the road were already out of business. Several more had just opened. Tahoe was a dream, a place where anything could happen, and everything did.

CHAPTER 15

Cheney wouldn't let him join the fun. He had Michelle brought in and told Paul to wait.

Stomach rumbling, Paul played back bits of the tape while he sat in the front room, a model of plain efficiency, observed by the officer of the day through his bulletproof window.

Michelle came through the door about one o'clock, smelling fresh as a baby's breath.

"Steve's coming to pick me up," she said. "The sergeant is ready to talk to you."

"Have a great trip. Tell Shanti in Reception I'll come by later to see the room." Paul stood.

"Thanks for helping us, and for making me do this. I feel better already. Tell Nina I'll see her soon, okay? I'm grateful to her. I don't think she's met our kids."

Paul nodded.

Michelle gave him a little wave. The outer door buzzed and she flitted off to pack for the land of aloha.

Fred Cheney's office, near the back of the South Lake Tahoe Police Department, which sat beside the

courthouse, which sat beside the jail, had an awesome view of a grove of tall pines. No other building
or human could be seen out the window, just nature.
Must be good for staying calm, because Fred was
the calmest man Paul knew. Pictures on his desk
confirmed that Cheney had a much younger wife, a
vigorous visage, and muscles where no man his age
deserved muscles. His hair, crinkly gray, was abun-
dant, almost qualifying as a modern Afro.

"Hey, there he is," Cheney said, and came around
his desk. They shook hands. "Been working out?"

"Some. You?"

"Keeps me sane. Sit down, Paul." They talked
about Carmel, and Clint Eastwood, who kept putting out a good movie every time somebody said
he was too old. Cheney held his calls and treated
Paul as a colleague. Paul found Cheney's attention
refreshing. Since Paul had left law enforcement
after getting kicked off the police force in San
Francisco several years before, he'd noticed some
cops thought it a betrayal. In law enforcement, as
with gangs, you were part of the brotherhood or
you were nobody.

It was worth being an outsider for the freedom,
though. Paul could still do what he loved best—right
imbalances, fix things—and make better money at
it, too.

"So. Speak of the devil," Cheney went on.

"Oh," Paul said. "Always great to be remembered.
But why might you speak of me in any way at all?"

Cheney cleared his throat. "A few things have come up, including your name."

"Oh? What things?"

Cheney closed the door to his office.

"You probably realize the Bee murder is a current and active investigation," Cheney said in his deep voice. "Not something we go around sharing with PIs from other areas without cause."

"So it is your case?"

"I'm handling the California investigation. Cyndi Amore was a resident of South Lake Tahoe. Douglas County Sheriffs has primary jurisdiction. Brenda Bee was killed in Nevada, but this is being treated as a double murder, because of the proximity in time of the two deaths and the probable motive for killing the housekeeper."

"You mean, because Brenda Bee saw him. Got a quick look, I mean."

"He thought she saw more than she did. That's the theory at the moment, based on the husband's statement."

"Let me help, Fred," Paul said. "I won't get in the way."

"So the Rossmoors hired you."

"That's right."

"A while back, wasn't it, Michelle's case?"

"Nina Reilly's first murder case," Paul said. "She had barely unpacked her shoes."

"They must have liked the work you did. Is Nina part of this?"

"No. She's got another whale to fry."

"I heard." Paul saw Cheney's thoughtful fingers tapping, then: "I've got some police reports you can copy."

"Thanks. Really, thanks."

"Ditto. You've already helped," Cheney said, "getting Mrs. Rossmoor in for a statement."

Paul took the file. "Read it and weep," Cheney said. "The first murder, the one at Prize's, doesn't look like a robbery. As for the death at the bus stop in Minden, Brenda's murder, nobody witnessed it or the perp. Whole thing went down in two minutes. No screaming, no signs of struggle. Her husband had just driven off. Our man snuck up on her from behind like the bastard he was. She ran, but he caught her, slit her throat from left to right. Nevada State Police did a good fast initial investigation. Some lab and toxicology reports to come, of course."

"Suspects?"

"Whoever killed Cyndi Backus, stage name Amore, that's our only person of interest at the moment."

"According to Michelle, Cyndi led a bit of a double life," Paul said.

"Even stripping ain't what it used to be in this recession. She had picked up this straight job as a receptionist six months before, and she was a model employee. Never the twain occupations mixed. Or something."

"Her weekend work might have led to more unsavory types with violent hands."

"I know, it's a consideration. She was married. I talked to the husband." Cheney picked up one of the reports and scanned it. "Johnny Castro. He has the marriage certificate but she never changed her birth name of Backus. She seems to have had a problem figuring out who she was. She wanted a straight life, the trips to Costco and the kiddies in footy pajamas, but then again she'd get bored, and her weekend job was pulling her back to her old bad habits."

"Drugs?"

"No, she had never done drugs but she liked whiskey. And she liked men. Johnny thinks she was having an affair. He thinks he knows who with, too, only I don't have a confirmation on that. The purported boyfriend is a mechanic down the highway by the Y. We talked to him, and he says the husband's wrong, that he was only helping her change her oil. Lubing her, ah, vehicle." Cheney gave Paul a couple of phone numbers. "You learn anything to the contrary, I expect to hear it."

"I guess my main question now is, was Cyndi Backus sexually assaulted before or after she was strangled? Or did she have consensual sex?"

Cheney held out open hands. "Wait for the lab reports, but it looked like signs of recent sex to the forensics team. A few bruises on her arms from being held down. Some blood on her teeth. A rape, or rough sex. It's possible we'll have both a semen sample and a blood sample. That'll help a lot. Bruise on her chin. Looks like he had sex with her, knocked her out, strangled her, and then fixed her up a little like maybe he was sorry. Sometimes I'm disgusted with the whole human race, Paul. I get from the husband that she really was moving into an ordinary life, about to retire completely from that world she had gotten sucked into as a teenager. She had a husband and a father and mother. The parents own a trailer park. They live in Arizona and they're on the phone with me every day. The mother's the hard part. She keeps talking about when Cyndi was a little kid. She says she warned her, told her she'd get hurt. I've been a cop too long. I've got kids, Paul. I lie awake on this one. The son of a bitch killed two women and I bet he sleeps like a baby."

"People are no damn good," Paul said. "That's my working theory."

Cheney gave him a pensive look. "Any chance you might need a PI down in that lovely little seaside town you work out of?"

"You mean you?" Paul said, astonished. "You'd move to Carmel?"

"That's what I mean. I've got twenty-five years in. I want to keep working, but not here. I've played this out, you know what I'm saying, Paul?"

"Yeah. Your wife okay with a move?"

"Yep. Loves the ocean."

"You seriously looking for a job? I hired a new associate, a kid, but he graduated from the Police

Academy and he's got a talent I'm helping him develop. I don't have anything for you myself, but I'll make calls if you want."

"Make it a quiet place with not too much action," Cheney said. "Somewhere featuring wineries or surf-boards."

"Listen, take that lovely young lady of yours out of here for a couple weeks, pronto. Stay with me at my condo. Bring your golf clubs. We'll play at Cypress Point. They're clients, so I get a discount."

"Maybe." Cheney rubbed his nose. "Might do that, Paul."

"On my advice, Michelle Rossmoor's taking her kids to Hawaii for a few days."

"She told me. I told her to do it."

Down the hill toward the lake from the massive redevelopment, Buck Tynan's office flanked Heavenly, with a broad view of Lake Tahoe toward the north, with its whitecaps, no boats, and a cloudscape reminiscent of a Florentine painter's.

A sleek, shaved-bald African-American man, Tynan sat with his back to the window. That meant the afternoon glare from the lake landed on Nina's face, half-blinding her. The marriage and family counselor wore well-designed clothing. Nina guessed Barneys, every item right down to the vest, tailored, tightly threaded, immaculate. He was no Californian, and as soon as he spoke, she heard the New York accent.

"Queens," he said. "How'd you know?"

But she was too worried to chitchat further. She looked at her cell phone. "He said he'd be here." A note flashed on her screen. She read it, swallowed.

"Oh. Something came up. He's not coming." Tears started up in her eyes.

Tynan nodded, as if he expected exactly that. "We can talk. Maybe I can help you clarify things."

Nina stood up. "No need. Nothing could be clearer."

"Are you okay?"

"No."

"I think I can help you."

"I might as well get some work done, not waste any more time on this—on this."

Tynan picked up a banana from his desk and gave it to her. "So you won't starve. Here it is Saturday. You should be home, right?"

She took it. He was a kind man. But even kind men can't work miracles.

CHAPTER 16

On that same hard-clear, windy afternoon, Paul drove down the hill, as the locals put it, to see Ronnie Bee. Bee lived in a cabin in the Nevada ranching town of Minden near the 395 freeway to Reno, which lay about fifty miles due north across the high desert. The Sierra massif Paul had hurtled down hung like a bright white weather front all along the western border of Minden. The seasons themselves were different because of the lower elevation; it was the beginning of spring here at four thousand feet, the meadows bursting with birdsong, colts running in their corrals, calves lying near their grazing mothers, poppies lining the road. By summer it would all be desiccated, but right now, anybody would want to live in this low-population, big-sky ranch country.

A young woman appeared in cutoffs, saying she was a niece, then Ronnie came out, a silver ruff around his skull, blinking in the sunlight, unshaved and disheveled, about sixty. He looked Paul over and examined his ID before inviting him into the cabin.

They talked for a long time inside the darkened living room, drinking lemonade. Although suffering, Ronnie was nevertheless taken care of. A tidy kitchen and warming fire felt welcoming.

"It's been strange days since Brenda died," Ronnie told Paul. "Every morning I wake up and I'm drowsy from sleeping. I feel cold. I turn to reach for her, then there's this moment when a void comes in and I sink into it." Ronnie's eyes turned inward. "I'm alone but I can't believe it. Where is she? It's fresh agony every single morning, you know? I'm dreaming of her and wondering if she's dreaming of me."

Paul nodded.

"You can't describe that kind of emptiness with words, you can only experience it. It's black and invisible, like a poison settling over the room. I realize she's gone. She is gone, not beside me. It's me and my cold feet and cold fingers and bleedin' heart."

"I'm sorry for your loss." Paul didn't make the statement automatically. He made it feeling the clenching of his own heart. How tremendous and cataclysmic it would be, permanently losing the woman you loved.

"What I can't understand is why there's been no arrest. My wife died on a public street in broad daylight!"

"I have to tell you, Ronnie, a few days aren't a long time when there's no witness. The police here run a tight ship. They do their best. They're more likely to find the killer than I am. But the Rossmoors have asked to see if I can do anything to speed the process along. They want to do right by Brenda."

"Bastard had the knife on him, ready to take her down," Ronnie said, absorbed by his own drama. "They must have been alone at the bus stop, so early. She worked so hard, so many hours. Sometimes she got to the motel by five a.m. I'm thinking he knew she'd be there, waiting, at that hour. Premeditated murder, that's what it is. A planned execution by someone who never knew her, who didn't give a damn about her worth in the world and how much she meant to other people. She must have been so scared." He buried his face in his hands. "I dropped her off that morning, you know? I kissed her, and drove away. I left her there alone."

"I'd like to help you, Ronnie."

"I hope you can. I want to know who could ever do such a thing to a woman who never hurt anybody. Everybody loved her."

"Except one person."

"The guy who left a dead body in the bed at the hotel, that's right. I described him to the police like she described him to me. Baseball cap." Ronnie teared up. "Maybe tall. That's all we have. You know, she has—had terrible eyesight. She never could have identified him."

"That does seem to be the motive from what I've gathered so far, that your wife was a witness."

"He rented the room at Prize's, right? He can't be that hard to find!"

"Actually, the room had been vacated early that morning but not rented again. The murdered woman was an employee. She took the key and met him there."

Ronnie sank back into his chair.

"How tall is tall?" Paul asked. "What exactly did your wife tell you?"

"She didn't say anything specific. I'm five ten. Anything over that was tall to her. Here's what keeps me awake. Why did he let her go that first time when she saw him, only to kill her the next morning?"

"Couldn't get to her before that," Paul said. "Circumstance. Maybe he'd killed that day for the first time and it didn't occur to him right away that he might need to kill again."

"I was watching out. I feel like shooting myself right now for letting her outta my sight. Okay. She told me he looked athletic, not like some loser. She was only fifty-five years old and she has—had her little boy in Virginia. Yesterday was the funeral. Hundreds of people came. Half the staff at Prize's." Tears dripped down Ronnie's nose. He picked up a napkin and blew into it.

Paul touched Ronnie's hairy forearm. Ronnie continued to weep, no force behind it, no storm, the weeping of somebody made of tears. His grief had incapacitated him for now. He had had no time to prepare emotionally. Death was devastating, and sudden, violent death was twice as destructive. Paul had seen it many times before. He usually looked first at the spouse when investigating a homicide, but Ronnie appeared to be experiencing such uncomplicated grieving, Paul felt pretty sure he hadn't had anything to do with it. "I've spoken to the police but I plan to stay in close touch in case they come up with anything. Meantime, I'll talk to the hotel staff. Casinos like Prize's rely heavily on security cameras. Unless this murderer is a ghost, they may have shots of your wife's killer. However, there's something you need to hear. You might not like it."

Ronnie dropped the napkin and looked Paul in the eye.

Paul explained that Brenda might have been murdered at the bus stop in a random act of violence by a local purse-snatcher, junkie, or gambler in over his head. Certainly, the police would pursue that angle.

"Nobody took her money. You're saying the police want to think she died for seventy bucks? That's utter bullshit."

"Oh, I agree," Paul said. "But there's a remote chance."

"You're suggesting that makes her suspect in some way, like she was involved in something dirty? You think she was conniving with drug dealers, or laundering money or something?" Ronnie asked, now red-faced with controlled tension.

"No."

"A housekeeper's lucky to clear twenty grand a year. Hey, I'm happy to provide you, the cops, and the media information on our taxes. Feel free to look at our checking account. It's a pathetic picture, okay? She was in cahoots with nobody. She came home at night talking about what products worked best to clean a mirror, for God's sake."

"I know."

Ronnie waved his hand. "Go nuts. But lemme tell you this. If my wife was murdered for no reason at all, I'm blowing up that place. I've got the means."

"I'd think like that, too," Paul said. "Maybe I'd do it."

"It's corrupt. Free money! Free drinks! Brenda and I, we never gambled."

"I get that, buddy."

"Her death better mean something, even if it's a sick shit who thinks she saw him. I can't stand the thought that she died for nothing. I loved her so much. I didn't deserve her!" Ronnie approached Paul and grabbed him in a bear hug and sobbed on his shoulder. Paul patted him on the back.

"It's bad, buddy. I'm sorry."

Paul rang Nina's bell promptly at seven in the evening, sun long down, dark long descended, energized by his afternoon travails.

She answered, covered, as advised, head to toe in warm gear. Hitchcock stood beside her. Paul held out a hand and Hitchcock gave it a respectful sniff.

"Bob?"

"Doing homework. Hitchcock on patrol. Father and uncle notified in case."

"There's no danger, Nina. I wouldn't put you in danger."

She shrugged. "I'm a mother. I think about these things."

Paul petted her dog. "He's not supposed to bark, though, is he? Isn't that the definition of a malamute?"

"Sometimes he barks. He's not a purebred." She eased the door shut behind her.

"We need a few things from your storage area before we go," Paul said.

They drove out to Pioneer Trail, turned left on 50, and left again onto 89 toward Sorensen's Resort. Nina was decompressing, listening to the radio.

Paul wondered how long he would remain free. He was taking an enormous risk bringing her along. But she was in a torment about Jim Strong, all mixed up and didn't know whether to believe Paul.

Nina's eyes closed. He wondered if she actually had the gall to doze off but noticed her bare hand in a tight, quivering fist on her lap.

Opening the driver's-side window, he inhaled the odors of the forest. Traffic was light. Headlights intermittently blinded him, then passed by. Although the blizzard of the night before had passed and the snowplows and sun of day had done their duties, the road remained fairly compromised, icy in patches where it wasn't slushy.

Driving uncharacteristically slowly, not for safety's sake but for the sake of remaining invisible, he clicked off the radio. They would soon arrive and he wanted his head clear. Where was that turnout?

At the time, two years before, in a snowstorm, with a body wrapped up in the trunk of his Mustang, he hadn't expected to come back to the place. His thoughts had gone like this: He needed to find someplace remote, where the body could never be found. He had considered hacking the body into pieces, as he had once fancifully suggested to Bob, but practically speaking, that had been retrospective wish-fulfillment. That snowy night, he had needed to get rid of it fast, and he had needed to hide it in a place nobody would be likely to stumble upon.

South Lake Tahoe hosted 3 million visitors every year, but every year at least twenty of them didn't gamble or drink themselves silly or go to shows or break an ankle ice-skating. No, at least twenty every year, the intrepid types, went out in all kinds of weather, climbing up frozen falls, hiking into remote, unwelcoming places they thought nobody else might have hiked before. And they found secrets of all kinds in the woods.

So on that night two years before, Paul had considered several locations, mentally tossing a coin between Christmas Valley and the road toward Sorensen's Resort. After ruling out the first area as too well traveled, he had driven toward the resort.

How difficult, tonight, to return to this place he had visited only in his bad dreams, watching anxiously for the broken-down bridge on the left and the ruins of old buildings that had marked the spot where he had turned off.

He glanced at Nina, whose eyes remained closed. He looked at the eyelashes sweeping across her cheek and listened to her regular breathing. Asleep or not, she trusted him. Whatever he showed her tonight, she wanted to see.

Paul had buried Jim Strong's body under snow and fallen logs and litter. Man, he had strained to make that sucker disappear forever.

He swallowed and took a deep breath. He had spotted the road that led over the remains of the bridge, past decrepit foundations of cabins that had once sat there. By now, Nina's brown eyes had opened to the wilderness. She said nothing, just watched him fumbling with the car. He found the powdery path that led upward and followed it until the road dipped near a stream. Then he stopped the car and turned off the engine.

It was one of those moments in life when you weren't sure of yourself or the world in any way. You rode with it.

"You buried him all the way out here?" Nina said, pulling on her ski gloves. She grabbed her parka from the backseat and buttoned it up, then covered her head with a wool cap. "A lonely place."

"So you knew."

"Where else could you be taking me? I'm ready."

Paul got himself suited up, then stepped outside

the car, clicking the door shut behind him. Nina followed. He looked around and listened to the melting snow, the two of them breathing, cars a dull roar on the highway a quarter mile away.

"Stop for a minute."

They stood together in the cold, breath making clouds.

He saw and heard nothing unusual. Cars made sounds interrupting the silence of the night. Wind breezed softly through the trees. He ferreted out Nina's shovel and a pick and locked the trunk.

"I'm amazed your car made it up this road," Nina said, looking downhill, stomping around the car to stand beside him.

"It's a Mustang. Mustangs are the princes of the car world. Snow tires help, of course."

The last time he had come up here, he had been seized by adrenaline fury and energized with purpose. This time, he felt reluctant and nervous. He handed Nina the pick and shouldered the shovel himself.

He walked toward where he thought he needed to go, memories dropping hints, leading him like old bread crumbs. Nina followed close behind. Everything appeared the same as he remembered except for a uniform layer of fresh snow. Along the edges of a clearing not too far from the Mustang, thick pines loomed like border guards. They made their way with difficulty, breaking through the hard crust of snow, falling a few times.

"How can we find him up here?" Nina said as they stared out over the clearing, and Paul heard the fatigue in her voice. "Snow. Trees. Piles of stuff. Miles of this."

"He's close by."

Pushing branches aside, he entered the dusky underbrush, looking for—ah, there it was, the huge treefall. Two years later, the trees had decomposed somewhat, but Paul felt it immediately.

Jim's body.

The unholy grail.

He approached the treefall, Nina right behind him, and began to remove the rocks in the pile.

Nina did what she could with the pick.

They worked for over an hour before the first faint signs of a grave showed.

"Here lies Jim Strong, murderer," Paul said, hoisting a rotten log off the spot, sitting in spite of the freeze. "These trees are his coffin, better than he deserved."

"After two years, nobody has disturbed his grave?"

"So it appears. Well, I feel grateful for that."

"Let's finish. I need to look at him and realize he's gone. He'll never come back to threaten me or Bob or my family. Seeing him might end my nightmares," Nina said. "And then I can finally believe everything you said. Sorry about needing proof."

Paul laughed slightly. "You're the lawyer."

After they had almost given up several times, had

a spat, rested, and tried again, they saw it, a bit of cloth or something. Paul got down on his knees and reached in with gloved hands and touched it. A torn piece of tarpaulin pulled out easily. He shone the flashlight, turned it over, and thought about many things, some things that he regretted now.

The tarp was still there. The earth continued to rotate at its usual speed and angled around its axis; his life was not upside down. Should he go any deeper? Why? The thing wrapped in the tarp was also still there, or the tarp would not remain. And he was getting cold now, his seat drying fast and chilling him, and getting spooked in this starless place, the way the shadows seemed to be moving in on him, bringing memories.

He pulled the heavy thing out, grunting, and shone the flashlight on the wrapped remains of Jim Strong.

"Pull the tarp away a little," Nina said. Her voice did not shake.

"You sure?"

"I need to see him."

Paul didn't want to do it, but he did. In the dry climate, buried in snow, even after two years, Jim's body was remarkably preserved. You could recognize his hair, the cut of his athletic body, even see long bits of skin. Decomposition had proceeded to the point where several of the limbs had disarticulated at the joints.

He was part bone, part flesh, the flesh mottled and

greenish. He stared from his half-skull vacantly at
Nina. His eyelids seemed to have disappeared. The
upper lip, what was left of it, was pulled back from
the white teeth.

Horrible. They had interrupted a quiet, eerie process. No one should see a human being like this, but
it had been necessary.

Nina stared at Jim's corpse under the cold light of
the flashlight for a long time. She said with remark-
able composure, "Question. What are the chances of
them tracing the tarp back to me?"

"Them? There is no them. Nobody, I mean
nobody, knows this place. Where'd you get the tarp,
though?"

"Some painters left it behind when I had the living room done. Bob put it in the storage area."

"You want me to take the tarp? I very much
doubt you or Bob could be connected to it at this
point."

Nina looked at the corpse of her tormentor.
"Never mind. Where's his wallet?"

"I threw it over a cliff at Twin Bridges. To complicate things."

"Was his driver's license in it?"

"Don't remember."

Paul pushed the piece of tarp back into the
vacancy he had made underneath the treefall and
hastily filled it in, working fast. Nina helped load
rocks and branches back on.

Then Paul shone the light around again.

The grave had sunk back into the forest. Here lay Jim Strong, murderer, desolate, shaded by tall trees and washed over by clean mountain air.

Paul pulled himself from the nest of branches, breathing hard. Seeing the remains had shocked him. A man amounted to nothing more than this, a jumble of bones in dirt. What remained of Jim Strong? Paul's mother used to say what remained lived in the memories of the people who loved you. Where did that leave Jim Strong? Nobody had loved him. Even his father had hated and feared him. If any small awareness of the being that once hosted Jim Strong lived on, it dreamed alone and unremembered, unloved.

The sky clouded over. Another light drift of snow would arrive, covering over their activities. Good. Paul laid the remaining branches haphazardly over the log and examined his handiwork.

In the daytime, it would be unfindable by anyone who didn't know what to look for.

He took out his portable GPS. He noted the spot's coordinates.

As they hiked back to the Mustang, Nina asked, "Have you ever thought about the moment of death, what you feel?"

"Yes."

"I think you go back to all the wrong things you did. We all do wrong things. You make them right. You come out okay."

"You have a religious background."

"So what do you think?"

"I think, for a few moments, it's like a dream, a crazy drama. Then you recede. You find yourself moving backward from all that. Finally you turn around and see what was really going on back there. Hey, you're shivering."

"He's haunting us."

"You saw him. That's all there is of him now. Look, you wanted to be sure. Are you sure now?"

"I guess so."

"You believe in ghosts. I should have known. Up the Irish."

"I'm more afraid than I was before," Nina said. "It's uncanny, the harm the dead can cause."

"Especially when money's involved."

"Secrets come alive themselves, maybe. They want to come out."

"It's not him. It's us. I don't like carrying his fucking body in my heart everywhere I go. I don't. I have to find a way to get rid of it for good."

"We feel guilt, Paul."

"I never thought I would when I did this."

CHAPTER 17

Eric Brinkman called Nina from the San Francisco airport at 8:00 a.m. on Monday and asked for a meeting in four hours at her office. Speaking in a hoarse voice, he kept the arrangements short. He had spent a long few days in Brazil and in the air, and he would be coming straight from the trip.

Philip and Nina waited for him in the conference room.

Paul had asked to come. Not an official member of the team, he had promised to participate only as a friend to Nina. He arrived shortly before noon, shaved, showered, and full of energy. The little conference room immediately began to feel crowded. He shook hands with Philip and sat down.

Moments later Nina and Paul heard Eric Brinkman come in and greet Sandy. She brought him in and took her own seat, shutting the door behind her. With the blinds drawn, the room felt tight and secure.

A place for secrets and straight talk.

"Hi, all," Eric said. He looked awful, as awful as

he could look, anyway. He hadn't shaved for a day or three—long enough to have developed a lush stubble. Puffy red streaks struck out from his irises. Nina imagined the jet lag he must be suffering. Let's see, Brazil was five hours ahead of California, and with the planes to and from southern Brazil, the trip had taken almost seventeen hours with layovers. His fatigue made him look younger. His face was thinner than Paul's, bones standing out in high relief. He wore a black T-shirt with a light gray jacket that had obviously gone to a foreign country and back.

Everybody shook hands some more. Eric accepted a cup of espresso, loading it with sugar. "I came straight here from the airport."

"We appreciate that," Nina said. "Now sit."

He sat across the conference table from Paul, looked at him, drank, and put his empty cup on the table in front of him, next to his briefcase. "It's hot down there. End of summer. I forgot how hot it gets." He accepted the bottle of water Sandy offered. Snapping open the case, he pulled out a file full of thin, stapled-together paper stacks. He passed them around, all brisk business.

"Copies of a new affidavit," he said. "One I got down there."

Nina glanced at her copy, then set it down. "Let's get to this in a minute. Did you see him? Did you see Jim Strong?"

"No. Got a lively song and dance from the lawyer about how as a fugitive he had changed his appearance and didn't want to give up his disguise. She said he has a right to contest the sale even though he won't show his face. She says she has never met with him, only talked with him on the phone. Her English is excellent, by the way. She's a solo practitioner with a fancy office in a downtown office building. I don't know how solid she is. Lawyers are experts at hiding their financial status and how they're doing." Eric rubbed a hand over his forehead. "Excuse my fatigue, Nina. Ordinarily, I don't make foolish generalizations. Let's just say she looked legitimate, and I didn't turn up anything to contradict that."

"Did you see video of him?"

"Nada," Eric said. "Same story. He can't let his new face be seen or he'll be caught and extradited."

"A tape?"

"The claim is that the voiceprint would give the authorities too much to look at."

"Fine, then," Nina said. "The fraud will be obvious to the court."

"Not so fast, Nina," Eric said. "Take a look at the attachment to this affidavit."

They all flipped to the last page, which held a copy of a California driver's license with a picture on it Nina recognized.

"It's Jim's license," Philip said. "My God, it's still valid! I've seen him flash it a million times. That sure looks like his signature."

"Must be forged," Paul said.

"But where would they get this?" Philip studied it, his jaw working nervously back and forth. "Unless—someone took it from him?" He shook his head. "He wouldn't give it up voluntarily." He held on to the license so tightly, his fingers whitened. "No, but this sure is an exact duplicate of the original. I remember because he weighed one ninety-five, he was always complaining about it, and he gave his weight on the license as one-eighty."

Eric said, "We can put a handwriting expert on it. And the other ones on the affidavits."

"Do you know if this is a duplicate or the original license?" Paul asked.

Eric shook his head. "I was handed these papers, which Michael Stamp, on Jim Strong's behalf, is going to file in your case tomorrow, Nina. About all I got you is one day's notice. At least it won't come as an awful shock in court."

"The lawyer down there must be in on it," Paul said. "What else did you find out about her?"

"No complaints against her. The local Guardia has nothing but praise. They aren't aware Strong may be living in their town either, at least so they say."

"This Brazilian attorney," Nina said, "I assume from what you've said so far she was not Marianne's mother."

"She was too young. No name match. Never lived in Rio."

"Did you talk to the notary?" Nina asked.

"Of course. He's a bank officer two blocks from

the lawyer's office. Said a guy with a beard and glasses and a baseball cap showed up at his bank to have this document notarized. He says he examined a passport in the name of James Philip Strong for identification. He claimed the picture looked like the guy in front of him, as far as he could tell."

Paul said, "Bull."

"It's kind of a big bull though," Sandy said. "The horns are kind of sharp. Time to bring out the really good picadors." Having said her piece, she disappeared back to the front office.

"How will this new information affect our case?" Philip asked.

All eyes swung to Nina.

"I haven't studied the affidavit," Nina said, "but it reinforces the claims that have already been made. Eric, what did you find that would add force to an argument that this is a fraud?"

"I can testify that the notary's statements to me indicated he hadn't really established the identity of the man who notarized this document."

"The lawyer's in on it," Paul said.

"Maybe not. No more than Michael Stamp. She's practiced law for twenty-five years and appears very matter-of-fact about the whole thing." Eric stroked his stubble. "I couldn't crack her façade, if that's what it was."

"I would have," Paul muttered.

"What?" Eric demanded.

"You came back with squat."

So much for Paul staying low-key, Nina thought, tapping her pencil, eyes locked at the image on Jim's license, now lying on the table, face-up. A grin on it.

"I did my job. The one you don't have." Eric turned to Nina. "What's he doing here, anyway?"

"Paul's an informal adviser."

"You don't trust me?"

"That's not it," Nina said, at the same time Paul said, "That's it exactly."

Eric said to Philip, "I can't help you anymore with this"—Eric took a deep breath—"with the highly opinionated Mr. van Wagoner second-guessing everything I do. Either you trust me or you don't. Hire him if you've got problems with my work, and good luck with that. Otherwise, I don't want him showing up and weighing in on things that are none of his business."

"Paul, I know you want to help, and I appreciate that, but Eric's right, this isn't your business," Philip said.

"Someone's defrauding you and running your business into the ground. I'm going to figure out who and how. And then—"

"To tell you the truth, when Nina asked if you could sit in today, I wasn't sure about it. Why insert yourself into this case?" Philip asked. "I don't like the implication that my investigator can't do the job. I trust Eric."

"That's right. Face it, Paul. Nobody wants you here," Eric said, arms folded in front of him.

"I'm here for Nina." Paul's face set.

"Okay, that's enough," Nina said, whacking her pencil on the table. "We're all here to get some work done and not get derailed, so let's get back to how to control this material."

But fatigue and macho prevailed. Eric unraveled. "You'd do a lot for Nina, wouldn't you, van Wagoner?"

"I would."

"Anything."

Paul avoided looking at Nina. He didn't say anything. Possibly he realized how patronizing he sounded. Maybe he had finally figured out this was a no-win situation. Eric also wasn't his best self today, as Nina's mother would have said.

"Now I'm wondering about something I heard, something about Jim Strong threatening Nina," Eric said, "and thinking about how you like to see yourself as her protector, not that she needs one."

"Wonder all you want, pal," Paul said.

Both of the men kicked their chairs back and stood. They glared at each other, classically posed, bodies taut, eyes bright with anger, raring to fight. They looked like wolves.

Nina also stood. "Enough!"

"I'll leave now," Paul said, "for Nina's sake."

"You'll leave because you're not wanted!" Eric's hoarse voice growled out of him.

Paul saw an advantage, his adversary close to out of control.

He smiled.

Eric's teeth ground together so hard, Nina feared he might bite off his tongue.

Paul took his time, beaming around the room, looking at peace with himself and the world again. Then he leaned over the table to shake Philip's hand. "Listen, Philip," he said softly, as if they couldn't hear him. "Don't trust this guy. He's got something wrong going on." Paul straightened up. "See you, Nina." He left.

Silence stifled the air.

"Look, we're all upset," Philip said to Eric. "You've brought us bad news, essentially, not that it's your fault." Philip patted the seat beside him. "Please sit down, Eric, so we can finish up and you can get a good sleep."

Which he sorely needed, Nina thought.

Eric looked out the window to where trees swayed in sunshine. He took Paul's copy of the affidavit and put it back into his file folder.

Nina waited until some sense of order and calm was restored. She cleared her throat. "Okay. Here we have Jim's driver's license with his signature and yet another painful affidavit to deal with, with almost no time. Tell us, Eric, how could someone in Brazil get Jim's license? Are these papers forged? What's going on? What's your professional opinion?"

"I can't give a full accounting yet, but I plan to follow up with the Department of Motor Vehicles," Eric said. "That shouldn't take long. However,

I should tell you they don't give out new driver's licenses by mail to anybody. Did you ever receive a bill to renew your license?"

"Sure," Philip answered.

"It's a fairly automatic process. But I don't think this constituted an easy renewal. Jim had to take the driving test because he had let his previous one expire. That was four years ago. This license appears current. Maybe Jim's alive and driving all the fuck over the land. Maybe he eats out in Brazil and raises orchids."

"You make it sound ridiculous."

"I never said I thought the people I met in Brazil were trustworthy, but I can't say your son is dead based on what I saw and heard."

"Tell us more about this lawyer's background," Philip said.

"I've told you what I know."

"Do you think she's conspiring with someone in this country?" Nina asked. "I think that's a real possibility."

Eric shrugged. "Maybe, but I think we have to make progress on that from this end. I keep thinking about Marianne Strong. I've been watching her since the original embezzlements. I'm meeting with her tomorrow. I should tell you something. I saw her last week—and this is really strange—I saw her coming out of the title company, you know, the one Hendricks runs?"

"Huh. Well, she's never made a secret about her

interest in the business. She might have a perfectly reasonable explanation for being there," Nina said.

"I called and asked her. She claimed she was clarifying business issues."

"So you were concerned enough to follow up," Nina said, curious. "I wonder. Eric, I'd like to come with you to meet her tomorrow. Would that be okay?"

"Sure."

"I confess to a certain—unease—about Michael Stamp. He's always at the center, though of course, it's my tendency to trust my fellow attorneys."

Startled at Nina's sudden levity, both Eric and Philip laughed. The mood in the room lightened just a bit.

"I have no reason to believe he'd do anything criminal. He's a well-respected lawyer in this town. However, I have a strong feeling I should talk to him and see what else I can find out about any possible link to these people in Brazil."

"I showed the attorney down there Stamp's photo, Nina. But nothing. She also claimed not to recognize Marianne or Gene Malavoy."

"What happens now?" Philip took the license in his hand once again, turned it over, and turned it again, looking about as exhausted as Eric at this point. Nina had seen that harrowed face before in a painting by El Greco: St. Sebastian tortured by arrows.

"The hearing is a day after tomorrow," Nina said.

"Your case is my first priority. Maybe I can get more time—"

"I'm really worried. This could crush the sale."

"Philip, I believe the sale will go through, but the entire net proceeds, the two and a half million dollars left after the sale, may go into an escrow account while you and Kelly and Marianne try to sort out your share from Jim's, and Jim's legal status finally is clarified."

"What a thing, Nina," Philip said. "He has no legal status in this world. He really is a ghost, dead or alive. You know, if that money is placed in escrow, I will be personally bankrupt. I can't wait several years for him to be declared dead. My share of the sale will go entirely to creditors. The same for Kelly and Marianne." He stood up. "I have to get over to Paradise. We have a broken quad lift and too many skiers for the number of runs we have. That used to be good news. Now I feel like I don't even know what good news is."

CHAPTER 18

Monday afternoon Paul stopped for a triple espresso at the Java Hut and skimmed the police reports regarding his new case, hunting for a direction. He was boiling about Eric Brinkman, but the boiling didn't seem to have much rational basis. It was the boiling of upper altitudes, cooler than it appeared. He had seen Brinkman's examination of Nina after he sat down, and it had made him extremely angry, and that was that, nothing to be done about it, unless Brinkman laid a hand on her, in which case he would—

He went back to his reports: autopsy reports on the two women, photos—Brenda's wound primitive-looking, as if an animal, not a knife, had done it.

The knife had been strongly wielded rather than efficiently wielded. The murder scene didn't look like the preferred place of someone who had committed similar crimes. Too risky.

Paul could not work this the way a cop would; he had neither the time nor the resources to be systematic. He needed to hit hard at the spikes, the things that jumped out at him, things that might open up.

Johnny Castro spiked first. He had been both the husband and manager of Miss Cyndi Amore, aka Cyndi Backus.

At three o'clock in the afternoon, Paul set his GPS for the address, driving along the highway. Mist clouded the lake and the road, and he bypassed a fender bender and spinout that had landed an SUV upside down on a hillside. Why couldn't people remember to put their lights on? Paul thought, rubbernecking to view the damage. Ah, nobody dead, only a few stunned-looking skiers talking with the cops, ambulances idling nearby. Traffic slowed, then narrowed to one lane, then a woman dressed in yellow plastic from head to toe waved him forward.

A small town a couple of miles away, south and adjacent to South Lake Tahoe, Meyers, with no town center and motley housing—cabins, trailers, and fanciful mountain homes jostling together in the forest—mostly lured people who preferred to live on the cheap or on the fringe.

Johnny Castro lived behind a larger home in an old cabin near Highway 50 as it headed out of town, deeper into California. The front porch had been boarded up into an inside room long ago. Fresh paint hadn't touched the weathered wood for ages. Paul parked in the dirt driveway, examining the black slushpiles of snow here and there—the old brownish snowman down on its luck meant children.

Paul found Johnny home on a weekday afternoon.

The door opened and the middle-aged widower/
father came out, sporting an extra forty pounds
and a tattoo collection that made his arm and chest
look clothed. Paul checked for gang tattoos but saw
mostly the skull, Bettie Page, and Virgin de Guada-
lupe type. Castro wore a small goatee; his hair was
cropped so close he was almost bald. Heat surged out
of the little house, hitting Paul like a slap in the face.

"Enjoyin' staring at my house?" Castro said.

"John Castro?" Presenting him with his card,
Paul explained his business.

Castro gestured toward the dim interior of the
cabin. Ironing board in front of the TV. Laundry
basket full of clothes, toys mostly neatly stacked in
the corners, a few of which Paul had to step over.
"We obviously have kids," Castro said. "I already
told the cops I don't know why Cyndi got herself
killed. I had to identify her. I'll never forget that.
Never." He flung the basket of clothes waiting to be
folded on the couch onto the rug.

Paul sat down in a clean spot.

"I don't have much time. Have to put on a sweatshirt and go get the kids. They're in an after-school
program." Castro shook his head. "They don't get
that their mom's gone forever. They keep asking."

"I'm sorry for your loss." Paul didn't like hearing himself say such a thing again in such short a
time. He didn't like imagining the harm such losses
entailed, the families left behind. Children. Lovers.
Friends. Moms and dads.

Grieving people.

Castro nodded, as if following Paul's sad train of thought. "No words for that crap, huh? No words to take in the whole in-fucking-credible loss of the mother of my kids. And how about the fact that I thought she was someone she wasn't?"

And no coffee here, Paul thought, glad he had fueled up. Like Ronnie Bee, Castro appeared devastated at the loss of his wife. "Mr. Castro, is there any chance you got to read the autopsy on your wife?"

"Saw it yesterday. Sergeant Cheney let me read it. Cyndi died of a blunt trauma injury followed by somebody smothering her."

"Asphyxiation."

"He tied her own underwear around her neck and suffocated her. My wife died in a hotel room with a stranger. And PS, this is not something I want the kids to hear, ever. Tell you the truth, I'd forgive her today if she came to me somehow and we could start this all over."

"Where were you around one p.m. on the day she died?"

"At work. I'm a cashier at the Raley's. Don't take my word. Take the word of my fellow workers, at least a dozen of them. Sergeant Cheney did."

Paul would check that claim later, but Castro sounded so casual, Paul believed him. "Is it your belief she might have been with another man that day?"

"What else? What else." Castro sighed, picked a pair of trousers out of the pile of laundry, and put them on. He searched for a shirt, rejected two, then settled on a brown knit polo.

"Tell me about her, Mr. Castro."

"Call me Johnny."

"Johnny."

"I met her at a strip club in Reno seven years ago. She was barely twenty-one. She hung with bad people, had a lot of bad habits. Once I started going down there on a regular basis, she started taking better care of herself. She stopped drinking. Once we got married, we both got clean and sober. Mostly."

"You had a substance problem, too?" Paul guessed.

"Had then, have again. I have an ongoing substance abuse problem. It's another thing to watch and manage. I self-medicate, but these days I work out a lot and eat better. I'm getting along. Improving. Not dragging myself through gutters."

"Did Cyndi keep stripping?"

"Dancing, yeah. Good money in that. Just once a week and no extras on Saturday nights at a little club called the Furnace in Reno. I didn't object. We needed the extra income. She liked her day job at Prize's, though, and the tips were drying up at the club because of the recession, so she planned to ease out of that scene."

"You have how many children?"

"Two. Boy and girl. Our kids hear things. They're burned down. I spend all my time taking care of them, taking them to school, keeping the house going, sitting with them at night. I can't work right now. I have to take care of my emotional problems and my kids'. My mother keeps us afloat right now. I'm looking for some way to make money at home."

"Hard to do all that if you have problems," Paul said. "What is it?"

"Bipolar. I have a good shrink and the meds were working on my depression pretty good. Then my wife, who I love, dies. And I come to find out she was cheating. I had some hints, but I ignored them. Mostly."

"Sorry to hear that."

"Ain't got no hope no more."

"It's natural to get angry when someone close to you dies," Paul said.

"Yeah, and it's even more natural to be angry when you start wondering if the kids you've slaved over are yours or not."

Paul now understood the man's hollow eyes and sepulchral voice. Johnny's reaction was so different from Ronnie Bee's. Johnny wasn't sure he was her victim. "Cyndi wasn't faithful?"

Johnny tipped his head at Paul. "She died in a hotel in the middle of the day at the hands of a stranger. I started looking into her phone records and so on. Where she spent time. I found a guy. I passed the information on to the cops. I'm pretty sure it's him."

"DNA tests are accurate. You could get the kids tested."

"That's what my lawyer said right before I fired him. What good would that do? I don't want to know. They're mine. I love them. Case closed on that. However, I'd like to see the boyfriend fried if he did this to her. In fact, I, personally, would like to shoot him dead." Johnny folded a few clean towels, placing them gently on the couch. "I think we might've gotten past this, if I'd found out." His voice cracked. "She would have told me eventually. She had a conscience. We were starting to go to church again. We were really close, once." Castro separated neat piles of clothing into two big white plastic baskets. "She had a good heart. She adored the kids. I can't work it out in my mind."

"The name of the guy you suspect?"

"Jesse Bancroft. Our car mechanic. I mean, she had the normal car trouble, but she paid him a bunch and called him a bunch of times I never heard about. That's not normal."

"Did you talk to him after Cyndi died?"

"Yeah, I confronted him a couple of days ago. Told him off. He argued with me. Denied it. You believe that? Arrogant asshole. He probably killed her. He took my wife away from her family, from me! Tried to get me arrested for assault. Cops came but nobody wanted to arrest me. They left me alone."

"You fought?"

"I punched him, yeah. He deserved worse. Bastard!" Johnny's face flushed. "He wouldn't even fight me back. Tell you one thing for sure. She had something going on, something secret, the last few weeks. She wasn't, like, all excited and breathy, like somebody who is in love with another man. But there were other signs. She bought new underwear. I should have guessed then. When you love somebody, you don't want to be suspicious. You don't want to get into their cell phone, check their side of the closet. I knew but I didn't know, you know? She was distracted and upset, is what she was. I'll tell you one thing, the situation was not making her happy. I thought I knew her better than anyone. Why wouldn't she talk to me?"

Sometimes you thought you knew someone well but you didn't, not really. Paul thought he knew Nina. But she still surprised him, not always pleasantly. "Her phone records show she was talking a lot with Jesse Bancroft?"

Johnny's teeth flashed. "Yeah."

"But he didn't admit anything?"

"Admitted they talked, no more than that. Said they talked about her car. Bastard! You going over there?"

Paul nodded. Castro leaned forward and jabbed his finger at him.

"Take him down for me, okay? The police say he's clean. He sounds convincing, all right."

Paul took down the mechanic's name and address. "Now, for a moment, let's go in another direction. What if it wasn't Jesse who was with Cyndi that day? If it was someone else who might take an interest in Cyndi—who might feel enough passion or connection or, I don't know, have something going on that he felt that need to kill her?'"

Johnny tucked his polo shirt into his pants. "A fan? She had a lot of fans. Guys came on to her every Saturday night, and I got to confess, she did like nice things. Saw her with a few pretty things in the months before she died, but she explained them away and I'm so dumb and I"—he paused— "loved her so much I bought it. 'Hey, where'd the pearl earrings come from?' 'Nobody.' 'Nice looking gold chain.' 'Oh, yeah, this guy comes every night. Wanted to give me something.'"

"Expensive things," Paul murmured, making a note. "Things a mechanic could afford?"

Johnny Castro stared at him. "If you made good money and didn't have two kids and a wife to support."

"Was Cyndi gone a lot? I mean, after work."

He shook his head.

"She didn't stay out afterwards. I mean, you kept track of her?"

"She didn't have a lot of free time to do much messing around between her gigs and her job and the kids. I guess that's why I'm pretty sure it was one guy." Johnny stood up. "Listen, I have to go now, get my children. Put one shoe in front of the other."

"One other thing. You have a sheet?"

Johnny eyeballed him. "I didn't kill Cyndi. I loved her," he said flatly. "I was at work. I expected that question you asked to come up and haunt me, so here's the full picture. I was married before her and convicted of domestic assault. My wife at that time accused me. I spent a year in jail. I have never touched Cyndi. Ask anyone. The truth is, I never wished her no harm. I'm in a fix now, with our kids."

Paul stood and shook his hand. "I'll go see"—Paul consulted his notes—"Jesse."

"He's probably at that gas station at the Y about now. Works afternoons and evenings."

They walked to the door. "You think that house-keeper at Prize's might have got killed because she saw the guy who killed Cyndi?" Johnny Castro asked.

"I don't know."

"Was she married?"

"Yes."

"Shit. Poor guy must feel as bad as I do." He stroked the goatee. "Cyndi's funeral is next week, but I'm not putting anything in the paper. This is private, this shit. Nobody's business but mine."

Jesse Bancroft was installing a tire on an ancient Chevy Suburban.

Paul walked into the garage and found him and, for once, no red tape. "I just need a minute," Paul said, introducing himself. A good-size, ropy guy in his midthirties, Bancroft looked a lot like Johnny. Apparently Cyndi gravitated toward tattooed bad boys.

Something discontented lurked in Jesse's expression. Stud in his right ear. Longish hair. A biker, Paul thought.

They walked around the side of the gas station and sat on a curb in the full sun. Paul put on his shades and Jesse pulled on a baseball cap and produced a cigarette. "That fool Johnny Castro sent you? He's bugging the hell out of me. Do you believe it? He thinks I killed his wife."

"I understand the police have cleared you."

"I was working right here that day. Besides, I never would have hurt her."

"I also understand there might be a question of paternity."

"Cyndi's daughter's mine. Not her boy."

"Is that so."

"Looks just like me, man. My coloring. Cyndi was a blonde, natural. Her old man has black hair, name's Castro, he's Michoacán. Me and Cyn's little girl has light hair and blue eyes. Everybody can see it once I point it out. She's me in a little-girl body. I knew it by the time she was two weeks old. She's got my spirit in her."

"Did you ask for a paternity test?"

"Not yet."

"She's four, I understand."

"Cyn begged me not to. Cyndi and I, we talked all the time. We were good friends. We talked and sometimes we had coffee. The sex ended years ago. I had nothing to do with her dying."

"Must hurt like hell, seeing your child raised by another man. I can only guess what it feels like having a little girl who can't call you Daddy."

Jesse blew out smoke. "I think, what's better for my baby? She has a sibling, a father with his own house. I live in the trailer park the city's trying to bury. I don't know. I have to think about things."

"In a way, Cyndi hurt you, not acknowledging your paternity."

Jesse stubbed out his cigarette. "Don't speak ill of her, man. Don't. I loved her and she loved me once. But she wouldn't leave Johnny."

Paul thought that maybe more to the point, Jesse didn't want the financial demands that came with raising a child for eighteen years. "Was Cyndi afraid of Johnny?"

Jesse's mouth moved around this way and that. "Okay, I got to say no. She was attached to him and the kids. Happy family, sometimes."

"You say your close relationship happened years ago."

"Our girl is four. You do the math."

"Lately you've been friends, not lovers?"

"Not lovers. Not for ages."

"Can you picture Cyndi with another man? I mean not you, not her husband."

"She wanted to be good," Jesse answered. "I'll give her that. When we got together? She felt really guilty. I was probably her best friend over the past couple years. I kept her car cherry, man."

"That's not an answer, is it?"

Jesse gave Paul a look. "The papers, the TV. They'll say she was a tramp. She wasn't."

"Who was he?"

"Usually, she didn't throw out names. It just came out one day. She was feeling bad and she told me somebody came after her and she rolled with it."

"Any details?"

"She said it's hard to resist when somebody falls that hard, gives you presents, says things like you never heard before. She said he was 'besotted.' That's the exact word she used."

"But she didn't love him?"

"Women don't love like men," Jesse said. "I could tell from the way she put it that she didn't love him like he loved her. You can bet he killed her for that. And now her old man blames me."

"When did you speak with her last?"

"The morning she died. We met up at Heidi's for breakfast after she dropped the kids off at school. She had to go to work."

"She get a phone call?"

"Not that time. Other times, yes. Could have been the new man." Jesse puffed furiously on his cigarette, held it between thumb and forefinger, then dropped it and stubbed it out. "Check me out. I was right here performing a fifteen-point inspection with an alignment on a 1987 Eldorado. Find who did it and call me, and I'll grab Johnny, and we'll both go over and explode his ass."

CHAPTER 19

After Paul walked out on the conference with Eric Brinkman, Nina spent the afternoon slogging her way through a long hearing in a contract case and worked out a settlement with opposing counsel, avoiding a ruling that might have been damaging to her client.

At least a few things were going right. She had time to shelve that file for the moment and make a few phone calls as the sky began to lose its light. She got through to Marianne Strong.

"Hello?" Marianne sounded rushed. People talked in the background.

"Hi, it's Nina Reilly."

"Yes?"

"You're seeing Eric Brinkman regarding some issues that are coming up with regard to the sale of Paradise tomorrow. I'm coming along."

"Why?"

"I have some questions."

"Such as?"

"Why you met with Nelson Hendricks."

"Are you kidding? He's in charge of information, in case you hadn't noticed. He's the man making the deals work. He merely filled me in on some financial background."

Or not, Nina thought. Hendricks had problems, a sick wife. Marianne had problems. Maybe they had worked out some solutions together. "Tomorrow at ten?"

"We've arranged to meet at the lift nearest the ski shop. I teach a class at nine. Novices. Snowplow." Marianne sounded dismissive. "Teaching them to fall without breaking their necks. Paradise's most profitable class, by the way."

Nina imagined Marianne, warm in her North Face parka and expensive snow boots, and herself in her lawyer-wear, standing around in the snow. "Ten is fine," Nina said, "but let's make it at the dining room at Paradise."

"Why?"

"Snow. Bad weather. Slips."

"If you insist. Tell Eric, okay? And I'd like my brother, Gene, you remember him, to come. If you don't hear from me by e-mail this evening, I'll see you both at ten."

"Thank you," Nina said.

"It's good. I want to talk to you, too."

Paul hadn't called, and Nina wasn't in the mood to try to reach his cell phone. She let the Strong case sit tight for a minute. Its issues had taken over the past few days and she had catching up to do.

* * *

Kurt called at five sharp as Sandy was gathering her purse to go home.

"I'll lock up," Nina told her.

"Don't forget you have a home." Sandy pulled the door shut behind her.

Nina said into the phone, "You didn't show up at the counseling appointment."

"True."

"No point, huh?"

"Listen, Nina, I've had to change my plans tonight. Can't take Bob to the movies. Sorry."

"I think because you were born in Michigan, I expected better from you. Midwesterners are generally so damn nice and reliable. You can't say the same for Californians. We're usually the ones all over the place."

"Nina, don't do this."

"He's counting on you."

"I said I'm sorry."

She had a moment that connected her to a bigger universe. She had picked Kurt due to a biological imperative—lust, desire, and some love mixed in. Disappointments, weaknesses, they came along with the body of the young forest ranger she had fallen in love with sixteen years before. Same body, different person now.

"C'mon, Nina. He'll find something better to do in two minutes." Kurt's voice sounded squeezed for air. He cleared his throat. "Tell him another time, soon, okay?"

"You tell him."

"Okay. I'll tell him."

"He's probably home."

"I'll call in a little while." Kurt knew that Bob loved seeing him and that Nina liked having a weekday night now and then in which she didn't have to make dinner and push Bob about homework. Kurt would show up and take Bob out for a while, and Nina would take a long bath and enjoy being alone. Like divorced or separated people with visitation rights, Nina thought.

As they seemed to be, come to think of it. "We should talk about—"

"Not now," Kurt said. "I have to go."

Nina hung up. Slinging her computer case and her bag over her shoulder, she went out to the RAV, frustrated and uneasy. She wished she could see Kurt. She didn't like getting cut off like that. She didn't like a newness in his voice, a strangeness.

Maybe she should swing by with something to eat, get a better bead on things? He loved her showing up with food.

En route, she passed a sushi place. Perfect. She swung into a sharp left across the highway.

Thirty minutes later, loaded with ebi, tekka maki, and California roll, she arrived at Kurt's apartment house. He lived on the second floor. She could see the living room light glowing. Pulling into the parking area, she located his car parked almost directly opposite his apartment.

A revamped motel from the sixties, the apartment house featured concrete stairs that seemed to hang in the air. The heavy material suggested stability. The creaking of her steps exposed it as risky and cheap. She climbed carefully, watching that she didn't catch a heel and go flying with all that good fishy stuff. She hadn't done anything like this with Kurt for a while, showing up spontaneously, and she felt cheerful at the thought. She'd keep the conversation light and go on her way to the next hungry male on the list, Bob.

Kurt's door hung ajar. She knocked.

Kurt stuck his head out.

"Look!" she said, smiling. "Sushi! Get out your chopsticks." She started inside.

"Hey, thanks." He stepped forward, blocking her. He took the bag and opened it. He sniffed. "Umm. Good stuff. But, uh—"

"Can I come in?"

An unfamiliar female voice spoke from somewhere inside the apartment. Before Kurt could answer, a girl appeared beside him, young, as tall as Kurt, pale and delicate, with long, shiny, light hair. The girl scoped out Nina from head to toe. "Hello, I'm Dana."

Nina blinked.

"Would you like to come in, Nina?" Kurt asked.

Nina knew she should go, but found herself

unable to. She shifted from one foot to another. Her
high heels hurt, suddenly and painfully. She wanted
to sit down, but instead she and Dana looked at each
other in an age-old way for which there are many
names, Nina cursing herself for not putting on lip
gloss before she had come. She licked her lips, noting
that Dana did not need to lick her lips. She had the
gloss thing down.

Kurt's intent eyes captured Nina's. "Dana arrived
an hour ago. Unexpectedly. Please. Come in."

Nina entered Kurt's modestly furnished living
room, where an overnight bag with those wheels that
rotate all the way around was propped against the
couch, a wad of ticketing stubs hanging off its handle. A huge, battered leather purse and a computer
case leaned against the bag.

Kurt went to the table and set down the bag of
sushi. Nina felt Dana looking again at her body,
making comparisons.

"Wine," Kurt said. "All I've got is Sangiovese."

"An excellent wine," Dana said. "You should
try it."

She had an accent. Well, she would. She was from
Europe somewhere, Sweden or Germany, Nina
couldn't remember what Kurt had said when he had
nonchalantly first mentioned her sometime back, or
later when he had equally nonchalantly mentioned
they were corresponding.

"I'll take some water," Nina said.

Dana wore a white T-shirt and low-slung jeans

held up with more battered leather. She smoked indoors, in California an act of such eco-evil, Nina could hardly take her eyes off the burning tip of the cigarette, the languid arm, the anachronistic romance of it all.

Dana went to the couch and curled up, holding an ashtray. Nina took a seat at the table, about ten feet away, and Kurt went to his tiny kitchen.

Glasses briefly clinked in the distance.

The two women sat together in excruciating and suggestive silence, Nina riveted on Dana's smoking, breathing in and out. Nina hadn't witnessed such blithely negligent inattention to personal health and the general welfare in years. Dana couldn't seem to take her eyes off Nina either. Her eyes fastened on Nina's shoes. Foot mutilators, yes, but red and oh so beautiful. Nina crossed her legs to show them off, enjoying her burning feet, reveling in the insane height of her heels. Dana, though, was making bare feet look chic.

Finally, Kurt came back to dole out drinks.

"In case you're wondering," Dana said to Nina, quickly touching Kurt's hand as he gave her a glass, shaking the ice, "he wasn't overjoyed to see me. I forgot to call, too. I think our Kurt"—she gazed steadily at him—"doesn't welcome surprises."

"Where do you come from?"

"Stockholm." Dana took a long drag and tapped the cigarette out into the ashtray. "Flew into Reno. The taxi up here cost a fortune."

"With notice," Kurt said to her, "I could have picked you up."

"Then it wouldn't have been such a lovely surprise." Dana's shining, poreless cheeks dimpled when she smiled.

"Cheers," Kurt said. He raised his glass in the air, looking uncertain, younger somehow.

They all raised their glasses, but to what? Their mutual destruction?

"God, I'm tired," Dana said moments later, her glass already almost empty, yawning. "I hope you're not going to turn me out, Kurt."

Like that, Dana had set forth her plan. She expected to spend the night with Kurt. Nina set her glass down, awaiting his response.

"Let's talk about that later," he said, voice almost a whisper.

The burr in Nina's stomach moved around. He should blow this interloper off in front of her, shouldn't he? Nina, never afraid of confrontation in the courtroom, ought to fight back, shouldn't she? Nina asked Dana, "What exactly brings you here?"

"You're a direct one, aren't you?" Dana took a handful of nuts from a bowl on the table. Nina saw that Dana didn't know what to say either, in spite of her cool expression.

"I find it better than being circuitous."

"Circuitous." Dana played the word like a dirty marble in her mouth. "Something to do with circles?

Anyway, Kurt and I have been sitting here having a chat. That's why I came here, to chat. Like you, I'm direct. I prefer face-to-face."

"And then I come along to interrupt absolutely everything."

Kurt sat down on the other end of the couch, his voice wobbly. He had tossed off a double in one gulp. "Should I feel I did something wrong?" he said.

"You did do something wrong. You don't belong here." Dana waved a dismissive hand around. "I can't believe this." They all looked around at his place, at the generic rented furniture, boxy beige. They regarded the shabby droop of curtains that never got washed. They observed how the grubby clutter on the kitchen counters competed with a leggy plant sporting unhealthy, brown-edged leaves. They probably all came to the same conclusion, Nina decided. Kurt simply didn't care.

Nina thought back. Kurt's place in Wiesbaden had been airy and light with high ceilings, windows overlooking a park, and sleek but comfortable furniture and striking artwork on the walls that showed how much he cherished his home.

"Mine own," Kurt said, emptying his glass fast, staring at the threadbare rug. "My life to date."

Dana sniffed, looked down at her drink, held it up for a refill, and said, "You've been here for months, yet you're not working."

"Jobs aren't easy to find these days. They never have been. Now's even worse." He scrambled for the bottle, like someone grabbing for something left floating after a boat capsized.

The two women watched him. Dana began smoking another cigarette and said to Nina, "I thought you were taking care of him."

"And I thought you were out of his life."

Dana ran a hand along her calf as if it ached after her long journey, or else to draw attention to its long slimness. She wore a gold anklet with a charm in the shape of a cross.

"Until last week," Nina continued. "So, Dana. What brought you all this way from Stockholm?"

A long draw, a final tap of ash. "I know you are an attorney. I suppose that means you're like a bulldog and can't let a delicate question go. What brings me here? Hmm, I haven't really put it to myself in those terms. I suppose I came to fetch him. I love him so much. Do you?"

Kurt got up. He provided refills for all, then plopped down on the couch opposite Dana. He had adopted the wooden face of the alienated male in a group of females. He would tolerate and he would survive, but he clearly did not want to participate, not at all.

"We have been calling each other," Dana said to Nina. "Right, Kurt?" She yawned deeply and unself consciously, like a kid. "A couple of hours a night. Thank God for Skype." She quit pretending to sit and stretched the length of her body out on the couch. Her sunny hair spread out over the pillow. She placed her bare feet across Kurt's lap. Her eyelashes closed as lightly as expensive feathers over her cheeks, and she yawned hugely again. It would have been charming, this little-girl act, in some other scene.

"Can we talk?" Nina asked Kurt, jerking her head toward the door. He nodded, extricated himself from underneath Dana, and got up from the couch. Dana didn't open her eyes. She was moving into the deep sleep of the jet-lagged traveler and would be hard to budge now. Kurt spread a woolen throw Nina had given him over Dana's slumbering form.

Nina led him through double doors to the outside landing. Night had arrived and the usual astonishingly clear stars danced in the sky.

"Dana's always been spontaneous, but I never dreamed she'd fly all this way without telling me. I suppose our last conversation got a little out of control."

Our last conversation confirmed the many intense ones that must have come before. Nina wondered if they had been the controlled conversations of two people trying to make peace with an awkward breakup, but suspected they had edged more toward emotional cliffs, injuries, recklessness.

"She'd call me at midnight her time when we were both half in a dreamworld. Things got said."

How reminiscent of a politician waffling, playing with meaning through the detachment of passivity.

He did not say, "I said something painful and intimate I had no business saying and so did she." Nope, things got said in that world and somehow things went awry.

"Remind me," Nina said. "How long were you two together?"

"For four years in Stockholm, right before I moved to Germany. She was a violinist in the same orchestra as me. Those paintings of hers you noticed on the walls of my place in Wiesbaden—she's a painter, too, as you know."

"So—Dana's going on that tour you've been invited to join. You didn't mention that. Why not tell me that?"

He said nothing for a few moments, just placed his hands in his pockets and stared up into the sequined black above them.

She judged his reluctance to answer and didn't like what she was thinking. "I'm not an enemy, Kurt. No need to mess with my mind."

"Of course we aren't enemies," he said finally.

"What exactly did Dana have to do with your invitation to this European excursion?"

"You're so quick, Nina."

Jab. He complimented her, and, oh, how betrayed she felt, recognizing the stall for what it was.

He gave himself another few seconds to think. "Dana knew about my money problems. She knows people. She promoted my involvement in the tour."

"Huh."

"I didn't know that until just now. I swear."

"You told me you broke up before you came back to me. Was that true?"

He nodded, grimacing.

"Why did you break up?"

"Who knows why women break up with men."

Nina steadied herself on the patio railing. If you felt low enough to consider jumping off a balcony, was that love or psychosis? So Dana had broken up with him.

"She's volatile. We fought constantly. Now she says she's got that all under control. Oh, why should you care? It's nothing to do with you, Nina."

"She's got things under control," Nina repeated. Her voice, usually so reliable, sounded cracked and troubled. She struggled to get a grip. "How old is she again?" Nina didn't really need to know. Dana was much younger than Nina, fresh, in love, tough. Nina needed a minute to pull together the vying parts of herself. She wanted Kurt. She didn't. Maybe she no longer had that first option.

"Dana's twenty-five," Kurt said uncertainly. "Maybe twenty-six?"

"I want to do this situation justice, so please, correct me if I'm wrong. Since your return to Tahoe and to me and Bob, you've continued to communicate with your old girlfriend, reigniting a relationship you told me was over but wasn't."

"Don't blow this out of proportion. You make me feel like I'm on the witness stand."

"You want her back?"

"I can't answer that! Everyone does it nowadays, staying in touch with old lovers. It doesn't have to mean anything. You work so much. I get lonely."

He said that last calmly and in a deep voice.

Nina pulled her coat around her. "You're hurting me." The old Kurt would never have been able to stand seeing her in pain. He would gather her in his arms, hold her, and whisper in her ear that he loved her, that he'd get this all sorted out.

He didn't look at her. His eyes flicked toward Dana, asleep in the other room.

"So, she'll stay with you tonight. Maybe again tomorrow night?"

"I guess."

"You guess."

He tore his eyes away from the vision lolling in his living room, back to Nina. "Now that she's here, I need to talk to her. She's an old friend. I'd like to know how things are going with the orchestra."

"Look at what you're giving up. Look at me."

Kurt shook his head, looked down. "I'll call you later."

Nina allowed him to lead her back toward the front door. Dana snored away softly, a tousle-haired, gangly girl, a girl who had known Kurt longer and apparently better than she, Nina, ever had.

Walking back down the unforgiving concrete steps toward the SUV, Nina thought about Dana.

Would Dana have got on a plane and flown six thousand miles to talk to somebody if she didn't love him a lot and if Kurt had not encouraged her?

No.

On the way home, she picked up barbecued chicken at a drive-through. Bob was waiting, and he needed his supper. They ate in the warm cabin, then took Hitchcock out for a walk.

Only when she was brushing her teeth to go to bed did she think about the thing she had done at Kurt's apartment, a thing that went against all her principles, all hard-won wisdom, all morality, and all maturity.

On the way out, while Kurt was distracted, she had tossed the sushi bag behind the couch, inches from Dana.

Nina looked up at the clear sky through the stars, hoping the fish dinner would rot there for a long, long time.

CHAPTER 20

The Lodge, a huge room with tall sky-lights, was full of people, but Nina sighted Marianne and her brother almost immediately at a table in front, their heads close in conversation.

Gene Malavoy stood politely and shook hands with Eric and Nina. Marianne didn't move, but she gave a nod.

Nina did not like Marianne Strong, but she had to admire the professional skier's beauty. Limiting her time to managing the ski lesson program at Paradise, at thirty-six Marianne no longer did aerial tricks in exhibitions. However, she still possessed sharply defined features and an aura of suppressed energy seen only in people whose lifestyle is devoted to sports or the military. Today she wore a purple sweatshirt, partially unzipped to show off smooth, round cleavage. Her black hair shone under the striped headband. With a gesture, seeing Eric, she removed it and invited him to sit down.

Nina sat down next to Malavoy. Also dark, younger than Marianne, he kept his sunglasses on.

His hair when she saw him last had been shorter than usual. Now it was cropped as short as Eric's. His thick eyebrows stood out all the more. He avoided looking at her. She had never understood his hostility toward her.

"So," Marianne said, holding her coffee with both hands. She had a slight accent, which Nina had thought was purely French, but Eric responded in another language, which must be Portuguese: "*Eu deseo que en estivesse esquiando hoje.*"

Marianne answered with a slight smile, "*Também, eu deseo que voce era, que voce parece forte.*" He responded by putting his elbow on the table and turning to her full-face, giving her a look of complete male attention.

"I like your boots," he said. "Frye, aren't they? Retro but so pragmatic."

Nina watched Malavoy. At the first foreign words, he had leaned forward, and his facial muscles tensed. She couldn't be sure, but she thought he might understand the Portuguese.

Thus had Eric, in one expert swoop, established a relationship with Marianne and also revealed that her half brother might know something about Brazil himself. Paul couldn't have done better. In fact, Paul couldn't have done it at all. So Eric did have some interesting skills, even if he hadn't been effective in Brazil. Eric said a few more things in Portuguese, and Marianne responded.

"Sorry," Eric said then, turning to Nina. "Marianne's mother was from Florianópolis, a city on the southern coast, exquisitely beautiful. You'd like it, Nina."

"I'm sure I would. Does your mother still visit there?" Nina asked.

"No," Marianne said. Her expression became formal again. She glanced at her half brother, Gene. Aside from their coloring, they did not look much alike.

"Your father was from France?" Nina said, turning to Malavoy.

"Yes, we both have dual citizenship. Why do you ask?" This came from Marianne, apparently the designated spokesperson.

"I'm trying to remember. You have the same father?"

"That's right. Gene has never been to Brazil, though I spent considerable time there as a child. He grew up with our father in France."

"So you don't speak Portuguese, Mr. Malavoy?" Nina asked, trying again to talk directly to the glowering young man beside her.

Marianne said, "You had something to tell us, something important about the sale and Jim. What is it?"

"You may know that Eric has returned from Brazil, where he spoke to the attorney who has caused two affidavits to be submitted, supposedly from Jim," Nina said.

"What did you find out?" Marianne said to Eric.

"Nina is of the opinion that the affidavits are fraudulent," Eric said.

"Of course she thinks that." Marianne nodded. "She doesn't want him to be alive any more than the rest of us. What did you find out, Eric? Give us a detailed report, okay? Philip hardly talks to us, but I understand he is paying big money."

"I can tell you this," Eric said. "I didn't see Jim. I didn't talk to him. I was handed the paper you already have a copy of, with his current driver's license attached."

"The lawyers in Brazil aren't all crooks," Marianne said, "even though you people probably think they are. It's a civilized country, and southern Brazil isn't that different from Europe. Maybe Jim's alive. Frankly, although I hate him, it would be great if he were alive."

"Why's that?" Nina asked.

"Because then we could settle the escrow problem and each of us could take a share. And then arrest him."

"How does it affect you financially if Jim is dead?"

"I'm sure you already know that. Jim's share goes to Kelly and his father."

"So the only disadvantageous situation for you would be if you have no evidence either way and if you have to wait three years for the legal presumption of death," Nina said.

"That's all very interesting, but you don't seem to understand yet that the sale itself is in danger if you don't resolve some legal questions very rapidly. We will lose the buyers. All I ask you to do is get the sale through. From my point of view, and Gene agrees, we need this to happen. Let Jim's share go into escrow, if it will ensure the sale. But make sure it's just his share, not all the net."

"The court seems inclined to place all the net proceeds in escrow. Either way, whether it's the entire net proceeds or Jim's alleged share, Philip needs it right now, to have something left over for him and Kelly to live on after the lenders are paid."

"Why didn't he think of that before he ran the resort into the ground? He should do whatever he has to so that sale happens. Nelson Hendricks said—"

Nina wondered yet again what Marianne had been doing at the title company and decided to assume she really had been there to quiz the man on finances. That was her obsession after all. "Nelson Hendricks isn't involved in this. And Philip isn't solely responsible for bankrupting the resort."

"Think what you want. The ski school was always run at a profit by me. Philip keeps the day-to-day operations of the rest of the resort to himself. Philip treats me condescendingly. I'm an owner of Paradise Resort and yet I have to teach little kids to slow down on the bunny hill. I could have helped prevent this disaster."

"Ever hear of any problems with the resort's accounts?" Nina asked.

"Only the allegations you made in court, that Jim was an embezzler, too. I told you, I was kept away from the money. From what I can glean, Philip stopped paying attention a long time ago. I wouldn't be surprised if he spends all his time playing poker downtown. Philip and Jim managed the money, and look what happened to a world-class venue. Now let's sell it. I have wanted to sell it since before Jim disappeared."

Marianne looked at her half brother again, and this time Nina wondered if she really was the boss she seemed to be.

"You might as well tell Philip this," Gene said unexpectedly. "The buyers are going to tell him tomorrow anyway. Marianne and I will be managing the resort after the sale."

"What?" Nina and Eric said together.

"We've reached an agreement to handle the general operations. The chief financial officer will be from the corporation, of course. But Marianne has worked here a long time. She's the face of Paradise, and she's able to handle it. She will become the general manager."

"I see," Nina said. "You're going to take over?"

"Yes, of course. It's normal. We know what to do. We know the staff, the weather, the lifts. The food here will change, I tell you that. We will bring in more competitions. We presented specific plans."

"Behind Philip's back," Nina said.

"Listen," Marianne said. "He doesn't care. He doesn't feel like working anymore. He'd like to find a way to make some money from the sale. That's his hope now. That's what you're not getting."

"That's not what he tells me," Nina said. "He tells me that the resort is everything to him."

Marianne made a sound like *pfft*.

Back in the smoothly rolling Porsche, Eric said to Nina, "She may speak Portuguese, she may know southern Brazil, but what has she got to gain in running such a dangerous fraud? She's going to get what she wants after the sale."

"Maybe," Nina said. "She should have talked to Philip about this."

"What about the brother, Gene? I checked him out when Jim Strong first disappeared. He's usually broke. He collects old vinyls of the British Invasion in the sixties—he's especially fond of Gerry and the Pacemakers. He goes back to France every couple of years. He has a green card, a clean record, and he rents."

"Girlfriends?"

"None have turned up yet. He works. He plays with his iPod. He hangs out with his sister."

"Why would the buyers give him a big job at the resort?"

"I'm going to check the details of this deal and get back to you, Nina. It's a surprise to me. My guess about Gene is that he'll stay in the dining room, but it's Marianne they want to keep. She's famous in the world of trick skiing, a real attraction as a celebrity, and she wants to go into management, show her face around, do publicity."

"I just don't feel like I understand everyone's motives. Even the legal situation is so fluid."

"Maybe you should ask Michael Stamp his theories," Eric said. "He'll give you a load of horseshit for free."

"I doubt he buys any of this. He's a lawyer. He's taking a position, that's all."

"Maybe Michael Stamp's our con man. As you suggested. He makes a deal with the lawyer in Brazil."

"I feel like it's deeper than that. Eric, I think the chances are very very slim that Judge Flaherty will lose all judicial acumen and order a fortune to be sent to a foreign country, based on a couple of signatures. Michael Stamp is experienced enough not to seriously try for that. He'll be satisfied if the money goes into a trust account."

"What good does that do anybody?"

"I don't know, Eric. But I watched and listened in court, and I'm right," Nina said so emphatically that Eric's eyebrows went up.

"I don't want it to be Marianne. She's got fine taste in boots," he said with a smile.

"Stamp wouldn't let the money leave the country. Whatever contacts he might have in Brazil, he couldn't count on having control of the money there."

"How did the driver's license end up in Porto Alegre? That's my question," Eric said.

"Jim's dead. Let's start with that. Beyond that, I can't imagine."

"You keep saying that as if it's an article of faith. Okay. If he's dead, then whoever killed him took the license."

Nina gave Eric a level look. Inside, she was shrinking and dying. Could Paul have—what? Lost it?

No—he had thrown the wallet away.

"Someone obtained a copy of it from the State Department of Motor Vehicles. Or Jim had a copy of it lying around his house or office that someone found. Even if it's really his license, Flaherty isn't going to go for it, Eric. I know him and this isn't solid enough for him."

"What are you getting at?" Eric asked.

"It's a stupid con, that's what I'm getting at. And everybody involved in this is smart. I'm missing something important."

Eric laughed. "I'll check on Marianne's mother, her whereabouts, just in case. Even though Marianne is smart."

"I personally wouldn't mind if it was Marianne. But you can't always get what you want."

"Sometimes you can, just by asking nicely," Eric said, looking at the floorboard on her side. "But if that doesn't work, a discreet theft usually does." He gave her the most unguarded smile she had seen yet and moved into the next lane.

Sandy Whitefeather turned her head from her mountain of work at the computer and said, "Supposed to warm up. Good thing. Our lambs don't like it cold."

"Good morning."

"Lots on the calendar today. You have to sign those pleadings I just put on your desk so I can get them over to the courthouse." Sandy wore her hair down her back in a shining black wave today. Only in her forties, Sandy always seemed older to Nina than she actually was.

Sandy went on to say out of the blue, as was her wont, "Five out of ten businesses cave. We need to be tip-top. And PS. We're making some money these days. Maybe you didn't notice, you're so busy making headlines."

"Are you saying I can buy some new shoes?" Nina looked down at her four-inch Jimmy Choos. They were spectacular and hadn't broken an ankle yet, but she had owned them for two years and they had lost some luster.

Strangely, that morning, she hadn't been able to find the right half of her pair of black Louboutins, the ones she had last worn to the courthouse. She had bought them thinking she owed it to herself for a job well done a month or so before, before the issue of the chairs came up.

Probably Hitchcock had absconded with the shoe, she decided, or else she had somehow dropped it at the courthouse out of the bag, damn it. The pair had cost her plenty at Nordstrom in San Francisco, and she loved the acrylic touches. She resolved to turn the cabin upside down until she solved the mystery once and for all. The shoe had to be somewhere.

"Wait until spring when the dough's rolling in," Sandy said. "We'll take care of everything then. Furniture. Decor. Raises."

"Is something wrong, Sandy?"

"You talked with the landlady about the mildew on the wall of our conference room yet?"

"She says she's stretched and 'a slight dark stain on the wall of my extremely reasonably priced offices' isn't going to be a priority."

Sandy picked up a pen, licked the tip, and made a note. "I'll take care of that."

"Right. Hold my calls until I get the papers read and signed."

"What do you expect tomorrow morning at the Paradise Resort hearing?" Sandy went on.

"I expect Mike Stamp to 'lose.' I expect Judge Flaherty to order two million five hundred thousand dollars of the sales proceeds into that title company escrow account for Jim Strong. Mike Stamp will exit the negotiations after that, I do believe. And I will feel like the whole thing was maneuvered that way."

"That's good?" Sandy examined Nina's face. "That's bad."

"That's no good. That money will do no one any good sitting in a trust account. But with the affidavits declaring that Jim strongly objects to the sale as a whole, we probably will end up with all the net proceeds tied up."

"I hear it in your voice," Sandy said. "You know more than you're telling. You and Paul should talk to me. My friend at the clerk's office says she heard from her friend at the DA's office that they have a theory Paul killed Jim. I know he was involved and I'm not the only one."

"Let's not talk anymore about that."

"Soon, though."

Sandy seemed to be looking at Nina for a reaction. Nina didn't react. Sandy examined a fingerprint on her lampshade.

Nina retrieved her briefcase from her office and stuffed paperwork inside, then went back to Sandy's desk.

Sandy was on the phone. "Mrs. Ravel? . . . You and I need to talk. . . . No, that won't do. . . . Nope, not Friday either." Sandy unspooled her black eyes in a straight line toward Nina's. "Three thirty this afternoon is perfect. Here's good, since that's where the creeping alien from outer space is based. . . . Uh-huh, mildew again." She hung up. The filing was done, the office functioned like a precision German astrolabe, and Nina felt a rush of gratitude.

"How much did you say these new client chairs will cost?" she asked.

Sandy showed no signs of joy or triumph. She merely fingered her lower lip thoughtfully. "About four hundred apiece. We need to replace all of them. Gotta match, you know. We have an image to protect. You're doing well in this town. People like seeing you are confident and successful. They look for signs of those things. And you show respect for our clients with nicer furniture. Comfort to butts in trouble."

"Okay, up to four hundred. Your choice." Nina signed a blank check and handed it to Sandy. "Go to that place in Reno. There's no place here at the Lake that'll have office chairs like the ones that are already so perfectly realized in your imagination."

Sandy nodded, tucking the check neatly into the pocket of her skirt. "Right now? What about the clients when you get back? I need to be here."

"Go. You know you want to. I'll be back in an hour to hold the fort." It was an old cowboys-and-Indians joke between them.

"You're in a good mood for someone shootin' from the Alamo," Sandy said. "Sure you trust me to choose?"

"I trust you. As for my good mood, you know how skulls grin?"

Sandy didn't say anything. She gazed steadily at Nina.

"I believe Kurt wants to go back to Europe," Nina

said. "I'm damned if I'll leave my home and country. Not that he's given me the option. If he goes, he'll likely go back with his old girlfriend."

"Well, if he does, he doesn't deserve you."

"I have a good life. It was good before Kurt came into it, and it'll be good again. I've got plans, Sandy. You're right. Let's spruce up the place. I'll get Bob a better music teacher. Buy some new shoes." Further positive thinking failing her, Nina sat down in one of the orange chairs, which felt threadbare and hard. "Get us the best, most luxurious, most beautiful chairs you can find, okay? Ones that will last a long time. Tahoe is my home. This is our business. I'm not leaving."

"Bravo."

Nina looked at the short lady in front of her. "You're a great person to work with, Sandy. Thank you."

"You're welcome. You're not gonna get all funny and hug me or something, are you?"

"Are you really writing a book? A novel?"

"That Paul. You can't tell a man anything. I did start one."

"About a woman lawyer?"

A slight curve of the lip showed Sandy was laughing out loud in her own way. "Yes and no. I want to write a bestseller. It's not me and it's not you. It's a fantasy. Kind of fun, I hope. A parody, but true bottom line."

"That's a relief," Nina said with a little chuckle.

"You know, you made me nervous thinking this had anything to do with our business."

"It does happen to be a woman legal assistant in a small law firm. She solves problems other people think are trivial, which aren't."

"And where is this little fictional firm?"

"Not far from here, fictionally. Down the hall, you might say."

"I see. Don't forget about fictional client confidentiality."

"I can invent my own stories. I'm not very far along, of course. But you know, legal assistants are the front lines. Like when our client's soon-to-be-ex nosed his Uzi through the outside door. Just the barrel. I ducked down and called 911, remember? I used that in the book, but I made the gun a Desert Eagle."

"Oh, good, nobody will make the connection then."

"Well, then, Reno here I come," Sandy said. "And they won't get one quarter off me I don't want to give them. You better get signing, then run. Meeting with Michael Stamp in thirty minutes." Nina finished her desk work, grabbed her briefcase, and hustled down the hall of the Starlake Building and out to the slushy parking lot.

Bluer skies, however. The sky was changing, clearing.

CHAPTER 21

On the short drive down the boulevard to Stamp's office Nina called Paul, who filled her in on his talks with Cyndi's husband and the mechanic. She found her mind drifting. How strange that Paul, in danger of being discovered by the police as the murderer of Jim Strong, could invest himself so thoroughly in another case.

He must have noticed her lack of interest. "You think I'm ignoring the Strong problem? I'm not. At this moment there's not a damn thing to be done. Meanwhile, it's business as usual for me."

Nina tried to focus on what he'd said. "I'm glad you're in touch with Michelle Rossmoor again. I'd love to see her. Catch up. Meet their kids."

"She feels the same."

Nina swerved to avoid a car that had spun out on the slick road. She could not wait for drier roads and snowless days. "I'm worried, Paul."

"Of course."

"Your future rests on the body of Jim Strong, and God only knows that's an awful place for it to lie.

Tomorrow's the hearing. If Judge Flaherty orders the money into escrow, what's the plan? You have a plan for those GPS coordinates?"

Paul, who didn't ordinarily do glum, did it now. "Maybe."

How long have I known Paul? Nina asked herself. A decade before, when she was a harried law student, she and Paul had come close to falling in love—Paul, with his violent temper and his love of freedom, who did not match her. She had thought she might someday have another child—Paul was not interested. Not appropriate for me and mine, she had decided. Her logical, linear mind had dismissed him, and much later, when Kurt came back, every fairy-tale image had fallen into place.

Until Dana came along with her smokes, her passion, and her unshakable honesty; a Hans Christian Andersen mermaid, a real-life fairy tale.

Meantime Paul lay as a substratum of everything in Nina's life. How many times had they said goodbye? How many times had she called for him? And he had always come to her.

It's not that I love him now, she told herself. It's that he needs me now and I must not fail him, as he has never failed me.

"I took out the garbage," he had told her back then when Jim Strong disappeared. Could Paul's handiwork ever be discovered in that godforsaken stretch of forest?

Not without help.

Nina wondered why she could never quite get her footing, never have peace in her life. In her balancing act she was constantly shifting weight, never standing still. Perhaps there was no such thing as balance in these terms, not even moments of balance. Maybe humans were all in a log-rolling game on a dangerous river.

Traffic picked up as kids got out of school. She knew she should get off the phone. "I'll call after the hearing." She rang off and swung into the parking lot of Caplan, Stamp, and Powell, a mile far from her own digs at the Starlake Building.

Gathering up her bag and slipping her feet out of her snow boots and into her heels, she recalled the first time she had seen these offices. Clicking the remote lock on the car, stepping carefully around puddles, she recalled the glamour and sparkle of the offices, and she recalled her chagrin. She had definitely felt outclassed. Nowadays, although the Caplan firm continued to do well and enjoyed a good reputation, Nina knew she had come up in the world. She had nothing to apologize for, and a lot to be proud of.

She could handle this chess game.

Punching the buzzer to their offices, she reminded herself to be humble. She didn't want to antagonize Stamp.

She walked down a neutral hallway decorated with huge, surreal Sierra photographic landscapes by Elizabeth or Olof Carmel. While waiting for the elevator, she admired the flaming aspens and rushing, blue, icy waters of a stream. The elevator arrived. She stepped in, sorry she had nothing but a small digital camera, which she mostly used to document Bob's amazing growth as a human being and Hitchcock's progress as a dog. Well, she had other strengths.

Michael Stamp's office proved to be an intimate refuge for predivorcées. She noted the lighting, uplights, downlights, focused lights, so that the room was bathed in a warm golden light she hadn't thought possible without candles.

Yeah, like gold, she thought, imagining how costly such renovations to an old building such as this one must have been. Then she noticed the overstuffed chairs, the cozy gas fire—and Stamp came to greet her, hand outstretched. "Glad to see you, Nina."

She shook his hand, inhaling the leather scent of the furniture and the polishes that kept all the wood desks and bookcases satiny and warm-looking.

He sat her down. She didn't like feeling shorter than she was, so she tried to sit upright, but the plushness of the chair made it impossible. To restore her strength of position, she crossed her legs, letting her skirt ride up. He wouldn't know who made the shoes, but he would certainly notice them.

"Ahem," he said, noticing as planned. "So, Nina, to plunge right into why you are probably here, because I'm dying to go home, let me reveal right away that I just got off the horn with the sheriff's office."

"Is it presumptuous to ask what you're going to do at tomorrow's hearing?"

"You mean, will we maintain the position that Jim Strong is alive until we know with absolute certainty he's dead? This is a reputable firm and we don't play games, but it's a reasonable position. Your own investigator apparently came up empty-handed on his trip there."

Nina said, "You have to know those affidavits are phony. How can you, in all conscience, push them as authentic?"

Stamp sat behind his cherrywood desk like Buddha, a paragon of equanimity. Behind him, Lake Tahoe, as expansive and beautiful as Nina had ever seen it sprawled through a silvery winter haze. "We don't know that. If we had reasonable grounds to believe Jim Strong was already dead at the time we were contacted by the attorney in Porto Alegre, of course we'd want nothing to do with a fraud. That's the short answer."

Nina took a breath. "Your intervention may cause the sale to fail."

The other lawyer looked surprised. "We'll cooperate in every way to make sure that doesn't happen."

"Mike, what do you think is really going on here? Don't you care that you're a dupe?"

Stamp's cheek twitched. "A dupe? Where's your evidence that he isn't alive?"

"Bottom line: we oppose an escrow account for a guy who is dead, as to the share he owns individually, and certainly with regard to tying up the entire net proceeds."

Stamp smiled. "Meeting of the minds. We're on the same side in the sense that we don't like the escrow notion. As you know, we have interviewed with a request to have the money sent to Brazil. It is not up to us to doubt or to determine the credibility of those affidavits, which are duly executed and have been filed with the court. We don't want an escrow account any more than you do. We want the proceeds from the sale that are due to Jim Strong to be sent down there to Jim Strong. That's what we should be working toward."

"Why do I feel like you're being disingenuous?" Nina leaned forward, feeling like a beggar, but willing to do what she needed to do to make her point. "The purchase and sale agreement has to be executed within the next four days. I need your help to make that happen."

"What exactly do you need from us, Nina?"

"A stipulation. Withdrawal of this false claim."

He stroked his square jaw. "I'm telling you, we can't ethically withdraw it. We don't know Strong's dead. We have legal documents on file that imply he is alive. All we need from you is for Jim's proceeds to be sent to Brazil. Then you can have your sale."

"If Philip Strong has to lose the resort, so be it. But to lose the resort he spent his whole life building, and come out of decades of work without a dime? You've played golf with him. Have a heart."

"Look," Stamp persisted, "the buyers pony up the sales price. We send Jim his individual share. Everyone's happy.

"Jim gets four hundred seventeen thousand dollars. Philip Strong takes one and a quarter million, half the net proceeds based on his share. And Marianne and Kelly Strong each receive the same amount as Jim Strong. We give up our claim to all the net, and of course our claim is overreaching a little, and I have even thought, and don't repeat this, Nina, but I have even thought that it was improper perhaps to object to the sale entirely."

"I'm almost tempted," Nina said, "to tell my clients their best bet is to get nicked for more than four hundred thousand dollars. Cost of doing business, right, Mike? You get your nick, a lawyer and a notary in Brazil get their nick, and whoever dreamed this scheme up takes the big money. Who are you really representing?"

Stamp swiveled in his state-of-the-art chair, which made nary a noise. "You know what? It angers me to be accused of fraud by a lawyer who's so emotionally involved she can't look at the fact that this asshole she hates may still be around."

"Mike, what's going on? Are you involved in this? Tell me, and I'll help you."

He stood up. "See you tomorrow."

"We're at an impasse, then."

Stamp nodded. "Yes." Nina stayed in her seat, stinging from his words, not willing yet to give up on him.

"You know I have to ask this," she said calmly.

"What now?"

"Would you gain from an escrow situation?"

He smirked. "You're too much, Nina. I was expecting that. First you ask me sweetly, then you ask me hard. Rather like attacking with a pawn, then revealing the queen attack, direct and forceful. So you think I'm really after putting all the net proceeds into escrow. Very interesting."

"How close are your ties to Tahoe Sierra Title?"

"We've used them for years. So has Philip. We trust them." He paused. "You don't?"

"You have any ties to Brazil, Mike?"

Stamp slapped his hand on his glossy desk and laughed and laughed. "Oh, God. You live up to your reputation. You're like a crocodile and your jaws are just aching to snap shut on me."

She listened, hoping her eyes said nothing. "I take it you deny any connection to Brazil."

"Listen, years ago, when you came to town and Jeff Riesner was a partner, he told us about you. He told us you were a loser single parent fleeing an ugly divorce. He said you were too good-looking to be smart. He said he would mow you down. He was wrong on every count. I admire you, Counselor. You've shown everyone, and I mean this entire town, you are a force. You've had success with hopeless cases, and this is a place that appreciates that kind of talent."

Nina nodded noncommittally.

"I promise you, I have nothing to do with these affidavits. I have no personal interest. I'm only sorry I took this case. It may be we're all being defrauded. But we have the case, and no proof of fraud, just a funny feeling. You have my word, Nina. I'm doing my job here, nothing more."

"Okay, Mike." A small part of her wanted to luxuriate in the pat on the back, but the bigger part thought he had resorted to flattery to obscure that he was giving her nothing, and of course he didn't doubt he could take her down. "So maybe the court will order that money into an escrow account tomorrow. What can you tell me about Nelson Hendricks?"

"We've used him for twenty years and never heard a bad word."

"I hear a *but* in there."

Stamp raised his shoulders. "I used to play golf with him, and I don't really have a bad word to say. That's the truth. He's like all of us. His family's suffering. Grown kids out of work. Wife with some health issues. We were glad to hire him, help him out."

Nina shook Stamp's hand on the way out.

"Glad to have you up here, Nina. I'd have asked the same questions. No hard feelings."

In the parking lot, though, she realized he had

scored, found her weakness. She was emotionally
involved, and if Stamp knew it, then Judge Flaherty
would know it.

In fact, her involvement was more than emotional. She could prove Jim was dead, and end all
this. I should resign and tell the truth, she thought.
She decided, if the hearing doesn't go well, I'm out.
She started the engine and returned to the office.

Kurt did not call to apologize. He did ask her to
stop by that evening. She got the message. All the
rest of the day Nina thought about him lying on
the couch making out with Brigitte Bardot between
bouts of Gauloise puffing.

She climbed the stairs to his apartment. As she
approached, she heard it—piano music pouring
fast and true through that cheap hollow-core door.
She stood behind the door for a time, listening, her
eyes tearing up. He was glorious. He played fero-
ciously. When the music finally stopped, she gave it a
moment or two, then knocked.

He opened the door. Unshaven and wild-looking,
his shirt gaped open to reveal the hair on his chest.
"Dana's gone."

"Hot diggity dog," Nina said.

He poured her a glass of wine and she took a sip.

"Going to join her?" she asked coolly.

"I suppose so." He hung his head, and it was real,
he was leaving her.

"Go ahead, then. We'll get by." Kurt seemed

relieved at her briskness. He didn't try to explain or plead or barter. He moved on.

"Listen, Nina, Bob has been IMing a girl in Stockholm. I talked to him an hour ago."

"You mean Nikki?"

"He wants to come with me. Nikki's the smaller part of it. The bigger part is the piano. He has a vocation, Nina. He wants to study at the music conservatory in Stockholm."

"No way. My son stays with me."

"Our son!"

"Whatever!"

"He's getting older now. He knows his own mind. Maybe you should talk to him."

At 4:00 a.m. she was already awake, and that was way too early.

In retrospect, how perfect life could have been. Write that on my tombstone and everybody else's, she thought, throwing off her covers, feeling for her slippers, ankles creaking. She got up for tea and drank it by the cold fireplace. When she had finished it down to the dregs, she peeked in at Bob, getting a good whiff of teenage boy. Reminding herself to do his laundry soon, she closed the door on the long feet that hung over the end of his bed. He couldn't leave. He needed her.

Back at her big pine four-poster, under the butter-yellow comforter, she kicked off her slippers. These slippers, old and battered, New Zealand sheepskin worn down to flatness, reminded her of her first husband, Jack. He had bought them for her when they first married, and she had laughed and sworn she wouldn't be caught dead in such ugly footwear, but they turned out to be soft and warm, perfect for the cold mountain floors.

She put her head on the pillow and closed her eyes. Visions from years before sprawled across the inside of her eyelids. That stupid plumber with his idiotic silver earring. The look on Jack's face when he discovered them together. Jack's own perfidy. They had both failed that relationship. Now she had failed with Kurt.

About seven, her pillow flat, tossing off covers because she felt hot, putting them back on because she was shivering, she lived through the avalanche again, and another man she had loved did not.

CHAPTER 22

The next morning was a bear, literally. A bear had broken into their much-defended trash and recycling and had strewn any and all unpalatable bits up the driveway and the street. Struck by the appalling number of wine bottles and packaged-food containers, Nina called to Bob, who was late for school, to help her toss everything back in the bin so that the neighbors would not know the truth about her, that she was a lush and a microwaver.

Running for the RAV a few minutes later, hands washed, dressed for court, Nina blew along in rain. She needed paperwork from the office.

Sandy called. "You have nine minutes to get here if you aren't going to be late for court," she intoned. "Eight minutes. Seven—"

"I'll be there in two! Have that stack of files I left on the credenza ready!"

Sandy stood outside on the steps, looking peaceful, enjoying a break in the rain, face upturned to a moment of sunshine. She handed off the paperwork through a window.

Nina tore toward the street, then rushed back. "My heel broke. Help!"

"I thought you kept those cute new shoes in the office."

"I lost one of that pair, okay? It disappeared after court one day."

"Not good," Sandy said. "You pay a lot for your shoes. You should keep track."

The Strong hearing therefore started off most inauspiciously, with Nina wearing pointy cowboy boots at least two sizes too large for her. Something about them was horsey. She was tired and nervous. She was hoping for more than she was likely to get, an end to all this. Too much else was at stake—Paul didn't have many options if things went badly.

Paperwork and presentations followed. Flaherty, in businesslike mode, with a full calendar and an unfamiliar court clerk who was obviously subbing and obviously suffering, was concise. "I understand your client has an offer in hand, Counsel?"

Nina said, "For a few more days, Your Honor."

"I have reviewed the second affidavit submitted to the Court by Mr. Stamp in support of the Complaint in Intervention. Your Points and Authorities don't attack the form of the affidavit, or disprove the validity of the attached California driver's license."

Nina began to argue, using Eric's declarations, Philip's declaration, and all the legal theory she could muster. Flaherty listened with impatient courtesy.

He turned to Stamp. "Your position?"

"Well, Judge, as we've said, we would like the proceeds from the sale that are due Jim Strong be sent to an account established by his attorney in Brazil. We see no need for an escrow account. That will only delay our client's fair share. However, of course, if need be—"

It was exactly as Nina had thought. Why in hell was the escrow account the true goal here?

Flaherty said, "All right, Counselors, the court has listened to and pondered your positions. The Court will order that, upon the completion of the sale of Paradise Ski Resort, all net proceeds, amounting to approximately two point five million dollars, shall be placed in an interest-bearing trust account with— what was the name of the local escrow company again?"

"Tahoe Sierra Title, Your Honor," Michael Stamp said.

"But, Your Honor, that deprives the other partners of their shares as well as tying up Jim Strong's share for an indefinite period," Nina said.

"I don't like it either. But from the evidence here, we have a live partner making a special appearance to object to the sale, its terms, its payouts, unless this court sends the one-sixth share to Brazil. This court is not prepared to release that share entirely, but that does mean the objection to the entire sale will need to be sorted out in further legal proceedings. If your clients want to complete their sale, they may do so, and they may make approved payouts to their creditors, but the full net proceeds are subject to further proceedings and findings that this court cannot make right now. Mr. Stamp, you will prepare the tentative order within ten days."

"But—"

Flaherty said to Nina, "Let me restate this as clearly as possible. You haven't given me any evidence he's dead, Counsel. There's evidence he's alive, but not enough for this court to send the money to a foreign jurisdiction. It's going to have to be held in escrow. We can't continue these proceedings forever; your clients have stated that they will lose the sale entirely. So I understand why you are not requesting a continuance."

"Yes, but—"

"We can't decide whether Mr. Strong is dead or alive today," Flaherty said, "and there's a way to protect the proceeds indefinitely. That's all I can do for you. You can have him declared dead in a few years without any more fuss, if he doesn't come back here for his share."

"But—"

Flaherty said to Stamp, "Is the title company willing to act as trustee for the proceeds?"

Nelson Hendricks, in the back, nodded. "Yes, Your Honor."

"That's that, then. So ordered."

"Next case," the court clerk said, *"Ramsey versus Minden Mufflers."*

A ragtag crew of people moved through the gate to take their places before the bench.

Nina called Paul from her car in the parking lot, looking at the evergreens around the court that were starting to show their more springlike light green colors.

"Good day today?" Paul started out.

"As bad as it gets. Judge Flaherty ordered all the net proceeds into escrow. Philip comes out with nothing. He lost both his sons and now he loses his resort, the one he built up for years, and gets nothing out of it for years."

Paul cursed for a full minute. "Okay, I've been thinking about what to do if you can't get Strong some of that money because they can't find the body. I have a plan."

"Is this something that I, as an officer of the court, should not be privy to unless I want my license ripped up?" She pulled off the boots as she spoke.

"Probably. I need you with me tonight."

"Oh, you do, do you?"

"Break whatever you have going with Kurt."

"Ha ha ha."

"What'd I say?"

"I have to go. Upsetting phone calls to make." Nina wiggled her toes and turned the car's heat on so that it flowed over them directly.

"Meet you at the Tahoe Keys Café at seven. It's on Lake Tahoe Boulevard."

"I know the place. I like their wraps. But, Paul, what are we going to do this time?"

"Don't be late and don't cancel. I'll greet you warmly, kiss that button nose, and we'll have fun. The dire kind, the skeletons dancing around—*La Noche de los Muertos*—well, you know. Remember last time."

"Agh. Why won't you just tell me! You make me crazy."

"Which has kept you interested lo these many years."

"This is serious!"

"I know that, honey," he said gently. "But let's pretend it isn't. We'll go out for a warm drink. Catch up on how much I like your curvy bits—"

"Oh, shut up."

Dog walked, boy fed and placed in mental chains at the kitchen table with threats to his future freedom if he didn't finish every lick of homework in a timely fashion by the time she returned, Nina set off for the café, which wasn't far from her cabin on Kulow.

At this hour, Lake Tahoe Boulevard hosted heavy traffic, playtime for the locals and out of towners alike. Scooting through yellow lights, stopping and going, Nina felt a vague sense of catastrophe ahead.

Anyway, can't get any worse, she told herself.

She parked, noticing the lack of lights over the sign and inside the café. Paul leaned on his Mustang, hands in his pockets, tall, blond, sexy, and sulky.

And really tough, not acting. She felt an honest-to-God sexual yearning and thought, It's been a month without Kurt, I've got to stay under control, this is no time.

"What's the problem?" She blipped her car's lock.

"They closed early. Hell."

"Well"—she looked at the dark back side—"it's a café. Most people don't drink coffee at night."

He slumped, saying nothing, kicking a foot in the slush like a little kid.

"What is it you need at this point?" she asked. "Why are we here?"

"Free Internet access."

"But I get the Internet at work or at my house."

"You don't get anonymous free Internet."

She thought. "Harrah's. They have wireless access."

"And my credit card number. And the soul of my first and only child, if I had one."

"Why's this important?"

"Because we're going to give out the GPS coordinates. We are sending them to the police so that Philip can put all his fears and emotions to rest about the whereabouts of his son and you can have another hearing. We can't give our names, though. Ponder this a second. I can see no other way."

She saw at once that he was right. His was the only possible course of action now. When the police found the body, she could arrange an emergency court session, and Flaherty would work with her, and they'd free up the money. She would have done her job, although there would be other fallout.

"Yeah," she said. "Yeah, let's do it."

She hooked her arm in his. "We register as Mr. and Mrs. Somebody. We rent a room using a fake name."

He stared at her. "Not so easy these days, Ms. Reilly."

"Oh, sure it is. Cash talks in this town. It may be going the way of the dinosaur everywhere else, but here, cash remains king."

Rather than go to Harrah's, where Paul was semiknown, and Nina might be known even a little more, they stopped in at the Valhalla, a motel overlooking the lake where the sharply dressed clerk happily accepted rent on an empty room.

In the motel room, Wi-Fi fired up, fake e-mail address up and running, they composed an e-mail to Sergeant Cheney, arguing over the language, and settling finally for something only a lawyer could love.

You will find the body of Jim Strong buried at these coordinates. The coordinates followed, checked twice for accuracy.

"*Après moi le déluge,*" Paul said. He pushed the send button on Nina's portable computer. Then they turned it off and looked at each other. "Fake address. Fake ID. Untraceable."

"I'm so worried about you."

"Not as worried as I am about me," Paul said. "And I have made you an accessory."

"Well, it's done."

They fell back on the bed together, side by side. For a long time, they lay there, barely touching, thinking their own thoughts.

"So you and Kurt," Paul said finally. "Ready to bring me up-to-date?"

"Over."

"Again."

"Last time." The words choked her.

"Can I ask why?"

"I will never understand the human heart. I loved him so much once, then not so much, no matter how hard I tried."

"Trying—that never works. Of course he felt that."

"Yes, he did. He said—uh—he said . . ." She found it hard to share what he had said, that she loved another man. Instead she turned her face toward Paul, took his face in her hands, and kissed him. She felt it strong in her again, how she wanted to stay right here, get closer, hold on tight, experience him—it had been a long time.

He pulled back. "Tomorrow, the police will dig up the grave of Jim Strong. And if something goes wrong, I might go to prison for a very long time measured in the life of a lovely lawyer." He stroked her long brown hair. "You are a dreamer. Underneath all that cyborg thinking, you imagine the world you want to happen, not what's out there."

"I dream that we will survive this."

"Ah, Nina."

CHAPTER 23

I rushed to unbury Jim.

I didn't have time to worry about the horror, but I did feel it. Some things you don't choose.

Once I located his body, the exact location at last, I had to work hard. The body was in rough forest under a pile of debris, which I hurled into the snowy hill behind me. I worked frantically, partly to keep my feelings at bay, partly because I knew the police were coming. They had the same coordinates. They would be searching for the body. I didn't know if I had an hour or several hours, so I threw forest debris left and right. I was wearing gloves of course, but felt bruises forming as the odd branch stabbed me, and as I stumbled over a rock.

I suffered moments of doubt. Was he really here? Did I have the wrong information? I doubled my efforts. In the blue mountain air, I felt the altitude, the crazed beating of my heart, the pounding in my ears.

Panic.

Nobody there yet.

I kept digging and lifting, hearing the ticking of a clock, although there could be no clock here, only a big wind blowing through the pines.

A full ninety minutes passed before I located the body. I threw myself to the side and breathed heavily, looking at my find, trying to stay unemotional.

A blue tarp entirely wrapped the body, and for that I was grateful. I wouldn't have to assemble the bones that moved around inside while I pulled the tarp out of the grave. Jim had lain here for two years. The body would now be decomposed, although to what extent I did not know and did not want to know. I finished the job, clearing the area around the area of mud, icy branches, and stink, making sure the tarp remained wrapped tightly around the body. Then I braced myself, pulling it out, slipping and bumping as I dragged him out of the wet hole that had been his grave.

"You're going back to the lake," I whispered to Jim before I took away the tarp over his face and forced myself to look.

Then I put him in the back of my truck and drove him back to the lake where he had always lived. All the way to my boat I thought of him, moving around in the truck as if alive again.

CHAPTER 24

Early the next morning, Nina went into her office, which was cold, dark, and empty. Sandy was no doubt thumping around on her horse on this fine clear morning, with Joe bringing up the rear.

Nina tackled one of the stacks of paperwork, only to find it required the kind of logical thinking she didn't have in her that morning. She decided instead to organize bills for payment, noting anything suspicious, piling them up for Sandy to take care of ASAP.

At 10:00 a.m. promptly the phone rang with the call she was expecting.

"Law Offices of Nina Reilly and Associates," Nina said automatically. She had instructed Sandy to use that phrase years ago and it had stuck. Well, if you thought of Sandy, Wish, and Paul, she had associates, didn't she?

"Nina, something amazing has happened. I got a call early this morning from the South Lake Tahoe police."

"What is it, Philip?"

"The police! They have received some kind of

anonymous information about a grave someone has found near Sorensen's. They think Jim may be buried there. Somewhere out in the woods. Buried. Not Brazil. Not Brazil at all."

She nodded. So Sergeant Cheney had received the anonymous tip. They were digging. Today, they would find Jim's body. Anxiety coiled in her.

"Such news," she said.

"I thought you should know. They're sending the equipment and men out about four this afternoon."

"I'm glad you called to tell me."

"I've called everyone, Marianne, Brinkman, Gene Malavoy, Kelly. It affects all of us, Nina. We're speechless. I believe it. Jim's dead. I wanted that for so long. I know it must make you glad, too, knowing he may have been found. I have to go now."

She hung up and found herself unable to call Paul. What good would it do, telling him they were going to dig up Jim's body? He must be thinking of it right this minute, wondering about his future in a jail somewhere, an ex-cop, not popular.

She thought of the cold grave, the constellations in the sky as they hauled those rocks away and revealed the body.

All day as she went about her life, she was also waiting for the follow-up phone call, the one that would tell her that Jim was officially dead.

That evening, Philip called her at home. She had been pacing, waiting for it.

"More news. Another police call." Something awful was in his tone of voice, thick, odd.

"Oh?" For a moment she had a frightening image of Paul caught, brought down by something found in the grave.

"The police finished digging."

"What did they find?"

She heard him mutter something, then say, "Nothing."

"Nothing?"

"A place where a body might have been buried, but no body. It's as though he got up and left. His second great disappearance. It's like a trick. Nina, is there a curse on me? On us?"

"Philip, are you all right?"

"Nina? Nina?" This came out faintly, as if he had dropped the phone for a moment.

"I'm right here."

"I don't feel very well. Awful pain. Something's wrong. Need a doctor." His gasping voice alarmed her.

"I'm calling 911 on my cell as we speak."

"Quite a bit of—"

"Stay on the line with me."

His phone clattered in her ear.

PART
THREE

CHAPTER 25

Nina picked up Bob and drove over to Matt's. The snow was melting, melting. Spring buds poked up hopeful heads alongside the cabins along Pioneer Trail. Bob sat beside her, hair uncombed, clothing slapdash, expression hangdog.

Nina tried to listen to the news but he kept changing the channel until she gave up and listened to his choice of music all the way there. She felt grim. Events seemed to roll on without any human control. This morning she would be watching all three kids while she and Paul tried to work out what to do next.

They arrived at the house and parked in the curve at the end of the road.

"Out," Nina commanded. "And don't forget your manners."

Bob slouched from the car, yawning, slamming the door with an emphatic smack, but was polite to his aunt and uncle before excusing himself with a smile on his face, eager to go upstairs and exact his vengeance.

Matt put his parka on, listening to the hoots and complaints drifting downstairs. "Makes 'em cantankerous, waking up early on weekends."

"Tell me about it," Nina said drily. She hugged her sister-in-law. "Happy birthday, Andrea!"

Andrea hugged her back. She looked healthy and young in a brown sweater that warmed her red curls and pink cheeks. "Any word about Philip Strong's condition?"

"They got him to Boulder Hospital within fifteen minutes and he came out of surgery all right. I'll visit him later."

"What happened?"

"Something to do with his heart."

"You know, in emergencies, people often freeze up," Andrea said. "You used your head, got him an ambulance in time."

"It was an obvious 911 call. He has been close to collapse for a while."

"Well, a morning out is a treat," Andrea said. "Being out of this messy house is a treat anytime! We're grateful to you, Nina."

Matt hugged his wife. "To misquote Taj Mahal, my wife deserves mo' better treats than we puny humans can give her."

"Aw," Andrea said.

Nina smiled. "Look at her blush. You two all set?"

"You sure you're up for this? You look like you're not sleeping. You're working too hard."

"I'm on it."

"Promise us no video games, no television," Matt said. "The sun is out, the sky is blue. It's beautiful. I want them outside."

"While you're at it, Matt, why not ask for world peace?" Andrea nudged him with her hip.

For a few minutes they dawdled over which jackets to wear. Finally they left.

Nina heard laughter that felt foreign to her ears.

She took off her extra sweater, kicked off boots designed to deal with slush, not fashion, and went into the kitchen to dig around for supplies. Eggs, milk, cheese, oh, some leftovers—

Almost an hour later, three teenagers emerged from upstairs, noses tipped up, sniffing. They ate fast and, finished, started slapping dirty dishes into the dishwasher, bumping against each other, complaining, and generally having a fine time.

Paul knocked on the kitchen door, peering in through the glass at them.

"Hungry?" Nina let him in. "I cooked."

"No. I'm here to freak out, not to eat."

"Jeez, Paul. Let's not go there yet."

"Hi, Paul! 'Bye!" the kids said, heading upstairs.

"Not so fast," Nina said. "Put on warm clothes and come right back down here."

"What? Why?"

"I'm the boss today."

A long groan ensued, then arguments followed by stubbornness, and finally, when they saw they could not win, capitulation.

Watching the kids run upstairs, Paul said, "It's the end of the world. You're babysitting. Is this what it means to be a woman?"

"Andrea and Matt managed to book a cham- pagne-brunch cruise on the lake. Our dad was supposed to come, but he's not always reliable, so I stepped in. Things still need to be done while the world ends."

"Isn't this kind of situation exactly why God invented the Net? Opiate of the children?"

She turned off the coffeemaker, restacked the pile of dishes in the dishwasher, filled the machine with soap, and cranked it up. They were alone for the moment. "Maybe I need to see my family, Paul. I didn't sleep last night. We gave the police an anonymous tip with specific instructions on how to find Jim's grave. They went there to dig him up and found nothing in the grave. Is it possible we sent the wrong coordinates? That they dug up something else?"

"I checked the e-mail we sent Cheney. Our infor- mation was accurate."

"Okay. Then I've come to the conclusion that we've been duped."

Paul nodded. "To move the scenario along a step further, who duped us? Who stole the body? How could anyone on earth know where I"—his voice lowered to a whisper—"put him?"

"Someone followed us to Jim's grave," she whis- pered back.

He shook his head. "I would have noticed."

"You have a better explanation?"

"He dug himself out. He's a freakin' demon."

They all piled into the car, suspending logical thought and talk until they got to the ice-skating rink at the state line. There, they all rented skates. The kids shot off.

Nina tried to remember how to balance herself.

"Hey, you know tricks!" Paul said, watching Nina spin.

"It's like a bicycle," she said, "you never— Oops!" Down she started, but Paul caught her arm. "You look good when you're cold and out of sorts," he said, steadying her. He stood there smiling at her like some kind of fool. They were both fools, spinning like tops.

She felt her eyes welling. "I'm scared for you."

"Stop that immediately," he said kindly, pulling her along. "We're having fun here."

They didn't last long and settled into a quiet corner away from the crowds. They watched the kids and other skaters, clapping as Troy executed a jump.

"Someone else besides you and me knew Jim Strong was dead." Paul kept his voice low in spite of the overall din. "It's hard to believe. Bob would never say a thing except maybe to Sandy, and Sandy wouldn't talk about it."

"Sandy didn't even tell Joe. I think she tells him everything, mostly."

Brianna had hooked up with a few girlfriends. Hanging on to each other, they lunged, laughing, attaching themselves to various young boys and then detaching, favoring none.

Nina, watching, thought of herself at Brianna's age, about the allure of young males with their hairiness, smells, and intensities, and about the way their chemistry compromised a young woman's intelligence. She could only hope Brianna could pump her way up and down that seesaw back to sanity before she ruined her life. Nina wondered if Matt and Andrea worried that way about their daughter. Nina sure worried about Bob, every single day, and now and then she thought of herself and Kurt, the young craziness, the young blissfulness.

"The missing body is connected to the sale of the resort," she said, continuing to watch, multitasking. "Somebody knows you killed Jim Strong, Paul. Somebody knows where you buried him. The body was taken because someone doesn't want the police to know he's dead. It has to be the same person or persons who are trying to nick some of that sale money."

"If that's true, the responsible thing to do is to go to the cops and get this off my chest for once and for all. I think I'm going to have to take it to Fred Cheney. He's an old friend. He'll believe me. Not to talk to the cops at this point is beyond irresponsible."

Nina found it hard to contain her fright at the thought. "You were a homicide cop. How can you suggest such a thing? Don't be naive. They'll eat you alive."

"Okay, Nina, you've got advice? Good. Spill your guts."

"You go to Sergeant Cheney, you open your heart. 'Yessir, I took the guy out because he was threatening Nina. He came at me. It was self-defense.' He may be your friend, but he has a sworn duty and an ethic, too. He may be sympathetic, but don't assume he'll treat you any differently than another police officer would."

"I don't expect sympathy I don't deserve. Fred's a dedicated law enforcement officer. I don't expect he'll let our friendship get in the way of what he considers his duty."

"You're hoping he will, though. Not officially, but you do hope for leniency."

"But Jim's body's gone. We did try to take care of this. The police will never be able to piece this elaborate story together and find who stole the corpse if I don't stop protecting myself."

Bob, Troy, and Brianna linked arms like a gang. Swooping around the rink powerfully, they took on all challengers.

"Paul, you need to hire a criminal lawyer, anyone but me. I know all the best ones. You'll be all right." Nina looped her arm over his shoulder. "You saved my life. We both know that. Whatever happened to Jim Strong, he deserved."

For some reason she lifted her face to look at him

as his face was coming down to look at her. They kissed naturally and simply.

"I don't think I want a lawyer anymore," Paul said. "I just want to tell the truth about how I came to kill him. I wish the Strong family—peace."

"That wish could land you in prison for life. Please, Paul. I'm a professional. Don't do it that way."

"I'll think about it. Enough for now."

They watched the skaters muscling their ways through tie-ups, laughing, having a good time. She clapped as Brianna made a small jump. "She's beautiful," Nina murmured. "So talented. Hard to know what life might bring her."

The three kids crashed suddenly. They got rid of the skates and demanded food. Again.

On the way back to Matt and Andrea's they stopped at Heidi's, Paul's choice. Everyone ate way too much, and the carbs made the backseat a calm and quiet place all the way home.

"Ahoy," Matt said. He poked his head into his front door nervously, as if he had expected the whole place to have gone up in smoke.

"Did you have fun?" Nina asked. She and Paul, silent on a porch swing, rose together leaving it to creak back and forth behind them, empty.

Matt looked at Andrea with adoration Nina had craved and had never gotten from Kurt. "Oh, yeah," Matt said. He kissed Andrea on the lips. "I'm a lucky man."

Nina filled him in on the morning, stretching out the part where the kids skated.

Paul walked Nina to her car. It was early afternoon, warm.

"I note you didn't mention the hour they spent afterward playing video games," Paul said.

"They won't squeal. Paul, can you please do this for me? Wait a little longer before you talk to Sergeant Cheney."

"Why? The court hearing has been lost. The body has been lost. The truth will never come out if I don't speak up."

"Don't you feel the lines of force? Something bigger than stealing Jim's body is going on. Can't you feel it? It's gathering. It's coming. I feel like we'll understand what's going on in a very short time. Let me think about this for one more day. You should talk to another lawyer—"

"All right." He ran his finger along the inside of her arm, a place that in other, more personal times he had described as "sexy with velvet." "But on the other hand, I'll do anything for you."

That afternoon at just after six, Lynda Eckhardt called Nina at home. Nina recognized the number and for a moment considered not picking up. She and Bob had given Hitch a bath and his heartworm pill and had dolloped his antiflea serum onto his neck. The three of them sat together on the couch, Hitch's head in her lap, watching a basketball game.

The Golden State Warriors were beating the Raptors 76–74 and the cool day was clouding up.

"Hi. Look, I feel terrible calling you at home. But you did give me the number."

"What's up, Lynda?"

"My blood pressure. I've been talking to creditors of Paradise all afternoon, making deals, setting pay dates. What a damn shame. I just saw Philip at the hospital."

"They let you in? I'm going after dinner."

"Not a heart attack as it turns out, but an arrhythmia. Kelly was there. She told me that they implanted a pacemaker and they're talking about releasing him tomorrow."

A sudden thought struck Nina hard. Would Philip have suffered this attack if she and Paul had come forward right away with Jim's body? She felt a rush of guilt and couldn't breathe for a minute.

As if mind reading and giving her one small hope that this was not entirely their fault, Lynda went on, "Turns out he had a minor attack a while back, but got himself to the hospital and told nobody. Has heart disease, that poor man. The debts and the sale together became too much for him. I really tried to prevent this forced sale, Nina."

"Sometimes you can't get the client what they want. You can only get them a chance to move on." Nina, breathing again, moved into the kitchen with the phone away from the television's distraction.

"I wanted to update you."

"I appreciate that."

"And one other little thing. A little favor I need to ask you."

"Er, Lynda, I'm kind of tied up at the moment."

"Doing what?"

"Visiting with my son. Petting my dog. Watching TV."

"Relaxing, eh? The noive of ya! Okay, let me be brief. You hooked up on Skype?"

"Yes."

"I've got a problem. I'm having a nervous breakdown, and I have one more big call to make. I can't manage it. It's to the lawyer for the buyers of Paradise. The Korean syndicate. She left a message for me to call her right about now. It's ten a.m., bright and early for her in Seoul."

"You want me to call *Korea*?" Nina had been pouring a tumbler of water on the nervous geranium in the window above the sink. She stopped and drank the rest of the water instead.

"Nobody else can handle this. It's simple enough. She wants a progress report. Her name is Su-dae Choi and she went to the University of Hawaii as an undergraduate. Great English, sharp gal, not all formal like you might think."

"Does it have to be right now?"

"It'll only be ten minutes. Guess so," Lynda said. "If you do this for me, I will stay sane, I promise. I will continue to be a contributing member of society. I will also be eternally grateful."

"Does she know about Philip's heart problem?"

"Well, no." Above all else, Lynda, who should really have been a gentle librarian, hated bearing bad news. "I know you can keep them from panicking."

"I see nothing to panic about. They want the sale, don't they?"

"What if, God forbid, Philip should get worse instead of better?" Lynda said. "What if he's incapacitated? The sale date might have to be extended, and you know what that means, some of their financing may evaporate. I think they're gonna panic. Like me, like I'm doing right now. I've popped enough Librium to make me sleep two days, and my eyes are still bulging outta my head. Please."

"You want me to reassure them that things are in order, that we can finish in time?"

"I'm on my knees."

"What's the number?" Lynda gave her that information. There were a lot of digits.

Nina went to the cubby in the kitchen where the big iMac was, looked through a couple of drawers and located the tiny camera, mounted that, and set to work getting the Skype software going. Then she realized the Korean lawyer would see her. She went upstairs and put on her blazer over her AC/DC shirt, put on gold earrings, and pulled her hair into a rubber band. Then she brushed her teeth and applied makeup.

A jiffy.

The game was over when she went back downstairs, and Bob was watching a *Simpsons* DVD. "Warriors," he said. "By twelve."

"Okay." She returned to the kitchen, turned the oven dial, got a pan of chicken and vegetables in to bake, drank half a cup of coffee from the morning pot, and called Su-dae Choi.

CHAPTER 26

"Aloha!" Ms. Choi said after her secretary put Nina on the line. On the screen Ms. Choi was a motherly-looking woman with a warm smile, and Nina's spine got to slump a little. Behind Ms. Choi there seemed to be another desk where another woman worked. Nina saw a watercolor on the wall. The office was not as sumptuous as she had feared.

"Aloha to you."

"How's the weather at Tahoe?" They compared notes on the weather. Ms. Choi's English was accented but fluent. "As a matter of fact I just returned from Honolulu," she told Nina. "My attorney friends are ready to retrain as surfers. Business is terrible. Too many lawyers. I told them, Korea is worse. Nobody's making any money. How about your neck of the woods?"

"About the same. You know, business for lawyers is supposed to be great in bad times, but I don't practice that kind of law."

"We're all going to be coloring ladies' hair in the

evenings at this rate. I see you are at home. Is Lynda all right?"

"I'm actually the litigating attorney in this matter." A lock of hair escaped Nina's rubber band and swung to her shoulder. "Lynda felt that I could give you more up-to-date information and asked me to make the call."

"I assume we are on track with the sale after the court hearing?"

"Very much so."

"Did it go smoothly?"

"The net proceeds will have to go into escrow."

"Yes, I checked on that with the court. Any other problems showing up? My clients call me every day. This is a big deal for them. First U.S. purchase. They own resorts in Switzerland and Austria, a big one here in Korea. We are fine at this end. The sales price will be wired to the two bank accounts on Tuesday and will be there for the Wednesday closing."

"Well, yes, something has come up." Nina watched a vigilant look flit over her colleague's face. "Mr. Strong has a medical problem. Unfortunately, he's in the hospital at the moment. He's scheduled for release on Tuesday. That's my information, and I assume he'll be able to sign the final set of papers in connection with the sale."

Ms. Choi took this in stride, and Nina gave her the details, thinking, Lynda could easily have handled this phone call, and I missed the one game I wanted to see. "I'll call our contact," Ms. Choi said then. "Marianne Strong. She has taken over in Mr. Philip Strong's absence, I suppose?"

"Not that I know of, but please don't worry. The resort will be managed properly for the next few days. It is possible Mr. Strong's daughter, Kelly, might oversee it if Marianne does not."

Ms. Choi visibly recoiled. "She was in a mental hospital."

"Not for some time. She has had problems, yes, but she has studied law and worked at the resort off and on for her whole life." No need to mention her experience towing cars and running snowplows.

"But—" Ms. Choi frowned. "This makes no sense. Marianne is the new manager. Why didn't Mr. Strong bring her in? She is taking over the general management responsibilities as soon as the sale is complete. Hasn't she informed you of that? Her half brother also has a management agreement."

"I just learned that," Nina said. "Mr. Strong wasn't consulted."

"He wasn't consulted? He doesn't approve?"

"Let's back up a little. I'm curious as to how Marianne Strong was hired to run Paradise after the sale."

"You don't know? That is so odd, forgive me." Ms. Choi frowned, eyes downcast, thinking. "Well, she is a minority owner of Paradise of course. She and her half brother"—Ms. Choi looked down at some paperwork—"Gene Malavoy first approached us about this potential sale almost three years ago. My clients' company was expanding rapidly at that time. We had interest. I'm not certain what happened, but someone dropped the ball in the negotiations for the past couple of years. Apparently, Mr. Strong was trying to find new financing to keep the resort. Marianne finally persuaded him that it would be wiser to let the resort go and contacted my clients again. She said that her father-in-law was ready to negotiate, at her insistence. We were, of course, grateful."

"Let me ask you this," Nina said. "Did Marianne tie the sale to her being offered the managerial position?"

Ms. Choi hesitated. "It was not a, uh, kickback, nothing like that."

"No, there would have been no reason to offer her the job as part of the negotiations because Mr. Strong was ready to sell."

"Honestly? He seemed hostile to the idea, but she was instrumental. She caused him to change his mind. She has many years of experience as the assistant manager there, and her half brother apparently has an MBA from the University of Chicago. She pointed out to us that he has been the chief financial officer at Paradise for three years. She said they would make a solid and stable team, and we were pleased to find them available."

"Excuse me," Nina said, "I'll be right back."

She got up and went into the living room and paced. She hated to think how disappointed Ms. Choi would be to learn that Marianne was only experienced at publicity and giving ski school lessons, while Gene was a high school dropout who worked as a host in the Lodge.

What now? She had to get back into the kitchen. The Koreans would have to fly in a manager at short notice. They seemed dubious about trusting Kelly, and she was the only other possibility.

No, worse. Working backward, the sale might be delayed and therefore fail. Would that be in the best interests of her client?

The phone seemed to buzz in the background. Was there an underground cable in the Pacific? Were coelacanths listening in?

Worse, this was the sort of bad news regarding which the bearer might get sued. Nina quickly reviewed in her mind a rather arcane area of tort law. The facts were not all in. If Nina told Ms. Choi about her sleazy new managers, would she be sued by Marianne and Gene?

Hmm. Hmm. Interference with advantageous business relation. Inducement of breach of contract. Those causes of action were just the beginning if the sale fell through. Philip might feel she had committed malpractice in volunteering such negative information.

Caveat emptor. Apt Latin maxims never die. She returned to the monitor.

Ms. Choi said, "Is Mr. Strong going to be all right?"

"We hope so."

"He couldn't, ah, suffer an event before Tuesday?"

"Life is uncertain," Nina said. "I am so sorry, it has been a pleasure talking with you, but I have to go. I hope I answered your questions?"

"I think I have a few more, now." And Ms. Choi would have a pantload more if Nina kept talking to her. Nina hurriedly said how much she would love to visit Korea someday—which was true, she loved Buddhist temples—and signed off.

Back upstairs, Nina pulled the rubber band out of her hair, sat on the edge of the bed.

Should she call Lynda? That would expose Lynda to the same legal and ethical problem that had unexpectedly landed on her. Should she call Philip? Paul? Eric?

Marianne and her morose half sib were completely unscrupulous. Nina wondered now if they had somehow defeated Philip's efforts to renegotiate his loans.

Had they used more than lies and chicanery to take over Paradise? Had they followed her and Paul to Jim Strong's body? If so, why would they take it?

She tried for one more connection. Could Gene Malavoy have been Cyndi Backus's secret lover? An adventurous woman might find him an attractive nuisance.

Did Cyndi ski? Did she meet him at the resort? And if that happened, how then did Marianne feel, with her young half sib taking up with a local stripper?

Nina's mind boiled over with possibilities, some outrageous, some that seemed to have a logical basis. The oven timer went off. Hitchcock sat at her feet, imploring her with big, steady eyes for some dinner. It was finally Sunday night, and she had laundry to fold while tutoring Bob for his geometry test, then she had to get over to Boulder Hospital.

She had to tell someone in authority at Paradise about the phone call. Philip was out of commission. She called Kelly.

Kelly answered immediately. She sounded rushed. Nina ran through the conversation. "I had heard Marianne make the same claim last week. I should have called you then. I'm very sorry. I know you have problems with Marianne and Gene. For that matter, with your father."

Kelly said, "I'm dumbfounded. They don't have the right."

"We have to approach this cautiously, Kelly. Will you let me figure out how to deal with this situation? We don't want to cause the sale to fall through."

"I don't know what to say. You better talk to my father, as soon as he's able."

"I didn't even tell you how sorry I am about Philip's illness."

"Seems like just one more evil twist. Okay, thanks for letting me know."

Nina hung up. Whew!

It was called compartmentalization, and men knew the feeling well. Nina plunked it all in a bow-tied box and picked up the pot holder.

Just off Emerald Bay Road, Boulder Hospital was small, intimate, and gave good personal care. Nina arrived well after dark.

She swung into the parking lot, remembering a story she had read a few years before about a bear which had stumbled through the automatic doors. The incident was caught on the hospital's surveillance video. Pulling into an empty spot, she wondered if most people in the world had as chummy a relationship with wildlife as people up here in the mountains, next to a colossal lake where Native Americans still fished. Bears had been bashing in windows lately when the human doors wouldn't give. One had even broken through the garage door of a local residence and eaten all the frozen chicken in the spare fridge.

The small community hospital treated roughly sixty-five patients at a time. It had a fully equipped Cardiopulmonary Department. Flowers in Reception held a big card with thanks from a former patient. Everyone seemed busy but happy. The rugs were clean. It was prime visiting time, but things were starting to quiet. Nina quickly found Philip Strong's room.

She hadn't had such a great experience with hospitals herself. Once she had been shot, sustaining a minor wound, and had been taken to Boulder. Giving birth to Bob had been tough, she thought, negotiating the corridors, remembering.

Back then, it had been just another hard time, Kurt not there, she young and lost.

The door to Philip's room was open. She stepped inside. Kelly sat beside Philip's bed, reading from a book by Roddy Doyle. Philip grunted now and then.

Nina put a vase full of flowers by his bedside, which already held four other bouquets. She moved some and set hers in a space under the window.

"Hello, Kelly."

Kelly looked up from her book. "Hello, Nina."

"Hi, Philip." Nina hesitated, then came over and hugged him.

"Understand you saved my sorry ass by calling for help," he said in a hoarse voice. "Thank you."

Relieved that he was making sense, Nina said, "I'm sorry you're having such a hard time. I wish I could make it all better for you."

"Would that the universe worked that way." He smiled weakly.

Kelly wore tan khakis and a sweater. Nina sat down on the only other chair in the cubicle, an adjustable office chair.

"How are you feeling?" Nina asked.

"I give myself a big two." He looked hopefully toward Nina. "Quit fussing, Kelly. Even if they put the money in escrow for Jim, Nina will figure out what's happening there. They'll find his body. Or something. I'm confident of that."

Nina plastered a smile on her face. He must know he was putting her in an impossible position. He might be doing it out of wishful thinking. He might be doing it to pacify his troubled daughter.

"Dad, now that Nina is here, I want to talk to you about something important. You need someone to run Paradise for the next few days. Marianne and Gene want to take over. Do you want that?"

Philip sipped from a paper cup. "Them taking over?"

Nina read tension delicate as spiderwebs forming between the two of them.

"Marianne's made some kind of deal with the Korean buyers. She's got a contract to manage the resort with Gene once the corporation buys it. Right, Nina? Nina talked to their lawyer in Seoul this afternoon."

"No!" Philip said, obviously shocked. "Marianne and Gene? Impossible. Isn't it, Nina?"

"Kelly's right. Marianne will be general manager once the resort is sold," Nina said. "She can do what she wants."

Kelly said, her tone so noncommittal Nina couldn't decide if Kelly was annoyed at the thought or happy, "The Koreans seem willing to play into Gene's dreams. He always wanted to run a resort. Marianne's satisfied running the ski school. I admit she's qualified to do that. But the two of them? I don't know."

"But Gene? He's a big nothing—a host in our restaurant, for God's sake!" Philip said. "He shouldn't be running anything more challenging than a gourmet appetizer! And Marianne. Oh, my God, I always expected it. She has invaded our family and taken advantage—"

Kelly went on, "The Koreans don't know any better. Marianne and Gene could fake a résumé. They do have some real experience at the resort. But you know, I wonder, and please, Dad, don't have a fit, I wonder if it isn't for the best? Marianne loves the resort, maybe even more than you."

At that very moment, the door to the room opened, and Marianne Strong and Gene Malavoy appeared. Their timing could not have been worse.

Gene held a huge bouquet of flowers, which he tried to hand to Philip. Philip turned his head away. "Get that out of my face," he said loudly. "What are you two doing here anyway?"

Marianne, dressed in yogic black head to toe, every muscular bone outlined, said, "How are you, Philip? Dad?"

"I'm not your dad and as if you gave a damn. I'm guessing it was bad news for you, hearing I made it through."

She tilted her head. "What a thing to say."

Gene tried to find a place for the bouquet, but there was no room on the ledge, and no vase to hold the flowers. He set them down on a cart and looked around. "Not even a private room for a man like you," he said.

"'A man like me,'" Philip said in a low tone. "You people. Traitors. You make me sick. You"—he pointed at Marianne—"married my son Alex to get your mitts on the resort, didn't you? And as for you, Gene"—Philip's face filled with disgust—"I gave you a job when you had no experience whatsoever, on Marianne's say-so."

"I'm guessing he has heard about our contract with the Koreans," Marianne said to Gene. She tapped Philip's hand so briefly he didn't have the chance to recoil. "Look, we have done nothing to harm you. Nothing. We have to go on, too. We made sure we wouldn't lose our jobs when the resort is sold."

"Maybe you engineered the whole thing some-how," Philip said.

"We didn't run it into the ground. You did that. If you'd kept it profitable, we wouldn't be taking over as managers, and I wouldn't be out of pocket my life's savings. Let's not be hostile. I've known you and Kelly a long time. Now I'm protecting myself."

"What do you want, Marianne?" Philip cried. "Why come here? Jesus H. Christ! You're vultures picking on dead meat."

"Let us get to the point. Gene and I are willing to run the resort as of Wednesday, the day the sale goes through."

The veins in Philip's face, already far too red and thready, throbbed. He did not answer.

"Since you are—incapacitated at present, it seems

to us that the logical thing now is for us to take over immediately."

"I begged Alex not to marry you," Philip said. "You've insinuated yourself into our family business to the point where you think—no, you believe—you deserve to take over."

"Dad, you shouldn't dismiss her without listening to what she has to say," Kelly said.

"Whose side are you on?" Philip pulled his sheet up over his shoulders. "God, it's cold in here."

Marianne sat down, speaking in a serene voice. "I understand this causes you upheaval, and I'm sorry about that, okay? But Gene and I will do a good job. We'll honor Paradise and its past, while ushering it into a new era."

Philip struggled to sit up. "I give you not one damn thing!"

A machine beeped. Within seconds, five medical people entered the room commanding them all to leave.

In the hallway, Nina put her arm around Kelly's shoulders. "Your dad's tough. He'll be okay."

Kelly, who seemed to be thinking hard, didn't answer.

Marianne shrugged. "It's a completed arrangement. We manage the resort as of this moment."

Kelly pulled herself together. She spoke in an ice-cold voice. "You manage nothing, Marianne. Legally, I have Dad's power of attorney. At the moment, he's unable to make business decisions. Right, Nina?"

Nina nodded. "That's right."

"So that leaves me in charge. So I hereby take over Paradise Resort for as long as the Strong family owns it. I'll manage it for as long as it belongs to my family, even if that's only a matter of days."

"Ugh," Marianne said. "I have nothing against you, Kelly, but your father gambled away a lot of money. He lost your family asset, not me. I don't think you're blind to that, either. Watch out for that family-loyalty thing you have. It can rise up and bite you."

"You don't know me," Kelly said, "so don't talk to me that way. I don't know you either."

"Oh, come on, Kelly, we are old friends. Let me be. I don't mean to hurt you or Philip. Don't be like this."

"Not until I sort some stuff out," Kelly said. "Maybe then. Meantime, I'll see you at Paradise at eight. Let's keep the damn place running. It's best for all of us. That we can agree on."

CHAPTER 27

Sondra heard the sound of the truck before she spotted it several stories below. Two slick-looking guys arrived at the receptionist's desk and were escorted into Sondra's office, where they asked politely where they should put the current shipment.

Arrangements agreed upon, they began the slow process of unloading a completely brand-new set of beautiful designer furnishings, including some original oil paintings of Tahoe before the logging of the 1800s. Sondra told them exactly where to place each piece and, when she was satisfied, handed each of them a fresh $100 bill.

"Wow," they said. "Thanks. That's the biggest tip we ever got."

She didn't waste time admiring her handiwork. Instead, she got busy on the phone. "Someone I'm wondering about," she said. "How sick is the wife, exactly?"

The new chairs arrived at nine thirty Tuesday morning, three for the front office, two for Nina's office, eight for the conference table in the library.

"Thirteen new chairs?" Nina said. "I don't remember anything about that many."

"Negotiated a deal for more chairs for the same money," Sandy said.

In Sandy-speak, that meant Nina would be devoting a little time to some free legal advice for the owner of the shop.

The Russian deliverymen took out their box cutters and got to work on the boxes in the front office while Sandy continued to field phone calls.

All the chairs were the same, hypercontemporary, veneered to a high luster, with rounded arms and copper-colored upholstered seats. As the chairs were freed from their wrappings and placed around the office, the whole place seemed to sit up and straighten its collar, and even the Russians started to joke around. Nina gave them espresso to keep them going, and in an hour the makeover was complete. One more *Do svidanya*, and Nina and Sandy were alone again.

They sat in the new chairs across the room from Sandy's desk. Nina stroked a hand along the smooth wood arm. "Very nice, Sandy."

"Nice?"

"Fantastic. Really improves the look and feel of the place."

Sandy seemed to like that better.

"Listen, I need you to cancel my ten-o'clock appointment this morning."

Sandy looked at Nina's schedule. "You mean the one at JoJo's Beautiful You?"

"I can't leave. All the disasters of the weekend have to be addressed. I can get a haircut when I'm dead." Although once in a while while she was alive would be helpful. Buns didn't work anymore. Even clips had a hard time keeping her flyaway blur of long hair controlled.

"You work seven days a week," Sandy said, eyeing Nina. "Go on, you have one hour."

Her hair must really need work. With this rare permission, and in spite of everything pending, Nina went down the street to the nearest haircutter, where she took out a picture of what she wanted and showed it to the stylist/owner, JoJo.

"Like you got, only shorter?" he asked.

"Well, you know. Like what I have, only work some magic on it," Nina said. They went to the sink and he washed her hair. "It's so flat on top," she said, eyes closed, his hands massaging her soapy scalp.

"Too heavy. Too long," JoJo said, holding a handful. "Blow all over the place. Not even a style. Bet you wore it like this since you were a teenager."

"You bet right."

"You a young woman yet. This?" He fluffed a towel through her hair. "This is not right."

"What do you suggest?"

"I have ideas."

"Two inches off, blunt cut, like the picture," Nina said, meaning the picture of the beautiful model with hair not at all as unruly as her own.

"I don't tell you how to defend clients, agreed? So

you trust me." JoJo giggled, then installed her in his swivel chair and began razoring her hair in sections and giving her tips on how to avoid split ends.

Eric Brinkman walked into the beauty shop. "Sorry to interrupt. This couldn't wait."

"Sandy told you where I was?" Nina said, mortified.

"After I lobbied intensely and resorted to some low fibbing. You look like a judge with that white band around your neck and the black cape."

"You want me to stop?" JoJo asked.

"God, no." Having already invested a good twenty minutes in this venture, Nina said, "Give us a minute, okay?"

JoJo went to speak with the girl up front. Around them, haircutters clipped, absorbed in conversations with their clients.

"So, Eric," Nina said, not happy to see him, her hair half-cut, a nylon bib covering her chest, feeling about as vulnerable and abased as any other woman on earth who looked like hell in front of an attractive man.

Eric stood in front of a shelf of hair products. He still wore his sunglasses; outside, the fickle day had begun with a brilliant sun but had now degenerated into a white overcast that might mean snow showers. "I have an appointment in a few minutes, but I wanted to update you on the tip about the body."

"Is this confidential?" Even though JoJo and the

receptionist were far enough away for privacy, Nina was careful when she could be.

"All in tomorrow's *Tahoe Mirror*, but I thought you might want to know ahead of time."

"I do. Go."

"First of all, I just came back from the hospital. Philip had a good night. No complications."

"Thank God."

"I also spoke to your friend Sergeant Cheney. He says the grave was thoroughly cleaned out except for the remains of part of a blue tarpaulin found under a couple of inches of dirt. The preliminary opinion of the forensics team is that there really was a body in there up to very recently. There were tree limbs moved, and the snow condition indicates the removal might even have happened within twenty-four hours before the digging equipment was sent in."

"Did they find any evidence as to who it was?"

"Not yet, though they're just getting started."

Nina said carefully, "What about the tarp?"

"They're looking at it today, testing it for body fluids, hair, that sort of thing. Evidently they only have a strip about six inches long that was accidentally left behind, so they're not expecting much. The anonymous tip is the thing Cheney's pushing right now. It has to be someone involved in the sale who didn't want it to go through."

Nina shifted in her chair. Quite a lot of hair had already fallen over her smock, and Eric seemed to be stepping on brown, hair too. "That sounds like good reasoning," she said. In the mirror, she looked strange. Halfway through a haircut, she thought. Normal kind of strange.

"The question is, did the same party who e-mailed the tip remove the body?" Eric asked.

"Why would someone do that?"

"I don't know. It makes no sense on the surface. Maybe the forensics have been faked and there never was a body in there. I'm going to find out. Nina, don't take this wrong, but I'm thinking van Wagoner is in this up to his eyeballs."

"What? Why think that?"

"I suspect he sent the tip. Turns out, it's a false tip. I don't know what his game is, but he's not trustworthy. I think you should separate yourself from him for the duration, Nina. He's not on this case, but he acts like he is. I don't like it."

"You suspect he sent the tip. Any evidence of that?"

"I'm working on it."

Nina thought, I am not going to out and out lie about this. What do I say? "What are you going to do?"

"I'm going to tell Philip Strong about my suspicions as soon as the hospital okays it, and make sure you're instructed to keep all further developments away from Paul van Wagoner, Nina. Sorry, but you're going to be compromised otherwise. I know he's your friend."

"Why are you focusing so hard on Paul?" A

female part of her felt vibes, the way he looked at her so intently, the way he was looking at the only part of her not covered by hair or cape, her feet in their extravagant designer heels.

"He appears so certain Jim Strong is dead," Eric said reasonably, moving his eyes back to match hers. "I watch and I listen. He's said it enough and I hear it in his voice. He believes it. He knows something. Stay away from him, Nina, please."

"I have to think about what you're saying. I may need more proof than—"

"You've got no business talking to him about my case."

Nina raised a hand out from under her smock. "We'll talk more about this."

"We'll stay in touch, okay? Meanwhile, I have to go. Be careful."

The tinny bell rang as the door closed behind him.

"He's upset," JoJo said, returning. His scissors, razor, and comb flew around her scalp. "You got man trouble?"

"No. He's a colleague."

"Had that look. You know, when I was in Folsom, I saw men like that. Jealous. I ought to know," the stylist said, and went back to his cutting. "He likes you down to your little toes." JoJo wore a long-sleeved sweater, but starting at the right wrist a huge blue dragon poked its nose toward his fingers. "Hold your head straight, darling," he commanded. "I did two to five for a drug offense. It worked out for me though. I found my religion and I learned how to cut hair. Also learned to avoid jealous men."

"That's interesting. I thought they didn't allow prisoners to use scissors at state prisons."

"Very dull scissors. Terrible haircuts. Now I have the best. I'm using a really good razor on you." He set down the blow-dryer. "No more flat head. See? How do you like it?" He handed her a mirror so she could see front and back at the same time.

Nina didn't recognize herself in the mirror, once all was said and done. However, on the bright side, she liked the woman with well-controlled thick brown hair that stared back at her once she recovered from the shocking change.

"It's a really hot style right now called a shag. Vintage. Jane Fonda in *Klute*. You come back, we'll put in some streaks."

She tipped a pleased JoJo, then, walking toward the door of the salon, called Sandy.

"How'd you come out?"

"Radically altered, kind of like our office."

"He is radical. That's why I recommended him."

"Thanks for the advance warning."

"And here's that address you wanted. She's home right now. Why are you going there?"

"Paul asked me to talk to her. Said she wouldn't talk to a man, didn't trust them."

"You should be focused on Philip and his troubles, not some random murder."

"I should, Sandy. But Paul said something funny.

He said the cases are connected. Said he could swear it. We couldn't talk long enough for him to tell me exactly why." Nina remembered that night, when primal instincts took over the Paul she knew. He had killed, and he could justify it. He could probably justify this.

"Well, don't be long. You have things you should be doing."

"I won't." Nina opened the door to exit the salon, and JoJo blew her a kiss.

"Beautiful you," he said. "Tell all your friends!"

Cyndi Backus/Amore's best friend lived in the Tahoe Keys.

Nina pulled up to a two-story stucco house that could have existed in Fresno and parked. She hadn't spent a lot of time in this area in years, not since her first murder case. She stepped out, locking her RAV with a beep. Today, so close to the lake, she felt an almost balmy day sweep over her like warm water. Maybe spring had come to the lake at last.

The Tahoe Keys, a beachfront development on Tahoe's shores that had been built in the early 1960s, held standard suburban houses with docks on small, man-made keys that fed into the lake. Euphegenia Delmonica, Cyndi Backus's best friend, did not live directly on the lake. She lived on the cheaper side, across the street, a few steps away from the water.

Euphegenia did not open the door after the first ring. Nina could see herself being examined in the sidelight next to the front door. Finally, the door opened, slowly and suspiciously.

Nina introduced herself. Tall as a showgirl and as pretty, with a perfect nose, a nice rack, and a pink cashmere sweater over gray wool pants, Euphegenia wanted to look at Nina's ID. Finally, she nodded at Nina and let her inside.

Right inside the doorway, without fanfare, Nina found herself dumped into a teal and purple living room.

"Take a seat," Euphegenia said, and brought Nina a drink.

Nina accepted the glass, sitting on a chair with arms barely wider than her hips. "You're—"

"Feel free to call me Genie."

"Right," Nina said, relieved. "Mind if I ask why you didn't want to see the man who is investigating Cyndi's death for the family? Mr. van Wagoner?"

"I used to like men. Not so much anymore. I look for a day when we can collect babies from sperm banks and dispense with the man thing. Leave them the hell out of the picture. Okay, granted, bed's good, but then you've got—what?—a child to raise on your own for eighteen, maybe thirty years, and you're stuck to a jerk for life who comes and goes full of demands, giving you not a damn thing."

Nina heard a world full of pain behind the words. She wondered if Genie had a baby to take care of alone, but she heard nothing except a distant radio playing. Well, it was not her business to know who or what had hurt Genie so much. She thought of her life raising Bob, mostly alone, and remembered that Kurt was leaving. Partly to give herself a little time, she took the iPad from her bag and quickly reviewed the crime and the few details she knew for sure connected Genie with Cyndi. "I'm here to find out more about your friend Cyndi Backus."

"A man killed my best friend. I hope he dies and roasts in hell for eternity. If you need to know my kindest thoughts on the matter." Her green eyes sparked.

Okay, generally speaking, the murderer, in Nina's limited experience, would not think and certainly wouldn't blurt out such a thing. Nina took a breath and a moment to take in her surroundings.

The home appeared to have been remodeled sometime in the eighties. Beams on the ceiling, once brown, had been repainted beige. A glimpse of the kitchen from the living room revealed not contemporary granite but sparkling, aging Formica on the countertops with an electric-coil stovetop. Fragile-appearing, tall, angular windows in the living room showed no sign of replacement by more modern double panes. On the plus side, a view out those large windows revealed a partial view of the lake as blue as her brother Matt's eyes.

"Tell me how you knew Cyndi."

"How? How about how long? I knew her since we were fourteen. We met in our English class when we were in eighth grade with Mrs. Rappaport. Cyndi transferred up here from Inglewood, showed up two weeks into the first semester wearing a skirt so short it pretty much exposed her butt, along with thigh-high leather boots."

"I take it that's not the way most of your class dressed."

"Oh, hell, no. But I had never met a girl like her, so sure of herself. So sure of her sexuality. She was a revelation to me. Most of the kids shunned her, but I made friends with her right away. Her mother liked me, probably because I revered Cyndi and she saw that."

"Did she have other friends?"

"We had a couple but we were both just off-key enough to be tighter. You know how that is?"

Nina nodded, trying to think. Eighth grade was probably one of the nightmare years for her. Her mother in trouble. Matt in trouble. Her in trouble. Friends? She didn't recall any friends.

Genie went on, "Cyn used to stockpile teen maga-zines under her bed. We painted her room baby blue. We cried about every single cute boy we ever knew. We stalked a couple of guys, if you call it stalking, hanging around where they hung around." Genie's head bowed, and the tears dribbled down onto her gray wool pants.

Nina thought she had a clue. "Your parents didn't like her?"

"They didn't understand her. You know, she had a different attitude. She liked sex."

"Did you have a relationship?"

"You mean sexual?" Genie laughed. "She liked men. She might have liked women later on, too. Certainly, that's not something she would have told her husband. I can't say I approved of her secrets and lies, but I never judged her. I'm sorry my parents didn't see that, that she was so good at heart. They were so narrow-minded."

"Did her open mind about sex stop you from being her friend?"

She shook her head. "Even after she dropped out of high school and started stripping. Loads of supposed friends judged her for that, but she was so pretty and never saw anything wrong in it. And guess what? A bunch of people I know did much worse and felt much guiltier than she did and never made a dime. By the way, up here? You make much better money stripping than you make doing child care, which is about all that's available to a normal, smart woman."

Nina decided not to plumb those depths and said, "Her death hurt a lot of people."

After a few minutes of sniffling, swelling, and a downturned mouth, Genie recovered herself. "Her poor kids. She had such a huge heart. She fell in love easily. Anyone really nice to her, she trusted."

Nina pounced. "Genie, please. Tell me who she was with when she died."

Genie left the room. Nina twiddled her thumbs, wondering if that meant she should leave. She waited instead. Not long after, Genie returned, holding an armful of picture albums. "I plan to transfer these to digital format eventually," she said apologetically, plopping them in front of Nina onto a table.

They spent the next half hour flipping through prints of Cyndi and Genie together and with friends. When they were younger, they had both worn much more makeup. As the years went on, they grew more beautiful. Aside from the photos of them in malls, hanging around in living rooms, playing on the lake, they were pictured paired with half a dozen young men apiece, mooning, kissing, hugging in badly shot flashes.

"Any of these guys recent?" Nina asked, hitting the final page of the fifth album.

Genie sighed. "The last one? There's no photo. We used to talk about her ups and downs with this one on the phone, but Cyndi never sent a picture. When I asked her why, she said her latest was a privacy freak."

Interesting wording. Not her latest man. "What else did she tell you?"

Genie sipped her flat Coke. "Tall, I remember her saying. Somebody she needed to keep secret. A scar on the belly, she said. Not a tattoo, some kind of injury."

"What else?"

Genie put her glass down on the table and burped quietly, politely. "Nothing, really. I miss her. I wake up in the morning and there's a moment when

I don't remember she's gone. Then when I do, I crash. I don't think I'll ever recover from this. I can't believe people have relationships for thirty years, and then somebody dies, and they walk around and accept that loss. How do they do that? I can't stand that she's gone. How could someone take her away so casually from the people who love her? We talked for hours every day. She told me everything and I told her everything. God damn it."

Nina set her empty glass down and patted Genie on the arm, feeling like a puny substitute for a friend. She murmured things, sincere things that sounded phony.

After a while, she got up to leave, disappointed at not knowing more.

Genie, tearstained but somewhat recovered, walked her to the door. "You know that story in the papers?"

"What story?"

"The one about the guy at the ski resort."

Nina pulled the jacket on and started to button it. "Are you talking about Jim Strong?"

"Yes! That was his name. Cyndi said she knew something about him. He disappeared, and she knew why."

Nina allowed herself a moment to feel startled, then thrilled. Paul had been right! The cases were connected. "What did Cyndi know?"

"She never got the chance to tell me more."

"Maybe that's why she was killed."

"I knew you might say that. I knew it. There's a lot of money involved. The family wants to sell the resort."

"It's a lot of money, yes," Nina said. "Genie, have you been questioned by the police?"

"I'm due there tomorrow."

"Go now."

"What? Why?"

"This guy might get some idea that you know about the tie-up between the sale of a big business here in town and a double murder. You might not be safe right now. And afterward, after you talk to the police, I think you should take some time off. Visit distant relatives."

"You think I need to get out of town?" Genie tipped her head. "For real?"

"Yes."

Genie pulled on her sweater. "This is harsh. You're saying there's something wrong with the resort sale. You're saying she told me stuff I shouldn't know."

"The sooner you tell the police everything, the safer you'll be. The information will be on file and doesn't—"

"Die with me?" Genie stood up. "Okay. I'm gonna err on the side of staying alive. My best friend's dead. Let me get my purse." She followed Nina back to the police station. Nina left her in the experienced care of Sergeant Cheney.

Driving back to the office, Nina thought, Was it Gene Malavoy? Ronnie Bee? Johnny Castro? Stamp, even? All of these possibilities defied rationality. Could any one of these men have slit one woman's throat and smothered another one? What would it take? What could motivate such desperate violence?

Think it through. Examine the result, not the confusion of the acts. What resulted from the murders was that the sale of Paradise Resort would probably go through.

And then there was the escrow account.

She and Paul needed to get closer to the escrow officer. Follow the money, she thought, changing her mind and making a neat right turn toward home, wending past the green lawns and elaborate baby gardens with their fragile shoots yearning toward summer. Paul loved tracking money, and that's what they needed to do.

She pulled into the driveway on Kulow, turned off the car, and sat looking into the golden windows of her house, watching for signs of Bob or Hitchcock.

She heard barking. She was home. She'd have a quiet lunch, then make a lot of phone calls.

CHAPTER 28

Tuesday arrived.

Philip was due home from the hospital today. His home would be put on the market and he would have to move, perhaps out of the state, as part of the settlements. Nina hoped he would have enough time to recuperate before that happened.

If all went well, the purchase-money wire would be received on Wednesday and Lynda could gain access to the funds in the main sales account to pay creditors.

Also, $2.5 million, the net after debts, was being wired the next day, separately, with Tahoe Sierra Title as trustee for a new escrow and trust account.

Nina drove to Tahoe Sierra Title Company in a peculiar frame of mind. Too much was happening. She couldn't catch hold of it; all she could do was surf along the ups and downs. Successful surfing involved staying in front of the wave, and she intended to follow her instincts and do the same with this case.

On the Highway, sharing space with the biggest bank in town, the Tahoe Sierra Title building sat behind a large parking lot. She parked and got out of her RAV, wrapping her jacket around her in the wind that blew off the lake a few hundred feet away.

Inside, Nelson Hendricks came out of his office to greet her, or *shambled* might be a better word. Maybe fifty, African-American, in good shape, lined and thin-lipped, he was formal and serious as he escorted her back to his office.

The loveless place had eye-crossing horizontal blinds lowered halfway behind him as he sat down. The requisite family photo showed him with a wife and a cat, and three young girls, who Nina recalled were now adults.

Nina remembered what Philip Strong had told her, that Hendricks's wife had multiple sclerosis. The photo didn't show her ill. She was an attractive Asian woman in her forties. Hendricks looked proud to be by her side.

Hendricks's hands shook slightly. Some people are nervous, some drink, and some slug down coffee. She didn't know the source of his shakiness, but then again, she didn't know him.

"I have everything ready for you to sign," he said. "Worked all weekend. The foreign connection and the court matter have made things somewhat complex. Here we go." He laid the court order authorizing the escrow, various stipulations Nina and Mike Stamp had made, and title-company papers for the accounts in front of her. Nina went to work reading and signing. The papers made Hendricks the officer in charge of the escrow account, subject to further court order.

The whole affair feels like a funeral, she thought, signing her name for the fifth time. "Has the wire transfer been finalized yet?" she asked.

"The money's wired but the bank won't post the transfer until tomorrow."

"What's the interest rate on the trust account?"

He looked at the papers. "Small. Sad."

Close to zero, Nina noted. The minuscule amounts would be rolled back into the account. Nina regarded Hendricks thoughtfully.

He felt her gaze and moved uneasily in his chair. "Is something wrong?"

"I think something is. What about you? Do you think something's wrong?"

"Well, yeah. A lot's wrong." He ran a hand over his scalp. "My wife—she fell down the stairs at our condo last night and she may have a concussion."

"I'm so sorry. That's wrong for both of you. She probably depends on you very much."

"As soon as we finish here, I go home. I'll take care of her like I always do."

"Philip Strong mentioned that your wife has MS. Was her fall related to that?"

"Everything relates to that."

"My mother had several chronic illnesses," Nina said, surprising herself.

"MS?"

"A group of conditions, really. All bad."

"How old was she when she realized—" He asked her a number of questions about her mother, which Nina tried to answer as honestly as she felt she could without tearing up.

"I find it hard to accept that my wife is going through such terrible changes. We looked forward to retirement. We made so many plans."

"Philip Strong said she was diagnosed very recently. It's a shock at first. Later, you'll figure out what the two of you can or can't do. It becomes part of life, and you make accommodations."

"A shock that shakes up a lifetime of dreaming. The shock that changes everything. Philip shouldn't have told you."

"I saw you were upset at court that day. He only offered an explanation."

"He shouldn't have! Besides, it's nothing to be ashamed of! It's a matter of privacy!"

"Tell him to keep it private in the future, then. Philip also mentioned that you know his investigator. How long have you known Eric?"

"Brinkman? Not long."

"I've been wondering who recommended Sierra Title to handle the escrow."

Hendricks took a drink of water and mumbled something. He appeared hugely stressed, and it might well all be connected to his wife, but Nina felt a duty to press him now, find out if he was part of the skein that had to be unraveled before she and Philip could move on with their own lives.

"We've done business here in South Lake Tahoe for two decades. Michael Stamp's firm has used us for years. They mentioned us. And Eric mentioned us to Phil Strong also. I already knew Phil, of course. We're old-timers, used to play golf together years ago. I'm happy to say that Sierra Title has a good reputation and we handle escrows for many large business transactions in town."

"Did you ask Eric to recommend you to Mr. Strong?"

Hendricks pushed his chair away. "How's that your business? What's going on here? I thought you came here to get the paperwork signed. Now you have this accusatory tone, as if I've done something wrong."

"How badly did you want this deal, Mr. Hendricks?"

His nose seemed to be running now. He ran a handkerchief along it. "What are you suggesting? In twenty years, I have never been accused of a crime. Our firm has an impeccable reputation. Yet, you come in here, suspicious with no reason at all. I mean, who are you, anyway? Another little lady lawyer scraping out a meager existence up here, defending drug dealers, petty thieves, and wife beaters. I confess, I'm totally at a loss as to how to deal with you."

"Don't deal with me. Just tell the truth. You know more than you want to say about all this."

"Perhaps you're overinvested emotionally in this case. I know about your relationship with the Strongs and about your husband, and actually I have been a bit worried about your ability to withstand the stress. I've done nothing improper. I've done nothing I'm ashamed of. You're out of line, coming in here with catty insinuations based on nothing."

She recognized the strategy: attack, never defend. Her father, Harlan, always recommended that course. She leaned forward and said slowly and deliberately, "Something is very wrong with this deal, Mr. Hendricks, and I would think you'd be alarmed."

"Oh, I'm alarmed, but not about the deal. I'm alarmed about you." He stood up and opened the door, saying nothing, with the expression of one much put-upon. His hand went into his pants pocket, then came out as he adjusted his pose. She didn't shake it.

Sandy said, "You have visitors. They don't have appointments." Eyes firmly fixed on the computer, she wore a visage as stony as Mt. Tallac.

The new chairs offered excellent support for the superbly toned rear ends of Marianne Strong and Gene Malavoy.

Malavoy jumped up and rushed toward Nina. Sandy put her fingers on the phone and said, "Breathe on her, I punch 911."

He pulled back his arm.

Marianne burst into tears. "You ruined my life!" she sobbed.

Nina said, "Sandy, my office," then walked swiftly into it, taking off her coat as she went, Sandy following.

Sandy closed the door and fingered her belt buckle. "You want me to get rid of them for you? They're outta control."

"Get the recorder out and turn it on and hide it. Then come in and stay here with me," Nina said, "and if he makes a move, make the call. Now bring them in." The door swung open. Marianne entered, followed by Gene.

"Sit down and control yourself," Nina said.

"*Ta gueule*!" Marianne cried. "You've destroyed us! I'll sue you! You've got Kelly in your pocket, and you've scared the Koreans."

"Sue me for what?"

"Gene and I—we know how to run Paradise. We're completely prepared. We've worked for this for so long, and here you come, tangling everything up!"

"Sit down," Nina said calmly, "or get out."

Marianne sat down, and after a moment, Malavoy did, too. "You called Korea. You lied about me and Gene."

"You're quick with a brick for somebody who lives in a glass house," Nina said. "And you're misinformed. I asked a few questions when I realized you had set up a side deal without informing Philip.

Then I had one of my investigators look at you and Gene a little harder. You don't have the qualifications you claimed."

Malavoy clenched his fist. Paul had told her he was only twenty-five years old. That meant he had come to Tahoe at twenty-two.

"Where's the proof of an MBA from the University of Chicago, for starters, Gene?" Nina knew how hard it was to get into that university. She had been accepted but hadn't had the money to attend.

"He's smart and he's quick," Marianne said. "He's as good as anyone."

"Someone with a real MBA from that school deserves it. Gene doesn't and has no business claiming it. He claimed a credential that takes unusual intelligence, a king's ransom, or a scholarship based on extraordinary ability and abnormal dedication to attain. And how about this assertion that Gene was chief financial officer at Paradise? He never was. Two minutes' research would expose that lie. The Koreans made a mistake not investigating our boy here."

"You know what you've done? You've demolished our lives," Gene said. "You've destroyed Paradise. Marianne and I would do a fantastic job there. We love the resort. It's our lifelong dream to run it."

"But you and Marianne had to destroy the Strongs first," Nina said. "I don't take kindly to that. I believe Marianne married Jim Strong's brother, Alex, to become involved with the family business and get a green card."

"I did not! And I didn't kill Alex! Ask anyone! Jim killed him! I wasn't there on that mountain. I had nothing, not one thing, to do with my husband's death," Marianne said. "I admit I wished him dead, okay? That's my confession. That's it. But Jim killed him, not me."

"The buyers will know by now that you two lied about who you were," Nina went on. She laid her hands on her desk, palms down, and looked, really looked, at them. Marianne was falling apart, her mascara in a pair of streamlets arcing down her cheeks. Malavoy looked more scared than enraged.

Nina looked at Sandy, who held her cell phone at the ready.

"We beg you. Call Korea. Tell them it's all right," Marianne said. "You may not see it right at this moment, but I swear it's for the best. The resort could thrive under our administration, grow almost as big as Heavenly. We are ambitious, and we know what we're doing. You think someone from Korea or somewhere else with a big degree will do better? No. Because we love the place. We have a decent contract with Korea. Because of you, they may back out. If you tell them we can do the work, we can do it! Do you have any idea how hard we have worked to be ready for this?"

"Oh, I don't know if Gene has been working all that hard," Nina said. "You had plenty of time for your girlfriend, didn't you?"

"Eh?" Malavoy said.

"You were Cyndi Amore's boyfriend, weren't you?"

"Who?" Malavoy said. "I don't know—"

"What are you talking about?" Marianne looked furious. "Here you go again, saying creepy things. Gene has no girlfriend."

"Gene here matches the description of the killer of a young woman who was afraid of him. The investigator has advised me that she told her friend her lover was pulling a scam involving the Paradise sale."

"What? What woman?" Malavoy said. Whether he was really innocent and wounded was impossible to tell.

"We'll see what you know and what you don't," Nina said.

"You think Gene killed someone? Are you crazy?" Marianne cried. "You're an idiot. What gall!"

"And so the pot calls the kettle black," Sandy said.

They all turned toward her stolid self, propped in Nina's doorway, arms crossed, phone in hand.

"Go on. Call the police," Marianne said. "Do it. I have nothing to fear."

"Okay." Sandy walked calmly toward the outer office. Five minutes later, she returned. "On their way."

Marianne got up, pushing back the new chair so hard it fell against the wall.

The left side of Sandy's lip curled up into a snarl.

Marianne recoiled from her expression. "We're

going. You're not thinking right. You're making a big mistake accusing Gene." She and Malavoy left.

Nina put her bare feet up on her desk, wishing she kept a bottle in her bottom drawer like a Raymond Chandler character.

Sandy frowned. "We should fill out a report. She damaged our property."

"She did?"

Sandy pulled the chair back into place, fingering a minor scratch on the back. Nina went over with a tissue to rub it. The scratch disappeared. "Did you really punch 911?"

"I should have."

Nina met Paul after work at the HQ Center Bar at the MontBleu Casino, which had taken over Paul's old favorite, Caesars Tahoe.

"Ordered the house white for you," Paul said, cocking his head and staring at her as if she had grown wings or fangs or something.

She tapped her frosty glass against his beer mug. "Cheers." She took a drink. "Ahh."

He continued his scrutiny until she felt so uncomfortable, she found herself fidgeting under his gaze. "What?"

"You look—"

She remembered her new hairdo. "I know. It's my hair. This guy? He's cutting away and I'm distracted and—"

"So young. You look beautiful."

For a second she couldn't speak. "Thanks, Paul. Really." She smiled at him, and he smiled back. His words and smile felt like water flowing into the desert.

They looked around.

"Hasn't changed that much since it was Caesars," Nina said.

"Too much blue light. I'm drowning. Not for me."

"You don't like change much, do you, Paul?"

"I liked those old plaster busts of Caesar everywhere. I liked the hookup with Roman depravity. At heart, I'm a traditionalist."

"Funny tag for a man who has had two wives."

"Hey, you've had two husbands. That's normal these days."

"Is that the new tradition? If it is, that's sad, isn't it?" For a few quiet moments they watched sports on the big-screen televisions that dominated the area above the bartender and listened to the innocuous background music.

"That guy over there." Paul indicated a direction with his mug. "Lost at the tables today."

Nina looked over at a sad sack drooping over a whiskey with a beer chaser. "Paul, how did you know the two cases might be connected?"

"It's a small town. Maybe I should have considered it before. I called Johnny Castro again. He said Cyndi found a new interest in skiing about the same time she brought home the new underwear. And she only skied by herself at Paradise."

"Wow. You were just guessing when you sent me to Genie. But now we know. Cyndi was killed because she knew his plans. She was killed to stop the leak."

"Not entirely," Paul said. "Remember Brenda Bee. And why did Genie escape the killer's attention?"

They both were momentarily distracted as the dejected-looking man finished off his drink, piled an undue number of bills on the table, and staggered for the door, reaching into his pocket for more cash. This night would not end well for him.

"Men don't understand how deep female friendships go," Nina said. "If she ever mentioned her friend Genie, the killer zoned out and got bored. He wasn't clued in on how women tell each other everything."

"But Cyndi didn't tell Genie who he was."

"He must have been very persuasive on that point."

"You tell Andrea everything?" Paul tapped his finger on the sleek wooden table. "Because I wouldn't like Andrea to know about me and you, and how it all went down. And I do mean all."

"Hush, you." Nina felt a blush creeping up her neck.

"Or, hey, you and Kurt. You and Collier. You talk about all your men."

She punched his arm. "You make me sound like such a slut, and a person who doesn't give a damn about other people's privacy. I spend all my time protecting people's privacy."

"I'm not suggesting any such thing, just wondering how big that luscious mouth of yours really is when it comes to your own life."

"I don't tell Andrea everything."

"Most things?"

"Probably more than I should."

Paul let air out from between his teeth. "Cyndi, Cyndi, Cyndi. She's key to this. Our killer was sleeping with her. It wasn't the mechanic. I don't think Jesse is the one, in spite of Cyndi's husband being convinced of it. Once we know who her lover was, we have our murderer. It's one asshole causing all this."

"I agree. I'm looking around at men involved in this case. Michael Stamp. Married, but let's face it, that's no guarantee of much. I have always seen him as honorable. Next, we have the escrow guy, Nelson Hendricks."

Paul said, "I checked into him. Never did a thing wrong, never strayed off the straight and narrow. Not so far, anyway. He's even friendly with Fred Cheney. They're both officers in the local chapter of the NAACP. Hendricks got the account through Eric's influence or maybe through Michael Stamp's. On the other hand, sick wife. Who knows what's up with that?"

"And then there's Gene Malavoy," Nina finished. "He and Marianne lied left and right to the Koreans. I confronted him flat-out today at my office and accused him of being Cyndi's lover. But he covered himself. His denial doesn't convince me, but he didn't give me anything new either."

"You accused him of being a killer?"

"More or less."

"Interesting technique. I don't use it enough. Look him in the eye and say, 'You did it,' and see what the guy does. See if he develops a telltale wet spot on his fly."

"Gene's fly stayed dry."

"So. You were observing carefully, eh? Well, here's my report for today. Get ready. This rates what the Brits used to call Certificate X. I went by the resort earlier today for a quick visit with Marianne. She wasn't at the ski school. I was invited to check her room. When she didn't answer my knock, I tried the door. It opened."

Nina shook her head. "You are so bad."

"Stepped into the semidark and found a body."

"What? Paul! Oh, no!"

"Not a dead body, Nina. An all too lively body. I stepped inside and what should I see but Marianne's white butt on the bed, wiggling in the refreshing mountain air."

Nina felt a smile creeping around her lips. "As always discreet, you apologized and left immediately."

"I waited like a gentleman for her to notice and change position. She's an agile one. So. Guess who she was with?"

"Please. I beg you not to tell me it was her half

brother, Gene. I hate that stuff. I avoid it at the movies."

He nodded. "It was Gene. But here's happy news, my secretly conservative but admirable soul. Gene's not Marianne's half brother. He's her lover."

"No."

Paul nodded. "Has been all along. Even when she was married to Philip's son Alex. Marianne imported Gene from France. She loves him. He loves her. They make loving fun."

"Are you sure?"

"Sure as shootin'."

Nina made a fist. "What a pair. All along, they've been conspiring to take over the resort together. Paul, it's hard to imagine any family so betrayed as the Strongs."

"Could be Gene. Cheating on his fake sis. Lies upon lies upon lies. But c'mon, let's get down to the obvious. I think it's Brinkman. He propped up the Brazilian bit. He got involved with the resort years ago, before Jim even disappeared."

"Forget that. Eric and I spoke yesterday morning. He suspects you, Paul."

"Of what?"

"Of everything." She recounted their conversation from the salon.

"Look, honey. He's got his eye on you and would love to take me out of the picture, that's obvious. The part that's less obvious is that by attacking me, he distracts you from looking hard at him."

Paul kept his cool, but Nina could hear the controlled anger in his terseness. She checked her watch. "I'm sorry to ditch so soon, but I have to go get Bob. He's visiting with Kurt."

"Kurt's still in town?"

"For another week or so. He's winding up."

"How are you with that?"

"Okay. Scared. Sad. I'll spill the gory details to Andrea, where I can freely indulge my fury without criticism. Don't get any madder, but Eric said he is taking his suspicions of you to Philip and asking him to forbid me from sharing any more information. He wants me not to talk to you until I'm discharged as Philip's attorney."

Paul didn't blow up as Nina had half expected. He was either controlling his temper better or hiding it better. He shook his head. "I'm glad you brought up Philip again. To continue an earlier, ongoing rant, his troubles are my fault. I need to tell him the truth."

She drank the rest of her wine and pulled her bag onto her shoulder. "How's it fruitful, thinking that way?"

"I've caused too much harm and continue to cause it. I don't like Philip losing the resort. I don't like his conniving relatives. But most of all, I don't like the heart problem. The stress of not knowing what happened to his son must be killing him."

"And you plan to resolve that how?"

"I plan to tell him what happened to Jim. Can't wait any longer on this. Then the cops."

"He just got discharged from the hospital. Tonight's not the right time."

"Okay, but this has to stop soon. I have an idea. Call Kurt and ask him to keep Bob for the evening."

"Why?"

"Because," Paul said, "it's Brinkman. He knows Hendricks. He wants that money and he's figured out some way to get it through that escrow office. I'm going to confront him. You in?"

"Don't go. I think you're wrong. It's not Eric and this is not your case. I've been warned off speaking with you about it."

"If we can stop a major crime and help Philip, to be thinking ahead about saving my own ass, but that's the way of my people, it may help when I fess up to Philip and the police. I'm going to Eric's place at Incline. Will you come?"

"Oh, for Pete's sake," Nina said. "Maybe I can keep you from making a huge mistake."

CHAPTER 29

"He seems to like risks. I wonder if he was planning to blackmail me," Paul said.

"Where are you?" Nina asked.

"Moving through Zephyr Cove. You?"

"I don't see you, but close enough. We probably shouldn't be talking on the phone."

"Focus, Nina. I think we need to have this conversation."

Nina and Paul were in separate cars, talking on their hands-free phones, driving up toward Eric Brinkman's place in Incline Village, located about forty minutes north of South Lake Tahoe.

"Why do you believe Eric followed you in the first place?" Nina asked. Beyond the tree line the moon followed her. She was beginning to tire but she wasn't going to say anything about that.

"Now there's an interesting subject. I think he's a rich guy who likes to play PI."

"He does it for fun?"

"My profession is fun, in a postapocalyptic sort of way. He got himself a license and he got himself some jobs around Tahoe, and one of them was to see who was pilfering from Paradise two years ago. Maybe he knew where Jim was in the days after he disappeared and was following him. Maybe he followed me that night from your house the night I took Jim out. Maybe he followed me when I buried the body. Then he would know where the grave was. Then he heard about the pending sale and realized he might be able to separate out some of that money and pounce on it, like a hungry lioness separating out a tasty emu."

"But the money will be in a bank," Nina said. "He might be able to separate it out, but how could he get at it? Ah. How about by offering Nelson Hendricks a share?"

"That's how the scam works," Paul said. "Hendricks has to be involved."

"The escrowed money gets wired somewhere else the minute it gets into his hands," Nina said. "Paul, that's tomorrow morning! Wednesday. The wire's due in first thing!"

"I'm realizing there's gonna be an embezzlement that'll stand as one of the big ones. Except for one thing. We're gonna prevent it. And it's Brinkman, like I keep saying. He forged the paperwork from Brazil. He dug up Jim's body when there was a danger someone might figure out Jim was definitely dead."

Nina wasn't convinced but had nothing else to offer as a substitute theory. "How about this? Philip said he called Eric to tell him about the grave being found, and about the tip. Eric could have gone straight there, if Philip passed on the GPS numbers, and taken the body right before the police arrived."

"Good point," Paul said. "It would take a couple of hours, but sure he could. Cyndi—maybe his girlfriend? He fits. He sure does. And Brenda saw him that day. He was worried she might identify him."

"You have nothing on Eric, really, though I agree we may have the bones of a conspiracy worked out, and I think Hendricks has to be one of the coconspirators."

"There's something off about this guy. He's dirty. I feel it. He's got secrets."

Nina zipped left toward Incline Village at Spooner Pass. The last of winter hung in the air in front of her headlights like tiny clouds, dissipating in the oncoming traffic, insubstantial.

"Actually, Hendricks doesn't even need to be here for the escrow. This kind of transaction's all done with smoke and mirrors. Maybe he's packing up, leaving town as we speak. Your phone is smarter than mine. Why don't you google Hendricks?"

"I'm truly amazed and agog and horrified I can google while driving late at night at sixty-two hundred feet above sea level through a deep forest split between California and Nevada," Nina said. She pulled over and played with her iPhone, punching and pillaging the Net. A few minutes later, she drew back out into traffic and called Paul. "Nelson Hendricks is a member of the Elks. And the Chamber of Commerce. The Methodist Church. The NAACP Big Brothers. Not a complaint to Better Business in decades of business. Not a hint that he's anything but straight."

Paul was silent for several moments. "I'm calling Wish on this. I'll call you back."

Silence. Nina listened to the radio. Then her phone sang its jarringly inappropriate song. She answered. Paul came on the line. "Wish is such a dog! Sandy should be proud. He's far more intelligent than he appears at first glance."

"What did he find out?"

"Listen, Nelson Hendricks's wife doesn't have MS. She has a blood disease. Something to do with anemia. It's not always fatal but usually is within a year or two. There's a new treatment but Hendricks's insurance company refuses to pay for it. They claim it's experimental."

"Wish got into an insurance company's private files?"

"I won't reveal his methods. When the insurance company denied Hendricks's request, he appealed and lost. I'm sure he's got a nest egg, but you know how expensive medical care is. Desperate times require desperate measures. Nelson and Rayanne Hendricks have been together for twenty-five years, since he was twenty-four and she was twenty. They have three kids getting started in the world, one in college, so no financial help there. They celebrated their anniversary and announced his upcoming retirement two months ago at a private party at the Edgewood Inn with fifty close friends. The *Tahoe Mirror* gave them a quarter page, they're that well-known and loved."

"And this pillar, this good man, Nelson Hendricks, made a deal with Eric Brinkman to steal the sales proceeds? For money for his wife?"

"Has to have. He's not the type to embezzle for anything less than saving his wife's life. Hendricks might get away with claiming he had nothing to do with it," Paul went on. "Brinkman would never be identified as the recipient of the funds. Neither of them could ever do this more than once on their home grounds."

"It all sounds sort of razor-sharp and extremely bold. Based on what you've said, though, I'd say the chances of Eric Brinkman succeeding in siphoning off the escrow funds are slim, Paul. I think he'd be caught."

"Maybe he wants to be caught."

"Maybe he thinks he's invulnerable," Nina countered.

"Yeah, that's him. What time is it?"

"After six. Never have an honest man for an accomplice," Nina said. "Nelson Hendricks is ripe to rat Eric out. He might be desperate, but he's not a born criminal."

"I've done things for you, honey. I can relate."

"I said an honest man," Nina teased, but her heart had gotten heavy. "Sorry. It's nothing to joke about."

"I'll ignore that gallows humor as being all too appropriate at the moment."

She turned up the hill toward Diamond Peak. Ahead of her a fast car came in the opposite direction. She pulled down the sunshade.

"Believe it or not, I believe I just passed Brinkman's Porsche Cayenne," Nina said with a calm she hadn't known she could possess. "I don't think he saw me."

"Which means he's not home. Excellent."

"Which means our plans are foiled. We can't confront him."

Paul said, "Park down the street, not on his property."

Nina pulled her RAV up a block from Eric's house. In the distance, she spotted Paul's Mustang.

Hidden behind a gate and a fence, a curved, short concrete-paver driveway led to Brinkman's low-profile mansion.

Paul met her near the gate, which was not locked.

"Let's explore the perimeter," Paul said.

She hesitated. He removed various items from a small pack on his back.

"What if his alarm system goes off?"

"We run," Paul said.

They walked up to the house like bold solicitors. No bells rang. No dogs barked. The surrounding forest was silent. A single light shone from the nearest neighbor's house across a sea of soft mule-ears. They listened to the breeze.

Paul said, "I'm now going to make the garage door go up." The door inside the gate rose, unresisting.

"How did you learn— Amazing! How could Eric not be guarding against it?"

"Here's the way things work now, honey. A controller controls things. Another controller actually bosses the first controller. Then there's the übercontroller, the big man, the higher power, whatever. That's what I'm using, the one that can override his security systems. It reads what he's doing and then jams or starts allowing electronic emissions in those frequencies. It's not going to work long. Pretty soon the private security firms will figure out how to block this fellow with an über-überfellow."

"Then you'll find an über-über-überfellow."

"Yep."

"Men exhaust me," Nina said.

He pulled a flashlight from his pack. They went directly into the garage. Beside them Nina could see a shadowy automobile. Paul shone the flashlight on a white convertible, which was empty, and on a large motorcycle, then looked at his handheld screen. "The back door of this garage connects to the rest of the house. Okay?"

His hand grasped the knob, which opened easily.

"Not locked," Nina marveled. "I lock every window."

They slipped out of the garage and up wooden stairs to an interior landing with a small mat at the door. Paul tried the handle, and it opened. "This is a bad idea," Nina said.

"Guy doesn't lock his interior doors."

"He didn't expect you to be able to open the garage. Agh, I don't like this."

"Shh." Paul yanked her into the house through the open door and turned on a light. "We're in."

A large, dim room lay ahead of them, curtains closed, blinds drawn.

"Motion detectors," Paul muttered, holding her arm, nodding toward a blinking light. He went to work again. While he fiddled with technology, Nina looked around.

"All clear," Paul announced.

"What if he's an innocent man?"

"No such thing. However, if he's not involved in the Strong scam, we leave and no harm done." They walked into Brinkman's living room.

A pebble-textured, black leather couch faced a large flat-screen TV next to the hearth. The room seemed impersonal to Nina. A few professional journals lay on the floor beside the couch. There were no rugs. A carved Balinese daybed, piled high with cotton pillows, ran along the length of the window that faced toward Lake Tahoe.

She inspected the view. A long geologic decline swept all the way down the mountain to the lakeside, miles away. The distant view was unobscured. You could see the mountains ringing the southern side of the lake twenty-six miles away. Redwood decking, cantilevered from the house, behind double doors in the living room, seemed to drift toward the lake.

She examined the items on the coffee table carefully while Paul made his own quick exploration.

What she saw first, on a side table, was an over-size, kitschy, white porcelain dog sitting on an ornate stand. Nina picked it up carefully, turned it over. "Jeff Koons," she said, recognizing the style now. "Brinkman spends money on art. He likes contemporary art." She replaced it gingerly.

"Is that what this is?" Paul called, and Nina turned toward his finger, pointing at a large aquarium near the hall door.

They walked over together, and Nina's disbelief grew: it was a fish, and that fish was not alive, but hanging from wires inside a solution she realized must be formaldehyde. "I know this kind of art," she said.

"This is art?"

"Well, it could be a biological specimen. Maybe he collects them. But I think this is an installation by Damien Hirst. His works bring the highest prices of any artist in the world. He's one of the most famous, too."

"It's got to be four feet long."

"The original was a fourteen-foot shark. It sold for millions."

"So, he has expensive taste." Paul continued to

stare at the fish. "I wonder if he caught it and pickled it himself. Where'd he get the money for this house and art?"

A large, bare room on the right, tableless and carpetless, had been turned into a gym. A ROM exercise machine had been set up in the center of the room.

"I've been wanting one of those for years. Keeps you hard working out just four minutes a day, if you believe the ads. He's dirty," Paul muttered. "I know it like I know my name. Come on. Here's the kitchen, and then let's find the office and his bedroom."

All the small appliances were European stainless steel. Every surface sparkled. "He had a decorator put the interiors together, I think," Nina said. "There's not much personal aside from the art. He's a clean freak. A little compulsive." She opened a drawer. Rows of utensils, sorted and matching. "Bet he's a Virgo."

"We haven't seen everything yet."

Since there was no dining table, the bar stools at the counter constituted the dining room. Nina went around the tall marble counter and on impulse opened the refrigerator door. She saw cans of Red Dog, a vitamin-caffeine drink, bottles of vitamin water, a box of Rice Krispies, a carton of soy milk, fish oil, and some dark juice in a pitcher. She saw prescription pills in their container and took a look—Provigil. What was that? She had been reading about it.

Right, a recreational drug. A *neuro-enhancer*, that

was the word. College kids took it without being prescribed it because it was supposed to make you feel more alert, more able to concentrate, maybe a little smarter.

She put the pills back and checked out the freezer, saying, "One sec," to Paul. A Dutch gin called Damrak, frosty on the top rack; frozen steaks below. A container of coffee ice cream. On the way out she glanced into the pantry; endless supplies of paper products and Duraflame fire logs and cases of water and juice, probably from Costco, the bulk-buy store in Carson City.

She had come to two conclusions: these cold cabinets did not hold Jim Strong's body, or any sign of it.

Also, she was finally getting to know Brinkman. He was self-disciplined; that was evident. He had an orderly mind and had sophisticated tastes. He needed to be in control.

Maybe it was nothing but a gut feeling, but she felt it strongly: Cyndi Amore was not his type. The whole situation would be too messy for him.

She didn't really want to go any further. If she and Paul turned back now, maybe she could talk their way out of a criminal trespass charge. The house was just the home of a wealthy, austere bachelor, exactly what Eric Brinkman seemed to be in spite of Paul's suspicions.

Paul beckoned at her from the door of the next room down the carpeted hall.

They went into Eric's office, another large room

with a long table facing the door serving as a desk. One wall of shelves made a library. There was a wood filing cabinet and another fireplace.

The bookshelves held paper and other supplies. Nina cast her eye upon the carefully shelved and sorted books—heavy art and medical books on the bottom shelves, books on languages, science fiction, manga, a collection of modern classics. Nina's eyes returned to the medical books, big professional texts. Paul worked the laptop, an ultrathin computer, trying to access the local airport. He looked up. "Can't get in. If Wish were here, he'd kick this shield to shit." Paul cursed again, picking up a file lying on the table. "Whoo. My name," he said briefly, and flipped through the paperwork.

As he read, Nina watched his face tighten. The cheekbones stood out and his lips wrinkled as his whole face seemed to become a bastion.

"He investigated me," Paul said, reading along, "looked for dirt. Has bank records and a credit report. Copy of my app for a PI license renewal last year. Notes on my connection to the Strong case. Notes on my connection to you."

"And this bulletin board."

"Obsessed with the Strong case," Paul said. They took in the board covered with newspaper articles, photographs, and notebook speculations.

"Why would he—is it possible he's intending to blackmail you regarding Jim? Did he know something?"

Paul examined the articles on the wall and began reading some posted notebook pages, obviously printouts from a computer, and only selections of longer ruminations. "He suspected me, for sure. It feels odd to be the prey, not the hunter." Paul looked genuinely shaken.

Nina indicated the electronic lock on the file cabinet. Paul disabled that quickly and they looked at each other.

"Ladies first," Paul said.

She saw her own name right away, toward the back in alphabetical order. She pulled out the file and saw herself as others saw her: medical records, credit scores, bank statements, what she had bought on her last trip to Reno at the Macy's store. As Paul had said, she felt endangered, as if a snake were coiling around her.

What had Eric intended to do with this information?

"Here's a file on Damien Hirst."

Paul said, "Give me Michelangelo. Nobody's been as good since." He continued to rummage.

"Paul? Maybe you don't realize this, but I don't want to get caught. Hurry."

Paul read through a longer notebook entry posted on the bulletin board.

"I can't. I have a child," Nina continued. "A son. Bob. Good kid. Needs his mother. Let's go. Right now."

"Nothing here to implicate Brinkman. But he's

as crooked as my grandma's nose." Paul scanned through every note on the board, flipped through every accessible paper. "Nothing. Nothing. Damn!"

"We need to go! Now!"

Paul straightened up. "He'll have a vault or safe or something. We need to check the bedroom, turn anything over that turns over." Nina, stuttering and unhappy, followed him into the hall and moved into Eric's bedroom. A fur throw lay neatly over a big bed, perfectly centered. No old socks littered the floor. Eric was preternaturally tidy. Nina checked behind the mirror. Paul ran his hand under the mattress. They moved stealthily like the couple of trespassing fools they were.

Nina opened Brinkman's underwear drawer where all the real secrets usually hid, but all she found were neat stacks of socks and folded white silk boxers.

In the master bath, which contained a separate shower that would fit two and a jetted tub, she leaned against the towel rack. "Ow." The rack was hot, a chrome rack beside the tub with no towels on it. For some reason, Nina turned the knob controlling the heat. As she did so, the long mirror above the marble counter that ran along one wall noiselessly slipped away, practically giving her a heart attack, revealing a small storage area about four feet high and the same in width.

"Paul, you need to see this! You aren't completely nuts. He is—" As she spoke these words, she stepped forward one step closer to the storage area, staring, and reached into it to take something. "Oh! Oh! Oh!"

An alarm must have cast its invisible light right across her path because the light flickered, and in the distance, somewhere in the house, she heard a magnified donkey blare, the amplified song of a humpback, an alarm that would definitely notify the police.

"We're out of here," Paul said.

Nina had the presence of mind to turn the knob on the towel warmer. The display case shut behind her. Running, Nina said, "I thought you disabled all the alarms!"

"Two systems. Oops."

They made it as far as the front of the house, then Paul put out a hand to stop her. "We're caught, honey. Nowhere to go from here." He touched her forehead. "Settle down, okay?" She struggled to contain her panting breaths. The alarm cried and cried in hysterical bursts.

Eric's Porsche Cayenne swooped up the driveway, catching them in its headlights.

CHAPTER 30

The Cayenne idled for a while, as if studying them. Finally, the lights dimmed and went out. Eric got out. "Hey, Paul, Nina." He tipped his head and spoke in a loud voice over the screaming beast. "Any reason we need the police here?"

Paul spoke before Nina could think of anything to say. "We tried the front door. Guess your alarm system responds to jiggles. Sorry. Nina warned me not to do it."

Eric took his phone out of his pocket and spoke into it, then went around to his trunk, punched a button, and watched the lid rise. Before he could reach into the trunk, Paul moved forward to see what Eric might be bringing out, but the only thing inside was a Raley's brown paper bag.

Eric carried his groceries up to the front door. He set them down on a bench by the door and used his keys to unlock it. The alarm inside continued to racket, and now the phone was ringing, too. "Why don't you two come on in?" Eric said, picking up a phone by the kitchen. He pushed buttons on a key-pad and the alarm stopped.

"Two separate alarm systems and companies," Paul whispered, following him inside the door, but stopping short of the kitchen. "Told you he's got something to hide."

"Paul, listen," Nina said, "you're right about that, but you're wrong about what he's hiding." She fought a sudden need to burst out laughing. "I—"

"The alarm companies know which room was triggered," Eric said, coming into the living room, eyes hard on Paul. "Systems are sophisticated these days. Strange you got as far as you did."

"No system is perfect. Malfunction all the time," Paul said.

"You want to explain to me why the hell you two broke into my home?"

"You have some interesting art," Nina said.

Now his eyes turned on her. She could see he wondered exactly how much she had seen of his collections.

"Is that a real Damien Hirst?" she asked.

"My parents collected modern art, and I've fol-lowed in their footsteps."

"Your home is stunning." She knew that was an idiotic remark the moment she made it.

"I'd be complimented if I had invited you into it," Brinkman said, cutting Nina short.

Paul did what he always seemed to do when

Brinkman was around, blew up like a puffer fish. "You're right. We came here to tell you we've got you figured out."

A half smile floated at the edge of Eric's angry lips. "How do you mean?"

"You're a man with secrets."

"Like all men."

"We know exactly what you've been up to."

A certain hesitation showed a decided unhappiness with how this scene was progressing. "What, exactly?" Eric asked, but Nina could see his nervousness.

"Nelson Hendricks."

At this point, something about Paul's tone must have signaled Eric. The half smile playing at the edge of his lips grew slightly larger. "The escrow officer for the Jim Strong case?"

"As if you didn't know."

"I don't know the man well. I only know the Strongs vouched for him and seem to trust him. My own research shows he's been in business a long time and there are no shadows on his record."

"Don't bullshit me," Paul said. "You two have cooked up a scheme to take that two point five million bucks tomorrow, the instant the money's wired to escrow."

"You're wrong, Mr. van Wagoner," Eric said. "I'd laugh if this wasn't so serious. Quit wasting your time."

"You forged documents that indicated Jim Strong

was alive. You love money, obviously." Paul looked around.

"You have nothing on me. Even you must know that. I inherited money. My father was a textile manufacturer. Maybe that annoys you? I understand your upbringing wasn't so easy."

"You're obsessed with the Strong case."

"You found my office." Eric offered them drinks, which they declined, but poured himself a glass of amber-colored liquid. "Okay, I'll tell you a few things that don't reflect well on me." He directed this comment to Nina. "This case has driven me crazy. I spent months on it, first trying to figure out who was embezzling."

"But," Nina said, "it was Jim, wasn't it?"

"I'm telling you now I never had absolute proof. I suspected all along that Jim masterminded the embezzlement, but Jim was dead. I went through a lot of possibilities, that he was mixed up with Marianne, that he had a deal going with Kelly. But I never found any connections." Eric set his drink down. "Two years I've considered this case and gotten nowhere. On the plus side, I met you, Nina." He smiled fully this time.

"You stink," Paul said. "I smell it."

"Why don't you get the fuck out of my house now, Paul? Nina, you're welcome to stay as long as you like."

He walked them to the door.

Paul left first. Before Nina could follow him, Eric took her arm. "Whatever you know about me, I know you and Paul broke into my house. I could cause you to lose your license to practice law."

"Don't even try," Nina said evenly.

"So." He reached into his pocket and pulled out a wallet. He put a $5 bill in her hand. "You're representing me in a small matter yet to be determined. You can't tell anyone anything about me. I'm your client. And I won't bring up the burglary."

"All I took was my own property back."

Eric rubbed his mouth. "Ah. I do apologize for that."

She took the five and put it into her bag. "You wouldn't want to do anything to Paul either."

Eric frowned. "Him, I'd throw to the dogs. You—I like."

She walked out, wondering if it was her he liked so much or something else about her. By the time she reached Paul's car, where a fuming Paul had taken the wheel and turned on the heat, she was chuckling.

Paul lowered his window. "What's so funny?"

"He's dirty. You are so right. But he's dirty in a totally harmless way. Paul, I don't think he has anything to do with scamming Philip out of any money. I think he's really tried to figure out what's going on, and he's failed."

Paul struck his steering wheel. "I don't like that guy."

"You're jealous because he's rich and attractive."

"Maybe, but that's not all. What did you mean back there, that I was wrong about what he was hiding?"

All the anxiety, the fear, that crazy alarm that made her heart beat five times faster than it should, caught up to her and she began to laugh again. She laughed until tears fell. Only Matt could make her laugh so hard, but here she was, crying with laughter.

"You're my investigator in this, and I'm his lawyer in this, so it's protected and confidential information, Paul. Do you agree to that?"

"Okay, okay!"

"I turned a knob in the bathroom and found Eric's secrets."

"What?"

"Shelves full of stiletto heels."

Paul reeled back. "He's a cross-dresser?"

"Not exactly. He collects shoes. He only needs one of a pair, though."

"Holy shit."

"He likes what they call limo shoes these days, ones where women can barely walk without help. And he had this." She reached into her bag and held up an outrageous pump. "My January mortgage payment, a red soled Christian Louboutin peep-toed stiletto. Soon to be reunited with its twin. I won't wear them again around him, though."

"His passion is shoes? That's the big secret?"

"He has a collection. Dozens and dozens. He must

steal them. I looked at the bottom of one of them and it had been worn. All of the shelves were lit tastefully like a mini-gallery."

Paul mulled this over. "Did he ever try to handle your foot?"

"What? No. Why do you ask?"

"Because that's molesting. Sick."

"He's only interested in the shoe. Maybe it's like the art. He has fabulous taste."

Paul shook his head. "I'd almost rather he was the killer. I'm feeling confused. Men aren't exactly men anymore. Except me, of course." He clammed up after that.

Nina shivered. "It's so cold. I need to go. Where will you be?"

"Out and about," Paul answered, looking toward Eric's house.

"Please, Paul. No more trouble."

"Nothing planned."

But he had a look she didn't quite trust. "Stay in touch?"

"You bet. I'll check in on you soon."

CHAPTER 31

With a quick cell phone call, Nina checked on Bob, learning that Hitchcock had already had his evening walk and that Bob had locked up properly after getting dropped off.

Her energy was fading, but she couldn't feel it. All she could feel was a driving worry now. She had been all too willing to go along with Paul's theories about Eric because she badly, very badly, needed to feel that her own case was controllable, if not under control. It had been a relief to say, He's the one, and know what to do.

They had found nothing linking him to the killings. Paul had jumped to a conclusion that was wrong. But if Eric was not the author of the Brazilian scam, she was at a complete loss. A huge sum of money was going to be transferred into a separate account in a few hours, and that money wasn't going to be secure. It might disappear, and she and Paul hadn't managed to catch the watcher. They had been weakened by their own distraction, their own vulnerabilities, Paul's jealousy, maybe.

Maybe they were wrong about Hendricks, too. It was all theory and potential motive, without any evidence at all.

An idea crystallized in her mind. She would call Nelson Hendricks right now and warn him strongly and demand that some further protections be put in place first thing in the morning before the money was wired. He could switch banks at the last moment, certainly change all passwords, notify the bank that there might be some attempt to forge his signature and thus to permit no wires out—he would have to listen to her—

She had Hendricks's number on her phone. She pulled over to the side of the dark highway before the turn onto Jicarilla Street and her own neighborhood and called.

The office recording took her to his voice mail. He didn't give any emergency number.

What time would the wire arrive? No one had been able to specify that. Sometime in the morning. Maybe as the doors opened. The rustlers would be there, but unlike the rustlers of yore, the ropes would be unseen and the calves wouldn't bellow and the sound of the gate's opening would be silent and electronic.

She went to Wi-Fi and onto the Net, clicking on the car light. Hendricks was on LinkedIn, but without a home address, not on Facebook, not on Twitter. Not a connected guy, and a cautious one, as she would have expected.

She went to a pay website that archived recorded real estate transactions and found that Nelson and Rayanne Hendricks, man and wife, had purchased property at Lot 36 in Block 12, as shown on a certain recorded map, in the City of South Lake Tahoe, State of California, for a valuable consideration, some six years earlier.

Now she accessed the County Planning department and its maps and found that the property was a house in the Tahoe Keys neighborhood, not on the water but close to it. All she could find was the Assessor's Parcel Number and a map, but it was plenty to find the house.

There was more. She was directed to a list of homes delinquent for more than a year in payment of property taxes, and the Hendricks parcel number was on it. Hendricks was in money trouble, as she had already been warned. The title company executive was not solid.

She decided to go to his house and talk to him. If he didn't let her do that, she decided to go to the police. She called Paul's cell phone. No answer. Irritation made her bite her lip.

She drove to the Keys.

Newer and more affluent than Gene's block, the neighborhood had bright streetlighting, but even though it was only nine o'clock, there was no activity at the tiny shopping center she passed. She found her way to the third house on the left on Clement Street. A standard-two-story model with a double garage in front below a small, useless-looking balcony, it had no cars visible. After all this adrenaline expenditure Hendricks might not even be home. She parked in the driveway, activating a motion floodlight, grabbed her purse, and marched up to the covered doorway, where the front door was already opening.

"What are you doing here?" Hendricks said, standing in the doorway in black sweats, his wife beside him in matching red sweats. Behind them Nina could hear a TV program, the frenzied music of which announced the climactic moment was arriving.

"I need to talk to you."

"What's happened?"

"It's what may happen tomorrow."

"Come to my office in the morning. We open at eight a.m." His astonishment was turning to suspicion, and for a moment she considered herself, a woman standing in a stranger's doorway at night making vague pronouncements. She might look nuts.

"The escrow account isn't safe," she said.

"What? How do you know that? Of course it's safe." But his face went ashen. "Better come in, then." He opened the door wide and Nina followed them into a big, clean family room dominated by a stone fireplace. To the right was a massive television on a massive stand. There were two couches, a chair and a lamp, a couple of unobtrusive pictures on the walls. It was the room of a vacation home, bare and unassuming, and she remembered that they were trying to sell the place. But she had seen no sign outside, and she had looked at the multiple-listing service on the Net without result. "Take your boots off, please," Rayanne Hendricks said, and Nina unzipped them and for the first time since 7:00 a.m. felt her toes in their damp socks. In the warm room she suddenly felt a wave of fatigue. She sat down on one of the couches uninvited, as Hendricks turned off the TV and sat down opposite her.

"Now what is happening?" he said. "What's this about the escrow?"

"I'm Ray," his wife said. She sat down next to him, close, their legs touching. She was Chinese-American, with sallow skin and big eyes. Nina's eyes went to the electric scooter visible in the kitchen. It seemed to sparkle under the bright kitchen light like a tiny, brand-new car. Yet Rayanne Hendricks had walked to the door, sat down. Nina flashed to her mother, who had also suffered from a serious illness that sometimes didn't show. She looked at the woman with sympathy.

"I'm waiting," Hendricks said.

"All right, I'll get right to it. I told you earlier today that the money being wired tomorrow into the account for which you are the trustee has been more or less channeled there as a result of false affidavits from Brazil."

"What do you have new to tell me? Besides the baseless information you already gave me?"

"You have to take additional steps to protect it." She explained her ideas. Hendricks frowned. "The body of Jim Strong was stolen from a grave it has lain in for more than two years, and the police will have forensic proof of that soon enough," she said. "But not soon enough to protect the wired money, if it comes in tomorrow."

"Are you going to court to ask for some sort of delay?" Hendricks asked. "Wouldn't that be more in keeping with your, er, procedures, rather than coming to my home late at night and repeating the same stories to me?"

"There isn't time. You can protect the money, Mr. Hendricks. You can refuse to accept the wire."

"A violation of my contractual agreements and fiduciary responsibilities," he said pompously. "And a court order. I can't do that. I am the only person authorized to withdraw money from the account once it is received."

"Whoever came up with this scheme in Brazil is a gifted forger who's had close contact with the Strong family. Who else would know how to mimic Jim Strong's signature so well?"

Hendricks paled. "Who exactly do you think could do such a thing?"

"I'm not sure. Someone you work with?"

"No one has access to my passwords and codes. We keep bank account numbers and so on in a safe. I locked it up personally tonight. It certainly is not one of my staff. I've known them all for years and years."

"Has any stranger been in your office recently while you were working with those numbers? Please think carefully. Who have you spoken with about this account?"

"Well, besides you, Philip Strong and his family, and Mr. Stamp, the lawyer. And Mr. Brinkman. I have spoken about this account in open court in front of Judge Flaherty. It's been discussed in the newspaper. Ms. Reilly, you're obviously very tired, and this has all been a strain on you. You're not thinking straight. I think you need to go home."

"Oh, please. I didn't invent those affidavits, and I didn't murder two women."

Both of them sat up straighter at hearing that, and Nina told them about the link between the sale and Cyndi Backus's lover. She saw Ray cast a quick glance at her husband and thought, She wondered there for a second if it could be him, but she doesn't believe it is. He's faithful and she knows he loves her.

Ray seemed shaken. "I don't understand. What a mess." Hendricks put his arm around his wife's shoulder and glared at Nina. "It's late, and you haven't brought me anything but wild suspicions. You should go. My wife needs her sleep."

But Ray had something to add. "I hate it here. I'm glad we are leaving the country, moving to Taiwan, where I grew up. This is a good example. Women killed over money, like they are nothing and nobody. I don't feel safe in the streets, and Reno, where I used to work, is worse. I can't stand it here one more minute."

"When—" Nina started, but Hendricks gave his wife a little push and said, "Darling, you're going to bed right now." He was firm but loving, helping her stand.

"Nice meeting you," Ray said. "Good luck. I'm sure Nelson will keep your money safe." She looked lovingly into her husband's eyes. "He's a good man."

Her husband blinked a few times, watching her progress as she walked slowly into the hall and shut the door.

Nina kept her eyes steady on him. She said nothing. She was processing the information his wife had given her.

A seismic shift took place in her mind, and Hendricks saw it.

"Now you get out of here," he said, voice as tight as his thin lips. "I'll sue you for blackening my character in the community. Now you've come around and upset my sick wife. I'm coming after you just as soon as this deal goes through. You won't get another client in this community. I'll make sure of it."

Nina didn't move. "Quit blustering. It's a major thing, moving to another country, and it's expensive. How can you afford it? I wonder. Are you expecting big money for some reason?"

"I expect I'll call the police." But he made no move to do so, and Nina felt a mad rush of excitement as the facts continued to realign in her brain.

Nelson Hendricks was breaking, knew that she was putting things together in her mind, that the notion they all had, that he was a good man, had crumbled with those few innocent words of his wife. He breathed hard, his body writhed, as if enduring a titanic struggle.

"You're part of it," Nina blurted. "You're in on it."

"Shut up."

She watched him hold back, wanting to give her a push out the door but restraining himself. A smart man, he thought carefully before he acted. "We can stop the escrow, Mr. Hendricks. I don't believe you killed those women. You needed money, you agreed to take part in an embezzlement, but you're not a murderer."

"A murderer? Never!"

"Who are you working with, Mr. Hendricks? Maybe you didn't know about the murders being connected to this deal. Maybe you can get out of this before you get yourself into serious trouble with the law. What good will you be to your wife then?"

Hendricks didn't move. Nina wasn't afraid of him. He seemed paralyzed by anger and indecision. His wife opened the hall door. Nina realized she had been eavesdropping. "Oh, my poor poor Nel," she cried.

"Shhh." He raised up a hand, as if he could stop her.

She held on to the doorway and wobbled.

"Please, go to bed," Hendricks said. "Ms. Reilly's

leaving. I'll handle this like I handle everything, okay?"

"You shouldn't have done this for me, Nel."

Her husband moved fast toward her, fast enough to catch her before she fell. She leaned against him, fingers tight on his arm. "I knew," she said in a low voice weighted by years of love and trust. "I knew we didn't have the money. Will they take you away from me? Then what will I have left? I need you."

"Nobody can take me from you. Nobody." He looked at Nina.

"Tell me who you're working with, Mr. Hendricks," Nina said.

"Lady, you do what you feel you should do, which is exactly what I plan to do. Meanwhile, stop hounding me and my wife."

"If you cooperate with me, tell me what the deal is, I promise to testify on your behalf later."

"Testify on my behalf? My job is to keep her well. And that's what I'm going to do. I've done nothing wrong and you have no business here. Go home. Kiss your husband if you have one." He looked at her bare fingers.

"You're not safe! She's not safe! Brenda Bee and Cyndi Backus were both killed because they could identify your partner. Your partner is a very dangerous man. Do it for your wife. Tell me who it is so I can put a stop to all this before you go to jail and lose everything that means anything to you!"

"Get out!"

Ray Hendricks, apparently fortified by her husband's support, lifted her head, rallied, sounding suddenly very like her husband back in his office. "Please. Go away."

"Okay. I'm going." Nina walked toward the door. "But I guarantee you this, Mr. Hendricks, there will be no transfer of funds in the morning. You won't manage it, because I have all night to put a stop to this, and I will."

At the door, she pulled on her boots and zipped them. Hendricks and his wife stayed across the room, whispering and touching. They seemed to have forgotten her.

Nina got into the RAV, drove around the block, parked again, and called Paul. Voice mail again. "Paul, you jerk, where are you? I'm absolutely convinced Hendricks is going to take off with some or all of the escrow money within ten minutes after it's wired in the morning. I'm sitting in my car. Call me!" She called Bob again. She had no phone messages at home.

So. Should she go to the police? What did she have?

What she had, right now, wasn't enough. Hendricks hadn't exactly confessed.

Cyndi's friend had linked the two cases. A double murder investigation was going on. Cheney would be interested in that conversation. But his interest was in the crimes already committed.

It's not so easy to preemptively stop a crime. Justice moves stiffly, cautiously. The evidence that a crime is about to be committed must be unequivocal. The opposing counsel in a civil case often tries to pull all sorts of outside strings to demoralize the other side. It's a chess game with an aggressive defense. She would be accused of making up the whole thing.

She called Michael Stamp's office and left a message. She went online to the state bar to try to get a home phone number or address on him, but like most lawyers he kept that information private.

She called Judge Flaherty's chambers and left a message asking for an emergency meeting at 8:00 a.m., *ex parte,* which meant without Stamp's presence, if she couldn't get in touch with him soon enough.

Thinking through it, she wasn't sure where to go now. What if Hendricks called his partner and the partner went to her home? She called Matt and asked him to go pick Bob up for the night. She started driving aimlessly. She called Paul again and left another message, then gave up for the moment, heading toward an all-night coffee shop on the highway to drink some coffee and take a moment to think some more.

CHAPTER 32

Paul hadn't been able to let Brinkman go that easily. A nasty son of a gun, he was after Nina, kinky, arrogant as hell, and begging for a lesson. Paul watched from down the block as Brinkman's garage door opened as soon as Nina left. The Cayenne slid down the driveway and Paul followed. It was the right thing to do. He was frustrated and pissed off and not finished with the conversation. He didn't like being dismissed. He particularly disliked being criticized in front of Nina. Besides, the other side of him, the curious, devilish kid he sometimes saw in himself, had kicked in. He was curious to see what Brinkman was up to at this time of night. Maybe he would betray himself yet.

After rolling downhill for a few blocks, Brinkman's Cayenne bumped up the winding path into the Village Shopping Center, which at this time of night was all closed up except for one place, the Bar Bar Bar. He parked right in front and went in.

Paul knew the place, one of only a couple of locals' bars in the affluent North Shore village of Incline.

Ostensibly a pizza parlor, it was a blue-collar oasis in a staid golf-and-ski-lounge culture, the last place he'd expect Brinkman to go for a drink.

Maybe that was why Brinkman had chosen it. Paul parked in front of the deserted post office and took a little tour around the dark parking lot, around the market and the secondhand-furniture store and a coffee shop, all closed and dark, making up his mind. Finally he opened the door to the pizza place.

The Bar Bar Bar wasn't big. On the left an actual bar sat, an unexciting slab embedded with quarter poker machines, upon which several bearded denizens leaned. To the right was a hole in the wall where a blond kid in a white apron rolled out pizza dough. Against the wall a few rickety tables had been set like afterthoughts, and at one of those Eric Brinkman sat staring at Paul, legs apart, a beer in front of him, moist and golden, one hand lightly held on his knee, ready for anything.

Paul sat down beside him.

"I don't like you spying on me." Brinkman seemed pretty relaxed under the circumstances.

"And yet it happens, as well it should."

"Why not have a beer, Paul. Take it easy for a change."

"I'll do that. I'll have some food, too." Paul went to the bar, where a pudgy, young lady gave him Jack Daniel's straight up with a Coors chaser, then went to the pizza window, knowing Brinkman was watching him the whole time and trying to figure him out.

"Do you have salad?"

"Salad?" The kid sounded as if he had never heard of such a thing. His face said, *Why no request for salmon croquettes? Look around, pal. Think this through.*

"Well, what do you have besides pizza?"

"Nothing." His badge said EDDIE.

"Okay, I'll take a slice of mushroom pizza, Eddie."

"We have pepperoni or sausage tonight. Oh, and a special, which is pepperoni plus sausage. That's it."

"I'll have the special."

Eddie slowly went about his business.

Finally Paul was sitting again, fantastically hungry. The slice of pizza disappeared fast.

Brinkman drank his beer, watching Paul reflectively. Finally he said, "For what it's worth, I know why you're here. You want me to promise to lay off her."

"You got that right, buddy." Paul finished the last bit of crust and drank down the liquor in a gulp.

Eric chuckled, running a hand through a haircut Paul found revoltingly fashionable. "So you find me humorous," Paul said.

"I find you a belligerent fool, that's what I find."

"You're the one going to an anonymous bar to get drunk after she walks out on us."

"I happen to be friends with Bev." Eric indicated

the manager—who had taken over from the frizzy-haired girl at the bar—a short woman in a tight T-shirt that showed off her amplitude, wearing high heels that forced her to lurch from table to table.

One of the customers hit a mini-jackpot playing with his quarters. Everybody leaned over to look. They all knew each other. The Bar Bar Bar was that kind of place. The men worked hard all day and shared cheerless apartments. Not a one was Latino.

That kind of place. Nevertheless, it had a cozy feel and people there seemed happy, laughing, knocking back a few beers after a long, hard day. Paul's pizza had tasted great. He should eat more pepperoni. Screw mushrooms. What they did here, they did well.

Paul said, "I may not be around for a while, and here's the thing I came here to tell you. I want you to leave Nina alone."

"Fine." Eric was watching Bev walk around to see the three sevens lined up on the poker machine. She gave Eric a wink.

The men ordered second drinks. They drank them.

Then they ordered thirds, drank them, too, and then things somehow turned more unpleasant.

"I believe you're not paying attention," Paul said. "I think I'm going to have to teach you a little lesson."

"No need. I'm well educated. Probably better than you. Columbia."

Paul stood up. "You arrogant ass. Let's go outside," he said, filled with rage, because tomorrow he was probably going to jail, because he was going to tell Cheney the truth, and then this rich dude who couldn't investigate his way out of a hamster cage would take over everything—the mountains, Nina, all of it. Paul's business, which he loved, Wish, the whole thing, everything would go to hell, and it was all his fault, but he had done the right thing, and—

Brinkman said calmly, "I'm a fifth-degree black belt. Don't make me take you out. Ever heard of the Lima Lama system?"

Eric had said the exact wrong thing, although maybe anything he said at this point would have been the exact wrong thing. Paul was a little fuzzy on that point. "Try it, buddy," he said. Bev was shaking her head. She jabbed her thumb backward toward the door. The customers watched them go.

They ended up by Paul's car. Brinkman said, "I'm not even after Nina, okay? Let's forget this."

"Liar. In for a pfennig, in for a pfund." Paul punched with his right. Brinkman grabbed his arm, twisted it over his head, and held it behind him, pulling him off-balance and putting the arm into danger of breaking. The whole thing took about two seconds.

Brinkman dropped Paul's arm and stood there, arms loosely at his sides.

"So you've got one move," Paul said. This time he feinted with his right and sent over a fast, hard left hook, but Brinkman leaned in totally unexpectedly and somehow got a snaky arm around Paul's neck and pulled him backward. He stepped back suddenly and Paul fell onto the pavement, landing on his side and damn near cracking his head open. As it was, his ear connected hard with the pavement.

He got up, touched his ear. Blood was flowing freely, but he could hear Brinkman say, "Use this."

Paul took the tissue and held it to his ear. "Let's go back inside, okay?" Brinkman said. "It's cold as fuck out here. I want to explain something to you."

"Not till I explain something to you." Brinkman's defensive arm came up fast, but this time Paul was faster. His fist connected with such knuckle pain he knew he had struck the jaw cleanly.

Brinkman staggered back. His eyes closed and he collapsed to the pavement.

Paul nudged him with his foot. "Wake up, Mother Hubbard." Brinkman opened one eye, saw Paul looming over him, and scuttled back. Paul felt much, much better, though his ear was bleeding again. "You tell Lima Lama there's a gap in the technique about five inches wide. It's called bare knuckles." The door of the bar opened and a grizzled man peered out.

"Come on in," he said. Brinkman got up slowly to his feet, holding his jaw.

"Is it broke?" the man said.

"I—I don't think so. Let's have one more, Paul."

"You talkin' to me? I'm not going back in there."

"I'll buy. Come on. JD straight up, right?" Warm air rushed out, and Paul thought, Why not cap off a great night? and went back inside. They sat down at the same table as before. Fewer than five minutes had elapsed. Nobody looked their way. The old-timers ignored them. It was a courteous place that way.

Bev brought their drinks. She smiled at Brinkman. "Like 'em?"

"Perfect copies of Jimmy Choo's 2010 collection," Brinkman said.

"I know you prefer 'em pointy," she said, and walked with small, careful steps back around the bar.

"How's the ear?" Brinkman said. "Let's have a look."

"Screw you."

"Speaking of screwing."

"I'm not speaking of screwing."

"Well, I want to speak of screwing, so why not shut up for a minute, Paul."

"Jesus Christ."

"You ever heard of an old book called *Psychopathia Sexualis*?"

"Krafft-Ebing."

"Right. A Victorian doctor. Sort of an early shrink. He wrote about various kinky things people get into about sex. You know, the dom-slave stuff, that sort of thing."

Paul drank his Jack Daniel's, which warmed him. "Do I dare even ask why we are talking about this?

Is it because you have about a hundred pairs of shoes lined up like little girls in your fucking pantry?"

Eric laughed. "Yes. Actually, I have even more. I'm a collector, Paul. I like women's shoes. High heels. Designer only. Beautifully made. Four inches or higher. Platforms turn me on. I like peep-toes, and as Bev said, the pointed toes are big favorites. I like them black, red, and gold. I'm not interested in earth tones like taupe. Boring. That doesn't do it for me."

"I can't believe I'm having this conversation. Do you wear them?"

Brinkman looked insulted. "What an idea. I play with them. I touch myself with them."

"Is this some—genetic aberration? Were you born this way?"

Eric shrugged. "Doubtful, but who knows? In my cups I'm not entirely my sharpest self, so I will tell you this. I had a piano teacher when I was fourteen, Paul, sexy as hell, but she wouldn't let me have sex with her. We did other things, and as time went on, I got to preferring her shoes. She was willing to help me out. You know—"

"Please don't feel the need to go into details."

"The red soles on the Louboutins—they're insanely sexy. Nina was wearing a pair. I wanted one."

"You bastard. She took back the one you stole after court that day."

"Yes." Eric looked disconsolate. "What a beauty."

"I guess we're even. We broke into your house. You stole her fancy shoe."

"But—the point I'm trying to make, Paul—I don't do women." Eric sat back.

Paul considered this. "You don't what?"

"Have sex. No interest there."

"You've never had sex with a woman?"

Brinkman smiled. "Only secondhand."

"You're extremely fucked up."

"See, now that's how you make me laugh. I'm playing. Lots of people like playing. I'm sure you do some things the media would consider unusual. Maybe you spank or you like threesomes or leather. Who's to say I'm weirder than the norm?"

"Okay, enough to focus on what's happening, I get that you're not going after Nina. And stay away from her shoes from now on." Paul drank down the rest of his drink. Brinkman sat there with his black belt and his shoe fetish looking like a nice golf dude. The whole thing was surreal. Paul felt compelled to question existence in general, the topsy-turviness of it all. He felt like writing a poem, or trying to beat up Brinkman again. "It's a crime," he went on. "Stealing them. You have money. You could buy loads of pretty shoes."

Brinkman leaned forward again. "I like shoes women have worn. I like watching them walk in them." He nodded toward Bev. "Now you know my secret, it's your turn, since we're playing truth or dare. Where's the body?"

"I don't know."

"Yeah, you do."

Paul thought, Oh, well, the world's going to be in on this in a few hours, what's the harm. Right then, he knew he'd be telling Cheney all this shortly. "I know where it was, but it seems to have gotten up and gone out clubbing."

Brinkman's eyebrows rose. "Now we're getting someplace. You're the one who sent the e-mail tip?"

"Yeah. I did."

Brinkman grinned. He slammed a hand down on the table. "I knew it!"

Paul told him the whole story. They had one more, which they really shouldn't have. They both had to drive but it was a night for being bad.

After they had shared far too many confidences, and Paul had learned much more than he ever intended to learn about really gorgeous, sexy, hot shoes, Paul had coffee and another slice of pizza. The special.

CHAPTER 33

By the time she got to the Al Tahoe streetlight, Nina had begun to think about Kelly Strong. She was a smart young woman who had been in law school. Maybe she was working with Hendricks. Maybe she had persuaded her father to sell, all for that escrow set-aside.

Through a process of elimination, Nina felt it was possible, but two things made her feel it was unlikely. First, she had spent time with Kelly two years before and found her to be honest but uninvolved with her family's business. Kelly had wanted nothing more than to leave Tahoe, as Nina recalled, but that brought up the second thing, which was that Kelly had suffered some sort of breakdown and had to leave school.

Kelly and Hendricks. Her part in it would have been to make sure the sale happened. True, she had gone from disinterest to strongly urging that her father let it go. And whaddaya know, the buyers in Korea had no manager all of a sudden, and she knew the business.

But Kelly hadn't killed Cyndi Backus and Brenda Bee, not with the description of the boyfriend they had.

Then Nina had a paralyzing thought: Could it have been Kelly who was having an adulterous affair with Cyndi?

Nina checked her watch—it was just before 10:00 p.m. She pulled over and did some more online research on her phone. This time it was easy, as she had Kelly's home phone number already inputted. Another paid service provided the address the phone was billed from.

She felt she could trust Kelly. Hiding something or not, Kelly was the one person in the Strong family who seemed to understand how troubling a story her family continued to unfold.

Kelly lived in a condominium over the Nevada line, near the Edgewood Golf Course. Her home sat back from the road with a crabgrass lawn in front and a lot of signs warning people not to park here and not to step there.

Nina climbed the stairs and rang the bell, feeling déjà vu. Two years earlier, she had talked to Kelly in another apartment, and Kelly had provided key information that had led Nina to realize that her own client Jim Strong had murdered his wife and probably his brother. Kelly was, Nina thought, a kind of Cassandra, a woman of deep understanding, but completely impotent in affecting events. Like Cassandra, she was viewed by everyone who knew her with caution, as someone who might hold together for a while, but could not quite be believed.

Kelly answered the door or, more accurately, opened it a crack.

"Hello, Kelly."

"What took you so long?" Kelly opened the door wide and Nina went in. The place was just like Kelly's old apartment, filled with books and prints on the walls. A fire burned in the small fireplace, and a yoga mat was laid out in front of it. Kelly wore leggings and a stretchy top that showed that she had gained weight. She pulled a pareu tight around her waist.

"My God." Nina went to the wall near the hallway, where a strange print was tacked to the wall, of a woman on her back, half off her sleeping couch, her eyes closed, sleeping. A small demon perched on her, leering. Looming above her, a hideous white horse, with white eyeballs, breathed horror into the picture.

"It's called *Nightmare*," Kelly said. "By Henry Fuseli. I think they have it at the Legion of Honor in San Francisco. You ever go there?"

"Not often enough. I think I saw it in a dream." It was so frightening, this painting, the woman in it so vulnerable and naked, and these monsters all around . . .

"Remember this one?" Kelly said. "It affected you a lot last time you visited me. *The Elephant Celebes*."

She pulled out a book and opened it to a page showing a dreadful surrealistic print of an elephantine monster-machine.

"Not an image I'd forget." Nina glanced back at the nightmare picture. "I'm afraid of horses. My secretary wants me to go riding. They're powerful animals. So strange."

"I was expecting you would come here. I suppose because Matt's been so good to me, and then there's the big thing. As we both know, the money for the sale of Paradise is due to be wired into the escrow account tomorrow."

"Yes, that's why I came."

Kelly sat down with a miserable expression on her face. Though she was young, she had something old and wizened about her, like a war refugee who has been deprived of sustenance and dignity.

"I also need to tell you what happened to your brother Jim."

"You know where he is?"

"No. But I know how he died. He came to my house the night he was last seen." Nina described it, the doorstep, the lockpicking, the crouched-over man with murder in his mind. She went on from there. All of it came out, in the compressed, analytical tones of a lawyer. Nina didn't want to feel any of it again. Kelly's expression troubled Nina. Not shocked, not grieving. Instead, she looked resigned.

When Nina finished, Kelly said, "So that's what happened. I imagined—worse."

Nina nodded. "Paul's going to both your father and the police. He'll make a full statement."

"Don't let him do it. Paul saved your life. Isn't that self-defense?" Kelly sighed, long and painfully. "Jim. Jimmy. He used to sing nursery rhymes to me in a funny voice. He also beat his wife and killed people. My brother. Holy crap, what a family."

"Anyway, this isn't over."

"That's right."

"I believe someone is working with Nelson Hendricks to steal the money that will be wired tomorrow morning from Korea, and I plan to prevent that."

"Don't tell me—are you thinking it's me?"

"I don't know. I'm lost. I want to stop what looks and acts like a train out of control. I don't want somebody stealing from your family. You have all suffered enough, your father especially."

Kelly nodded. She got up and came over to Nina, and suddenly her face was right there close to Nina's, her blue eyes, the folds of flesh that had come too early to her, an intensity that made Nina want to move away at any cost, but before she could do anything, Kelly said in a gravelly voice, "Where do you think he got it from?" Then tears seemed to spurt from the eyes so close to Nina's.

Kelly blinked the tears back hard and moved back a little. "Where did he get it?" she repeated.

"Who?"

"Where do you think Jim got his tendencies?

His lying. His stealing. His possessiveness. Oh, how blind everybody is! I could laugh! I could laugh! You think Jim started it because that's what you want to think. Who started it? All of it?"

"I don't know," Nina stammered.

"Yes, you do. You remember Jim's wife? She was not loyal. She went elsewhere to find love."

"You—you mean—Heidi?"

"That's who I mean! Heidi! And so, who slept with Jim's wife Heidi?"

"Kelly, let me get this straight. Are you accusing your father of something?" Nina let that fact come back. Heidi had had an affair with her father-in-law, Philip. It had broken Jim Strong.

"Who slept with his son's wife? Who set Jim off on his revenge killings, set off all of this? Oh, God!" Kelly fell onto her knees on the floor, sobbing. "Maybe I'm the same. I've got a defect, like my brother and my father."

So this was what Kelly had been hiding. What a burden. "Philip?" Nina whispered. He had had an affair with Sandy's mother and his own son's wife. He was a womanizer.

Was he a killer like his son?

"My father ran Paradise Resort into the ground until there was nothing left. Of course he's working with Nelson! He's known him for decades! He played on Nelson's love of his wife, her sickness, his honesty!" Kelly rocked back and forth. "He's had half the women in this town. I'm surprised he never went after you. He always has a girlfriend but he's not interested unless they're married or committed. He needs that. He needs to destroy."

"Kelly, are you saying Philip's planning to steal the money tomorrow morning?"

"Of course he'll steal the money! All of it. Who's to stop him from wrestling every bit from the resort? He feels he's owed. He hated Jim stealing, pilfering. He was so mad, for a while there I wondered if he had killed my brother."

"But now you believe he didn't."

"True. But don't you get it? He set up this escrow scam to get Jim's share of the resort. And Marianne's share. And mine."

Nina shook her head. Kelly stared at her as if willing her to understand, those young-old eyes riveted.

Nina dropped her head, put her hand to her forehead.

"That's right," Kelly said. "Now you get it."

"Give me a sec." Nina let it all in, Philip's gambling, his creditors, his broken family, his single lifestyle, his many lovers, all of it.

Everything fit. "Jesus, Kelly, why haven't you talked about this? Why didn't you tell me? You work with my brother. I have always trusted you."

"Because I can't prove anything. I never can. I don't care about myself anymore, Nina. I'm out of hope. He's turned my whole life into a nightmare of twisted—of horrible—" Kelly couldn't finish.

Nina put her arms around her and let Kelly cry on

her shoulder. Kelly calmed a little, while Nina riled up. She understood suddenly how Paul felt, like a poisonous creature puffing up, preparing to fight.

She had been lied to and manipulated, first by the son, then by the father. They had both put her to work for them. Philip was a scum-sucking liar who had cost her precious sleep and made both her and Paul feel guilty for not saving him. She felt humiliated. She had made the same mistake twice with this family.

"Kelly, do you know where your brother Jim's body is?" Kelly, lost in her own world, said nothing. "Where is he?" Nina asked again.

Kelly seemed to shake off a fog. "He found Jim's body and took it. Of course he did. He found Jim and dug him out of his grave. I guarantee, my brother's gone forever. Nobody will ever find him."

"I'm not sure I follow you. Who found Jim?"

"Who else?"

Nina struggled for clarity. Kelly, Jim, Marianne, Gene— "You can't be suggesting—"

"My father. Philip Strong. He's responsible for everything."

"But—why do you believe this?"

"Call me crazy. That's what my father will say, not to believe a thing I tell you. But I was there when the police called, in the hall."

"Where?"

"At the resort. Outside the main office in the Lodge. The police called in the morning first thing, when we were opening up, and I heard him talking to them. 'I want to be there,' he said. 'This afternoon?' he said. 'Where do I go?' he said. He wrote down some numbers."

"GPS coordinates?"

"I don't know, some numbers, and he was—oh, he was livid, frightened and furious and I don't know what all. He left, and he was gone all day. That night he had the attack."

Nina was holding her hand over her mouth.

"That's right, the police told him they were going to go dig up a body, and it might be Jim, and he got there first, okay? I think about this all day long. I dream about it at night, our father digging up his son." Kelly sat back on the floor in front of the fire. "He never liked Jim. He was glad when Jim was gone. You know that?"

Nina nodded.

"So now Jim's gone for good, Nina. You'll never find the body. It's gone. Jim couldn't just show up, if Jim's body was found, why, that would be the end, no wired money, nothing to steal. Dad has a new girlfriend already. He can't stand life without one. I don't know who she is, he calls her and says things, and I hear, but—do you think I'm crazy? Do you?"

"No. No." Nina got up. "I'm going to go and see how well he can lie to my face. My own client."

"Don't. He may be just out of the hospital, but he's dangerous. He'll lie and lie and then I don't know what might happen."

"I'll be careful, Kelly. I promise. And after our talk, if he hasn't completely satisfied me of his innocence, I'll go straight to the police."

"Don't go. Don't. He's a dangerous man."

"I'll call you later."

"He's not innocent. He's bad." Kelly sounded frantic.

"Don't worry." Nina remembered the day Philip had come into her office looking for help, insisting on using Brinkman, not Paul, acting like a poor beleaguered father who has heard news that has burned his world to ash.

And he and Hendricks had cooked up the whole thing.

CHAPTER 34

Paul finished his story. "So it's all over but the penitentiary."

"Come on. They won't indict you."

Eric wasn't such a bad guy, even with the shoe thing. In fact, knowing that Nina might lose a shoe, but not her virtue, had relieved Paul immensely. He repressed a smile and touched his abraded and bleeding ear, which would give him that artist look for a week or so. "Wanna bet?"

"Ten bucks says you'll never see the steel toilet with no lid."

"Done." Paul felt even better, as if maybe Eric were right, he did have a chance.

"I'm going home," Eric said. "Are you safe to drive?"

Paul indicated his tall water glass. "I'll be okay."

Eric left. Paul paid the tab and headed out to his Mustang. The sky was awash in stars, the mountains lightless silhouettes on the horizon.

He headed back toward Harrah's at Stateline,

back to the South Shore where his action was. There wasn't a thought in his head.

Except a wee one.

Oh, yeah. Hadn't checked his messages in a while. He fished his phone up on its cord from the passenger-side floor. "Whoa." Ten messages. He was near Sand Harbor. He went a little farther to a turnout where he could watch the starshine on the lake.

The messages were all from Nina. Fifteen minutes before, on her last call, she said she was going to Philip Strong's place. That last message had a small amount of profanity, very unlike Nina, which showed this was major.

Paul swung back onto the road, sped up, drank more water from the bottle.

The front door to Philip's house was unlocked, no lights showing. Nina didn't bother to knock. She made her way through the cold, dark living room with its smell of an old wood fire. He would be in the bedroom upstairs.

Nina burst in. Philip looked up in surprise. He was lying in his big four-poster reading a book in the lamplight, a tray table full of medicines beside him, a walker alongside the bed, the picture of a peaceful convalescent. On the wall side of the bed was an open window with a view of the sky. The room was cold, but he had a down comforter. Nina reached into her purse and turned on her portable recorder, then set the purse casually on the dresser by the door.

"Hello. Hope you don't mind me dropping in. The door was unlocked."

"Damn nurse," Philip said. "I'll talk to her in the morning. She just left." He set the book down.

"I've had a talk with Kelly. And your buddy Nelson Hendricks."

Something unknowable chased through his eyes. "Aren't you going to ask me how I'm feeling?"

"Okay. How are you feeling?"

"Like shit. That's how I feel. And not in the mood for visitors."

Nina stayed away from the man in the bed. "I resign as your attorney. Anything you tell me from this moment on is no longer confidential or protected by any privilege. Do you understand?"

"Your work's about over anyway," Philip said, face impassive, his knuckles white on the book.

"How dare you. How could you?"

He fell back onto the pillows, saying, "I'm so tired. I'll be glad to talk to you about anything at all tomorrow."

"After the money gets wired? That's why I'm here, Philip, to tell you that money won't be wired if I have to wake up every cop in town tonight."

Philip's face crumpled. He murmured. Nina couldn't make it out. She moved around to the side of the bed.

And a still-powerful arm flew out. Strong pulled

her onto the bed, onto him. He rolled over on her, both of them thrashing, and somehow grabbed a pillow. Then he had her pinned, the pillow hard on her face, her breath cut off, his legs pinioning her arms as he crouched over her.

She fought with her legs, trying to buck him off. He sat on her chest, holding the pillow down with terrible ferocity. She kept struggling, but nothing was working even with the strength her boiling rage and fear gave her. He adjusted one knee that had been holding down her arm at the elbow, and she managed to get her arm free. She reached between his legs and he let out a yowl of pain.

But he didn't let go, he held the pillow tightly. Down, thick, a deadly weapon.

She couldn't take in a breath.

She must have passed out for a second. She heard a high voice.

He fell away from her. She jumped off the bed and ran to the doorway, where Kelly stood with a small-caliber pistol in her hand.

Philip did not attempt to get off the bed. He pushed out his lower jaw.

"Do it," he shouted. "Go on, do it!" Kelly stood there, blinking hard, the gun shaking. She put her free arm around Nina.

"You all right?"

"Yeah." Nina was recovering swiftly. She looked back at Philip. For the moment, her body seemed to have no more emotion left in it. Philip seemed spent, but she wasn't going to get close again. His gray face was covered with sweat.

"Kelly, give me the gun," Nina said. Kelly didn't move as Nina took the pistol and examined it. She held it on Philip.

"Now where were you, Nina?" Kelly said.

"He was starting to say something truthful for a change."

Kelly turned back to her father. "You planned to leave Tahoe. You were going to leave me. Leave me dead broke with everybody looking at me, the daughter and sister of murdering thieves."

"I'm sick."

"Answer me!"

"I'm going into heart failure."

"Liar!"

"I never meant to hurt you."

"You fucking liar. You never thought twice about me. You never cared about Jim or me, just Alex."

"I supported you."

"If I had money, I'd throw it in your face."

"It's not my fault how Jim turned out."

"Are you talking about before or after you started screwing his wife? What did you think he'd do?"

Philip groaned and pulled up his sheet so that it covered his shoulders.

"I know about Cyndi Backus, too," Kelly said.

Her father's face tightened. He gritted his teeth, seemingly in pain.

"You killed her, didn't you? You were sleeping with her."

"I'm lonely, sweetie, I fell in love. Please try to understand. I didn't intend for that to happen. Yes, we had an argument—but I never hurt anyone before. I was trying to keep her quiet—"

"You slit that other woman's throat!"

"A horrible thing. Yes. Horrible." He looked at his daughter. "Please, don't look at me that way. I needed a fresh start. I thought I might help you. That was my intention all along, to help you. You've had such difficulties. So much pain, with all of this."

Kelly walked swiftly around the bed to her father. She slapped him stingingly, once, and stepped back quickly. Her mouth was trembling. He didn't move, though his skin reacted, pinking. "Don't even try to blame me."

Nina said loudly, "Get back from him, Kelly. Don't touch her, Philip, or I'll shoot you."

"You won't like where you're going," Kelly said, "and don't get any ideas about preventing it." She looked over the bottles on the table and began picking some up, throwing them in the purse on her shoulder. "I'll leave the aspirin. Nina, let's go."

Kelly took one more look at her father, her eyes hailstones. "You're lucky I don't have the family penchant for murder."

"Sweetie, don't leave me. Don't, please, I need you. You have to forgive me. I'm your—"

"Don't say it. I never want to hear that word again." Kelly looked around the room. On the bureau sat a framed picture of a woman in a sixties bouffant. Kelly took the photograph and went back to her place at the door. Her bravado was beginning to desert her.

Philip stared down at the covers, his lips working as though he was talking to himself.

"Do you need a doctor?" Nina said.

"I think I need a lawyer."

"You sure do."

"Well? You've been good to me," he said.

Nina said, "I will say this: there'll be a sale all right."

"It's all Jim's fault. So much. He's responsible for me losing the resort. I was doing my best for my family."

"Jim's just a chip off the old block."

Strong shut his eyes.

Paul appeared behind them. "Hi, honey. Sorry I missed the calls." He had a bandage on his ear.

Nina handed him the pistol and allowed herself to sag against the wall. Paul said, "Have you called the police yet?"

"Philip won't leap up and run away, Paul," Nina said. "We were finishing our conversation, me wondering if he's capable of showing any real regret at all for what he's done, and finding he isn't."

"Are you recording him?"

"Of course, including my resignation as his counsel." She turned back to Philip. "Where's your son? Where's Jim?"

Philip looked confused. His mouth hung open.

"Jim? Jimmy. Your son. Where is he?"

"Oh." Philip let out a long breath. "Jimmy's at the bottom of the lake. I see him there, nights. I see his bones and wonder what is going on with him. Do you know, do they live on after they die? Do they think about us?"

"You beat the police to Jim's grave, then?" Nina asked.

"I couldn't let his body be found. That would have stopped the escrow account from being opened. I found it very hard, digging out my own son. Very, very hard. Though, yes, I had come to hate him. May I have some water? I'm so thirsty."

"I'm sure the police will give you some," Kelly said.

"How cruel of you, Daughter."

Kelly put her face in her hands.

Paul turned to Nina. "Make the call, my phone's out in the car."

Nina reached into her bag and pulled out the recorder first, still going. She clicked it off, rewound it a short way, then clicked it back on. "—*digging out my own son.*"

She clicked it off, took out her phone, and made the call.

Strong rolled over on his side toward the window, and Paul said sharply, "Don't move." But Strong kept moving as Paul propelled himself toward the bed. Philip rolled over to face the window. Then he pulled himself up. Then he stuck his head out and his torso out. Paul, who had jumped onto the bed, reaching for him, missed catching him, too late.

They heard a noise below, and it was Nina's turn to put an arm around Kelly, holding her while Paul pulled himself to the window. He leaned out.

Paul pulled his head back in. "It's rocks down there. Not good. Nina, you and Kelly wait here for the police. Don't let her downstairs—and don't let her look."

CHAPTER 35

Two hours later Nina and Paul lay in an exhausted heap on her couch in front of the smoldering fire. Philip Strong had been taken into custody and they would be reporting to Cheney in the morning, right after making the calls to Stamp and Korea that would stop the wiring of funds into an escrow account.

Paul had his big, muscular leg over Nina's. He snored rhythmically. Nina's mind drifted from point to point, thinking about pianos and horses and how it was all right to rest. She had to sleep—she felt the pillow that had almost taken her life pressing down. She felt she had traveled beyond some personal boundary and would never be able to feel the solace of sleep again, so she opened her eyes and watched the fire burn.

The phone rang. She pulled her arm gently out from under Paul's and checked her watch. Two-forty a.m.

She disengaged from Paul, who did not waken, and padded into the kitchen.

Fred Cheney spoke. "Thought you and Paul should know. Philip Strong died while we were trying to get him moved to an ambulance for transfer back to the hospital. The paramedics were right there, but his injuries were too great, too much blood lost, and his heart probably gave out."

"Thanks, Fred. Did you call his daughter?"

"She wouldn't have anything to do with him. Somebody needs to come take charge, make some arrangements. Do you know anyone?"

"No. No, I don't. We'll see you in the morning, Fred, good night."

"Sleep well," Fred said. And just like that, she did.

Bob came down the stairs. "Hey, Paul."

"Hey. Isn't it getting late, even for someone who plays until all hours like you, or me?"

"What are you doing up so early?" Nina asked.

"Spanish again," Bob said. "Mr. Acevedo. He's tough on us. Quiz once a week. I don't get Spanish. It would be better if I was learning Swedish. At least I remember some of that. But as for right now? Mom, I'm hungry."

Nina got up to microwave a burrito with green chili sauce, which Bob ate with gusto.

"Done studying?" she asked Bob as he headed for his room.

"It never ends."

"Bob, it's going to be a difficult day. I want you to go to Uncle Matt's after school."

"Again?"

She felt bad, looking at his easy smile, at his for-
giveness.

"Just giving you grief, Mom." Bob smiled bigger.
"I'm old enough to know how to crack the skull of
an interloper, if one shows up."

"Interloper? Wait, no!"

"Oh, Mom, don't work yourself up. Anyway, I've
got Hitchie here to protect me." The dog bowed his
head under Bob's hand.

"I'll lock all the doors."

"Of course you will," Bob said, emitting a long-
suffering sigh as he closed the door to his room
behind him.

"Matt's phone number is—" she called out.

"Got it. I know Uncle Matt's number by heart,"
he called back, "just like for the past many years. Oh,
and I decided not to go to Sweden with Dad. Not
right now, anyway. You couldn't handle it. You need
me too much. So, okay, see you later, Mom."

Paul made a phone call.

Nina listened on the sidelines as the voice coming
through his phone rose in tenor, argued, and finally
came around.

They suited up against the snow shower that had
sprung up and went outside.

"Let's take my car," Paul said. While she was
getting into the car, he pressed his fingers so hard
against the steering wheel she heard them crack. "I

want what's best for you, even if it means going to prison. I mean that, honey."

She put her hand on his, the one closest to her, and felt the tension leaching out of his skin and into hers.

"Last escape route comin' up," Paul said. "Keep going and head down the mountain to Reno. The airport's there. We can take the next flight to somewhere."

"You're not serious?"

"No. I was wrong not to wake you that night two years ago. I was wrong not to call the police."

"I've thought so much about that night. What you did for me and Bob. I've thought about everything. I have dreams."

"I can't make it okay this time, sweet one. This is bad."

She put her hand on his. They turned onto Ski Run Boulevard, then toward Cheney's office.

"Hope you got more sleep than I did," Cheney said, letting them into the building himself after they buzzed, waving off the uniformed officer of the day.

They sat down and spent a little time talking about Philip, the murders, the escrow. "Hendricks is in custody," Fred said. "So let's get a statement from last night."

He asked them numerous questions, and both of them reported what had happened to the police stenographer who was making notes. Nina kept hold of Paul's warm hand.

Finally it was over. The stenographer left to prepare written statements for them to sign, and Cheney offered them coffee. "Job well done," he said. "You should have called us earlier, though, Nina. It was too dangerous to go to Strong's house, even if he was bedridden."

"I never would have known somebody as sick as he was could still have so much strength in him."

"Desperation will make almost anyone strong for a few minutes." Cheney pushed his chair back, and Nina saw how weary he was and felt twice as awful, because he wasn't finished yet.

"Fred, there's another statement I need to make, on a related topic," Paul said.

"Oh?" Fred yawned. "Let's get to it, then."

"Are you recording this?" Nina asked.

Cheney shook his head. "You know, Counselor, I have to notify you before recording." He cleared his throat, pushed a few papers around on his desk. "You saying you want me to?"

"No."

"All right, then. Let's hear what this is about, before we start recording things."

"Right," Paul said. "We're here to talk about Jim Strong."

"Paul, let me tell him," Nina said.

"In a minute."

"Please."

Paul sat back in his chair.

"Two years ago," Nina began, "Jim Strong was

my client." She recounted her nightmare to Fred and to Paul, describing the way Strong had traversed along the top of the hill and caused the avalanche that killed her husband. "He used to say he took whatever you loved most. Then came the night he came to my home to kill me."

"How can you say you know what he was thinking?" Cheney asked, fingers thrumming the scarred wooden desk.

"I do know," Nina said. "After months of working with him, I knew what was going on in his mind. He hated his family. He wanted them dead, Kelly, his father, Philip, everyone close to him. He hated me. He understood I had betrayed him."

"Did you?"

"Yes."

"You lost his case intentionally?"

"Yes."

"You believed he had killed his wife, Heidi?"

"I did, and for that I paid such a price. He killed my husband when he realized that I had guessed."

Cheney shook his head again.

"I was there on the mountain that day my husband died. I saw what happened. I spotted Jim up there, watched what he did—" Nina took a long minute. "He had violated me and my family and I continued to be scared to death of him. A few days later, after he had disappeared and everyone thought he had left town, I even thought he might be outside, watching my house in the night. He wanted me dead. I called Paul to tell him how panicked I felt. I had already sent Bob to my brother's, where I thought he might be safer."

Cheney had picked up a pencil and was either doodling or taking extensive notes.

"Why not call 911?"

"To say I was afraid? I had Paul."

Cheney gave Paul a look of disappointment and sadness, like a father who expected so much more. "Strong showed up?"

"I watched from my car as he went to her back door," Paul said, taking up the story.

"And then?"

"I watched him jimmy the lock on her back door. I watched him pull out a folding knife, snap it open."

"Ah."

"I—engaged him."

"You told him to stop. You showed him a weapon. You called the police."

"Not exactly."

"But you went there to protect her. He was out there breaking into her house. With a weapon?"

"Like I said, I saw his knife."

"And you felt Nina was in imminent danger."

"Yes. So we fought."

"He used the knife?"

"I did. The knife nicked an artery. He bled out fast, while I tore off my shirt and was trying to use it as a pressure bandage. Couldn't believe how fast he went."

"You didn't mean to kill him?"

Paul said honestly, "Hard to answer that. Once I realized I hadn't killed him immediately, I did try to save him. I couldn't. Then I buried him in the grave you excavated later, Fred. I took a tarp from under Nina's house, wrapped him in it, and buried him. Like I told Nina, I took out the garbage." Paul explained that he and Nina had sent the e-mail tip-off about the location of the grave.

Cheney nodded his head slowly. The room was quiet. Outside, Nina could hear a clanking noise, like the jailers coming to lock them up forever. But it was only a deputy's equipment banging against his hip as he walked past outside.

"Why not come and tell me then, Paul?" Cheney asked. "We're old friends, or so I thought. I consider myself a fair man."

"I should have," Paul said, "but you know, I had a problem with the idea of being locked up. I didn't think I could take it."

"What are you saying, Paul?"

"Back then I decided that I'd—well—kill myself before that happened."

Nina bit her lip.

"What about leaving Strong's family not knowing he was dead?"

"It caused them a lot of emotional distress and other harm, as it turns out," Paul said. "I honestly never thought of that. I thought they'd be relieved. He threatened all of them at various times. I believed they thought he was a monster. I believed they'd be relieved that he disappeared."

"Hmm," Cheney said. During the next long silence, Nina kept her gaze on Paul's boots, covered with wet mud.

"I see the problem," Cheney said. "You covered it up for two years. You ought to be ashamed."

"Was it wrong, Paul protecting me? That man came to my home that night to kill me. His sister-in-law, Marianne, told me he told her that," Nina said hotly.

"I'm disappointed in both of you. I should take you both into custody."

"I don't know what is right anymore, Fred," Paul said quietly. "I'm leaving it to you."

"Hmm." Cheney made a loose fist and began hitting it lightly with the palm of his other hand. It was exactly like an old-fashioned cop on the beat hitting his hand on his truncheon as he talked to a couple of juvenile delinquents.

Paul put his hand on Nina's knee, giving it a squeeze as if it were the last time.

"It's not my job to be a judge, but here I am. I know you people." Cheney pointed to Paul. "You killed a man. Not going to the police, burying the body, wasting law enforcement resources—we looked long and hard for this fool—bad judgment, Paul. However, I find it really hard to believe a jury would convict you of much." Cheney tilted his head. "You read Shakespeare?"

"Not lately," Paul said.

Nina remembered a night at Sand Harbor in August, warm and beautiful, the lake shining behind the set. They produced Shakespeare plays every summer, and she had seen most of the performances over the past several years.

"'Which is the justice, which is the thief?'" Cheney said. "That's in *King Lear*, and it is a line I remember. I wish I knew the answer to that question."

"I'm not good at literature," Paul said, "much as I admire it. But, Fred, please, what's your point?"

Cheney paused for a moment and wrote notes with an old-fashioned pencil. They listened to the *scritch scritch scritch*. "Philip Strong killed his own son and buried him in the woods. Years later, after an investigator came close to discovering that he was the one embezzling from his own business, he dug his son up and permanently disposed of the corpse in Lake Tahoe. He had the idea that he would steal the escrow funds and leave the country, escape before he got found out, and before everything went to the debtors."

"But Philip hired Eric Brinkman to look into the resort's finances. Why would he do that?"

"He realized his daughter, Kelly, and daughter-in-law, Marianne, were catching on. He was delighted when Eric Brinkman never found any proof. So he looked around for a fresh start. He killed his girlfriend because he had told her what was going on and she wasn't about to go along with it. He killed that poor Minden woman, slitting her throat like a monster. All to spare his own curly tail."

"People are no damn good," Paul said.

"Maybe I'm no damn good either," Cheney said, "but I'm not going to do anything with your information because I earnestly do not believe the district attorney will do anything with it. I'll note you made a full report to me. I won't go into particulars."

"You're not even going to take this to the district attorney's office and see if they feel it warrants an indictment?" Nina said.

"Those kids? I'll save them the time," Cheney said.

EPILOGUE

Under a mountain sky, four bodies lay side by side, dreaming. A warm breeze shifted the bushes around them, and in the distance children laughed and ran in and out of the water, their splashes faint. Dogs barked, but the sound drifted over the lake and far away.

Nina dreamed she was flying—no, riding on the back of a beautiful, fast animal. Tall pines whipped by, and she could smell the grass they ran through. They ran together out of sheer pleasure, not to escape anything, not to go fast, to feel the air slapping her cheeks and the thump of hooves, of life.

Next to her, in Andrea's active imagination, her children, Troy and Brianna, banged on a door, begging for her attention. The next door over, the women that she worked with every day, victims of violence, hammered as hard. She opened both doors and let the flood commence.

In Matt's mind, Nina's and his dead mother, Margaret, offered them advice: help your kids however you can. That serious thought led to another, much more exciting: Andrea and him waving good-bye to the kids, who were going off somewhere good, such as to school or a fabulous job, and then the two of them falling into bed as they had when they were young and full of lust.

On the other side of Nina, Paul lay, receiving the strong, high-altitude sun like a kiss, dreaming of a dead man thrown into the cold waters of Lake Tahoe. He watched the ruined pieces of a body flutter under its glassy surface and land in the smooth sand far below. Was that peace for a dead man? Did he think anything, two years after his death, drifting toward his final resting place?

Did he deserve peace?

Living people had such vivid dreams. In Paul's mind, the dead did not dream. They lived on in the living, and that was all.

"Ouch!" Nina cried, sitting up suddenly. Her howl woke her fellow sleepers, who groused around in the hot sand.

"Sorry, Mom." Bob picked up the Frisbee from next to where she lay on a faded beach towel. He whispered, "Troy's athletically challenged."

She dusted her sandy feet, pushing sand off one foot with another. "But a brilliant student."

"Only because he does homework," Bob said, frowning, then kicked up sand, running off to toss a hard pass to Brianna, who caught it easily.

Andrea stretched out her arms. "Too much

simple carbohydrate added to too much wine at lunch."

"Enough to get the neural passages relaxed at last," Paul said.

"Hey, I drank Coke and fell asleep," said Matt. "What's with these corporations and their promises? Where's the mega-caffeine jolt when you need it?"

"Sunshine. Warm weather. The lake so swimmable," Nina said, enjoying how the sun stroked her skin. "The kids, for once, too busy for angst."

"Thermos of coffee," Andrea said, rooting around in the basket. "Cups." She made up people's orders, sugar here, cream there, and handed the cups around.

They drank, but soon fell back upon their sandy towels, watching the kids, who had given up their game and run for the lake.

"Got anything chocolate?" Matt asked, and Andrea dug around in a bag for some fudge-iced biscotti.

"What a day," Nina said, taking a bite out of her biscuit. She watched billowy clouds skim across the sky.

"You must be glad Bob didn't go to Sweden," Paul said. "You're not ready to let go of him."

"You're right about that. He's in school here, in another band," Nina said. "I think he's doing great. I can't wait to see what he'll do someday."

"Typical motherly optimism," Paul said. "But he is an exceptional kid."

"Yep, he is," Nina said.

"Kiva's my favorite beach," Andrea said, up on her elbows, watching her kids mess around in the lake. "Where locals come, where dogs are allowed. Easygoing. Right for us and right for Hitchcock."

Hitchcock was on a leash, and Bob was teasing him with smelly bait, driving the dog crazy.

"Who knew you were so provincial?" Matt sprinkled Andrea's stomach with sand. "Who knew you harbored bad feelings about outsiders?"

"I like being in the know. I like being local," Andrea replied. She took a handful of sand and piled it on Matt's stomach, then rubbed it in.

"You bad girl," he said, brushing it off.

"You bad boy." Andrea smiled at him. He smiled back at her.

"Hear anything from Kurt?" Matt asked Nina.

"Often. He's good about staying in touch. He's living with Dana. They have a two-bedroom apartment in Stockholm, I guess hoping that Bob will visit soon. Frequently. And I think he will visit them soon. He does miss his dad."

"Doesn't that hurt?" Andrea asked.

"Kurt is Bob's father," Nina said, thinking, And my first real love. "We did a pile of good together, making that boy. I want him happy. That's better for all of us."

"Most women like seeing their exes slapped," Andrea said. "It's unusual but admirable, you enjoying his happiness."

"How about Kurt's music?" Matt asked. "He's had issues. He find a way to play and stay in the game?"

So Nina told them all about Kurt's music, how well he was doing, but really, she was looking up at the clouds, how the shapes changed, how she loved being here in this moment, on the hot sand, watching the kids play mindlessly, next to all the people she loved the most. She knew she needed more sunscreen, but torpor stopped her from moving.

"Okay, well, I've made a personal pledge not to trash the guy," Paul said, "even though I have negative thoughts on the topic of him, his music, and his personal choices that would amuse the world if I blogged." Paul turned over onto his stomach.

Nina hadn't seen him in a couple of months. He looked like the lion that lived on in her imagination, the way former lovers did in idealized versions: fit, tanned, confident. After things settled down, and it was clear Cheney was not interested in ruining Paul's life, Paul had returned to Carmel and his life there. He and Wish were doing well. Economic meltdowns didn't faze investigators. People were always stealing, and a bad economy meant they stole more. Paul and Wish found themselves in great demand and weren't hurting for business.

"What happened to Paradise Resort?" Matt asked. "Not much in the *Tahoe Mirror* since the secretive Koreans took charge. I know there's some local criticism of the sale, but I drove by there a couple of days ago. The changes look good to me. Anything to benefit the local economy, I say hooray."

Nina took a drink of her coffee. She lived in this place that had moods as drastic as any negligible human but continued to draw her, strong as gravity, holy as air. She had no plan to leave the mountains where she had raised her son, where her brother lived, where her life was. "Marianne and Gene are in charge at the resort. I talked to the Koreans and they were surprisingly okay with their deceptions. They like those two because of how connected they are to the resort, and how much they love it. They're working on making it a destination year-round, you know, hiking, biking trails. They're agitating for a gondola like the one Heavenly has. Their backers are receptive to the concept, even though nobody in the world has money for any such thing these days."

"And Kelly?"

"That's a good outcome. After her father died, she straightened up and went back to law school. I'm really happy for her. You know, Paul, what you did, confessing what happened to her brother? That mattered to her. That helped her."

For a few minutes, they drank their coffee, watching the kids harass each other.

Andrea's red hair glowed in the sun. Nina thought, What a marvelous human being. How wonderful that my brother found her.

"Time to pack up the day," Matt said.

"Not yet," Andrea said, and closed her eyes.

All three other adults followed suit, closing their eyes and giving in a little longer to the mellowness of an August day at the lake, so beautiful you could hardly breathe.

The clouds moved over the sky. They listened to the sounds of dogs in the distance, barking and scrapping, and kids screaming their joyousness.

Lake Tahoe lapped along the shore.

"I am in heaven," Andrea said.

"Paradise," said Paul.

They chatted and dozed, and the time passed in a summer blur of lake, cloud, blue sky, and towering mountains.

"Mom?"

Nina awoke again to the sight of Bob, in his baggy swimsuit, hoisting a sand-encrusted inner tube.

"I'm cold."

She blinked, looking around. Even in the summer, the lake changed every five minutes, and right now it had changed to something threatening.

"I saw lightning over Tallac," Bob said. "Really bright."

"Oh, that mountain is notorious for thunderstorms. Nothing to worry about." She thought about the lightning strike up there, deaths. She didn't pray often, but she hoped anyone up on that mountain was taking care.

Bob, his worries set aside, went off to find his cousins.

Nina nudged her fellow sleepers. "Time to go."

Laden with dirty towels, baskets, and umbrellas, they began trudging toward the cars.

"We should make the kids help," Andrea said, heaving a trash bag into the trunk of their car. "They need to learn—"

"Let them play," Matt said, shutting the trunk. "How long does it last, this moment when the sun is going down, and the lake is driving us nuts with how pretty it is, and the sky's strange and we love each other?" He put his arm around Andrea's waist, and they walked back to the beach.

Paul put his arm around Nina's waist. They walked behind Matt and Andrea back to the beach.

"Here's a fallen tree," Paul said. "Let's sit here. See how bad the storm is. See how long the kids last. Before it's dark."

"Before it's dark and we have to go home," Nina said.

After the police left, Sondra's employer, Riley Fox, called her into her office, asking her to please sit down on the new white leather Palermo love seat. Sondra sank down into the cushion, wondering why she had been called in. She thought through the past few weeks and couldn't think of any mistakes she had made, but you never knew how another person really thought. You never knew how another person might judge the exact same situation. Maybe she had canceled a client that turned out to be the biggest, best case, but that would really surprise her. As always, she had evaluated recent clients the way she evaluated men, with a cool and thoughtful eye, and an acute nose for the nasty ones.

She had ferreted out a nasty one, hadn't she? The sick wife, the compromised husband, all in cahoots with a greedy murderer. Well, she couldn't exactly spell it out, but her boss had taken her hints and run with them. Surely she recognized Sondra's part in solving the case?

"You continue to surprise and please me, Ms. Filo-plume. You figured out what was going on before I did, and you gave me that lead. You had the guts to call in help when we needed it, when I wanted to go it alone. You know I have a lot of trouble with that guy, and I had resolved never to hire him again if I could avoid it. So"—Ms. Fox handed Sondra a glass of bubbling champagne and clinked it with her own—"a toast to you, Sondra. You saw how much trouble we were in, and you stepped right up to do something about it."

"But I had nothing to do with Raul coming up here," Sondra protested.

"Yes, he mentioned that you didn't want him to tell me anything about your role. Ms. Filoplume, you are a humble woman, and I appreciate that, but I'm glad I know. He told me all about how you persuaded him to come and help us, even though I had done everything in my power to stop him."

They sipped champagne for a moment, watching the ancient lake through the picture window as it ran through the rainbow colors of evening, a sight that always made Sondra's heart soar.

"Oh, and I've got something else for you." Ms. Fox reached into her desk and pulled out an envelope. "A bonus. It's not enough, but it's all we can give you, along with my undying gratitude and appreciation. And by the way, I wondered if I could come out to your ranch for a horseback riding lesson soon."

Sondra nodded. It was about time Ms. Fox learned such a basic skill.

Sondra locked the door carefully behind her, knowing what she knew, and knowing when not to interfere, and knowing all's well that ends with a big bonus.

T h e   E n d

ACKNOWLEDGMENTS

The authors are indebted to Nancy Yost of Yost & Associates Literary Agency, who, with her usual wisdom and grace, played an especially critical role in the publishing process this time around; to Abby Zidle, our sharp new editor at Simon & Schuster, who showed great patience and discernment; to Louise Burke, our excellent publisher at Simon & Schuster, Inc., who has been kind enough to extend deadlines for us and has given us steady support; and to the many staffers at Simon & Schuster who worked on the book, including Tony Mauro, for such fine work on the cover art, and Steve Boldt, our skillful copy editor. We would also like to express our appreciation to Maggie Crawford, our previous editor at Simon & Schuster, who helped us tighten and organize the manuscript and was a valued adviser in an earlier stage of publication.

Many thanks to the following friends and family who supported us through the writing process with good humor and special encouragement: Andrew Fuller, Brad Snedecor, June Snedecor, Kevin Neal,

Cori Snedecor, Katie Bedard, Connor Snedecor, Creda Wilson, Meg O'Shaughnessy, Stephanie O'Shaughnessy, Nita Piper, Beth Vieira, Jenny D'Angelo, Caroleena Epstein, Bruce Engelhardt, Esther Bueno, Ardyth Brock, Steve Parker, Walt Kondrasheff, Kathy Choy, James Starshak, Sally Backus, Ann Wright, Dr. Ellen Taliaferro, Sylvia Walker, Frank Menke, Ann Walker, Dr. Ruth Bar-Shalom, Sandy Polakoff, Lynn Snedecor, Beverly Sheveland, Karen Snedecor, Elizanne Lewis, Joan Westlund, Joanna Tamer, Helga Gerdes, Hermann Gerdes, Pat Spindt, Ruth Dawson, Bill Dawson, and Jim Nicholas.

See how Nina Reilly got her start in . . .

SHOW NO FEAR

Now available from Pocket Books

PROLOGUE

Monday, November 26, 1990, 3:45 p.m.

I needed to take control of a dangerous, tumbling situation. She presented the worst threat I have ever experienced.

I waited for her to return to the run-down little cottage where she lived. Her old car struggled up the hill. While she parked, awkwardly, too far from the curb, I assumed a bland expression, getting out of the big white rental car to approach her. She turned around, arms full of groceries, her strangely impassive face pale.

"Why are you here?" Her voice sounded interested, although I heard an underlying suspicion.

I couldn't answer, naturally. All hell would certainly break loose on this quiet street, so I lied, trying to keep that exterior calm of hers going long enough for me to get her into the car. Ideally, I could somehow convince her to come along with me, but she was too smart, onto me somehow, spooked but not sure.

She jabbed her key in the lock with her right hand. "I'll just drop my groceries inside." And drop them she did. Glass shattered, and some clear liquid pooled on the worn wooden floor. She tried to close the door in my face, but she's relatively feeble and I'm not. I shoved my way in behind her.

I showed her the gun. "We're going for a ride. There are things we need to discuss. No need to get worked up."

She eyed the phone, asked to make a phone call. I felt the urge to laugh.

"I'm a mother," she said. Her otherwise clear eyes clouded.

But I knew for a fact nobody needed her at home that afternoon. "Out the door," I said. "Now."

She had guts. She definitely caught me off guard, taking off like a young and nimble runner, dashing for the kitchen. By the time I overcame my surprise at her ability to move so fast and followed her, she held a big butcher knife. "Get out of my house!"

I could shoot her right then and there, but I had a better plan. If she was going to make things harder for me, I'd make things harder for her. I stepped straight toward her, slapped the knife away with the butt of my gun, slapped her face, not too hard, just letting her know where we stood, and watched her wince at the pain.

She locked up carefully. We walked down the steps, me following her, gun hidden but present. She climbed into the car without another word.

We drove in silence past Carmel on Highway 1. I

kept one hand on the wheel, the other on my gun. The only sign of her fear was the way her hand gripped the dash as we took the curves. I glanced sideways at her, watching her look out the car window to her right. Carmel Highlands lay behind us now, and she scanned the gray sea off Garrapata Beach.

"I didn't think my life could get any worse. Just goes to show."

"Keep quiet."

"Are you going to shoot me?"

I didn't bother to answer.

"Where are you taking me? At least tell me that."

"To a beautiful place."

Just then we swung around a sharp curve. Bixby Creek Bridge lay ahead of us. I saw the scenic turnoff on the cliffside where tourists stop and admire the view of the old Depression-era bridge between two cliffs. It's steep by the turnoff, several hundred feet, a vertiginous drop to a confluence of Bixby Creek and the Pacific Ocean.

I pulled over and stopped the car.

A stiff wind harassed the low brush on the hillside on the other side of the road. The ocean glittered far out and I could see cloud shadows racing down from the north. The hairs on my skin stood up like tiny needles, irritated by the weather. I waited for a good long break in the occasional line of cars.

"Get out."

"No." She stared straight ahead.

"Get the fuck out!"

Slowly, laboriously, she took her seat belt off, adjusted the strap of her bag on her shoulder, and buttoned her jacket. She emerged too slowly, blinking in the cold breeze. I took her arm and led her the few feet to the edge.

We both looked out into the radiation from the horizon and down across the solid ocean flecked with whitecaps. She opened her mouth to shout something into the wind.

A wayward sports car passed, swerving along the curve. I ducked behind the car so that anyone in that car would see only one person. She had no chance against me. She stood about three feet in front of me, right at the edge. I found her back insulting. She had no right to hide the mortal fear she must be feeling.

I rushed at her, hitting her with my shoulder like a linebacker, with a whump, hard. She toppled away while I caught myself, fell to my knees.

She disappeared.

Her last shriek, animalistic, harsh, and loud, startled me. But she had time only for that one final sound, heard only by the two of us, muffled by the sound of distant surf. I jumped back into the car and turned around and headed north again. A semi roared south as I rounded a turn and I almost sideswiped him in my excitement. For the rest of the way, I made an effort to drive extremely carefully, hugging the mountain side of the road.

Yes, first, this fast breathing, this feeling that I had been very close to the edge myself.

Then—I don't know. Some glee. Ruefulness. Regret, I guess.

And finally—relief. The worst was over.

CHAPTER 1

September 20, 1990

The law offices of Pohlmann, McIntyre, Sorensen and Frost surrounded a courtyard in a low, white-painted adobe building in the town of Carmel-by-the-Sea, California. Lush flower bushes, pines, and succulents bedecked the hilly front yard where steps led to the main door. In the bright sun of mid-September the building looked overexposed, bleached like the sand on the beach at the foot of Ocean Avenue. Now, at ten in the morning, streams of Lexuses and Infinitis already cruised this side street, hungry for parking spaces.

Nina Reilly grabbed a pile of mail on the receptionist's desk. She had worked as a paralegal at the law firm for the past year, having snagged this coveted job simply by submitting a résumé. Her mother called it Irish luck, but Nina suspected it had more to do with another Irish character trait. Her father, Harlan, knew Klaus Pohlmann because he hobnobbed with everyone, but he would never confess to having pulled strings with Klaus.

Nearing eighty, Klaus was a legend in the community, the most daring and successful lefty lawyer south of San Francisco. He only hired the best, and that included Jack McIntyre, Nina's latest crush. Jack was over at the Monterey County Superior Court at a settlement conference.

Nina called out to the receptionist, "Back in an hour, Astrid. I promise."

Hurrying down the walk, she caught her sandal on the edge of the stone steps and stopped herself from falling by dropping the mail and raising her arms for balance. She dusted the letters as she picked them up, then tossed them through the car window to the seat, counting to keep track in case one fell between the seat and gearshift.

Could mean the difference between a future and no future at all, getting every one of those envelopes to the post office. If she was going to be sloppy about details, she might as well slit her throat today and skip the stomachaches and nights of worry altogether, because in the legal profession, as in medicine and architecture, a minor oversight could be lethal.

Nina had finished college a few years before with a degree in psychology, studying film, art, and people in the luxurious fashion of a girl-child awaiting her prince. She wished now that she'd had better guidance from the adults in her life, who should have known— what? The future, what real life held for a single mother in her late twenties entering a slow economy? Her psych degree had not even prepared her for service positions in the restaurant business.

But she was making up for that now, between law classes, paralegal work, and Bob, not in that order.

Fog murked its way in front of her. She scrutinized the hazy road for patrol cars, then executed a swooping, illegal U-turn, arriving at the post office in downtown Pacific Grove, heart pounding. She shoved the letters into the metered-mail slot.

Relieved to be rid of her latest emergency, she fired up the MG along with the radio. Moving out into the street, she narrowly missed a waiting Acura. She swung onto Pine Avenue, drifting toward the middle line as she rummaged in her bag for the address for Dr. Lindberg. She located his card, swerved to avoid a jaywalking tourist family, and turned left onto Highway 1. The pines loomed on either side as the fog drizzled over the Pebble Beach road. She drove swiftly the few blocks to her mother's cottage, parking in front of the huge Norfolk pine in the front yard.

Honking, she reminded herself about the miserable people she saw every day at work, injured on the job, alone and poor. She conjured these images to steel herself for the sight of her mother carefully locking up, pausing every few steps, looking down as if she weren't sure where the sidewalk was. Her mother had ordered her not to come to the door. She didn't like being reminded of the changes in her health.

In the one minute she had to herself Nina leaned back and closed her eyes. Breathe deep. In. Out.

Let's see, Wills and Estates tonight. Professor Cerruti made it her favorite class, but she also liked what lawyers called the "settled" law of that ancient and noble subject. Unlike environmental law, for instance, which fluxed through revolutions every time a new president came in, with Wills one could learn rules that had stuck for centuries. How nice if she could apply a few firm rules to the tatty loose ends of her own life.

I'll read the cases while I eat dinner, she decided. So much for school. As for work, she had all afternoon to obsess about how much she was falling behind there. Deal with it when she got back to the office.

As for friends, ha ha, they must think she had moved to Tajikistan, for all they ever heard from her; a boyfriend was not an option, she didn't have time, though she had fallen into some casual overnighters a while back that had left her feeling worse than lonely. But she did feel warm whenever McIntyre came into her office. Her mind began bathing in a certain bubble bath—but right now here came her mother, struggling down the concrete walk.

Today, the skin on her mother's face looked tighter than usual. Nina opened the passenger-side door from the inside. Ginny paused to remove her right glove, uncovering a hand scrimshawed in pale blue lines. She leaned in and touched her daughter's hand. "Honey, why not let me take a cab? You're a busy woman."

"God, Mom. You're like ice."

Nina's mother had changed so much. Always a handsome woman with sparkling eyes and a daunting energy, she had gradually seemed to lose all color and character. Her skin stretched as tight as a stocking mask over her cheekbones, even pulling her lips back as if they were shrinking. Her once mobile face now looked somehow both flat and puffy, due to both the illness and the steroids used to treat it. Still she tried to smile.

"You always look so cheerful," Nina said, giving

her a brief hug after she had maneuvered into the low-slung car. "How do you do it?"

"The right attitude makes me feel stronger. You know how much you hate it when people condescend to you, 'Oh, poor Nina, raising a boy on her own, working so hard'?"

"Oh, come on. I don't pity you."

"Sure you do. Anyone with half a brain would." Ginny patted her shoulder. "Let's just admire how delightful the leaves are at this time of year, okay?"

Maybe it had been better, those days of not knowing what was wrong, because of the hope they'd had then. Did her mother still hope?

Nina drove quickly to Dr. Lindberg's Monterey office on Cass Street. Would she have time later to run by the school library for that book on reserve? She had a mock trial coming up in a week in her Advanced Civil Procedure class and a paper due for Gas and Oil Law that demanded lengthy research. If she hurried, she could pick up Bob at nursery school, drop him with the babysitter at home, stop by the library, and be back at the office by two. Would Remy notice she had been gone longer than her lunch break allowed?

Gritting her teeth, she thought, Remy would notice.

She parked at a meter and ran around to the side of the car. "Need help, Mom? Those stairs are pretty steep. Let me help you up them at least."

Her mother let her help her out of the car, then shook her off. "I rise to all occasions. That will never change. Please don't fuss so much, Nina."

"If Matt doesn't show up to pick you up, promise me you'll leave a message for me with Astrid. I'll come get you."

"You're a worrywart."

Her mother trusted Nina's brother, Matt. Nina hoped she would call if Matt didn't show up. Again.

A few blocks north of Dr. Lindberg's office, Bob attended a preschool chosen after Nina had looked at a dozen of them and settled on this one as the least of all evils. The playroom walls were covered with outsider art Picasso would have envied, committed by three- and four-year-olds who were never given fill-in-the-blanks coloring books. Children were making collages at each table, and she spotted Bob, dark hair fallen over his round, delicious cheeks, smearing a magazine tearout onto gluey paper à la André Breton or Max Ernst.

Seeing her, he called out, "Mom, look!" Resisting an impulse to check her watch, she pulled up a tiny preschooler plastic chair and sat next to him, nodding at the collage.

"Finish up, honey, we have to go." Thank God he loved the place and was reluctant to leave. "What's this?" she asked, pointing at a tray of wooden puzzle pieces alongside the collage.

"My job." He reached over and with startling dexterity stuck the pieces into their slots to complete a duck puzzle.

"Oh. A duck! Cool!"

"But now watch this." He dumped the pieces onto the table, then stuck them across the middle in a snaggletooth row. "My keyboard," he said with a grin. "Like at home."

"But this one you can't play."

"Huh?" He ran his fingers up and down the wood

pieces, humming. He was playing a sea chantey CD at home these days. "'Way haul away, we'll haul away home—'"

"But you ruined your puzzle."

"We can go now."

Taking her son's backpack and his hand, Nina ushered him to the door. Bob currently loved the cheap battery-operated keyboard she had found at a discount store. He didn't want to learn real songs yet, just loved making noise, but sometimes she caught him fingering the same notes over and over with a thoughtful expression on his face. She would have to find a way to pay for piano lessons when he was older. Never squelch potential talent, Ginny always said.

As they pulled the door open, an aide handed Nina a paper bag full of dirty pants. "He had two accidents today," she remarked, carefully noncommittal. Nina took the bag. Bob looked up at her with a worried expression. "Mommy, don't break my heart," he said, watching her face. She smiled and patted his hot cheek, hustling him outside, chastising herself for her impatience.

On the way to the parking lot, she ran into an old friend she hadn't seen for ages.

"Well, look at you," Diana said.

Nina hugged her, remembering how much Diana favored flowery perfumes. "When I told you I was pregnant, you never said a thing about being pregnant yourself."

"I was scared," Diana said. "I'd already had two miscarriages and began to think I'd never have a child. Her name's Cori." They stopped to watch Diana's curly-haired daughter gather up her backpack.

"So you settled down," Nina said.

Her old friend waved a set of flashy rings. "He just wouldn't let me alone. Good thing. He teaches chemistry at the community college."

"You always said you'd never marry."

Diana corralled her daughter and nudged her toward a red minivan. "Yeah, surprise! I turned out normal. How about you?"

"No surprise. I didn't."

Diana tilted her head. "So what if you never go about things the way other people do. You're exceptional. Not abnormal."

"I decided to get everything out of the way at once, be a single mother, go to school, work like a cur. That way, I'll have earned the right to a long commitment to some quiet loony-bin spa by the time I'm thirty."

"I gotta scoot." Diana started the battle to get her daughter strapped in. "Let's gossip soon."

"You back at work?"

"Part-time until the little gal's ready to launch. Two more years. I couldn't find full-time child care I can trust that would have her." Diana latched the seat belt across her daughter's car seat with a sigh.

"It's like getting them into a good college, applications, interviews."

"And then they reject you or your child, or your private financial status." Diana shrugged, slamming the door against her cranky child. "I discovered passable child care involved dark rooms with peed-upon plastic mattresses, watery peanut butter, and drunken college students. I realized, hey, I can do that and pay nothing."

How nice for her, Nina thought. Diana had a

partner to help and an option to stay home with her daughter. How might that feel? No doubt good, no doubt fortunate.

"Take care," Nina said, strapping Bob into his own car seat. He had a new book to study, so he let the process happen peacefully for a change. Suddenly starving, she climbed inside her car, rustling around in the MG's glove compartment for a snack. She found nothing to eat there, only an old brochure for a restaurant she could never afford. Disgruntled, she raised her head to another unwelcome vision.

Richard Filsen leaned against the brick wall of the church that bordered the parking lot, smoking a cigarette.